PRAISE FOR CALIA WILDE

Wilde splices the action with heated scenes that breathe inti-
macy and urgency

— BOOKLIFE

The way in which Wilde displayed sexual passion upon the
page was a fair mix of realism and metaphor, which is what
I like…I think *the payoff* can be more explosive or have a
greater impact if much of what happens on the page can be
experienced through the reader's imagination. Wilde hit the
nail on the head.

— LIVE FREE LIVE RICH

ROSES ARE DEAD

SKILLETSVILLE DESTROYERS MC BOOK #3

31 DAYS OF TRICK OR TREAT

CALIA WILDE

MISFIT INK BOOKS
MARYLAND, U.S.A.

Misfit Ink

5257 Buckeystown Pike, #215

Frederick, MD 21704

MisfitInkBooks.com

Ordering Information:

For details, contact theAuthor@CaliaWilde.com.

Disclaimer:

This book is a work of fiction. Any references to historical events, real people, or real locales are used fictitiously. Other names, characters, places, and incidents are the product of the author's imagination, and any resemblance to actual events or locales or persons, living or dead, is entirely coincidental.

The following is an indication and acknowledgement of potential content that may be upsetting or triggering, but is clearly not exhaustive:

Vulgar language, abuse (physical, sexual, emotional, verbal), child abuse or pedophilia, animal cruelty or animal death, sexual assault, excessive or gratuitous violence, needles, kidnapping (forceful deprivation of/disregard for personal autonomy), death or dying, cancer, cult or religious references or practices, and blood.

Roses Are Dead is a work of fiction that contains emotionally disturbing content. While there is ultimately a happy ever after for the main characters, they and other characters are depicted as living through painful experiences. Please be aware of your own tolerance for the triggering content mentioned as well as use your best judgement about reading when your own emotional reserves are low. Sometimes it is the little things that can tip the balance into dark spaces.

Cover design: Created by Clarise Tan of CT Cover Creations, www.ctcovercreations.com. The 31 Days of Trick or Treat logo and artwork used with permission.

Cover model: Sam Miller, Licensed photography from r+m photography (https://www.rplusmphoto.com/).

CONTENTS

To my ancestors of the oak,
Thank you for your guidance.
I broke the chains and closed the circle.

To my Snow White and Rose Red,
Thank you for your love.
May you always know grace, hope, and beauty.

To the witches,
Thank you for your perseverance.
Stay strong.

To my readers:

Roses Are Dead is both a tribute to Halloween and is part of the 31 Days of Trick or Treat collection of books released in October 2025.

But it also is Book 3 of the Skilletsville Destroyers (https://caliawilde.ccm/skilletsville/) series. If you picked up this book without reading the preceding stories, don't worry, I've tried to make it as stand-alone as possible.

The Skilletsville Destroyers books are available at Kobo, Amazon, Google Play Books, and more.

1

ROISHIN

Fair is foul, and foul is fair. - MacBeth

Don't be fooled by a pretty face, or by a pious countenance. Sometimes both hide the darkest secrets. Case in point, Carl Windgren. A preacher's son, he was heir to the divine-infused, velvet-cushioned throne at the back of a broad stage in my hometown. He was also a notorious drug dealer who lived in the lowest-rent neighborhood of Harrisburg, Pennsylvania, where he ruled as lord over a criminal empire. Since he couldn't crown himself king of a church, he found the next best substitute. Drugs.

I'd done my best to gnaw my arms off to get free. Not only from that church, but from Carl.

So, why was I willing to put those shackles on again?

Beth. My best friend. My *only* friend.

In every way, she was the opposite of Carl. Beth Windgren-now-Smith was my savior, my first love, in a sisterly way, and the kindest person I had ever met. A mother to two boys and two girls, a devoted wife, a full-time stay at home mom, and a front-line volunteer for anything that helped make people's lives more livable, enjoyable, or beautiful.

And she was dying.

The culprit? Aggressive Non-Hodgkin lymphoma. It was a deadly kind of disease.

No prayers could fix that. And believe me, there had been many.

Medicine and science had answers, perhaps not firm solutions, but offered hope. But even hope needs a nudge now and then.

~

I hid behind Carl Windgren's couch for the third time that month and measured my breaths so Carl's criminal visitor wouldn't kill me. As I lay on Carl's beige-gray carpet, I inhaled the rot of mildew, ancient pet stains, and the pervasively sharply "green" aroma of pot shake while the drama unfurled in graphic detail.

It started simply enough. A knock at the back door. Another minion coming to buy, right?

Carl checked his closed-circuit TV system and ordered me to hide. Missing were his joking manner and the veiled threat to make me witness his power play. Whoever it was, warranted Carl's fear. I dipped behind the couch because he was already opening the back door.

"I thought Sketch was coming." Carl's voice was clear.

The other's wasn't. I tried not to listen. But whatever he had to say, Carl didn't like. "What do you mean, you didn't bring it?"

This time, the voice was clearer because the guest moved into the living room. "I checked the bag, it ain't there. Someone fucked up. I'm calling, okay?"

"My time is valuable," Carl reminded him.

The guest didn't bother to answer. "Yo, Bear. I left Sketch's and —" he was cut off by whoever he called. "Fuck. Sorry about that. I didn't know. I picked up the car he said would be fixed. It was fixed —" a pause went on for longer than the last interruption. Answered with a vague, "No shit? Daaaaaamn."

I didn't have to look to see Carl's face. He didn't mind most swearing except for two instances. Damn, or goddammit. I knew that sour, holier than thou squint, followed by the slightest downturn of both corners of his mouth. The tight whiteness that replaced his natural pallor, proving he was stockpiling words like an arsenal but guarding it stronger than any army would.

"Cool. I'll let him know." The tone shifted because he must have had his back turned and now faced Carl. "Sketch is on his way. Maybe ten minutes, tops. He's got your shit."

Carl's voice lowered to a hiss. "*He clothed himself with cursing as his coat; may it soak into his body like water, like oil into his bones.*"

"Yeah. Right. Anyway, that's going to be sixteen K."

A drug drop. *Lovely.*

"I'm not paying you." Carl's voice was calm.

"Listen, if you don't pay, we fuck you up, and you don't get your shit."

I bit down on my urge to reveal myself. He hadn't truly threatened Carl yet. And I'd heard this same refrain at least once before. Carl was a big boy, he could handle himself.

"Per my agreement with your boss, remember him? Jackson? I *can* ask for twelve days from delivery to payment."

"What? You ain't good for it?"

"No wonder they call you, Whoosh."

"What's that supposed to mean?"

The noise that came from Carl used to make me curl into a ball and cover my head. It wasn't loud, or even all that violent. Just a sigh of contempt. At least one person died after that nonverbal assault.

"Sit. We will wait for your friend in *silence.*"

"I don't have to be quiet. I'm a Destroyer. Go fuck yourself."

Ah. It made sense that Carl's supplier was the notorious motorcycle gang that thundered down the roads in packs. Good, god-fearing folk warned their children to stay away from that type of criminal.

It made me want to peek around the edge of the couch to see what one looked like up close to satiate my curiosity. But I knew better than to move or make a sound.

"You are not a Destroyer, yet."

"I will be."

"Not if you drive to a drop, forget the product, and then anger the club's best dealer, you won't."

That shut him up. For a few minutes. Then he prattled away about nothing important. I settled into a more comfortable position so I could ignore the deal going down. Sketch showed up, and the argument went much like I expected. Lots of posturing, some threats, and through it all, Carl being his infuriatingly calm but slimy self, only agreeing to pay half up front because Whoosh was rude to him.

Then all hell broke loose. It started small, a thump with the telltale crinkling sound of broken glass. The kind you hear in a car accident, but muffled by the house walls and the distance to the back alley.

"What the fuck was that?" Whoosh asked.

Sketch moved. His shoes were harder and heavier than Whoosh's or Carl's.

Another thump. Then a scream.

My blood ran cold. That was a woman, not an alley cat, and too high-pitched to be one of the gang members that slinked in the grimy valley between the row houses. Sketch swore and tore open the back door. Carl quickly tapped in the security codes to the alarm system; the beeps were barely audible over the yelling. *Bang!*

I covered my head to protect myself from the expected return gunfire. But instead, the heavy tromp of Sketch's boots grew louder as he strode from the kitchen to the living room. "Do you know which gangs wear purple?"

"That would be either the Fifth Street boys, or fucking Maleanta's asswipes." For Carl to swear meant he was beyond excited, or pissed. They'd argued over the payment terms, the amount, and everything in-between without him raising his voice.

"Does he buy from you?"

Carl's hesitation made me hold my breath. He was going to lie to a Destroyer. Probably an armed one because someone fired off that shot from Carl's back porch.

"Cut him off." Sketch didn't bother to wait for Carl's lie. The shuffling of money was distinct. I'd heard the same thing only an hour ago as Carl meticulously counted the cash he'd need for this deal. "Where does he live?"

Carl gave Sketch an answer that not only included where they lived, but what cars they drove, full names, and where their favorite fast-food restaurant was.

The Destroyers left, and Carl reset the alarm. Cautiously, I crawled out of my hiding spot. His gaze landed on me, and I froze. "Come here, Rose."

Shit.

I stood and joined him, pretending that this kind of thing happened all the time. That life was as normal as… well, some crime drama.

"Do you know who those men were?" He pointed toward the alley.

"Destroyers."

A soft noise of satisfaction emanated from Carl. "That's right, Mary-Rose."

I hated the way he said my name like that. He traced the rows of tiny lines carved into the door frame. The house was so old, the scars weren't out of place, but there was something incestuous about his fascination with them. When he reached the bottom of the rows, he traced four small lines under it with his thumbnail. Then he sighed. "You were listening. If they ever find out you were here, you're dead. They don't leave witnesses." His tone shifted to the same pace and cadence his father used during sermons.

Then why are you still alive? I stuffed the question deep, along with any defiance that would betray me.

"Look at the very top mark."

I did.

"Touch it."

It was a fight not to disobey him. But I did as he asked.

"That is ours, Rose. You and I made that mark."

He was certifiably crazy. And I was even more insane for ever thinking I could bargain and reason with someone clearly trying to outwit the very Devil himself.

My silence kept him talking. "Remember that day? You wore a dress. I could see up your skirt. Your thin little legs, virginal white panties, those ridiculous light up tennis shoes you wore. There was pink lace on your socks."

I hated pink. Most any color now. Except black.

"Your point?"

He grabbed my hair and forced my face against the rough wood. I hadn't had any warning. "These are deaths, Rose. All of them. Count."

There was no way I could. "Okay," I said to placate him. That was the game. Placate Carl. Pretend to be obedient so he'd do what I wanted. Give up my life to keep him happily amused for long enough to get his compliance. It had been such a rough September. But I'd never complain. Too much hung in the balance. "I'm going to bruise. And we have the doctor's appointments next week."

He let go of my hair, and I straightened the pins for my braids so nothing hung loose. As I did, he traced down my cheek with a fingertip. "I don't think you'll bruise. It's just a little red. Put a cold washcloth on it."

If I didn't know better, I'd think he cared about me. The soft tone of his voice was deceptively sweet. But it was all an act. One he'd insisted upon. Carl the kind. Carl the merciful. Carl the forgiven.

What a crock of bullshit that was.

And an even bigger crock held my own deception. I wasn't this meek version of myself. The button-down beige and pastel clothes were echoes of a different life.

Now that he'd let me go, I counted the marks. He made it easy, lining up the neat hash marks in rows of five. Only the top line and the bottom row with its lightly scratched ghosts broke the pattern.

Sixteen and four to come.

If Carl was to be believed, he'd had a hand in those deaths. Details on those would come in handy if I needed to blackmail him. Yet, a part of me didn't *want* to know. If Carl had escalated his bloodlust, I was in deep trouble. And those ambiguous final four had to remain quiet. Because, while Carl gave the Destroyers exactly the information they needed to hunt the gang down, he hadn't precisely done anything wrong. And he had a point. No one narced on the Destroyers and lived. He'd found people more diabolical than he was, and that was not only dangerous, but deadly.

What if he's playing a game with me?

Then I'd have to play a better game is all. He fought proxy wars by making others do his dirty work. Carl rarely took an active role, knowing full well how a single crime could bury him. Or ostracize him. I smiled. I'd been his downfall once. I could do it again if he didn't do what I needed him to do. Hopefully, before he killed me.

I needed to break free. I needed an escape.

I needed *hope*. But that wasn't what grew in my heart. The spark born there was vengeance. A thirst for violence when despair becomes desperation.

The only light I could see was that after the blood donation procedure, this farce should be done. I'd be free if everything went well. Carl had complied with all the medical orders, taken the shots to boost his stem cells, and all his tests came back perfect. I'd made plans to move in with Beth's family to help her focus on her recovery and to eliminate "temptation" from Carl's life. Hopefully, by the time she got better, I could figure out a way to return to my old self and remain out of Carl's crosshairs.

Despite that, an invisible noose tightened around my neck. Carl had manipulated my life to fit his plans. I couldn't trust he'd let me go. That meant I needed to give fate a little "nudge."

A few nights later, I slipped out, prepared, but not knowing if I'd find a suitable location. My requirements were moving water, a place to stand in the in-between, and the new moon. I couldn't look anything up on my laptop because Carl would find out. I couldn't use my phone because I wasn't certain that Carl's hacker hadn't touched that, too.

The weather got worse as I crossed the bridge. A late hurricane drove moisture up the eastern seaboard and despite breaking up over twenty hours ago, the clouds churned ominously.

But that worked in my favor. The threat of more rain kept sane folk inside. A flash of lightning lit up the sky as I drove west along a tributary to the Susquehanna. The flash bounced behind the clouds, giving a soft glow to the surroundings. In that brief reprieve to the gloom, I spotted a chained driveway. I stopped the car. It was a boat launch. Perfect for what I needed.

I unhooked the chain and drove in. I hid the car from view behind a monstrous bank of drooping gooseberry bushes.

The dense canvas of my coat barely snagged as I slipped through a gauntlet of thorny brush to reach a broken dock that jutted into the river. The right side had solid planks that creaked as I walked onto them. I took the jacket and my dress off to face nature wearing nothing but the sky. Then came the hard part. Unbraiding my hair.

And meditating.

I always had problems with that part. My spirit was too wild and volatile to reach calm. I was at my most focused listening to the heaviest metal music complete with throaty screams and wild drum beats, not some tranquil chiming of bells or worse… silence.

Silence was deadly, like a church.

Thankfully, the wind and the water were loud. I merged with the violence easily as I prepped the spell.

I stood on the non-broken spur of the pier. There, I balanced between the land, air, water, construction, destruction, cultivated landscape, and untamed wilderness. The skies obliged sending not one, but two fast concussive bolts of searing white light from one end of the horizon to the other.

This is powerful, my soul cried.

The wind picked up, casting sticks and debris into the maelstrom.

My hair whipped around, blinding me, and binding around me. The egg in my hand had Carl's name scribed seven times across the surface. The words inked in a mixture of wax from a black candle and the ashes of intent written in my blood.

Being a good little witch was beyond my patience. This magic suited me much better. The strength of it coursed through me as easily as breathing. My will focused on one thing, getting rid of that man's influence on my life. A single word encompassed my entire future; I was working a spell toward *freedom*.

I whispered the word to the egg, conveying the desired outcome of the binding into the spell. There was no vision of how this change would unfold, only the sensation of finally owning my destiny and experiencing joy. Maybe holding my best friend's youngest in my lap? Or better yet, watching that child graduate from high school and cheering almost as loud as Beth as we celebrated June's passage into adulthood. *Yes*, that would be the reality I sought.

Another sheet of lightning sizzled above me. My hair lifted into the wind as if two unseen hands held it aloft. I felt the magic in my bones. My heart called to it in the short span of time and space we lingered together. It simmered in that moment of held breath, will, desire, and natural energy. I cocked my arm back and screamed a curse into the void. Then threw the fragile carrier of all my hopes and desires into the rushing river.

The last of the light faded as the churning water ate the splash.

The wind blew straight, wet, and cold, chilling me so quickly it sapped my energy with each sideways, stinging raindrop.

I slipped in the mud as I climbed back onto the bank, still naked, and drenched from the water pouring from the sky. My clothes were wet and muddy. I put them on anyway. Luckily, I'd planned for this possibility and slid onto the tarp-covered seat. At most there'd be a little mud on the floorboards, nothing for Carl to yell about. Barely a sign that I'd defied him once again.

Right before I drove away, I swore I saw a wild animal in the bushes. I blinked and it was gone. Strange. And fortunate. Sneaking out of the house and using Carl's car was dangerous enough, but having to fend off an animal crazy enough to not get out of the rain was not on my agenda today.

Hexing my ex-boyfriend and tormentor? Absolutely.

2

———

BEAR

There were exactly two hours before a rare mid-week "prayer" meeting at the club. Enough time to slip in a run. I scanned the clouds. The day started ominously and marched vindictively toward the promise of a late season downpour spurred on by moisture coming up from the south and a hard-edged cold front creeping down from the north. This far west in Pennsylvania the remnants of most fall hurricanes were gentler than if I lived on the gulf or the coast east of here, but lately it seemed as if the planet wanted humanity washed off its surface. Or blown off. I could appreciate the sentiment, as long as it wasn't aimed at me.

The wind picked up.

I tied my running shoes and prayed no one saw me. At six-five and pushing two hundred and eighty pounds, it was hard *not* to see me, but what I really wanted was for no one to take one look at my tattoos, my mohawk, my bulk, and then see the bright as fuck neon pink running shoes and laugh their asses off at me.

Slow. I didn't mind being called fat because I could have another eighty pounds of beer gut and still kick the speaker's ass. But slow? That was a death sentence. And I loved living too much to be a corpse any time soon.

So, I'd started… *slow*. Fuck, I hated that word. That meant a treadmill tucked inside the safe room in my basement. When that got boring, I toyed with the idea of jogging the multi-purpose trail behind my house. And with that fool notion, I'd let some idiot salesman talk me into bright pink running shoes. They were an embarrassment of epic proportions. One that kept me from starting any public workout until it was almost too late in the season to make a habit of it.

With two hours to kill and a storm keeping everyone inside, I slipped onto the bike path behind my house and ran away from the city. The first leg was easy. Then the asphalt ended, and gravel took its place. *Whatever.* I'd keep going for twenty minutes, path or not. Then come back, take a quick shower and haul my ass to the impromptu Wednesday night meeting at the Destroyers' club house tucked into a junkyard across the river about two miles north.

What? You thought I meant a *Christian* prayer meeting in a church? Hell, I'd be struck dead walking into one of those. I was a proud pagan follower of Odin and Thor. I wore a heavy silver hammer pendant around my neck like those folks wore crosses. And despite my wild black hair that I kept braided in a stripe from forehead to neck, I was biologically, and more importantly, animalistically, Norse. I was born an ancient soul in the modern world. That's why I'd found a home with the Destroyers MC. They were the right kind of drunken, pillaging idiots I enjoyed.

But if they saw me in pink shoes, damn. My reputation would go right into the shitter. I pounded out those thoughts as the gravel crunched under my feet. The path took a turn toward the river, avoiding the industrial park where the club owned four warehouse buildings that brought in over ten grand in lease income each month.

That was another thing that had changed in the last few years. It used to be that the Skilletsville Destroyers barely had any legal cashflow outside of dues, the junkyard, and accompanying automotive or motorcycle repair shops. But then the dumbest idiot of the bunch slept with his half-sister… not biologically his half-sister, mind you… but damn that whole concept was kind of ball-shriveling for some of us, and then, fool that Sprout was, he married her. At least there was a perk besides sex. She inherited almost nine-hundred-million dollars and didn't mind sharing it with her husband or his club.

I know what you're thinking, no fucking way. And yes, way.

Now we were not only rolling in dough, but appointed as the people responsible for building this town beyond its little steel industry roots and straight into gentrification. I hated it. One day, this running path would be finished, and all the wildness would be gone. That hurt.

But the money was great, so I shut the fuck up and did my part. And just to make sure no one invited me to any groundbreakings or soirees, I added more tattoos to my skin, piercings to anything that could get pierced, and gave up wearing anything normal.

Fuck normal.

And *fuck* pink. I slapped my foot into the middle of a puddle, turning a neon abomination into a muddy one. I searched for another puddle to complete the set. That's why I didn't notice the surroundings until the flash of lightning silhouetted a—

Was that chick naked?

I froze in my tracks.

She stood on the end of an old boat dock. We were supposed to tear that down next week as part of the park renovation. It wasn't *safe.*

Neither was standing over water during a lightning storm. But I'd be damned if I said anything.

Did I mention she was *naked?*

And she had the longest hair I'd ever seen in person. It wrapped around her and swirled like a living thing. The kicker? Every few seconds, there'd be a flash of boob. Or ass.

Oh, and those delicate little divots of flesh behind her knees. They lured me like a siren.

I wanted to *possess* her.

A lesser man would have. She had to realize how dangerous this was, didn't she? Any predator would love to nibble their teeth into a chunk of that.

I stared down at my singular pristine pink shoe and crouched so the weeds would conceal my monstrous form. No sense in scaring her once she turned around. But if anyone else came down this path, I'd fuck 'em up. Whoever she was, woman, or nymph, she had my protection. Whether she liked it or not.

And she had my attention.

She cocked her hand back and screamed something into the storm. The object flashed white for a moment, then splashed into the river half a second later.

That wasn't a rock. I knew a binding spell when I saw it.

Whoever was on the other end of that curse was a dead man. Assumptions aside, no woman pisses off another woman that hard. Nope. If the rare instance happens, most women do one of two things, well, most of the times both. First, they get quiet. That's because they are plotting murder. Then they admit whatever plot they've concocted to their sister in spirit to compare notes and viability, and all's forgiven and forgotten. It's a damn fine thing that women are not the fragile creatures men think they are because one serious cat fight would have wiped out the planet.

But when that anger pointed at a man? Well... that's when there's an edge to the pain. Instead of theory, desperation takes over. Because while women aren't fragile, they can't take down a man my size and still have enough left over to slice his neck. Not without losing a piece of their own hide in the process. Which is why I assumed whoever this creature was, it was a *man* who'd made her angry.

All the more reason to keep my ass hidden until she left.

The rain began to blow sideways. It would be a pain in the ass to run face first into it to get home, but I'd made the dumbass choice to pick tonight for my first foray into outdoor jogging, I'd deal with it.

She struggled up the bank, wrapping the length of her hair around her arm at least three times. Her wet clothes were tucked under the other.

The dress she slipped into was homespun. Odd. But it gave me a clue. There were Pennsylvania Dutch settlers in this region. Varying religious sects made this area home, too. From Quakers to Amish, there was a hodgepodge of "folk" who made their own clothing. And then there were the new cults popping up among the Evangelicals who believed in trad-wives and that stuff. It fit with the long hair. Or, she could be one of the homespun pagan types who created their own ritual dresses. That was a puzzle piece I'd figure out later.

She shrugged a man's utility coat on. The color might have been pale orange once, but age had frayed the cuffs and faded it to a dull tan.

And it was soaked. She was soaked.

I was soaked.

Despite that, I crawled to a break in the grass so I could watch her climb into her car... Gods *damn* it. I ducked back behind the weed cover.

I knew that car. It was *not* hers. There was only one F8 green Scat Pack Dodge Charger R/T in the county. And while we all "heard" Carl Windgren boast that he had a woman, no one I knew had ever seen her. No one in their right mind would ask him if he was lying, either. Because Carl had a reputation.

A *weird* one.

He moved at least 100K of our product every year. Had done so for at least five years straight. He was solid, careful, and meticulous. He rarely overindulged, and had a head for numbers. His house was a rathole in one of Harrisburg's worst neighborhoods, and he didn't do flashy. Except for that damn car. And everyone knew if you touched it, you'd die.

Well, the assumption was you were dead. He had an uncanny knack for making people disappear. *Permanently*. Even the Destroyers respected that. He was soft-spoken, rarely bragged, and didn't hesitate to word his threats in such cold, calculating phrasing that you just *knew* he already had your murder plotted and it was all a matter of semantics at that point. Carl was our homegrown Norman Bates of the drug trafficking industry. And he really had a woman. One he hadn't made disappear like so many others around him. I didn't know if I felt sorry for her or not.

But I smiled as the woman drove away.

He'd pissed his woman off.

Old Carl didn't know it, but he'd signed his death sentence. It would be fun to watch it all unfold. Which reminded me. I had a meeting to attend. If I wanted a front row seat, all I had to do was *volunteer*.

I dumped my muddy shoes on the patio outside my living room. There was a barrel that caught rainwater next to the edge of the concrete pad. I splashed that over my legs and feet to clean them off before walking inside.

"Where the fuck were you?" Jackson, our regional president, took in my shorts, the soaked thermal shirt, and my general state of disorder, and then asked, "And what the fuck are you wearing?"

I looked down at my hairy, tattooed legs. "Shorts. I was running."

"From who?"

That was Jackson for you. He was a biker through and through. Born into the life, raised in a whorehouse, and never once ran from a fight. He was pushing fifty, with a brand-new wife and a smart-ass teenager, and still had the body and shape of a twenty-eight-year-old, and the mind of a fucking fifteen-year-old.

He was also my neighbor and the guy I was supposed to protect. Hence, why I needed to stay in shape. Because with his smart-ass mouth and graying hair, he was guaranteed to piss someone off at least once a day. Apparently, that person was me today.

"From the scale." I tore off my shirt and dumped it onto the tile in my kitchen. Better there than the wood laminate in my great room.

"You ain't fat."

"Thanks."

"Slow, maybe…"

My hands fisted. "Watch it…"

He chuckled. "Lay off the expensive whiskey and get laid more often. And forget about that fucking scale, will ya?"

"Can't."

He cocked his head to the side to study me. "Are you still pissed off because I took Bandit on the last tour?"

Tour. That was a hell of a word. He'd nabbed the regional top spot and went on "tour" to visit each and every club in his kingdom. He wanted it all done by Christmas. His reasoning? He needed the boots on the ground view of his troops. He wasn't about to sit back and let news come to him, he wanted it in his greedy hands, *yesterday.* And that meant getting up close and personal with every club east of the Appalachians from the Canadian border to Florida. I was supposed to be the one he took with him.

Instead, he had me on kiddie detail. And because of that, I remained quiet. Because, damn straight I was pissed. I pulled a towel off the handle of my kitchen stove and tried to dry off.

"Bear." I'd heard that tone long enough I knew he was trying to appeal to my good nature.

"He doesn't *know* you."

"And he *needs* to. Pittsburgh hates my shit right now. This is politics, not me slighting you. I need his approval to get *their* approval so they can forget my woman shot his president."

His wife didn't shoot Shock.

I knew that because I figured out who did.

Kiddie detail included sleeping over at the house next door when Jackson was four states away. And Kate, biker First Lady she was, went with him, knowing full well if she didn't, he'd get some whore pushed on him. That meant Zoe, their sixteen-year-old daughter, stayed home… alone. Not truly. I was there as her bodyguard and hormonal punching bag. And sure, I knew I was protecting the one thing Jackson valued most, but it still rankled. And her being left behind was kind of crappy because that poor kid still had nightmares about the murder of her mom's husband. Not Jackson… the *first* one.

What a fucked-up mess.

Shock, Pittsburgh's dead president and Kate's first husband, was lucky he was dead. Because if he'd have lived, I'd have stripped him of his skin from scalp to toenails. Then cut his back open and splayed his lungs out across the bloody breathing carcass. He'd stolen and raped Kate when she was barely seventeen. Jackson helped her get free of his child-creeping ass. But this year that bastard found her again, and she and Zoe made the right decision. They came home, to Jackson, and this club, to let us sort it out.

Which meant Pittsburgh thought Jackson killed Shock to take his wife since he'd already gone there biblically, leaving her with a kid for evidence. Zoe was the spitting image of Jackson, but cuter. With that sin on his hands, it was an easy leap to think he'd done more.

Murdering a brother was against the rules. Didn't mean it didn't happen. I knew damn well that it did. My former role as Sergeant at Arms here in Skilletsville prepared me for the inevitable fuck up of someone pressured to squeal on us. Luckily, I never had to eliminate a brother.

"How's Kate holding up?" I asked. Getting him talking about her was a great way to divert the conversation.

Jackson smiled. Even though it was a happy one, he still looked like the diabolical devil he was. "She's perfect. Tired of the bullshit, though. She wants to stay home next trip."

"You're going to need me with you, then." I said that because Kate trusted me. She knew I'd tell her if Jackson had some whore forced on him. So far, he'd given up all his womanizing ways. But pressure and distance can fuck with a man's head, even if his heart was solid.

"No can do."

"Jesus-fuck, man. Who ya taking?" He'd better not say Bandit, because that asshole *wanted* Jackson to fuck up.

"Griz."

I made a noise suspiciously close to a growl. "Kate's going to hate that."

"That's why I'm also taking Hollywood. Figure I can pawn off any sweet butt or three his way and Griz'll scare off the rest of 'em."

"Who's on Wolf?" Griz was Wolf's Sergeant at Arms now.

"Tits."

I frowned at him. While he was right, Wolf's wife also wasn't a man. Despite her being deadly enough, the optics looked bad. "Seriously, who's on Wolf?" We were in no position to let our brand-new president be guarded by a woman who was also a member of a different club, no matter how competent she or her road sisters were.

He cocked his crooked eyebrow and chuckled. "You."

The towel went down in a heap on the counter. "And who's on Kate and Zoe?"

"You."

"Fucker. I can't be both places."

"Then delegate. It's time you start learning how to lead. I'm not president here anymore."

I'd heard this refrain before. "You know damn well I suck at leading." I did. Point me at a problem, I'd fix it. But herding a bunch of screw-ups? Hell no. I'd rather put my arm between Fenrir's jaws than do that.

"You don't suck. You just *think* you do. Like you *think* you're fat, or slow."

He wanted me to argue with him so he'd win.

But he wasn't going to. I *was* getting slower. My body wasn't at that golden cusp of fitness that peeked somewhere between twenty and thirty-five. I'd slipped into forty this year, and no sooner than that milestone hit, so had my first injury. And rehab. And doctors poking at my ass talking about BMI and blood pressure and shit.

I was dying.

Slowly.

3

ROISHIN

Something fuzzy hit my face and startled me out of a sound sleep. I pulled it away and sat up, clutching the covers and whatever it was, to my chest. I double-checked to make sure I was still wearing the ugly nightgown I'd pulled off a discount shelf at a chain store. I was. The ruffles and purple flowers mocked me. I'd never wear something like this if I had my way.

But it kept Carl at bay. The shapeless flannel and the crown of braids I oiled with un-fragranced castor oil were an additional layer of deterrent to any "plans" he had on my person. I wore its ugliness like armor.

"Put that on," Carl ordered.

I examined the garment. It was a cilice, or in simpler terms, a hair shirt. I'd never seen one in real life. "Why?"

"You took the car without asking."

Damn it. He'd figured it out. But I had no idea how. "You gave me the keys." Right after the mechanic upped the list of things wrong with my car. Its demise strangely coinciding with my deal with Carl.

He took a step forward and ripped the comforter away. "Put it on, or I will put it on you."

I scrambled to pull it over my head, then tug it over the night-gown. Technically, I'd put it on.

His eyes narrowed. "You will wear it all day, tonight, and into tomorrow. I will tell you when to take it off. And, in case you think I didn't notice your defiance just now? Let me be clear. It will be worn against your skin. Do not wear a bra today. Understand?"

I nodded.

Carl didn't smile. "We're visiting Beth today."

Right. The stem cell donation and hopefully the end to this horror show. I scrambled out of bed and pulled on a pair of jeans before anything else. Carl watched me fumble with the process of pulling my nightgown off from under the cilice. As the fibers met my bare skin, I flinched. There were jagged pieces woven into the wool. Hair, or something sharper poked at my skin, causing it to twitch in irritation. But I knew better than to scratch because, while I'd never seen one, I'd heard about their torturous results.

From the Devil himself.

Carl smiled and took a step closer. I froze.

He ran a hand down the wool, caressing it, not me. I held my breath as he swept over my breast.

His eyes locked with mine and his hand stilled…there. Slowly, his fingers curled and dug in.

I clamped my teeth shut so I wouldn't cry out. This wasn't about sex. It was about control. My tears or my pain would egg him on. I detached my body from my spirit. I let that unnatural beast shine through my eyes. He could never touch that. No matter how degrading he got, my will would only hate him more. Eventually, I'd kill him.

Maybe tomorrow? It begged to be set loose.

Two months. That was the maximum span to confirm his stem cells multiplied inside Beth and formed her own healthy blood cells. I could do this.

Especially since after today, I'd be free of him. I'd promised Beth I'd leave.

I'd be her slave forever if it kept me away from Carl. I'd be *anyone's* slave if they kept me out of Carl's "tender" clutches.

He let go. "Blue shirt. Wear the cross."

Like hell I'd wear the jewelry. "The clasp is broken." I'd done that when I returned that night. He couldn't force me to pretend piety.

He dug inside the jewelry box he'd purchased when all my blessed jewelry went missing in the move.

When he found the cross, he looked at the broken clasp and the empty slot where the pin should be. I'd lost it in the floorboards. Tragic… *not.*

"You did this."

That wasn't a question. And moreover, the real question was, "Do you dare to defy me?"

"Yes."

He wrapped it around his hand. The frail gold chain snapped as he made a fist.

I waited for him to hit me.

But he thought through what *that* would do. Beth would notice. Moreover, her husband, John, would. And he'd call the cops, without hesitation. I doubted Carl wanted to spend his next two months in jail.

My tormentor's mouth curved upward. "After."

Whatever. I kicked the delay can down the road, hoping I could appease him enough to soften the blow.

I put on the plain, button-down, blue shirt. It was too tight to wear without a bra. The cilice helped to smooth the front panels and hide my nipples. But that only meant that the added pressure poked the sharper fibers into my skin with more pain. I bore it knowing after the hospital visit, there would be worse.

His mom hugged me, then frowned. "You're not wearing a bra." Her tone clearly implied I was a morally loose person for it.

"Your son wanted it that way."

"Carl!" The admonition was sharp. I refrained from showing any emotion because it would be misconstrued.

"She has a rash, mother. I was looking out for her comfort, that's all."

It was amazing how easily he lied.

"That's my son. The Lord says, 'Each one of you also must love his wife as he loves himself.' Ephesians."

Carl rattled off the chapter and verse before his father could. "I remember."

"But as the representative of his household, she should learn better decorum, and deal with the discomfort. And let me remind you, she's *not* his wife, yet." His mother was obviously not convinced of my value. Her tone implied that it would be a cold day in Hell before Carl and I were married. And *that* was a topic I wholeheartedly agreed with her on.

John, Beth's husband, interrupted their "discussion." "Beth's checked in. They're allowing only three visitors; did you want to see her?"

Carl's mother lifted her chin and looked to her husband for direction.

"We don't want to tire her out too much. I'll come in after to pray with her."

"May I visit with her?" I asked Carl, not John or his parents. John would say yes, enthusiastically. His parents? Hell no. They were still piqued at me for living with Carl for the last few weeks. But I knew that this entire farce would wear thin if I stayed in this room too long. It must have shown on my face, because Carl nodded.

"Shame," Carl's mother muttered.

I didn't bother to listen to the rest. John had to rush to keep up with me.

"Walk any faster, and they'll know you hate their guts."

I stopped. "They've known that since I was twelve. I've made no secret of it."

He laughed quietly. While Beth and John had been together for almost as long as humanly possible, it wasn't nearly as long as the history between Beth, Carl, and me. Despite that, John knew all the gossip, and anything I'd ever confided to Beth. "How long are you going to keep play-acting with Carl this time?"

"I'm leaving tonight."

"Will you need a ride?"

I might, but if I told him that, he'd show up. And then Carl would have one of his drug buddies shoot him. A tragedy, it would be called. A father of four, husband to a terminally ill woman, dead at age thirty. "No."

John shook his head. "Call."

"As soon as I can. Don't wait up."

"You know it will be a long night with kids. They're upset she won't be home, so…"

He'd be up. And he'd need help taking care of the kids tomorrow so he could get some much-needed rest. "I saved a little cash for a cab just in case."

"Make sure Carl doesn't find it," he whispered.

"Don't worry about that. I have it covered." I had it in a Ziploc bag I taped under the cilice. The irritation from the tape was almost more comfortable than the bits of hair and metal woven into the fabric.

I scrubbed my exposed skin, donned the protective gear, and masked up before entering Beth's room.

She was pale and had lost more weight. "Hey." I tried to put as much positive energy into my smile so it showed in my eyes and transferred to her.

"You made it." Her voice was barely a whisper.

"Wouldn't miss it. This is going to do the trick. I just know it." The cancer had come back despite being in remission for years. I knew the odds were grim, but not impossible. And that little sliver of hope I shoved to the front of my thoughts, willing it to be real.

Her smile faltered. "Is Carl behaving?"

I nodded. The very last thing I wanted was for her to worry about me. "I've been watching him like a hawk. You've got nothing to worry about. He's probably going to live to a hundred with me cooking for him and keeping his house clean." But after today, all bets were off. I'd lace his food with arsenic or hemlock as soon as Beth was better. I kept that sentiment inside.

While John suspected the deal with Carl was all an act, Beth *knew* it was. She'd been there when I listed all the reasons I'd never marry such an awful human. So, when Carl announced our engagement in front of the whole family and all of Beth's doctors in attendance, I had to think fast for an excuse to placate her. I'd come up with the rationalization that I was living with Carl so he *couldn't* do a damn thing to jeopardize his sister's treatment—not wouldn't, because we both knew he would if he *could*.

So, it was partly true.

She smiled weakly. "John's parents are going to help with the children. But I told them not to mention it in front of any of my family. You're covered just in case you need a little more time to get away safely."

"I don't need it. So, I guess I can focus on spoiling the kids rotten, then." I winked.

"Like my parents aren't trying to do the same thing," John muttered. He picked up Beth's hand and their fingers intertwined like they had been doing that for years.

And it struck me, they had. They'd been in love since middle school. Right about the same time I fled from anything that hinted at love. Of course, with Carl, it wasn't love. It was obsession…or something more… *evil*. Definitely not pure like what Beth and John found. I was happy for them, but worried because they'd had it too good.

Love sucked. If this treatment didn't work, they'd have maybe four months left. And in her condition, Beth was barely able to sit up, let alone be a mother or a wife. She was dying, and while doing so, torturing the man she loved, because he refused to let her do this alone.

That's not how it was supposed to work. If anyone deserved a happily-ever-after, it was these two.

I shifted, causing another bout of itchy pain to pick up in a new spot.

"Are you okay?"

Lie? Not to Beth. "Your brother's idea of torture sucks."

"What did he do?" She struggled to sit up, but John didn't let her wear herself out, opting to lift her instead.

I laughed, trying to make light of it. "He made me wear a wool corset instead of a bra. Your mom noticed and bitched at him." I smiled, remembering the moment.

Beth rolled her eyes and shook her head. "Only a few hours more."

"Yup."

I settled in for the few minutes of the visit we had left to give my support and imagine my new life. One helping Beth get stronger every day. Where I'd be free of Carl.

But until tonight, I was his. That meant helping him into the car after the donation.

"That fucking hurt," he complained as I buckled him into the passenger seat.

"You'll feel better tomorrow."

He grumbled and shifted positions. "Did you know the needle they use is four inches long?"

Wait a minute… "I thought you were donating stem platelets, not marrow."

"I was. They showed me the needle for the next step when this fails. I'm *not* doing it."

His word choice sucked. *When.* Not *if.* And he claimed I was dramatic. "It will all work out. She'll get better after this donation, and you'll be spared."

He stared at me. It was uncomfortable to be scrutinized so viscerally as I drove his car.

"What?"

"I had to sign donation paperwork."

Obviously.

"They want the marrow from my bones, Rose."

An itch poked at my spine, and it wasn't from the hair shirt or the eerily lurid way he said what he said. "Only as a last resort," I said, hoping to comfort him so he would just drop whatever was gnawing on his mind.

"Our deal is going to change."

Oh Goddess, not now. *Please.* But if he was going to renegotiate, so was I. "I'm going to John and Beth's to help with the children."

"No. You're going to stay with me."

My nostrils flared. I chanced a moment to glance away from the road and meet his eyes with a glare from mine. "No."

He gripped the seat near my head, snagging a stray wisp of hair in the grip. "You will obey me. That was the bargain."

"I will do nothing you say. We had a deal that ended today. I'm going to your sister's house tonight. And, when Beth is in remission for a full year, then we'll renegotiate."

He tightened his fingers, and the hair pulled out of my scalp. He noticed and twisted the strand around his finger. "I bind you, Roishin Black. You are mine to control."

Was he using magic against me? "You need blood to make that stick." I spat onto the palm of my hand, curled it shut, and held it toward Carl with the horns of my pinky and forefinger poking out. In Latin I spoke, "Contrere brachia iniqui rei et lingua maligna subvertetur."

"Witch."

I wore that label proudly. Carl didn't like my lack of reaction, however.

He reached across the console and grabbed the steering wheel. His yank pulled us off the road, and I slammed on the brakes to avoid hitting a fence post. The car barely stopped in time.

"You could have killed us!" The car hissed, and every warning light was lit. I tried starting it, and it wouldn't turn over.

Carl smiled. "Oh, so sad. You can't use my car tonight." He pulled out his phone and called one of his buddies for a tow.

If I had my own car, this wouldn't be an issue. But I had a sneaking suspicion Carl paid someone to vandalize it. He'd definitely paid the tow and repair guy to delay its return.

"I hadn't planned to."

But Carl wasn't listening. He was making plans to torture me.

The same guy he'd called for my car arrived and surveyed the damage.

"Oh man, your poor car. What did she do to it?" He stuck his hands inside his overalls. It wasn't lost on me that he was fondling his junk.

Carl told him I grabbed the steering wheel and tried to run the car off the road. And oh, poor him, he just got out of the hospital. He barely got the car stopped in time.

Lying sack of shit.

"I could take her off your hands for a night. Teach her some manners." He tipped his hips at me so I could see the tent his cock made as he stroked it. "Bet she needs them *beaten* into her."

Carl laughed. "Do you want to know a secret? I think she'd enjoy that. Right Rose? Whipping is more your style. I can make that happen. How much?"

"Hell, I'd do it for free." The tow truck driver laughed.

Carl pulled out a gun. He must have stored it inside the car because he hadn't carried it into the hospital. "I meant, how much will you *pay* me for her?" True to form, Carl wanted to profit off my misfortune.

The guy swallowed. "I was just kidding man." He took his hands out of his pants slowly and held them in the air.

The sight of them made Carl grimace. His face twisted up like he smelled the stink of dirty cock on them. "Don't make jokes about my Rose," he warned. His glance strayed down the street and he pocketed the gun. A second later, a police cruiser drove past, slowing down to assess the situation. He pulled in front of the tow truck and turned his lights on as he backed up.

"Not one word. I know where your kid goes to school," Carl warned the driver.

Then he plastered on a friendly smile.

And lied once again. This time, his story was that I'd been spooked by an animal crossing the road and swerved to avoid it. No harm, no foul. And Carl played the hospital card once again, begging for a ride home.

Too soon, we were dropped off outside his house by the officer. Carl shook his hand, then waved at him as he drove away.

Then he did something I swear he'd rehearsed. "You are trapped by our bargain. If you leave me, I will call that policeman back and tell him you tried to kill me. And he'll believe it. Because I *pay* him a lot of money to believe anything I say. I have *everyone*, and *everything* in my control. Don't ever disobey me again, Rose. Because if you do, you will lose what little freedom you have. *Forever*."

And just like that, I was *fucked*.

4

———

BEAR

Whoosh had a vested interest in monitoring Carl Wingren. He also had street connections in Harrisburg. Which meant that when his buddy witnessed Carl getting dropped off by a police cruiser with quote, "some frumpy chick" in tow, he knew within hours, maybe even minutes. I found out almost as soon as I walked in the door of our clubhouse because, like Jackson unfortunately pointed out, he wasn't president anymore, and it left a void when Wolf filled his shoes. And Whoosh targeted me as next in line.

Rumors the club could ignore. In fact, rumors were good for business. I didn't mind anyone spreading the word that the Destroyers were "bad news," and "don't mess with them, because they'll kill you." As long as no one mentioned names, and certainly not to the police. But if that last part happened, it became not only something to handle, but something that needed to be handled *urgently* by me.

And that fit my plans perfectly.

Before I went into Carl's house, guns blazing, I needed more than a rumor for information. "Who is the chick?" I snapped my fingers at our tech twins, Hickey and Skinner. "And which cop was it?" Then to Whoosh, "Your guy, he's cool, right? Does he need anything for the tip?"

Whoosh shook his head. "I go way back with this dude. Maybe an invite?" He said it tentatively.

I stuck my thumb in Sprout's direction. "Waterskiing at the house."

To which Sprout asked, "Aren't we waiting for Wolf?" At least he understood hierarchy, but failed to understand *urgency*.

"We'll catch him up when he gets here. If the cops are asking around to figure out who and what went down last week with Whoosh, Izzy, and Sketch, this can't fucking wait."

Not more than a week ago, Sketch and Whoosh tangled with a lowlife, pissant gangbanger named Victor who stole the car Izzy sat in right out of Carl's backyard. That asshole and one of his buddies ended up dead behind an Italian restaurant. Whoosh stepped up that night, big-time, tagging one of the bodies. Sketch took care of the other.

A day later, two other members of his gang disappeared without a trace—courtesy of yours truly. I knew exactly where they were buried. No one else did. I planted Whoosh's unregistered gun at one of their homes with the hope that the cops would think this was an internal gang dispute and look no further.

But there was one person who could take Sketch and Whoosh down—Carl. He was present when the whole mess started and was instrumental in identifying the leader. That was a problem. One we needed to correct ASAP.

With Wolf, our president, on route, and Griz, the club's sergeant at arms, out of town, and no one filling the VP role yet, Sprout technically was the highest-ranking officer present, and I should be listening to him. But taking time to listen to the village idiot wasn't what this club needed right now. So, I barked orders, fruitlessly hoping they'd be listened to.

But maybe it wasn't a bad idea to kiss his ass?

"And Sprout? Unless you want the VP role this minute, can you please make a good suggestion for damage control?"

"Naw, I think you're covering it. Bear for VP, anyone?"

Several "yeahs" sounded around the table.

I had to squash that shit fast. "Who's on kiddie patrol then? Anyone want to tangle with Jackson's spawn for me? I'd *gladly* hand that over." I waited to see who'd bite. No one did. *Obviously.* "Fuck off to all of you assholes. Let's just work this shit in front of us and worry about the other steaming piles of excrement later, okay?"

Hickey snorted. "Steaming piles of excrement," he muttered as he tapped away on his laptop. "Might have a hit." He flipped the unit around and showed Whoosh a picture. "This her?"

I peeked over his shoulder. "Yup."

The room went quiet.

Whoosh broke the silence by stating the obvious. "Considering it was my friend who saw her, not me, I can't say, but Bear seems pretty convinced. Are you clairvoyant now?"

Fuck.

"I saw that chick climb into a green F/8 Charger last week."

"And that's how the mighty fall…" Sprout propped his arm up on the table and made creaking noises until his hand hit the table. "Boom. Snatched up by the pussy."

My fists curled in on themselves. "Are you calling me a pussy?"

Sprout's grin was a little too broad.

I might have to wipe it off his face.

He hesitated, knowing full well I'd clean his clock for giving me shit.

"Seriously, you kept a sighting like that secret?" Hickey asked. "We need intel on this guy. He's been a good earner despite the obvious 'serial killer' vibes, but if he's talking to cops, and this mysterious 'woman' shows up all of a sudden, that just smacks of a task force making moves."

It did.

And Hickey was right. Which meant I needed to own up to my bullshit. "I got distracted."

"By pussy," Sprout stage-whispered.

I glared at him. "Now you're calling Jackson a pussy?"

Wisely, Sprout wiped the smile off his face and pretended to be interested in something very far away.

"How'd you find that photo?" I asked.

"Tracked a rumor to a mega-church directory. Found Carl, he's the pastor's son, and this woman? She was his sister's best friend. They're in a lot of photos together from a decade ago and older. Not as many recently. Carl's sister has cancer. There's one of them prayer request sites online for her."

"Name? I mean, for the woman, not the sister."

Hickey tapped a few seconds more. "Huh." He sounded stumped.

"Is that a good *huh* or a bad one? Skinner?" I asked Hickey's counterpart, who wasn't as easily distracted by unnecessary details.

Skinner stopped searching the police databases to see who was dispatched yesterday and looked over. "Name change." He scanned farther.

"At age twelve. Whoa, and age six from the one she was born with. *Damn*. She's used up her quota."

These guys and their trivia. A few years back someone discovered you can legally change your name three times without incurring a fee. Trust one of these two to remember that tidbit but not give me a straight answer.

I drummed my fingers on Wolf's desk because I didn't have a name…yet. This was *why* I didn't want the damn VP job. No one *listened* to me. If Jackson or Wolf had asked for a name, they'd have it. No commentary, no side convo. No fucking trivia.

They didn't get the hint. "Well?"

"Current name is listing as *Rosin Black*. That screams alias. Figures, she picked it when she was twelve." Skinner pronounced her first name like the stuff in the bag you use on pitching mounds.

That couldn't be right, not for a woman as alluring as her. I looked at what Hickey had dug up. The spelling was Roishin. Pretty name. Perfect for the cute little divots behind her knees.

"It's pronounced, ROEsheen. It's Irish. And Black? That's Irish, too."

Hickey stared at me.

"What? You think I can't know things?"

That shut his mouth. Skinner jumped into the breach. "It's just that you seem to know a hell of a lot about a woman you saw climbing into Carl's swamp green Scat Pack."

I counted twice on my fingers. "I don't know why she's with him, *or* whether she's working with the cops, do I? That's what I need you two for."

Hickey tapped some more. "She ain't working with the cops. She ain't working period. 'Got fired from a local pharmaceutical research facility last month."

That was too coincidental. I spun my thoughts out loud. "Pharmaceutical? Carl loves his pill customers…"

A set of nods followed my logic.

"Do you think she's a cook?" Skinner asked.

A methamphetamine cook would make sense. More sense than someone actually being in love with the asshole. Then again, would he let his cook drive his car?

That didn't fit with what I knew of Carl. He never did anything decent unless he could profit off it, or get favors for it.

"I think we need to give him a visit."

"You got a mouse in your pocket? *You* need to give him a visit." Hickey said.

Sprout chimed in. "Once Wolf approves it."

"Thanks, VP." Giving Sprout a promotion sounded funny in my head. But no one else was stepping up. It might as well be him.

The men around the desk laughed. I pointed at the idiot they all thought so little of. "We all know he's the power behind the throne, don't let him fool you."

"That'd be Danielle," he fired back.

"She's the power *under* your throne," Skinner said.

"Between your knees," Hickey joked.

Sprout rubbed his crotch. "Hell, yeah. That's the best part of being married. Except the whole pregnant part kind of fucks with her being on her knees for very long."

"When is that woman finally gonna pop?" She had to be due any minute now. She was as big as a house. Not that I'd say that in front of Sprout. For that, it was a sure bet that he'd knife me.

Everything else ran right off him. But bad-talk about his woman or his ma? *Boom.* Suddenly, he turned into his father.

Don't get me wrong, Sprout's deceased father, Jolly, was a great man, and left big shoes to fill when it came to enforcer legends. I was trying my best to live up to his example. I couldn't imagine the weight of it on Sprout. No wonder he was a fuckup — he had less to prove that way. My epiphany was cut short.

"She's due December 25th."

Damn, no separation between Christmas and birthday presents. "That poor kid."

"Hey! He's going to be spoiled rotten."

"That'll be Ma's doing, not yours." Hickey laughed. "Poor kid."

"All you all can fuck off."

"You sure it's not a girl?" I asked.

"The Great Dane does not shoot X chromosomes."

Dumb ass. He willingly gave himself a nickname ripe for ridicule.

"Uh…" Hickey started, finger in the air, but I interrupted him.

"That boy won't understand," I warned.

"Right." Hickey nodded and tapped away on his laptop some more.

"Understand what?" Sprout asked.

Skinner stood up, determined to make a point. "Your ma?"

Sprout matched him, expecting Skinner to lay down fighting words. I moved my chair back in case this came to blows. "What about her?" Sprout challenged in his lowest register.

"She put in half of you. That means there's at least a fifty percent chance you'll get someone like her." He stated the obvious much more kindly than I ever could have.

"Damn straight, and it would be an honor to raise another biker babe like Ma. But it's a boy. I got the picture of his dick to prove it."

"Oh Gods, spare us." The last thing I needed was him passing around that grainy ultrasound picture again. I swear he mistook the umbilical cord for the kid's penis.

Wolf finally showed up—just in time to debrief and divert us from Sprout's insanity. I ran through what I had so far, including seeing her get into Carl's car.

"Bear's got a crush on her," Sprout added.

"Do not," I fired back.

"When you saw her, what was she doing before she got into Carl's car?" Wolf asked.

I smiled. I'd saved this part, the best part, for my president. "Standing naked in the rain."

He blinked.

The rest of the room laughed, thinking I'd made a joke. It died down because Wolf didn't laugh. Instead, he let everyone get uncomfortable, then said, "No shit?" He'd read through my poker face.

I nodded. "She was probably casting a spell or a curse."

He tensed. His eyes fell to the hammer pendant hanging from the chain around my neck. "On who?"

Sprout interrupted, "Wait a minute, Bear, you didn't say you saw her naked."

"I saved that for the man who matters. So, fuck off." Then I addressed Wolf's question so he wouldn't have to dig it out of me like I had to in order to get answers from these knuckleheads. "I'm guessing… Carl."

"Interesting. He's due for his second payment soon."

There was a reason Jackson picked Wolf as his number two guy then passed the mantle of presidency off without looking back. And it wasn't the same reasons he'd had for VPs previously. Apparently, Jackson had seen the writing on the wall and knew it was time to reach for a higher rank. For that to happen, he needed someone just as smart and just as ruthless in his spot. Wolf's sharp mind was already weaving my information into a plan. I added my two cents in before he got too far off track. "With the cop in the mix, I think it's time I go pay him a visit and remind him what happens to snitches."

Wolf nodded. "I'd say take Griz, but he's with Jackson. Who do you want with you?"

"I can handle Carl."

He scrutinized me. "Yeah?"

"I can." I wasn't *that* slow, I wasn't weak, and I wasn't stupid. I'd have my Glock as backup.

And if the gun needed a backup, I had my buck knife and my fists. "I'm there to talk and remind him about the payment, not make him piss his pants."

That argument Wolf could get behind. He nodded. "Make sure someone is close, just in case."

For that, I tapped Skinner. Not only was he good at surveillance, but also a damn good shot. In addition, he blended in well. He slipped his nondescript utility van into an empty spot in the alley. He stuck an electronic tag on me. It monitored two things. My heart rate and body temperature. Nothing else. The signal it emitted should get lost in the clutter of smart devices and cell signals nearby. But with those two metrics, he would know instantly if I'd been shot between the eyes.

Behind Carl's house there were floodlights, monitors, cameras, and Hela-knows what else back there giving him fair warning if anyone approached. They 'worked better than a dog,' according to that lunatic.

Funny thing about him saying that, there was a dog kennel in the neighbor's yard. It had been empty for a while now.

Which gave me insight I really didn't want to know about the man.

I stood at the back door, staring at the camera facing the stoop.

He'd open the door, or I'd hear the front door open if he rabbited. I didn't need to knock, did I?

One full minute later, he opened the door.

"Hey, Bear, is it?"

Fuck answering that. My name was sewn right over my heart. "Let me in, we need to talk."

His eyes widened slightly. I couldn't get a bead on whether he was surprised or scared. I was hoping for both. And I wasn't asking. I was *telling*. Maybe that pissed him off?

I pushed past him and strode through the enclosed porch and into his kitchen. There was a pot simmering on the stove. Stew, by the smell of it.

The house felt different since my last visit. Instead of the tension of factions wondering if they could trust each other not to screw the other over, it felt…

Homey?

What the fuck?

I realized it was because of the smells. Not only was a pot of stew simmering on the stove with the promise of slowly tender-ized, savory beef scenting the air, but there were layers to the aromas.

Freshly baked bread and clean surfaces. Those were highly unusual smells for Carl's house. Sure, he liked things clean, but it was never truly *this* clean.

I scanned the room, figuring out quickly that the two lumpy towel-covered shapes on the counter were where that fresh bread smell came from.

My dick got hard. Sue me.

Carl might have a cook, but it was the best kind, not the drug-dealer-serial-killer kind.

"Are we alone?" I eyed the bread. I bet if I held a hand over the fabric, there'd be heat emanating from the covered loaves.

"Yeah."

Really now? Lying right out of the gate? Carl, Carl, Carl… shame on you.

I played along. "Cool. Turn that shit off and sit with me in the living room. This might take a bit."

Carl sucked on his cheek. Odds were, he was biting the inside to keep from telling me off.

For incentive, I reached inside my vest and casually took out my gun. I walked into the living room and plopped my ass on the couch. Then, set the gun on the armrest where it was inches from my fingers.

Taking a bit of comfort from the fact that I hadn't just killed him outright, Carl smiled and took the hard-backed chair across from me, rather than the recliner. Smart.

"I heard a rumor," I said.

The corner of Carl's mouth went up. "Rumors are generally good for business."

Some were, so I nodded, but added, "Some are bad. Like hearing you got dropped off at your house by a cop."

The tense line of his brows relaxed, he leaned back in the chair, losing a bit of the stiff posture he'd held as he sat down. "That was my guy on the inside. I wrecked my car."

"I don't give a fuck who it was or why. You spooked a few people."

He laughed. Downright guffawed.

I was exactly three inches away from killing him, and he thought what I stated was funny.

"Anyone who didn't understand who dropped me off, *deserves* to be spooked."

Was that a threat?

Or was it an insult?

"Like I said, I heard a rumor. But maybe I need to spell things out." I leaned forward and placed my hand on the gun.

The smile fell off his face. "Proceed."

The command was issued as if he were in charge here.

Fuck that. "Eight grand and silence."

"I'm sorry?"

"That's what you owe us for the last drop. It also is the amount of difference between where you peaked at three months ago, and where your orders are at now. You're down to sixteen grand in one month from us. Not twenty-four. And not a damn word why." I got a little more comfortable. "And I know that the local boys run at least thirty K. Now, that's just one group. This area is good for forty-six thousand a month, but last month, our cut went down. I know consumption isn't. Before we get to the second part of what you owe, who is pissing in our territory?"

Carl's posture stiffened again. "Everyone."

His answer was a buzzkill, despite it being a known problem. Solving the decline in our reputation and our business was a delicate path. We couldn't do either of the things we needed to do, which were knock heads and seize control, because honestly? We were getting out. But we really had to make sure it was on our terms not on someone else's. Otherwise, we'd never survive the fall.

"Everyone's wrong."

Carl studied me. "Perhaps."

I stared him down. "Does *everyone* include you?" I knew damn well it did. We'd cut back on our deals with him deliberately so he'd cultivate other assets. Twenty-four K is a lot of product tied up with a volatile asset like Carl. But if in the act of cultivating he'd run afoul of the feds or something worse, we needed to know.

"Don't threaten me."

That was Carl. That holier-than-thou attitude he'd honed seeped through his tone.

"Why can't I? What's stopping me from drilling a hole through you and that fancy-backed chair?"

A noise sounded behind me. There was barely space for a rat to crawl behind the couch, so it startled me. I stood up, pointing the gun downward as I tossed the heavy sofa into the center of the room.

Carl jumped out of the way of the moving couch, but the chair he had sat on so primly took the brunt of the hit. It clattered to the floor, breaking into a skewed mess.

I barely glanced at it.

The woman I'd seen driving Carl's green sports car cowered in the space that had been between the sofa and the wall.

"Who the *fuck* is this?" I knew damn well who it was, but I also needed to play this to the nines. Scare him. Maybe even make someone piss their pants. I rammed the point of my gun against her head. "You said we were alone!"

Carl stretched to see the woman without getting too close to me.

"She's no one." His tone dismissed her and tempted me to pull the trigger.

I grabbed her by the frumpy housedress she wore and pulled her to her feet. Her hair was all wrapped up in a braided crown around her head. I could have held her more securely by that, but I didn't want to hurt her.

She weighed barely more than an SUV tire. And that housedress? Already torn and revealing an odd woolen undershirt. The dress ripped farther as I shook her.

Her hands gathered the fabric around her body and tried to cover what she could. But her legs were bare.

Distractions rarely bothered me. Unless they were shaped and scented like a woman.

Like… *this* woman.

Her feet were bare, too.

I was staring. Carl would catch on to my weakness quickly. I blurted out, "She doesn't look like no one. Name, now!" I shook her again.

"Roishin," she said right as Carl said, "Mary-Rose."

I glanced between them. "Which one of you is lying?" I pointedly glared at Carl because I knew she went by the new name.

His nostrils flared. I tightened my grip and turned the gun from the woman to him, hoping he wouldn't make me use the weapon. It was one thing to shoot with distractions. And a whole different thing to shoot someone with an unpredictable bundle of hissing she-cat barely controlled in the opposite hand.

"Forgive me, I'm used to her… *dead* name."

What interesting phrasing. And he spoke it casually, as if I weren't holding a gun on him at all.

"Roishin Black." She had a lyrical voice. The notes of it were quiet, soft, and utterly feminine in quality and timbre.

"Did I say you could talk?"

Carl stepped forward with a raised hand.

I stuck the gun out, aiming in a deadline for his nose. "Did I say you could move?"

He froze. Slowly, he lowered his hand.

Even more slowly, a smile grew on his lips. "Do you like her?"

This was not going as I expected. When did he gain the upper hand? I had a gun on him. "Not if she's a fucking narc. You know what happens to narcs. Is she one?"

Carl was cool, calm, and deliberate as he spoke. "She's not. She's… how to put it?" He pretended to think for a moment. Then, that macabre grin got bigger. "She's property."

"Of you?"

"Yes."

Fuck.

I let go, practically dropping her. "I see. No harm. No foul." I even tucked the gun away to prove to Carl that I was going to let this all go. But I wasn't. There was a red mark across her arm. It was ugly bright, with the center of it turning darker by the second. Something hard and narrow did that. A cane or maybe a crop. I didn't know. And nothing nearby gave me any clues.

Notably, she didn't retreat to Carl for protection. She remained where she'd landed on the floor, barely moving. Her dress was ripped all the way down the back. She'd hunched it up to cover her ass, but that strange undershirt was completely exposed. So was the reddened skin near the armholes and neckline. That was either an allergic reaction or chafing. And it had to hurt.

But she barely moved. Not even to breathe. It was as if she was trying to avoid attracting the attention of a predator.

Or two of them.

5

———

ROISHIN

When Carl made me hide, I thought I'd been spared from his anger. I don't know if it was the pain from the procedure or wrecking the car, but he was in a mood. Or maybe he was ready to enact the retribution he'd promised?

I tried everything to avoid it, appease it… control it. I baked bread. I made the stew recipe his mother made for him. I didn't mention the cilice, or his promise to let me remove it. None of my efforts worked. He blamed me for the pain. He said vile things about his sister. And he was breaking his promise.

"I'm done suffering at your hands, Rose. You're going to suffer now." After that declaration, Carl came at me with the broom. I blocked it.

I yelled back, "If you kill me, Beth and her husband will know it was you. They'll tell the cops, and your parents."

He growled because he knew I was right. But that didn't stop his rage. "I won't kill you tonight. But you're going to wish you were dead. I swear it!" Right before he swung again, an alarm started beeping. Carl set the broom in the corner of the kitchen, checked his computer, and told me to hide.

Whoever the huge man on the monitor was, he scared Carl so much that my misery could wait.

That scared me.

The intruder stood at least a hand's width taller than six feet. I'd heard the nickname "Bear" mentioned. It fit. His arms were thicker than my thighs. One fist could probably fell a small tree.

And he was hairy.

The wiry brown hair on his arms matched his beard. There was so much of it you could barely see the tattoos underneath. Both sides of his scalp were shaved, and tattoos coiled around his skull randomly. They even encroached on his face.

Metal piercings glinted at his eyebrow, ears, and lip. More objects were embedded in his beard and hair.

Like his beard, his hair was dark and long. But he kept it controlled by a thick mess of twists and braids that ran from his forehead to the nape of his neck before trailing down his back in a waterfall of smaller braids, shiny beads, and bits of wood or stone wrapped into the pieces like they'd been trapped there as it grew.

It was wild, like an animal's.

No, like a *feral* animal's mane.

Something shiny glinted at his throat. I tried to see what it was without moving my head to look. But my angle was all wrong. I'd have to move.

Which would be a mistake. One I couldn't afford to make.

Carl might be evil and cruel, but he wasn't nearly as strong as the man named Bear.

He'd thrown the couch one-handed.

A whole couch.

It made Carl's fit with the broom look like… amateur hour. With that strength and that gun, Bear had the will and means to make good on his threat to kill Carl.

And then?

I'd be free, but Beth might die without him alive to donate again. And I would not risk that. Not until I *knew* she was getting better. When Bear talked so casually about killing Carl, I couldn't help the catch of my breath. It swamped me with how fragile life was. How all I'd suffered so far was for naught if Carl's drug-dealing antics ruined everything.

And as much as I wanted to be at Beth's house right now, I couldn't just leave Carl with this man. Not until I was certain that his donated stem cells were enough to kick-start Beth's recovery.

Then I'd gladly hand Carl over to Bear myself. Maybe even ask for the gun so I could be the one to shoot him.

He deserved it for ruining my life.

Carl's smarmy voice filled the room. "If you want her, she's for sale."

Not this again.

Bear laughed. "I'm here, bitching at you for being seen with a cop and shorting the club on profit opportunities, and you think selling me some gash is going to make me forget that you're putting my club at risk?"

What did he call me?

"Ah. Then I think we both need a gesture of goodwill," Carl said calmly.

"I need you not to be sticking your ass out in front of the cops and freaking out buyers. What the fuck, man? We *own* you. The only reason you're where you are right now is because you *didn't* attract attention." Bear was unhinged. His words spat out at a rapid pace, the Destroyers skull on his vest adding weight to his words.

In contrast, Carl was calm. "Times change. Maybe profits are down because I'm getting out."

Bear fired back, "Times can go fuck themselves. You want out? *Buy* your way out. And do it without the fucking cops involved, got it? Otherwise, you and I both know that me and my brothers have no problem with losing you, *permanently.*"

There was weight in the silence that echoed through the house. I could feel the touch of the Goddess in this moment. The hair on my skin prickled, electrified. It burned where the cilice had rubbed me raw. I almost groaned out loud, but I managed to clear my head and think only about the presence of magic surrounding this place. It hung in the air, waiting…

Bear broke the spell. "You owe us eight grand. And another

eight grand for losing out on one month's *best* earnings. Pay me tonight and we'll wash our hands of you. But we'll be watching you. In or out, it doesn't matter. *Watching* you. Got it? No more cops."

Carl didn't hesitate. "My payment date is in three days. You'll get your money then. But I have a question, perhaps two. One of your hookers takes in what? Four hundred a night? Maybe even more on a good day, right?"

"What are you getting at, Carl?"

He grabbed me by the hair and lifted my head. "She's yours for one month. Do *anything* you like to her, but I want her *alive* when you return her. And don't go stashing her somewhere she can run away and *snitch* to the cops. I need her visible and seen with your club for one month. That's all. When the month ends, I'll buy out any remaining debt and even pay extra for the best earnings you should have had, and we'll *both* be done with each other.

"With the use of her, that's at least thirty grand in addition to the double payment. Plus, you're guaranteed another witness to your club brothers' indiscretions is silent, and I'll not have to deal with her insubordination for a month. That's *more* than generous enough. Do we have a deal?" Carl shook me. I realized this was his way of making me suffer. A way that wouldn't trace back to him. He hadn't changed one bit.

Carl wasn't selling me for money; he was selling me for time. And in one month, I might know whether his stem cell donation had helped Beth. And in one month, if it didn't, I'd have to return to Carl and beg him for help. Or, in one month, Beth would be alive and thriving, and I'd be… dead.

Getting me back from this terrible man alive was only a means to an end. Carl was working a game. One he'd just looped Bear into. I could walk back into this house without a scratch on me, and Carl would see to it that my dead body washed up somewhere the next morning with all the earmarks of torture. And since he wasn't connected to me for over a month? He'd walk away, free. That's how he operated.

I needed leverage.

"I'm not buying her," Bear said.

"Of course you're not. She's on *loan* to you as a gesture of good-will and insurance of that silence you want so much."

I searched Bear's face for some hint that he wasn't worse than Carl. I needed hope. And found none.

His scowl deepened. "This goodwill? You go to the cops and say, 'the Destroyers took my woman' and fuck us. Is that your game?" He pulled out his gun again and pointed it at Carl.

In a voice too calm to be real, Carl slowly spoke, "You're not listening. I need her trained to behave, and quite honestly? I know you and your club would do a much better job of breaking her than I ever could. Do *whatever* you want to her. I don't care. I'll pay sixteen grand to you—not as a buyout—but for teaching her how to be a *good* slave. And remember, if she can't behave, it's your reputation on the line. One that's been a bit…tarnished lately. That's all this is."

"And between then and now?" Bear prompted.

"I'll lie low. No more cops. No rumors. You won't even know I exist."

All hope fled. I'd walked right into Carl's trap. Freely.

"One month?" Bear asked to clarify.

"One month. You can return her on All Saint's Day. Do you know when that is?"

"I'm not stupid. It's right after Halloween."

"It's the day to celebrate the martyrs!"

I flinched at Carl's uncharacteristic volume.

Bear, however, didn't balk. "…And the dead."

That pleased Carl. He let go of my hair, then rubbed his hand against his jeans. "Go with him."

Was this really happening?

"She got any clothes or shit?"

Carl laughed. "She won't need clothes."

"To get her ass where I need to get her, she needs clothes. I'm on my bike tonight. You, Rose or whatever it is, grab enough shit you won't freeze or get me pulled over. You got one minute. Go!"

I ran to my "room" which was more like a closet than a bedroom. I grabbed what I could and stuffed it into my laptop backpack. I slipped the device into the padded back pocket and stumbled, overwhelmed by the futility of it all.

I ripped off the dress, but couldn't untie the hair shirt quickly so opted instead to toss a sweatshirt over it. Then jumped into my jeans and my good boots, no time for socks. I stuffed a bra into the side pocket of the pack. The clock in my head was ticking.

From downstairs, Bear yelled out, "Don't forget whatever woman shit you need. I ain't buying tampons!"

I froze.

I hadn't even thought about all that stuff. My hair products, my makeup, my…

My leverage.

I tore through the bathroom, spilling my products out of their box and only grabbing a handful. If I wasn't going to see Carl for one whole month, I'd have time before he killed me for this mess. As soon as I had enough stuffed in a pocket or two, I reached behind the toilet tank. Carl had a stash point in this bathroom. Whenever one of his dealers came for a buy, he'd finish by walking up to this bathroom and hiding the cash in the little hinged hole in the wall.

I pulled out the twin stacks of bills hidden there and shoved them under the spot in my pack where the lining had worn thin. The padding for the laptop worked away from both sides. I tore the wrapper bands off the money and flattened the bills out at the bottom of the bag where they were concealed by the half-inch foam. I'd lost pens, coins, lip pencils, bobby pins, hair ties, and receipts in that gap, swearing each time I'd replace the bag. But I never had. It was about time the black hole of doom swallowed something else. The cash I needed to buy my freedom. I ripped off the tape holding my cab fare to my skin, pulled the money out of the Ziplock, and stuffed half into my makeup bag as a decoy, and the other into a package of facial wipes. I used folded pieces of the tape to secure the ripped hem of the lining so the larger portion of cash couldn't fall out.

Carl would eventually miss his money. When he did, I'd bargain with it.

And if Beth was better by that point? I'd hand it over and walk away.

Finally *free*.

Just one more month. I could do this. I'd endured worse.

"Get your ass down here!"

Bear was much more vocal than Carl. I grabbed what else I could and zipped up the various pockets and swung my pack over my shoulder. Then scrambled down the stairs to face my new fate. Whatever the Goddess had planned for me, I'd accept it. I'd asked for freedom. And I was getting it. Just delayed by one month. There was always a price for magic. Nothing was without cost. And everything worked on the world's timeline, not the individual's.

And maybe this wasn't exactly how I envisioned my freedom would start. But I wasn't about to question the will of the Gods.

Carl stopped me and yanked the pack from my shoulder. "Not so fast. I gotta make sure you didn't take anything that wasn't yours."

My heart threatened to escape my chest. If he found the money, I'd never be free.

Carl searched through the bag, spilling the loose bottles and tampons onto the floor, shaking out my laptop and my clothes to join the clutter at my feet.

He unzipped my makeup bag and took the cash I'd stuffed there.

Satisfied I hadn't pilfered anything of his, he tossed the empty backpack at me. "Clean that shit up."

I stuffed everything back into its place under both of their watchful eyes. Bear took the bag from me, then Carl groped me. His hand poked at my crotch and squeezed my boobs hard as he made certain I had nothing stuffed down my pants or into my shirt.

His grin as he smoothed along the cilice was awful. His hand paused where the tape residue made the fibers in the fabric dig in worse. He leaned close and whispered, "Try to keep this. I'll want you in it when you return."

Then he shoved me at Bear. "You'll love her under garments. They're custom made."

The night air was chillier than I had anticipated. I shivered as Bear herded me onto the back of his bike. Carl watched us leave, standing in the doorframe, lit from behind. Almost like a parent bidding their child goodbye. Light bounced off his sinister grin.

Bear fired up the motorcycle, and I grabbed onto his coat to avoid being tossed off by the violent jerk of power as he tore out of Carl's realm and entered his.

I was truly screwed. Loaned to a biker with less care than a library book gets. I should just let go and roll to my death.

One thing kept me clutching at the dirty black leather coat Bear wore.

It was doubt.

What if Beth didn't get better? What if I needed Carl to save her again? If I were dead, no one would be able to con or bargain with him to help. No pleas for mercy would be heard. That was beyond his ability to care. Carl only helped himself. I knew this long before I'd approached him for a deal. It was a miracle he'd agreed.

It was an even bigger miracle that he hadn't demanded more.

6

———————

BEAR

This wasn't in the plan. I drove—not exactly paying attention to the road as much as I was trying to figure out the point in the conversation where Carl took the upper hand.

I'd reacted as expected. I got a good deal. Carl's promise of eight grand on time and a buyout at the end of the month was better than good. We finally could cut Carl loose without him setting us up.

So, why did this sit all wrong?

The girl clinging to my back was one good reason. The other was Carl's utter lack of fear. The only times he showed any emotion were when he dangled Roishin by the hair and when he corrected me on the date.

What kind of nutjob gets that worked up about a fucking holiday? And what was that shit about martyrs? I had some research to do.

Good thing I could delegate. I slowed down and pulled over along the highway. Out of habit, I put my hand on Roishin's leg and said, "Stay seated, just making a call."

She squirmed.

What if she bolted? I tightened my hand and tried to scroll for Skinner's number with my thumb. It wasn't working well and took longer than I wanted it to.

The connection finally went through.

"Yo, you out?"

"I am. Got a rabbit hole for you. Why would someone call November first the day of martyrs?"

Behind me, Roishin made a noise.

"Call you back." I disconnected the call and twisted around to lay down the law. "When I'm talking to my brothers, you don't listen, and you don't make a sound. Got it?"

"In the year 609 or 610, Pope Boniface the Fourth stole, sorry, *converted* the Pantheon from use by the polytheist worshippers in Rome to reconsecrate it to the Virgin Mary and the martyrs of the Christian church. It was celebrated on May first until Pope Gregory the Third stole Samhain from the Celts and designated *that* day as the day the Church would remember the consecration. It was named All Saint's Day for the martyrs—of which, they collected like Pokémon by that point."

Her eyes dipped to my neckline.

I glanced down to where my hammer had worked its way out of my shirt from the vibration of the bike. Then looked at Roishin, where she waited for a response.

"Fuck those assholes."

She smiled. "I agree. Not literally, just in a spit on their tombstones sort of way."

A snort snuck out. "That's a funny thought. Traveling all the way to Rome to spit on the floor of a church."

She spoke loudly enough that I heard it. "I'd do it."

Hell. I wasn't supposed to like her, or discover a common thread of discontent lacing her voice with anger. She was a far cry from the docile woman I saw at Carl's.

Which begged the question, *was this an act?*

Her diatribe told me one important thing, and no, it wasn't that she was interested in pagan things. I knew that already. What I hadn't known was that Rose, Roishin, whatever, was a very smart woman. And I shouldn't underestimate her. Carl likely hadn't.

She squirmed, pulling her shirt away from her body with a grimace.

"Off."

I didn't give her time to protest. I stood up and braced the bike while practically pushing her off with my free hand.

She stumbled a couple of steps, giving me time to lock the bike down. Rose stood still, likely in shock, waiting to see what I'd do. A truck screamed by, buffeting us in its wake.

Even I didn't like what I was going to do. I backed her up against the Jersey wall. There was a stone sound barrier behind it, so she had nowhere to run.

"Take off your shirt."

She clutched at it instead.

"I didn't fucking stutter. Take it off."

"It's cold." She glanced at the highway where cars buzzed past without even slowing down. It was late enough that half of them probably didn't even see us on the shoulder.

"Take off the shirt, or at least prove to me you aren't still wearing that goddamn fuzzy thing you had on earlier."

Her eyes went wide.

Fuck. She was wearing it.

I flipped open my knife and turned my back to traffic so they wouldn't see it. "Easy way or hard way?"

She scrambled to take off her sweatshirt and reveal that horrifically ugly garment. As soon as she did, I realized no one in their right mind would willingly put on something so heinous.

What kind of hold did Carl have over her to make that happen?

"Take it off."

I grabbed her sweatshirt and held it up so the traffic wouldn't see her unraveling the string ties holding it together. "I promise I won't stare at your tits." That was a lie. No sooner than she got the left side loose, the soft curve of her breast peeked out. The glow from an ultra-high LED headlight set bounced off the cement wall behind her, giving me a perfect view of her skin.

Reddened.

My anger boiled like a fucking volcano. I glanced away, deliberately counting the lines carved into the wall to absorb sound. Carl was a dead man. She tugged the sweatshirt from my hands. The rustling of her pulling it over her head clued me that I could look again.

Rose had the hair shirt in her hand. I took it from her and squeezed it. It pricked me as if it had steel wool or fiberglass fragments in it. "You wore this?"

Her head dipped once.

"Willingly?"

Her response was silence as she stared at the ground. I shoved the thing in my saddlebag and cursed. "We're burning this fucking thing, understood?"

Rose's mouth opened.

I waited for a protest to come out.

Her mouth closed.

Like I said, *smart.* I pointed at her. "New rule, no arguing with me."

"Argument isn't the same as requesting an adjustment to your course of action."

I barely heard her over the rumble of a truck passing by on the opposite side. Sarcastically, I said, "Really? Enlighten me on your brilliant plan."

"I was going to ask if I could light the match."

If she hadn't still been looking at the ground, I'd have guffawed with laughter. But the situation wasn't funny. Somehow Carl had gotten inside her head so far, she was afraid.

Of what? An asshole who was now firmly in her past? I had one month to come up with a solution to shove down that son of a bitch's throat that would allow me to keep Rose. His quote was a hell of a lot of money to lose out on. But I was willing to offset the loss with my own money if I had to. And if he didn't let me keep Rose, bullets for my 50-cal were less than five bucks. I should bypass the offer and save myself a lot of scratch. I didn't even have to wait that long to do it, either—only three days.

One thing held me back. The *why*. Why would someone as obviously smart as Rose—*Roishin*—willingly wear a torture device? What would she possibly fear more than constant pain? That mystery had me rethinking my plan.

"Get on the bike. I've got a grill at home."

She swallowed her fear and climbed back on. Before we took off, I pulled out my windproof jacket liner and zipped it up over her hoodie. Even with the bulky layer under it, the thing hung on her and covered her hands. It puddled where her ass met seat.

"Are you warmer?"

Roishin nodded.

"You know that whole 'don't talk' thing I bitched about at Carl's? That isn't a rule, just don't interrupt me when I'm talking to someone with this coat on. That's disrespectful. Even if I'm only on the phone with 'em. Got it?"

"Got it."

Good. I scanned traffic to find a hole to pull out into, but something held me back. Instead, I pulled out my phone again. I held it high enough and pointed at my coat to let Roishin know I was calling Skinner again. "Bro."

"Bear, what the fuck? Since when do you hang up on me?"

I did that shit all the time. "Fuck off."

"I suppose you got another rabbit hole for me, don't 'cha?"

"Naw, I need to meet up. How far out are you from the tattoo shop? I got stuff for you."

"I'm fifteen minutes from there now."

"I'm twenty."

"Where the fuck are you?"

A truck blared past, drowning me out, and hopefully telling Skinner what he needed to know. "I had to stop to call you."

"Get a fucking Bluetooth like everyone else."

"I ain't wearing no pansy-ass piece of radioactive shit on my head."

Skinner tried to log a protest, but I cut him off.

"Remember our curious little puzzle I went to solve?" I asked Skinner, reminding him of Roishin and Carl.

"Yeah?"

"It got weirder. Brace yourself."

Twenty minutes later, I pulled up to the back door of my tattoo shop.

Skinner's van sat in the little lot off the alley. I tucked the bike beside it. Roishin got off and waited as I crab-walked it into place.

"Where are we?"

"My shop."

She looked around. This side of the river walk was still in a state of renovation where old and rundown met new. Some of the buildings were occupied, many weren't. A restaurant opened two buildings down. Their dumpster was still so pristine it didn't stink. That would change. And when it did, I'd bitch. Food was meant to be enjoyed, not left out to rot.

Her eyes fixed on the lighted street.

"Are you thinking of running?" I asked and braced for the lie.

"I'm supposed to be at my friend's house." Roishin licked her lips.

That was a tell. There was a lie in there. "Who's this friend?"

She clammed up.

Of course she did. I hadn't exactly been all warm and fuzzy. "Do I need to pull my knife again?"

Even in the dim light of the alley, I could tell that the blood left her face. She shook her head, ending it seriously with a hard-pinned stare at me. "I—my friend, Beth, is in the hospital. I was supposed to go over to her place after dinner and help take care of her children."

The dinner I'd interrupted. Stew and fresh bread. Carl had something that sweet in life and gave it up transactionally. That was... foreign, bizarre, *inhuman*. More proof to me that he was fucked up in the head.

"Can you call?"

"I think I left my cell phone at Carl's."

A grunt escaped. I hadn't exactly given her a lot of time to bug out. "Do you know the number?"

She nodded.

"Cool. There's a phone in the shop."

She took a step toward the door. I stopped her. "Just so we're clear? I'll be listening in." I raised my eyebrows to convey what I wouldn't say.

Because while I should make it clear that this wasn't a kidnapping, and that she was much safer in my hands than in Carl's, I also didn't trust her. And I *couldn't* trust her until I figured out the game those two were playing. Therefore, I had to play the role of the bad guy and be the asshole everyone assumed I was. I shouldn't have even offered the phone call. But even I couldn't be that much of a dick.

On the plus side, if she truly had to be somewhere tonight, calling and canceling would keep me out of the hot seat should this blow up in my face.

"I understand."

I hoped like hell she did.

Skinner was inside. I slapped hands with him and theatrically swept my hand to introduce Rose.

"Meet Roishin, or Rose. Last name, Black."

Skinner shot a sharp glance at me. I smiled and gave him a little smug lift of my chin.

Roishin watched us carefully. She must have deemed me a bigger threat since her glances settled on me. That was fair. Skinner hadn't pulled a gun or a knife on her… yet.

I pulled down a book of tattoo flash from the shelf and handed it to her. It was heavy, and she needed two hands to hold it. As I handed it off, I took the backpack off her. Then ordered, "Go in that room, shut the door, and look at tattoo designs. *Don't* listen to anything we say."

She measured us with her gaze but relented, going into one of the private rooms, setting the book down, and closing the door.

That didn't guarantee her ear wasn't plastered against the wood. I kept my voice low. "Skinner, she's got a laptop and Gods know what else in that bag. You got any of your scanning gear with you?"

He shook his head but took the bag from me. Then hissed, "What the fuck, man? *That's* Carl's woman?"

"Yeah."

He stared at me with the oddest expression on his face.

"What?"

He glanced around as if checking for an audience. Seeing none, he blasted me. "What in holy God's name are you doing? You were supposed to talk to him, not kidnap his girlfriend."

I knew that. "I did both, sue me."

Skinner's eyes narrowed. "Tell me how it went down."

I straightened. Times were, I outranked him. Now I didn't. Which meant I probably should try to appease him. "I go in there, Carl claims he's alone. There's fucking signs he ain't, right?"

Skinner nodded, encouraging me to continue. Meanwhile, he slipped the computer out of its compartment and did a quick swipe through the pocket to feel for anything else in there.

"So, I'm in the middle of negotiations—"

Skinner's snort interrupted me. "Negotiation isn't your strong suit, Bear."

"Shut up and let me talk."

Coming up empty in that pocket, he moved to the others.

"And I hear this squeak come from behind the couch. It's her. I throw a fit and Carl…" I tried to play the scene back in my mind. Even in the memories, it seemed just a bit fuzzy, like there was something in the air that made it all not make sense.

"Carl what?" Skinner piled her clothes and other shit on a bench. "This receipt is a month old. Women, I swear…" He pocketed it. Strange man.

His tangent gave me time to really think about the scene. "Carl offered to sell her to me."

Skinner froze. His head turned to the room where Rose hid. The stare he gave that door was loaded with apprehension, then he turned back to me and said, "Do *not* tell me you *bought* her."

"I didn't."

He relaxed for a moment. "Then, why is she with you?" The squint he narrowed at me tried to make sense of things before I could defend myself.

"I told you it got weird."

"How *weird?*" His voice was steeped in sarcasm.

This was going to look bad no matter which way I said it. "Apparently, she knows about that little scene with Sketch and Whoosh. Carl offered her to me for a month to keep her silent, and—"

"You fucking moron." Skinner checked his volume before continuing in what was obviously supposed to be loud, but wasn't. "He set you up."

"He tried."

There was a pause in the conversation that went on for too long.

"Keep your mouth open for any longer and something's gonna crawl in it." I pointed at his gaping face.

"Apparently, he succeeded because you got her, and he doesn't. Or am I reading this wrong?"

"It wasn't like that."

He rolled his eyes at me and dug through her bag with more fervor.

"What are you doing?" Roishin stood in the doorway, the book in hand.

Distraction time. "You find anything you like?"

She slammed the book down on a workstation table and strode over to where Skinner had her shit strewn all over the place. "That's my stuff!" She tugged the empty bag from his hands and began shoving things back into pockets.

"We were checking for trackers," I admitted.

"You have no right to do that," she shot back.

"But Carl did?" I tilted my head and glared at her.

Her movement halted for all of two seconds before she went into double-time mode. "What is between Carl and I is none of your damn business."

"It is my damn business if you're dragging trackers into my house."

Skinner released a sound that was somewhere between a gag and a squeak.

"Shut up." I didn't need his commentary right now.

Roishin reached for her computer.

Skinner slapped a hand on it. "No fucking way." He even went as far as to put his hand on his gun.

Rose stared at his gun hand. "I need it to find work." Her tone was almost defeated.

"You can use mine for now," I offered.

Her eyes met mine. "You're going to let me work?"

Apparently, Carl didn't. That was pretty plain to read on her face. "Maybe?"

She braced herself visibly.

"Listen, think of this as a vacation," I started.

"Bear," Skinner warned.

"I told you to shut up."

Funny how both Roishin and Skinner had similar expressions on their faces. Skinner was pissed at me—I could easily read that. And Roishin was angry, too. Nice to see I was batting a thousand.

"Listen up, both of you."

They waited for me to come up with something better than barking orders at them both. As the seconds ticked by, their faces fell into scowls. I was losing them.

"Okay. Back at Carl's was weird, right?" I looked to Roishin for verification that it wasn't just me.

"Carl is always weird. He was born that way."

Skinner's eyebrow rose with that revelation. She had his attention, at least.

"Okay, now that we got that established, I've been charged with taking care of you for one month. Maybe not to the letter of what Carl requested, but nevertheless, for one month you're *mine*."

Skinner went from open-mouthed to shaking his head. And I couldn't let that lie.

"What?"

"Jackson is going to have your balls for this."

Ah shit. I hadn't thought that part of my responsibility through. His wife, Kate, was a real sweetheart, unless you treated women like shit. Owning one for a month, no matter how well-intended, or weird, was going to get her screaming mad. And that would go straight to her husband.

And Jackson didn't fuck around with any preliminary warnings or that shit. He went directly to murder.

Skinner's comment deserved a response, however. And it wouldn't be one he liked because I had to walk the tightrope of doubt. What if Roishin was a plant? What if Carl and her were working together, and this was all an act to see how we operate? I'd basically just outed us, if that were the case.

"And when that month's over and you go back to Carl and tell him everything about us…" I shot my gaze to Skinner.

His face changed from a scowl to enlightenment.

In contrast, Roishin's expression went stone-faced. *Interesting.* "…you're still gonna be in one piece. I promise that. But I will do everything I can to protect my club from whatever bullshit he's got planned, or any fallout from what you may or may not have seen or heard. Understood?"

As I looked directly into Roishin's eyes, her face fell. Then, her head moved, denying something in my statement.

Luckily, I didn't have to wait too long for her to cut me.

"Carl's bullshit? It'll take you down. There's no way you're prepared for what he can do."

"He's one man," Skinner noted. Then, he made a finger gun and pulled the trigger. His eyes glittered as he did it.

Roishin studied us. "You can't kill him."

Both Skinner and I laughed at that. "Try us," I said.

"No. You can't. I'll abide by whatever rules you have. And I'll hold up my part of this bargain." She took a shaky breath and stared into space. "But when the month's over? I can't protect you anymore."

It was almost as if she'd said something else. The skin on my neck prickled. In my mind, I heard different words. Maybe it was her expression, or maybe Freya herself had just whispered to me.

But I heard, "I can't protect myself anymore."

7

ROISHIN

Carl knew what he was doing, sending me off with Bear. Instead of just one man to deal with, there were many. As I listened to their whispers and the names dropped, I realized that where you saw one Destroyer, there were many more behind the scenes eager to help.

And they all were armed and dangerous. Even Skinner, who didn't seem intimidating at first, was quick to threaten me.

Bear? He'd done nothing but threaten me. I had no illusions that these men weren't deadly.

And yet… I felt safer with them than Carl. And they truly didn't know how far Carl would go to prove a point. He adhered to one thing, his vow. And he'd vowed to make me obey him. But it wasn't the obeying he wanted. It was something darker. He wanted to break my will, destroy my sense of identity, and reform me in his image. That was his goal.

I realized that about him a bit too late.

"May I make that phone call?" I had to warn John that Carl was probably going to come after him or the children now that I wasn't there to distract him.

Skinner was easy to read. He silently warned Bear that this was not a good idea.

Bear shot him a glare meant to intimidate and handed me a cell phone. "Remember my rules?"

"Completely."

"What are they?"

I rattled off all the demands he made by counting on my fingers ending with, "You'll be listening in. Did I get everything?"

He frowned.

Skinner, however, paid attention. He should never play poker because his eyes spoke volumes. Most of the expression was one of dumbfounded shock. But there was admiration in there, as well as anger. I'd managed to prove to him that I was a threat.

Bear, however?

He wouldn't know a threat if it bit him in the ass. He'd relied too long on his strength to understand that some battles can be won with wits. In fact, most battles were won by strategy rather than strength.

Satisfied I wouldn't be interrupted, I dialed John's phone.

It rang five times before he picked up, announcing himself. He really shouldn't do that.

I stared at Bear, waiting for him to get angry.

Surprisingly, he didn't. "How are you doing?" I asked.

"Hi, yes, Beth is doing fine. And we're holding up well."

I paused. John wasn't usually cryptic. I lowered my voice in case there was someone on the other end of this conversation listening in like Bear was. "Is someone there?"

Bear frowned, obviously clued in on the fact that I wasn't talking to my friend.

John paused. "It's okay, I got home from the hospital and my parents are here to help out. Her brother stopped by just a bit ago to see if we were doing well."

Oh, fuck. Carl was there. "Is Carl behaving himself?" I looked Bear in the eye, hoping he'd get the information I was feeding him.

Bear scrambled to get a pad of paper and scribbled something on it to pass to Skinner. Meanwhile, I paid attention to John's rambling to read between the words as to what Carl was doing.

John paused and spoke to the audience on his end, "Hang on, I'm going to step outside so I don't disturb anyone."

I heard the screen door open and shut. John hurriedly spat out. "Where are you?"

"I'm with two men, one is named Bear, the other is named Skinner. They're bikers."

John hurriedly asked as much as he could, "Which bikers? Are you safe? I called, but Carl said you'd left, and when you didn't show up here, I got worried."

"The Destroyers MC. Let me guess, Carl showed up there to make sure I didn't arrive, right?"

"Worse."

My stomach twisted. "Oh Goddess, what did he do?"

John's anger was palpable. "He demanded to hold June."

"He hasn't hurt her, has he?"

"No, I got Dad watching him like a hawk."

"John, you can't let him near the children." I motioned to Bear to give me a piece of paper and his pen.

"I know. He—hey, Carl, do you need a ride home? You look kind of… tired."

I heard Carl's voice in the background. It gave me goosebumps knowing he was so close to John.

On the paper I scribbled, *John is Beth's husband, friend.*

Bear read the paper and raised an eyebrow. He scribbled back, *You should have told me before the call.*

That didn't need to be addressed.

John spoke, this time to me. "I appreciate you for calling, I'll let Beth know you're praying for her."

Praying? *No.* Doing anything in my power to help her recover, yes. But Carl tied my hands by sending me to a bunch of over-testosterone-laden bikers. I wouldn't be able to break free of this trap. "I probably won't be over."

"Absolutely. I think it will be a week or two before she can have visitors. Right now, it is family only. Call us then, okay? Thank you for the well-wishes." He hung up the call.

I checked to see it was disconnected before deleting the call from Bear's history.

"Wait, what are you doing?"

He grabbed the phone right after I hit delete.

"You deleted the number?"

Skinner chuckled. "I'd have done the same thing."

"Stay out of this," Bear grumbled. Then he turned on me. "Why is Carl at your friend's house?"

"Beth is Carl's sister."

Neither of them were shocked by that. *Maybe I'd underestimated them?*

"Let me guess, you already did a deep search on Carl."

The guilty glances they sent each other was enough of an answer. Noted, these bikers had collective intelligence.

"What is Carl to you, anyway?"

Skinner asked the right question. "A means to an end. And I'm guessing there's no love lost between you two and him, either. And that announcing my plans isn't going to get me killed, right?"

"What end, and what means?" Bear was quick to put his hand on his knife sheath.

"The end is getting what I want. The means seems to have changed in the last hour. Carl wants me to suffer at your hands. But you two don't look like idiots who just do what other people want." I made certain to appeal to their pride.

Funny, this time it was Bear giving me the scrutinizing look, not Skinner. He looked like a man who had experience with women using him for something. He proved me right. "Nice try. We're going to do what we're going to do, Carl or not."

I shook my head. That kind of thinking would walk them right into any trap Carl set for them. "You are going to regret thinking like that."

"Who are you to tell us what to think?" Skinner stood up, laptop in hand. "Bear, good fucking luck with this one. She might be able to recite your rules, but she ain't going to listen to them."

He shot me a look and said, "Not unless it serves her end game, that is."

He left in a huff, taking my laptop with him.

Bear stretched his legs out from the rolling stool he'd perched on. He balanced there with easy grace. In fact, as I looked around, he'd probably spent much of his lifetime on a stool just like that. "This is your shop?"

"I said that. You forgot that part?"

"My understanding of motorcycle gangs is that—"

"Buzz. Club. Not gang." His heavy boots hit the floor with a thud.

Club my ass. I let my eyes drop to his gun holster. "My understanding of motorcycle… clubs… is that property is co-owned."

"Where'd you hear that bullshit?"

"Books." *And movies.*

He had the nerve to laugh. "Books ain't going to teach you jack shit about our club." He sobered and looked me dead in the eye. "Life as you know it, it's over. You're going to live in *my* life for a month. That means, *my* world's rules apply."

"You told me the rules."

"Naw, I told you *my* rules. The club has more. Number one is respect. Respect the club. Respect the brothers. And most importantly, respect the symbols."

"Symbols?"

Bear scowled, apparently not used to teaching. "The patch. The coats… the vests, the *bikes*. Unless you're asked to touch, *don't*."

I logged that information right alongside of the memories where he ordered me on and off his bike. I'd touched his coat, his bike, even his patch. All without asking. But I guess, orders could be construed as "asking."

"Rule two, fuck authority."

"Not literally, correct?"

He coughed, trying not to laugh. "Of course, not literally. Geesh." Then he got a glint in his eye I didn't like. "Rule three, women are property."

Oh, *fuck* that rule. There was no way I was abiding by that one.

He grinned and pointed at my face. "I see you have a problem with that one."

Shit. I was usually much better at controlling my expression than that. I had to be that way around Carl. *When had I let my guard down?*

Bear laughed. "Now I see Carl's game."

"No, you don't."

"No, I do. He was having trouble breaking you. Wasn't he?"

I slipped easily into the neutral expression I donned around Carl. "Breaking?"

Bear studied my face. "Yeah, breaking." He nodded to himself, or at his words, I didn't know which. "And that's where he fucked up." He stood up and stretched. "I don't suppose you had a chance to actually look at any of the flash inside the book while you were listening to Skinner and I, did you?"

I scrambled for a lie. "I'm thinking something with a tree." In my mind's eye, I saw branches snaking down my body, even to my fingertips. It felt right, but I'd never go that crazy.

Oblivious to my thoughts, Bear scratched his beard. He walked over to the book and flipped open the binder to a page, and practically found what he was looking for first try. "Like this?"

He turned the binder around and held it out.

On the right-hand side, a gnarled ash tree spanned the entire width and length of the page. From top branches to deep roots, it filled out in a neat oval.

If I ever did get tattooed, this was really close to what I'd want.

Woven in the branches were runes. I scanned their patterns.

Protection, life, happiness… fertility.

Nope.

"Can it be changed?"

"Of course."

I pulled over the paper I'd written on and drew out a symbol. Then added the right glyphs around it. As the design branched out, Bear leaned over to see my work.

"Protection, strength, wisdom…" He nodded again. "Good choices."

I froze. He knew how to read witch's marks? I'd outed myself.

He grabbed the pencil from me and laid a transparent sheet over the book. On it, he began positioning the items I'd drawn.

"Any thought on where you'd want it?"

"I don't want a tattoo right now."

He turned his head to send me a look I couldn't read.

A yawn hit. I tried to stop it but couldn't before Bear saw it. "You're tired. Got it." He packed up the book and papers and dug in a bin. He pulled out a coat with the shop's logo printed on it. "My house isn't far."

Carl would have enjoyed my suffering.

He certainly wouldn't have tucked my hands inside his coat pockets like Bear did on the short ride to his home.

A light came on inside the house next door as Bear pulled into his driveway. He made a sound of frustration and braced the bike to quickly text a message.

A woman walked out of the house, phone in hand. "Just checking it was you." She stared at me. "I didn't realize you had company."

Bear dropped his hand on my leg again. "Yeah, should have warned you. Speck doing his job?"

"His name is Kane," she replied.

"I know that. All the same, he ain't out here and you are. Tell him he's in trouble for that."

The woman shook her head and laughed quietly. "You bikers. Good night, Bear."

"Night, woman."

"Kate."

That must be her name. The way she fired it at Bear was exactly how she mentioned the other's name. Kane. Speck… was that short for prospect?

Kate stared at me for a moment. "Good night, whoever you are. Good luck with this one. He's a handful and a half."

With that, she went inside.

Bear didn't move. He stared at the door well after it closed and the light went off.

"Everything okay?" I asked.

His fingers squeezed my leg. "Just fine."

He lied.

"What are you waiting for?"

My question nudged him into action. He pushed a fob that activated the garage door. Inside, the automatic lighting revealed an SUV, a jet ski on a trailer, and another motorcycle. He had more vehicles than Carl. And a nicer home. It wasn't lost on me that this subdivision was so new most of the lots didn't have grass growing yet. Bear's only had straw laid down to stop erosion.

He stopped the bike inside, and I took the rumble of the garage door coming back down as a cue I should climb off. I was much less clumsy this time. I'd practically fallen when he ordered me off the first time. The second time, I was a bit too nervous to execute the maneuver smoothly. But this time, I almost handled it like a pro. Except for my heel catching and my boot sliding off, leaving me lopsidedly barefoot.

I hopped around to avoid setting my flesh on the chilly concrete. One braid threatened to fall loose, so I slapped a hand on it as I bent over to retrieve my boot.

Bear laughed. "Are you always so…"

"Clumsy? No."

His gaze was glued to my ass.

"Are you always so lecherous?"

That gaze slid up and locked on my eyes. The corner of one eye twitched into a squint. "You'd be prettier if you smiled more." The corner of his mouth lifted.

I opened my mouth to berate him, but the gleam in his eyes stopped me. He was enjoying this. Far be it from me to entertain him. I shoved my foot in my boot and waited for him to lock the bike down and open the house.

8

———

BEAR

No wonder Carl called her "Rose." She was prickly as hell. My quip barely dented her composure. Which was disconcerting. She'd already picked up on my tells. It took Jackson all of a month to figure them out. Wolf? Hell, I don't know if he figured all of them out yet.

Most of the guys in the club had given up on understanding me long ago. If I didn't want to be read, they had a hard time with it. Barely an hour with Roishin, and she'd seen through my sexist comment for what it was. A way to rile her up.

And she chose non-violence. Which made sense, given my size and the number of times I'd threatened her tonight. Yet, instead of flinching in fear, my last threat barely registered on her radar. An eye dip to the knife I'd covered, and she plowed right on.

If it had been anyone other than Skinner with me? They'd have taken offense. Skinner was smart enough to see through it and warn me.

Was I going to listen?

Hell no.

The more I found out about this woman, the more I liked her. And that was a huge problem. My phone buzzed as I pointed out the particular important sections of the house. Bathroom, food, bedrooms… I had three. "Pick one," I said and checked to see who was calling. "I gotta take this." I ran my fingers across my lips reminding her to shut up.

"Hey, Jackson. What's up?"

The noise in the background meant he was at one of the bars or the clubhouse outside Atlanta. There was another stop planned in Tallahassee before he, Hollywood, and Griz came back. Kate was smart to stay home. Those clubs were too close to rival territories to be safe.

"My wife tells me you're playing hooky tonight."

I glanced at Roishin and said to both of them, "Hang on a minute."

I walked down the stairs and out the back and didn't stop until I was deep in the woods that flanked the running path. "Sorry, had ears eavesdropping."

"Kate said you had a woman with you."

"Yeah, about that…" I really should tell him everything. But what could I say on the phone?

"Kate said she wasn't wearing a shit ton of makeup like you usually snatch up. Where'd you find her?"

I cleared my throat. "Carl's."

There was a pause on the other end. Jackson was so quiet, I could hear Griz yapping in the background. Finally, he said, "Fill me in."

"He got a ride home today from a cop."

More silence.

"I went over to chat and met his girl. And… uh, weirdest thing, she came home with me." That wasn't the whole truth, but I really couldn't say all of it over the phone, so I said what I could, "Carl *wanted* it that way."

Jackson sucked in a breath. "He's playing you."

"No shit. Skinner said the same thing."

His voice skipped into innuendo zone. "She any good?"

"I don't fucking know."

"Come on, man. Give me something. Ass shape, tit size, something…"

"You're married now, bro," I reminded him.

"So?"

Wow. If Kate heard him talking like that… "Kate's going to have your nuts."

"I don't need 'em. Got Zoe, and Kate and I definitely shouldn't make another one like her. Seriously, is Carl's girl ugly or pretty?"

I hesitated.

"Woof?" Jackson laughed.

"No," I protested.

His mirth ceased. "What do you mean, *no?*"

How could I tell him? "She's… interesting. Pretty, yeah, but not… you know, caked makeup, pushup bras, and all that stuff that makes 'em prettier."

"That's what Kate said. She isn't your usual type."

"Exactly." I did have a type. Brass, bold, loud, brightly patterned, and easy to scrape off. I'd never picked anyone like Roishin, and never would. She was too soft, delicate, small…and too vulnerable against a monster like me.

I gave Jackson more to chew on. "Listen, you're right, he's playing games, but I think Carl's also playing a game with her. He pushed her on me, and it *wasn't* her idea. Now, I know you know I'm not *that* kind of man but I had to pretend I was because she was bruised and scared as shit. I needed to get her out of there. But maybe he's testing me? Maybe he thinks I'm weak enough to take the bait, or he's trying to get dirt? You know him better than I do, what's his game?"

Jackson gave it a moment of thought. "You're right, he never does anything without a reason, and that man can twist reasons out of smoke. If I were you, I'd watch my back. She might be the one to stick a knife in it. Or, Carl is using her to create a reason to make you fall. And by proxy, *all* of us."

He didn't give me time to talk before he rambled on. "You're going to have to pretend this was her idea, and get that girl on board, fast. Say she's scraped Carl off for you and get her to sell it. You'll know if she's faking this for him or not soon enough."

I rubbed my ear because there is no way he said what I think he said. "You're kidding me, right?"

"No. If he's trying to make up a false accusation, and she's in on it, or even if she isn't, you could get in serious shit. You're right to think it's a trap; you'd be fucked either way. Right now, it's really close to… how to put it?" He trailed off an I heard the unspoken "on an unsecured line" part of his thoughts.

"Trafficking?" I offered.

"Damn it, Bear."

I laughed. "That ain't what this is. She's been opening up since I got her away. When I was there, she was quieter than a mouse, but this lady's got hellfire in her veins."

"I thought you said she wasn't your type?"

"She ain't." Immediately my mind flashed the memory of her naked legs and that hair whipping around in the storm. I pressed the heel of my free hand against my junk to remind it to settle down.

Jackson laughed long and loud. Griz rumbled in the back-ground, asking what was so funny.

"Bear's met his match."

Aw, fuck. I'd never hear the end of this now. "Go fuck yourself."

Jackson laughed harder. Griz must have said something to make him wheeze.

"What's her name?"

I told him and gave him the rundown on the name changes Hickey found. Then added, "Why shouldn't I just set her up with Ma or something?"

There was a minute before Jackson sobered enough to answer. "Well, first off, Ma ain't exactly a good influence on women. It took her all of two hours to teach Zoe and Kate how to shoot. Second, knowing Carl? He's got you watched. And if you start passing off this Roishin to someone else, he's gonna know you wussed out. Worse? he's likely to pick up his vendetta with Ma. And *none* of us wants that to happen.

"Also, I'd hate to think what our enemies would do with the knowledge we're taking in strays. I ain't exactly on solid ground right now, Bear."

Shit. Especially with him brushing up against two major factions where he was. "Okay. Aside from that, gimme one good reason why it should be me. Why not Cutty or Poke?" They were better with women than I was.

"Because both of them would stick their dicks in it without thinking twice or being careful about it. And that, Bear, is a trap. One I know you know how to escape. And if this woman is both dumb enough and smart enough to be with Carl, still be in one piece, and not buried in some basement somewhere, then I need someone *smart* on this. And face it, Bear, you're the only single smartass capable of that right now. Griz is here with me."

Fucker. "I'm telling Kate you asked about Roishin's ass."

"Do that, and I'm making a coat out of you when I get back."

"That's if Kate doesn't kill you first." I laughed because this new, married Jackson was so much easier to rile than the single one.

"Listen, just give me some juicy fodder for when I call Kate back and have phone sex."

"I'm not doing that. Find your own spank material."

He laughed. "See? She's safe with you, Bear. Safer than with anyone else. You may pretend you have no morals whatsoever, but you're an honorable man. I wouldn't have you any other way. So, I'm begging you, fake it… for the cops Carl's going to sic on you, for the ol' ladies who'll sic Wolf's woman on you, and I don't need to remind you that Tits will skewer your ass if she finds out you made a deal for this woman, and lastly, do it for the club. We don't need the heat right now. You have got to make it look like you're legitimately dating her or some shit. And make sure she's treated better than any of your priors, got it?"

I couldn't argue with a direct order like that.

"I ain't seducing her."

"No one said you had to do that. Just turn on the charm. Be nice. Women appreciate nice."

Griz's mutter was loud. "Bear ain't got charm, and he certainly ain't nice." There was more I didn't hear, but it made more than one person on the other end laugh at my expense.

"Fuck off, all of you." I hung up. Jackson had a full trip to get over the slight. It served him right for not taking me with him. If he had, none of this would have happened.

Or at least not to me.

I walked inside, and caught Roishin staring at my altar. Her hand hovered over my little statue of Thor resting on his hammer. It was a replica of a marble carving from the 19th century. Sprout's wife found it online and bought it for me.

"What are you doing?"

Roishin snatched her hand back. "I was admiring your altar. Thor?" She indicated the statue and the red candle.

I nodded. It didn't look like she'd touched anything, but I checked just the same. The last thing I needed was for some witch to fondle my junk and screw up the energy of it.

As I straightened the bottle of Trappist Ale, I spoke, "Since you recognized it for what it is, and because of those marks you drew back in the shop, I'm guessing you're pagan. And likely a witch. Did you have an altar? Maybe you can set one up somewhere in here."

Her silence was curious.

"Roishin?"

She swallowed, and her eyes were haunted. "I had one, at my apartment. But it's all gone."

Carl. She didn't even have to say his name, and I knew that sanctimonious son of a bitch did something.

"How long ago was this?"

"Barely a month," she whispered, head hung low.

"Any chance you can get it back?"

Her head barely moved, but the side-to-side motion ignited my fury.

"He fucked with it, didn't he?"

She turned away and I might have caught her wiping an eye, but she rallied. "I think I'll sleep on the couch in the basement."

That wasn't a bedroom. It wasn't even set up as a proper room. All my exercise gear was down there. "Why?"

"Because if someone breaks in, the last place they'll go digging around in is the basement, and if they do, they'll trip over your barbells, and I'll hear them."

"You ain't sleeping in no basement."

Her head tilted, jaw set. "It's my choice, isn't it?"

Ah, there she was, that hellcat daring me to lay down the law again. I smiled. Jackson had shit for brains. He thought everything could be solved by sex. "I vow it is." I laid a hand on Thor's head and expanded. "On my honor as a warrior, and as a servant of the mighty God of Thunder, I swear your choices will be your own. The only thing I ask in return is that you respect my ways, my people, and my decisions."

Her eyes narrowed.

"No."

I tried again. "On my honor, you can sleep where you want in this house. Be it in the basement, or at my side, I will not take that decision from you."

"At your side?"

Maybe some things could be solved Jackson's way? I resisted the urge to picture her naked form again. But I could at least be honest, right? "If you want to. I wouldn't turn it down." I raked my eyes down her body.

She hesitated. "What's the catch?"

"No catch. However—"

"Oh, here we go…"

I smiled my not nice grin. "Carl's going to try to cause trouble."

"Duh. Do ducks quack?"

Ignoring her sarcasm, I plowed on. "The more people who see us together, and see you *willingly* with me, the better."

Her mouth hung open slightly. "Do you want me to *paw* at you in public?"

Put that way, *no*. "I want you to make it look like this is your idea to stay here." Her mutinous face wasn't showing conviction. "Because when Carl starts pulling his bullshit, who's going to pay?"

Her shoulders slumped. "You're right. Carl might not take a

direct approach if he suspects something." She walked over and knelt at my feet.

I took a step back, stunned.

She held both hands out, palms up. "On my word, by the life in my blood, and with the spirits of hearth and home as witness, I vow to be convincingly willing in public."

That was sincere enough for me. "Accepted." My stomach growled. The fragrance of baked bread still clung to her skin, and I could smell it. "Are you hungry?"

This fake relationship would start as normal as it could. I'd make her dinner. Tomorrow? Maybe take her shopping?

I shuddered. That wasn't my style. Everyone knew it wasn't. I'd have to figure something out, fast. Because Jackson was right. Carl would be watching.

9

ROISHIN

*W*hatever it takes. I made a vow to the Goddess on that for Beth's sake. But staring at Bear's altar reminded me that while I might not always like the sacrifices asked of me, they were part of a greater design.

Why else would Carl hand me over to a man like this? If he wanted to torture me, giving me to the tow truck driver would have been a better move. Bear might be grumpy, irritable, rough, dangerous… okay, not ideal, but he also had a thread of honor running through him that he hid from the world. Carl missed that.

I'd missed that because Bear had acted his part so well.

Until I noticed his home. The things he surrounded himself with were far from the character he portrayed to the world. On the altar, he'd spread sacred plants. Angelica, chamomile, clover, and yarrow, as well as a scattering of acorns and dried rose petals. Gifts to the Gods to bring harmony and peace into his space.

Outside his home, his backyard butted up against a forested section. I explored that after he left in the morning. A trail snaked through it, growing less visible the farther I followed it. When the asphalt turned into gravel, and that turned into dirt, I found a secluded park. I watched the small river for a while. Then I searched the area and the path.

Bear had used this trail for running almost as soon as he was awake. It must be a regular thing. The evidence of a prior run was imprinted in the dried dirt. I traced the zig-zagged tread of his shoes.

"That's where the mud came from." Bear had expensive running shoes and treated them poorly.

I followed the trail of footprints. He stopped at this point in his run, crouched at that point. The heavy imprint of the front of his shoes told me that. I crouched, too, searching to see what he might have been looking at.

Gooseberries.

Why did that seem familiar? I scanned the tableau. A post stuck out of the water. It was the remnants of a pier.

"Oh, shit."

I picked my way through the thorny bushes blocking the water and walked along the riverbank.

In the dried mud above the high waterline was the imprint of a bare foot—my *bare foot*.

I walked to where I'd parked Carl's car and turned to where I'd seen the animal.

"He saw me."

My knees gave out, and I plopped down on the dirt. A crow called from the meadow. Another answered it.

"Dear Goddess, I hope you know what you're doing." Whether I spoke that to my deity or to myself, it didn't matter. Bear had seen me completely naked. Vulnerable. Alone.

And done nothing but observe.

Sure, I could be reading this completely wrong and it was merely a coincidence, but the signs were everywhere. This was meant to be.

On the walk back, I threaded stalks of chicory flowers into a small wreath. I laid it at the entrance to the path before stepping into Bear's yard. The day was warm, one of the few clear, bright, and gentle days left for the year. It would be a good day to sit in the sunlight and bathe in nature.

An hour later, I emerged from the house. My freshly washed hair was down. I held a drying towel to catch the drips, and had barely more than one of Bear's super-sized thermal shirts on. I left a small food offering near my flower wreath for the pixies.

Then, I curled my toes into the deep carpet of grass and clover Bear hadn't mowed in weeks. The scent of fall was in the air. It was different from the growth and flowering of spring and summer. There was an earthy quality to it. As if the very last molecules of life were lifted into the atmosphere, rich with flavor, but fleeting.

"Whatcha doing?"

I startled. A teenage girl, probably late teens, with reddish-blonde hair and a quizzical cant to one eyebrow stared over the fence at me.

"I was just drying my hair." I tried to be polite, but hadn't expected anyone to pay attention to me. This area of the subdivision wasn't over-populated… yet.

Except of course, the neighbor next door. This must be Kate's daughter. They looked similar, except for the eyes.

"You have really long hair. That must take forever."

I laughed. It did. Especially because I tried to let it dry naturally rather than force hot air into it. The latter only made it brittle.

"Days like today help."

"I'll bet. I'm Zoe. You must be Bear's new girlfriend."

Yikes. I scrambled for something convincing to say. For some reason, I didn't want to lie. It stuck in my throat. I settled for, "Girlfriend is a relative term."

"Oh right, fuck bunny, whatever. Same difference."

I swallowed. That's all women were to him? "Does your mother know you swear like that, Zoe?"

A voice from the house's balcony piped up. "She does. And Zoe, knock it off. Don't bother Bear's woman."

"I was just talking. Can't I talk now?" There was an angry bite to her words.

Late teens. I remember those years… not fondly. I'm certain the people around me then didn't remember me fondly, either. I waved to Kate who had stepped out onto a balcony attached to the second floor. "Hi, Kate."

"Hello. We met last night, but I didn't catch your name."

"Last night? OOoooOOoo." Zoe made it sound nefarious.

Which, technically, it truly was. I ignored her tone and addressed her mother. "It's Roishin."

Kate barely blinked. "That's a pretty name."

"It's Irish."

Zoe butted in, "Who named you? My mom named me. At least that's better than 'Mini-Me,' which is what the guys are calling me now because I take after my dad."

"I named myself." I swallowed, preparing the sanitary version as to why.

"That's so cool! Mom, can I name myself?"

"Not until you're out of this house."

"Mom!"

"Don't 'Mom' me. I brought you into this world and nearly died doing it, so show some respect.'

I couldn't help but smile. While their argument seemed harmful, it was completely normal. Someday they'd look back on this time and laugh.

"So, Roishin? How did you meet Bear?" Zoe asked.

"How?"

"Yeah, were you at the club?"

The motorcycle club, a building like in the shows? "No."

"Cool. That's different. I wanna hear all about it."

"There's nothing to tell." Literally nothing. Unless... A devious thought entered my head. "He saw me dancing naked."

"Oh, you're a stripper. I didn't guess that."

What?

My question must have been on my face. Because Zoe rambled on. "Your hair would kind of get in the way of the pole, if you do that, and a lot of the clubs—"

"Zoe Regina Nist, finish that sentence and I'll..." Kate leaned over the balcony. "I apologize for my daughter. I'll be right down to set her straight."

"It's okay. I'm not a stripper," I called up.

Kate froze.

"You mean, he really saw you dance naked and it *wasn't* at a strip club?" Zoe climbed higher so her arms could rest on top of the fence. "When was this?"

"A few nights ago. I was casting a spell in the rain." Her smile encouraged me.

"One of Mom's friends does that. She's Wiccan. Dad says she walks around skyclad all the time."

"She doesn't." Kate's head popped up next to Zoe's.

"I don't either. I'm a witch, but not Wiccan. Hi." I held my hand out to Kate and then Zoe.

"That's how Bear knows her. He's Pagan, too." Zoe was a font of information. I wondered if her mother ever told her not to tell strangers other's secrets.

"I guessed that from the altar and his hammer."

Kate took in my lack of clothing. My feet were bare and grass-stained.

When she met my eyes, she spoke sincerely, "I'm so glad he finally found someone like him. Those other girls…" She clammed up, trying not to speak ill, but I could tell by the guilty way she looked away that she didn't think much of the women in Bear's life.

With that reminder, my insecurity made me nervous. "How many girls?"

Kate's eyes went wide.

Zoe, on the other hand, snorted. "You put your foot in it, Mom. I'm not helping you get it unstuck."

"A few," Kate settled on a vague number.

"This month?" I said it with a smile on my face and a joking tone. Inside, I was seething. But reminded myself that this was temporary. It was a blip on the radar. I shouldn't read anything into Bear's plans or the arrangement we had.

"Good to see you're not the jealous type." Kate's smile wavered nervously.

"I'm not. How long have you lived next to Bear?"

"Since late June."

That explained the straw on the sod. "Would you like to come over? It would be more comfortable than hanging on a fence."

"Heck yeah!" Zoe's head disappeared and a portion of the fence moved open. The wooden slats of the gate melded perfectly into the pattern.

"Zoe! Are you sure it's not an imposition?"

"Not at all, you can keep me company while my hair dries."

Kate did another scan. "That's a lot of hair. I'd kill for that thickness."

"If I could, I'd let you borrow half."

Kate almost looked like she was going to take me up on that. Zoe on the other hand, plopped down on the picnic table where I'd spread out my conditioning oils and braiding supplies.

"What's all this?" She picked up the castor oil and sniffed it. "Gross." Her gag stopped short as she looked at me. "Sorry."

"It's okay. I need to infuse it. Smell the yellow one."

She picked that bottle up and sniffed. "Lemon... and flowers?"

"Lemongrass, sage, and pennyroyal." I picked it up and sniffed, forgetting what else I might have blended with it. "Oh, and I found a jasmine essential oil for that the unfinished one. The other bottle is a coconut oil-vanilla blend. I was trying to decide which I was going to use today."

Zoe took her time comparing the two scented versions.

"Bear loves food, I'd vote for the cookie smell."

Kate joined us. "Ditto. If you smell like a cookie, he'll never let you go."

I laughed. We sat in the sun, watching the leaves rustle and talking about their Wiccan friend, Crystal, and the times they helped out at her shop in Maine. They reminisced about the festivals they took part in.

My side of the conversation explored similarities of practice and finding out more about these two. They'd moved here when Kate reconnected with Zoe's father. He'd been the leader of the

Destroyers chapter here until that point, then got a promotion and was now the regional president.

"This is the first trip he's gone on solo." Kate said with a furrowed brow.

"Are you worried about him?" I kicked myself as soon as I said it.

"He's quite capable, I worry about everyone else. He's bound to be short-tempered by the time they make the next stop. He called last night to check in. I kind of have a confession that I knew your name already. I didn't want to seem like a creeper or anything."

"How'd he find out my name?"

"Bear," Zoe offered. She busied herself by helping me crush the wild mint and chamomile I'd found.

"Oh, right. That must have been who he was talking to."

Kate mused with a shake of her head, "They gossip worse than we do. Oh, that reminds me, there's a ride this weekend. Are you going with Bear?"

He hadn't mentioned it. "I don't know yet. I guess, if I can."

"Where do you work?" Zoe asked.

"Up until four weeks ago, I worked at a pharmaceutical testing lab in Harrisburg. I'd taken it as a temporary job while I'm down here helping a friend who's sick." But Carl ruined that. Luckily, I'd finalized my lease. Otherwise, I'd be in dire straits. "Right now, I'm looking for something comparable." Or anything, really.

"I can ask Regina, she's a nurse. Maybe she knows of an opening. What kind of work did you do at the lab?" Kate asked.

"Mostly sample testing and analysis. I have a degree in biochemistry."

Zoe's mouth dropped open. "Really? I want to go into Marine Biology, but I'm worried the transfers from Maine to here screwed up my STEM classes."

Kate listened while her daughter and I discussed the course requirements and any college application insights I had for her. I found myself opening up about the college I went to and the options there.

A commotion from the front of the house had us all craning

our heads as Bear came in. He carried several bags. He dropped them onto the kitchen island when he noticed our group in the backyard.

He didn't look happy.

Of course, his size, piercings, beard, and tattoos probably had something to do with that. "What are all of you doing out there?" And he didn't let us answer before asking Kate, "Where's the speck?"

"Nathan went home."

"Who said he could?"

"Wolf. The alarm is on."

Bear glared at the fence, and the open gate. "And it didn't go off?"

"I know the codes for the zones." Kate tilted her head and shot Bear a look that clearly challenged, *what are you going to do about it?*

He took a deep breath. "I wasn't here. You know there is supposed to *always* be someone here."

"Roishin was here," Zoe supplied.

He finally noticed me. His eyes fixed on my loose hair. It was almost dry and the oil I'd combed into it made it glisten in the sunlight. The brown turned slightly golden as it hung loose. His eyes trailed down to my bare legs and feet and the traces of mud and grass on them. "How long have you been outside?"

That was directed at me. "At least three hours."

His jaw moved, causing his beard to lift. "Alone?" He gritted out.

"No, Zoe and Kate have been here keeping me company for at least an hour."

His nostrils flared. He turned away from all three of us and took in a huge breath.

I braced for a bellow, or possibly even a blow. But he let out the air and slowly turned back to us. "Kate? Please?" There was a note of begging in his tone.

"Bear, I'm armed. Zoe is too."

His eyes didn't move from her. "That's not good."

"It's okay. No one is actively trying to kill me anymore."

He swallowed. Suspiciously, his eyes drifted to me and back to Kate. "It's not safe."

Of course it wasn't. I'd forgotten about Carl. I picked up my jars and the ground mixture Zoe had worked on. "I agree. We should have been inside. You're welcome to come over, after you lock up your house."

"I'll do that." Bear strode through the open gate and made quick work of securing Kate's house before herding us inside.

I pushed one of the bags aside so I had room for my things. "What is all of this stuff?" There were large bags, smaller bags, and some heavy boxes.

"I picked up a couple of things." His face turned red. The lie was evident in the pile of purchases.

I peeked inside one of the large paper bags. "Sage?"

"And sweetgrass."

I stacked the bundles and pulled out a small besom. "Are you planning a ritual?" He had way too much here. I pulled open another bag.

Crystals spilled out and hit the counter hard. I ran a hand over the faux stone hoping that they hadn't scratched the new counters. There were at least a dozen stones in the bag. Onyx, quartzes of varying size and color, tiger eyes, moonstones… "Bear?" This was too much.

"Open this one." He held out a plastic bag.

I peeked inside. The bundle of black fabric didn't tell me anything. I shook it out and stared at the pattern.

Zoe leaned in. "Whoa, that's seriously cool. Where'd you get it?"

"I stopped by a place in Mechanicsburg."

"Crystal Dawn had one like this in the shop. You know, she could have shipped all of this to you at a discount," Kate observed.

I brushed my palm down the fabric. The black cotton was printed with an intricate pattern of roses, feathers, candles, and crystals. It wasn't a Norse design. If I didn't know better, I'd say Bear picked it out especially for me.

"I picked up a little table. It's in the back of the truck. As soon as I get it in, you can spread that out and set up."

There was a crease of worry between his eyes.

"You shouldn't have."

His beard moved again. "Too late now." He grunted and retreated to the garage.

"He bought all this?" Zoe whispered.

"Looks like it," Kate whispered back. And then a smile grew on her face until the smug satisfaction was plain to see. She glanced at the door to the garage and back to me, then leaned in. "Don't you dare hurt him. Zoe and I *do* carry guns, and we're not afraid to use them."

She straightened as Bear banged the table against the wall. I rushed to help him with an end but he wouldn't let me. All the while, I tried to put my emotions and thoughts into neat boxes where I could analyze them later, because things were moving too quickly for me to keep up. He positioned the table next to his. The two altars engulfed the entire length of the wall.

Zoe handed me the cloth. "Go ahead."

I spread it out. The black of my cloth matched the dark fur on his. The design was completely different, however. His altar had red runes painted on the white inside of a smaller hide, mine was a combination of lavender, gold, and deep metallic violet. But once I got it straightened, it almost looked like they belonged together.

My nose prickled. I forced down my emotions and began opening bags. All of the items needed a good cleansing, but I wasn't about to complain. "You know I can't use these right away, don't you?"

Bear shrugged. "Do or don't do what you want." He glanced at Kate and Zoe, then leaned in and smelled my hair. "May I?" His hand hovered in the air, not touching me.

I realized we had an audience. I took his hand in mine and leaned in. I put my head against his chest and tried to make the hug not look awkward. This wasn't like riding on the back of his bike where my only thought was self-preservation when I wrapped around him. This time, I was acutely aware of his body heat, the broad expanse of his chest, the difference in our heights. The top of my head barely reached his shoulder.

Moreover, he had a nicely tapered difference between his chest and his belt. It wasn't narrowly cut like body builders. However, I could wrap my arms around him at his waist, but I doubted my fingertips would touch if I tried that around his chest.

And best of all, he smelled like leather and trees. Not a cologne, just naturally outdoorsy smelling. I liked it. The scent was grounding, and moreover, safe. I glanced up at him, searching his expression for something that told me I was doing this right, or that it would all be okay. I hadn't felt safe like this since…

I broke the embrace, embarrassed to be caught off guard like that. I tried to smile and put on a happy mood so Zoe and Kate wouldn't catch on.

"Since when do you intrude on witches dancing skyclad?" Kate asked.

Bear stiffened. His mouth fell open. He glanced around, searching for the traps. "I…"

He was obviously in grave peril. I decided to toss him a rope. "I took a walk down your running path."

His mouth snapped shut. "I didn't look."

Funny, when he lied, his eyes shifted to the left. I poked him. "You did. Don't lie."

"Yeah, well Zoe doesn't need to hear this."

"Do too. Besides, Crystal Dawn does it all the time. Not like Roishin's the first witch I've ever known. I grew up my whole life around that sort of thing. More women should go around naked."

Bear's face flushed deep red.

"Zoe? Please don't tease Bear like that," Kate admonished.

They didn't fear him.

Normal people would, or at least should.

No one was supposed to know I'd seen Roishin naked. Well, besides the people who needed to be told, and that didn't include Kate and Zoe. Now that little tidbit would run through the telephone chain up to Jackson.

If Wolf hadn't told him already.

Lay my ashes on the ground and put a stone marker down, I was screwed. And Jackson's plan to be "nice" to Roishin? That was backfiring on me something awful. It took three hours of my morning to haggle with the shop keeper at the store. I had no clue what Roishin needed, and that meant the clerk tried to sell me the damn store.

And was it worth it?

You ask me. That anemic hug she gave me wasn't a thank you. Buying her affection hadn't worked. And obviously we were not physically compatible because she skittered away from me like a frightened squirrel.

It didn't matter that her hair smelled like macadamia nut cookies, and was softer than kitten fur, or that her eyes were pools of rich amber brown. Now that everyone knew I'd seen her naked, I couldn't get that image out of my head. I'd look at her and it was easy to remember that luminous flesh. A man had to be a saint not to want that.

Or give in to the maddening desire to wrap her hair in my fists and trap her close…

Don't even get me started on her lips.

I wasn't a fan of kissing. Most of the time I didn't have to bother because the women who hung around the club were interested in one thing, your position. And if they weren't patch chasers, they were attracted by the motorcycle. It didn't matter if it was me or someone else, they just wanted to get that Milwaukee vibrator between their legs. I was a means to an end, not a person to them.

But when Roishin stared up at me, I swore she saw me. Her lips parted, and I wanted to kiss that gasp. That desire must have risen to the surface.

Because I frightened her. I was a monster. First, by my act at Carl's, and by assuming she'd be here long enough to need an altar. Then, letting my urge to devour her show on my face.

Gods, I was an idiot.

She'd seen right through me. How was I going to keep her?

It took everything I had not to grab her loose hair and pull it to my face again. I wanted to drink her down, eat her essence, and bathe in her softness.

And that was wrong. I'd pitched Jackson's idea at her and didn't get her full buy-in, then pushed her. What did that make me?

Worse than a monster. I was in danger of becoming the kind of man I hunted down.

And it was only day two. I had twenty-nine more to go. No matter what anyone thought of me, I wasn't that strong. I wouldn't last.

Kate and Zoe left after dinner. I don't know how Roishin did it, but she managed to make the meager food in my refrigerator into a meal for four.

She wiped down the counter as I washed the last of the plates.

"Thank you for dinner," I said, trying to keep a wall of politeness between us. Maybe that would work?

"You don't have to thank me."

No, I did. I told her as much. "I should go grocery shopping."

"I noticed you have a lot of protein powders and shake ingredients."

"Yeah." Hopefully, she hated that.

"Are you… I mean, I can do the shopping and cook your meals if I know what you like, special dietary needs, and other preferences if you want?" She sucked in her lower lip and chewed on it nervously.

I frowned. She was being too accommodating. Was that out of fear? "Did Carl make you do that?"

Her eyes widened. Then her expression flattened. "It wasn't that difficult." Her glance away told me that there was a lot more to the story.

I put the towel in my hand down and curled onto one of my stools. It took an act of will to relax my fists. "Let's talk. Okay?" Like adults. We were adults, cohabitating and learning how to get along. I didn't have to capitulate to her. I just had to be polite and listen.

She mirrored my position, but was a lot less comfortable, so I started.

"We'll share household duties. I don't expect you to do everything around here and I'm more than capable of cleaning up after myself."

She glanced at my damp hands. "Okay."

"And now that you've met Kate and Zoe, I guess I gotta tell you a bit to explain why they're protected as much as they are."

"I gather Kate was in trouble with an ex," Roishin said.

"Yep. He was a fucking asshole. Now, Jackson ain't much better as a human, but for his family? He's… he loves Kate and Zoe with everything he's got and will do *anything* to keep them safe. I think if something happened to one of them, he'd lose all touch with any good he's got left inside.

"So, I hope you understand why I'm asking that you stay away from them as much as possible unless I'm here."

She studied me. "Are you afraid I'll screw up?"

Hell no. But *maybe*? "Don't tell them anything about Carl. Not even if you're all doing that girl sharing shit you do. He's the one thing I'm going to demand you don't mention."

"Why?"

I took a deep breath. "This is in confidence, okay? Kate would try to fight your battles. And that?" My head shook from side to side as I tried to find the words that would impress on Roishin how dangerous this was. But she cut me off.

"Carl would use that against them and quite likely kill them, or use that information to get you or the club in trouble. I understand completely."

She was a piece of work. Frail in stature, mighty in will. Funny, but I hadn't noticed how thin her wrists were or how delicately the little lines of her blood vessels peeked through her skin. It all disappeared once she breathed or spoke, or simply stood. Then she became a mighty goddess warrior. A Valkyrie of sheer power. I was slowly becoming enthralled by her and wondered if she would be my doom or my salvation.

I quickly changed the subject back. "Groceries. I usually spend about two hundred a week, but always seem to run out. Then I eat like shit. If you can figure out a way to make that work better, you'd be doing me a favor."

We stuck to the safer topic of food for a while.

When that topic was exhausted, she stood up and stretched. "May I get your help to move the table to the patio doors?"

"Why? It'll block the exit."

She hesitated. "I want to let the items you bought bathe in the moonlight. Just for tonight."

That's all? She made her request seem like a Herculean task. I picked up the table, rocks and all, and put it in front of the sliding doors. Tonight's moon was waxing toward full. In another week the light would be much brighter. But from what I knew, waxing was good for charging magic.

"Roishin? Don't be afraid of me. Just ask when you need my help. I'll do it."

She swallowed.

Time to set her straight. "We're stuck with each other for a full month. You need to bend around my ways, sure, but I can do some bending, too. And I don't have a problem with your practice." Unlike fucking Carl.

"You truly don't?"

"Do you perform blood sacrifices?"

"No."

"Then I don't have a problem with it."

Her eyes searched mine for answers. As they did, I wondered if my favorite whiskey was darker or lighter than the center color in them. "Are you really Irish?"

"Yes. With a little Scottish on my maternal grandmother's side. And you?"

"Norse."

She laughed. "You are about as Nordic as…"

"Be nice. My father was as blond as you can get. My mother? Not so much. But I got my coloring and hair from her mother who was from Poland I guess. The whole family lives north of Pittsburgh."

Since we were opening up, I asked, "What about your parents? Where are they?"

Roishin clammed up.

"Rose?"

She glared at me.

"Roishin?"

The fire in her eyes dimmed slightly. "They live in Franklin County."

"Do you see them often?" Sure, I was fishing. Aside from John and Beth, she hadn't mentioned friends. And I needed to know who was going to be hammering on my door when Roishin didn't surface for a month.

"I haven't talked to my parents in fourteen years."

Holy shit. I did some quick math with what I knew about her and asked, "What? Were you twelve? The fuck?"

Her eyes fixed on me with unwavering strength. "Yes. I was put in foster care with Beth's family at twelve. Age fourteen, I was handed off to a different couple because, and I quote, 'she's a bad influence on Carl and Beth' end quote."

"So, you're to blame for Carl?"

"No."

Funny how one word can shut down a conversation.

I searched for something to fill the silence. "Do you need a phone? Maybe check in with your friends again?" I could pick up a burner the next time I was out.

"I'd appreciate that."

I pulled out my personal phone and handed it to her. "Go ahead."

She stared at me as if I had two heads.

"Seriously, call your friends. I want you checking in with them every day."

The disbelief on her face disappeared. "That way you won't get blamed when I go missing, right?"

"Something like that." If that is what she wanted to believe about my motives, then it would be a good thing. I was the bad guy here. She'd never understand that I was trying to be nice.

I tried not to listen in as she spoke with John and ultimately Beth this time because he was at the hospital. But I did catch that Carl had gone home, and wasn't expected back today. That information was good. In fact, if he made a habit of visiting, I'd have the skinny on his whereabouts. There had to be a way to exploit that. Wolf would need to know.

Like before, she deleted the call log before handing my phone back. Now John had two phone numbers from me. And I still had none. But I had Hickey and Skinner. One request and I'd have the number in minutes.

Roishin didn't need to know that. I planned to let her play those games for as long as she wanted.

"Is your friend doing okay?"

"As well as can be expected. We won't know for a few weeks."

"What's wrong with her?"

Roishin studied me. "She has Non-Hodgkins's lymphoma, and if your club brothers did their research, you'd know that already."

"Maybe."

Roishin sighed at my non-answer. "Listen, I'm tired. Do you mind if we save the inquisition until tomorrow?"

"Is that what you think this is?"

"Isn't it? I mean, if I were in your shoes, I wouldn't have been half as nice."

"I'm not nice."

She stood up and fired over her shoulder, "You *are* nice. All of this stuff you gave me is above and beyond nice. I don't deserve it."

"Don't." She was being too hard on herself. And she was bossing me around. I didn't like it.

"What? Don't complain? Don't caution you about spending money on me? I'll be gone in a month."

I shot back, "That doesn't mean you have to suffer like you did at Carl's."

She shut her mouth.

"If I'm buying you shit, I'm buying it. And it will be the best shit I can afford. Got it?"

Her face ran through a bunch of expressions from anger to mutiny. Finally, she said, "*Fine*. Buy what you want. Dress me, pamper me, I don't care. It *won't* work. Oh, and you forgot to buy me an athame." After firing that parting shot, she beelined for her lair.

Once she disappeared into the basement, I did a quick search on my phone for what the hell she wanted.

A *dagger*.

Jackson's words haunted me. *She'd be the one who'd stick a knife in it.* And I'd be the dumbass idiot who handed it to her. I stared at the table. There was an overhang that blocked the moonlight from one corner. I pushed the legs a few more inches to the right so the entire surface was illuminated.

She needed a knife. I'd seen those decorative letter openers at the store and dismissed them. Why buy something cheap and store-bought that might hurt more than actually kill? If I was gonna get stabbed in the back, I wanted it clean, sharp, and deadly. I knew just the person to call for one of those.

"Who is this and what the fuck you want?"

Fin was never friendly, but he'd gotten even more cantankerous over the years. "It's Bear. I need a knife."

"You know what to do, haul your ass down here and tell me what you want in person. I don't take orders over the phone."

Then he hung up on me.

Which was just fine. Fin might be the grumpy sort, but he made good steel. And his wife, Betty Jo, was an expert judge of character. She also worked magic with leather. If pretending Roishin was my woman was what it took to convince people that this wasn't what Carl said it was, I'd do this the right way.

Poor Roishin didn't know what she was in for.

11

ROISHIN

I woke before Bear did and moved the table and all the altar paraphernalia out of the way. His running shoes sat outside. They had to be damp with the dew, yet, as filthy as they were, I didn't blame him for not bringing them inside.

There was a bristle brush under the sink. It was brand new, never used. Which was a shame. Tools should be used. I sat down outside, bundled up in a blanket and shivered while I sloughed off the remaining caked mud and grime. The fancy running shoes would never be pink again, but they were a far cry better than before. And I needed to atone for my outburst last night.

"What are you doing to my shoes?"

Bear was dressed in workout sweats and a performance thermal shirt that clung to his chest and abs. I got slightly distracted by the muscle definition so didn't answer right away. Realizing my gaffe, I quickly replied, "They were dirty. I cleaned them." I handed the shoe I was working on to him. The other wasn't much better, but they'd do.

He looked at them. A sour expression scrunched his face into a grimace. "I hate pink."

"Why did you buy them then?"

"The salesperson was good."

"Really? You know there's dye."

"Yeah?"

"A good leather dye would make them almost any color you want."

"Black."

I smiled. His pants were charcoal, the thermal, black. The bands at his wrists were black, and his piercings varied between silver or black. He definitely wasn't the pink type.

He snapped his fingers. "That reminds me, we're riding today."

"Not tomorrow?" I asked.

He froze as he slipped on a shoe. "What do you mean?"

"Kate said there's a ride tomorrow."

"Ah, right. There's a ride today, too. Then church."

I waited for him to ask me, rather than demand. But it never came.

"I'll be back in an hour." He took off at a light jog, turning right as he hit the T in the path where it intersected with the trail.

Breakfast was ready when he returned. He stopped at the doorway, dumping his shoes outside and inhaled deeply. "Sausage?"

"And eggs, I made biscuits, too."

He stood there, hovering in the open door.

"You're letting the cold in." I'd finally warmed up. The basement didn't hold heat well, and I shivered most of the night.

"Sorry. I… I'm not used to breakfast."

I stared at his supplements. "I would understand if you didn't want to eat my cooking. I can always save your portion for later and maybe make a casserole or something with it."

A heavy hand dropped onto my shoulder. His body was directly behind me, the heat of it both welcome and not. I tried not to flinch. "Thank you for cooking for me. I appreciate it."

My sigh of relief slipped out before I could stop it.

He squeezed my shoulder. "Bet Carl didn't appreciate you enough, did he?"

That didn't need to be answered. The less I heard that name, the saner I felt. "Please don't talk about him."

"Why?"

I had the pan of hot food in my hand and had the overwhelming urge to smash it against something. Like his thick head. But I calmly set it down and turned until I wasn't so close to the stove. "I do not want a whole month of comparisons. That will get old."

The blow I'd braced for didn't come.

Bear slowly nodded, agreeing with me. But then opened his mouth. "On a scale of one to ten, with Carl being the one and your dream man being a ten. Where do I rank?"

Right now? A two. But that was unfair. He'd done nothing so far to deserve to be lumped so closely with Carl. "A four. You pulled a gun on me, and a knife."

"And if I hadn't done that?"

"A seven, maybe?" *Maybe an eleven?*

He smiled. "Good. That's what I needed to know."

With that, he pulled the plates down and arranged two settings. I took the side seat, knowing he'd want the short end of the table. It was all cordial and polite, and yet I wanted to scream. Rail on Bear for the unjustness of this situation. I wanted to cry, too. And the more I stewed on that, the greater the urge got. I barely finished my eggs and half a piece of toast before I couldn't stand it anymore. I got up and began washing dishes so I wouldn't have to think.

"You gonna eat your sausage?"

I should, but the thought of food made my stomach queasy. "No."

A scrape of fork on plate and the rustle of his clothes answered me.

He chewed loudly.

Carl never did that. Carl barely made a sound. At least I knew where Bear was. That was comforting, I told myself.

Even when he finished and brought the plates to me, I heard him.

He stood next to me, handing off the plates and drying the clean dishes before putting them back where they belonged.

A minute into it, he grabbed my arm. I almost dropped the glass I had in my hand.

"What happened here?" He had twisted my arm to reveal the long black, purple, and green bruise from the broom handle.

"What do you think?"

He stared at it, not letting go. In fact, his grip got tighter. Not horribly so, but enough that I didn't dare move.

"He's a dead man."

"No."

Bear forcefully inhaled and prepared to berate me for my disobedience.

"You can't go around killing people. It's wrong. And for the one month I'm here, can you just forgive?"

His jaw went to the side. "Forgiveness is a Christian thing. I don't have that word in my vocabulary."

But he let go of my arm and pulled the glass out of my hand to dry it. I studied him. Such a contradiction. A warrior, built for domination. Yet, domestic chores were not beneath him. He didn't have to prove himself because he truly walked the walk and talked the talk. It was refreshing.

"I wanted to consecrate some of the things you bought for me yesterday."

"When we get back. It will be late. You can do that by moon-light, right?"

"Do I have to come along?"

"Yup."

No explanation, no clues, no politeness. I downgraded my estimation of him. "I don't get a say on it?"

"Nope." His lips pressed together, almost hidden by his beard. If I didn't know better, he was trying not to laugh.

At me.

"Where are we going?"

"South."

I counted to ten. "Where south?"

He chuckled.

"It's not funny."

"I'm taking you to an old road dog's house. He's going to make you an athame. And his wife? She's going to get you outfitted for riding. If you're going to be on the back of my bike tomorrow, I need you looking the part."

At least that wasn't a one-word answer. "Was that so hard? And maybe you want to *ask* next time?"

"Nope."

I growled in frustration.

He smiled and took the last plate from my hands and set it in the drying rack. Then he turned me to face him.

"Roishin Black, I don't ask. I'm not that kind of a man. And I certainly don't beg." His fingers tightened on my hips.

My pulse sped up. I barely tried to breathe because my whole body braced for trauma.

But he smoothed his hands down and loosened his grip. "I don't want to scare you, either."

I took a shaky breath. It didn't go unnoticed.

"Riding. I should dress warm, right?"

"As warm as you can. I'll bring some of my thermals down for you. But you want to dress in layers for when it gets warmer, okay?"

That was as close to a request as I'd get. "Understood."

His jaw shifted. It was his thinking face, and what he was thinking about, he didn't like. I liked him better for it.

What I didn't understand was how anyone would enjoy freezing to death on a bone-jarring, butt-numbing torture session across the border to Maryland. We stopped at an ancient farmhouse set on the edge of an aging subdivision. Bear parked the motorcycle near the largest barn and yelled out, "Yo, Fin, where you at?"

A woman stepped out onto the porch and yelled back, "Stop bellowing you oaf. He's right there in the barn. Can't you hear the hammer?"

That's what that rhythmic clang was. Bear indicated I should get off, but I was stiff from riding and almost fell lifting my leg high enough to clear the seat.

"Who's that with you? She looks half frozen and dressed like you slapped her together with duct tape. Don't you got any sense at all?"

I liked this woman already. Anyone brave enough to berate my captor had my loyalty.

Bear stuck a thumb at me. "This is Roishin. She's mine."

Really now? I glared at him from where I stretched my legs.

"Then treat her better, you fucking idiot. You, Roishin, get your ass in here, I got something to take the chill off."

She motioned for me to come in the house.

Before I could, Bear stopped me. "Don't let her get you drunk."

What?

He didn't elaborate, instead, locked the bike down and disappeared into the barn where the noise came from.

"Here." Betty Jo handed me a warm coffee. Then spread her arm to the left to show me the fixings. Including whiskey. It was before noon.

I opted for cream. "Thanks. That was a cold ride."

She nodded, looking at my layers of clothes. I had to resort to almost everything I owned and two of Bear's thermals. All of that still didn't keep me from feeling like a popsicle that had been run through a cheese grater.

"You need some proper shit to wear. You a size six?"

"Mostly."

She squinted. "I'd guess that mostly is your scrawny ass, but you're a medium up top, right?"

Since she'd nailed it, I just nodded.

"Cup size?"

"What?" I choked on my coffee.

Betty Jo cleared her throat and grabbed my chin. "Bear brought you here, half frozen on a bitch of a day to ride wearing practically nothing that would keep the wind from giving you hypothermia. He's going to pay dearly for that mistake. I'm going to load you up with at least seven hundred dollars of clothes. You got a problem with that?"

"No?" *Maybe?* "I'm not a charity case."

She laughed hard. "No, you ain't, but that doesn't mean that overgrown idiot doesn't deserve to fork over some scratch. Cup size?"

"C."

She scanned my bulky clothes. "Thirty-four, right?"

I nodded again.

She led me through the house to a workroom that had stacks of fabric and leather, three sewing machines, including one contraption I'd expect to see in a factory, and racks upon racks of clothes. Not just any clothes, *biker* clothes. Male and female styles, mostly in black leather, and at least two more racks of outfits you'd see at Fantasy conventions, or Renaissance fairs. "You made all of this?"

"Sure did."

Wow. I might have stepped through an enchanted gate. And this woman who, despite the tattoos and heavy makeup, was my fairy godmother in black leather.

"When you're not dressing like a Mormon hobo, what do you like to wear?"

I looked down, embarrassed. She'd pegged the style. "Goth or dark fairy-core but it's been a while." There was no need to dress up when you wore a lab coat for work. And since coming back to help Beth, I hadn't had time to find a scene, let alone been free enough to go.

Her eyes lit up. "Screw seven hundred, let's try for seven thousand." Under her breath she muttered, "Stupid Bear."

The first thing she held out was a leather trench coat. It was best described as, *what if the Old West met Lord of the Rings Mordor-style*. I loved it.

I had to take off three layers before I could try it on. As I took off the last shirt, I forgot I was only wearing a white T-shirt underneath. Betty Jo caught my arm and stared at the bruise.

"Tell me Bear didn't do that."

"He didn't."

She stared at it for too long. "That was from a cane or something thicker. Which idiot do I have to kill?"

These bikers and their threats. "No one."

"Don't."

"Don't what?" I asked.

"Don't *lie* to me." She took the coat out of my hands.

"I'm not lying, you don't need to kill anyone."

Her eyes went a little scary-dead as she studied me. "I'll let you in on a little not-secret. My ex-husband, may he rot in Hell forever, used to beat my ass. I know that mark because I had one or two myself. Sometimes on my bare butt. Who did this?"

I swallowed. What could I say that would get her off this subject? I had a feeling if I lied, or tried to misdirect her, she'd send me home naked. And while that wasn't the absolute worst thing that ever happened to me, it would be terrible enough that I hesitated.

"Well?"

"In a month, maybe two, it will be resolved."

She glanced out the window. Through it, I could see the barn. "He ain't roping my husband into anything, is he?"

That I could answer honestly, "No. I hope not."

"He better not be." She quickly changed the subject, handing me the coat back, but first adding a long-sleeved turtle-neck in a soft grey-black.

The yarn was softer than cashmere, and loosely woven. The neckline wasn't strangling tight, either. I slipped it on and marveled at how good it felt. "This is amazing."

"That's hand wash only. Cold water. Lay flat to dry."

I could see why. "What's it made from?"

"Mulberry silk and alpaca. Got a friend in the yarn business who trades me supplies sometimes." She pulled out a damask dress. It had a lace-up bodice that squashed my tits higher when I tried it on.

"I had one like this." But not nearly as nice. "Store bought, of course." I swished the skirt so it would flow outward. My old one didn't flare like this one did. I felt like an evil queen in it. "This is beautiful."

"Try on this, too." She handed me a combination of tight black leather pants and a push up top.

"That's not my style."

"No, but it's Bear's. I want to see his eyes bug out of his head, just toss it on."

"Toss? I might need a shoe horn." I laughed, feeling much freer than I had in ages. On the heels of that, I wished Beth was here to make fun of my choices. *An outfit in every color, as long as it's black.* She'd quip.

"Try it."

I tugged on the pants and stuffed my boobs into the top. Betty Jo helped lace up the back. "How am I going to get out of this? I can't breathe."

"Stop bitching. Do you always wear your hair like that?" She tugged on the clamp that I'd pinned my braids with and the loops fell free.

"Holy shit. How long is your hair?"

The braids fell well below my ass. "Mid-calf."

"You ever think about getting it cut?"

Never. But that was a lie. I thought about it almost every day I had to go through the ritual of detangling it, trimming the damaged ends, and braiding it again. The only times I let it flow loose were when I was working magic or getting it dry after a washing. Both were sacred times for me. "I've had it cut."

Not voluntarily.

"Well, if you ever wanna donate to cancer victims, that'd probably make three wigs."

I stared at her in shock.

"What?"

"Nothing." Did she know about Beth?

Betty Jo frowned. "It ain't nothing, and I can see that. But maybe I could have been a little more tactful with my words. Fin lost his best friend to cancer. I was there at the end. It's tough business."

I nodded. It certainly was.

"Who?"

"Beth, my best friend."

She made a sympathetic sound and hugged me.

I stiffly hugged her back. It had been so long since anyone, even

Beth, had hugged me this well, I almost cried. As it was, I had to clear my throat twice to speak. "Thank you."

"What kind if you don't mind me asking?"

"Non-Hodgkins lymphoma."

Betty Jo thought for a moment. "That one has a good recovery rate if you can find a donor."

"She did."

I didn't know this woman at all, but maybe a perfect stranger would be the right person to tell. I turned my arm and showed her the bruise again. "Him."

"*Oh.* That's why he ain't dead yet." Betty Jo dusted off her hands and gave me the coat she'd taken from me. "Put that on, and keep your braids down, I wanna see."

I did, moving my hair outside of the collar and letting it fall with three braids to the back and two snaking down the front. I turned and looked at myself in the mirror.

And liked what I saw. This woman had power. The person I wanted to be stared back at me. I lifted my chin slightly to let its sharp angle jut out. I felt like I'd just conquered a kingdom.

"You need jewelry. What's your flavor of Goth, pentagrams or crosses?"

Neither. "Do you have any moons?"

She smiled. "I got a few. Diana or Hecate?"

"I'm not picky. The power predates the names."

She stared at me oddly. "You should meet Sierra. You two might have something in common."

"Who is Sierra?"

"She's one of the wives here. Her grandmother sees the future. I think Sierra inherited some of that woo-woo." With a quick change of the subject, she asked, "How'd you meet Bear?"

Funny how she'd picked up on that. I decided to test my theory. "He saw me casting a spell. Naked."

Betty Jo laughed. Her whole body shook. "Oh boy, that'd do it. I only had to flash my ass at Fin." She wiped her eyes and said, "Welcome to the fucked-up family."

12

———

BEAR

It was a mistake to let Betty Jo dress Roishin. My wallet thought so. At least Roishin balked once the total topped a grand. A set of saddle bags were already stuffed with clothes, and if I had to guess, Roishin left what she'd worn here out. At least some of it. Hopefully, it was the frumpy shit. I liked the new clothes much better. She stood taller in them as Betty Jo made her model them for me.

And she smiled. I hadn't seen one of those on her before. At least not one that lasted. Without a doubt, Fin's wife was a miracle worker.

She even convinced Roishin to leave her hair down. Albeit, braided, but after yesterday, I never wanted to see that tightly-pinned crown of braids again.

Nope. I wanted to immerse my hands in her hair, play with the strands, and slide my fingers through it. Hell, I'd even volunteer to braid it just to get that chance. But Fin saved me from making an utter fool out of myself.

"Bear here says you don't have a dagger. And he also thinks you got specific tastes. Enlighten me."

Roishin's eyes went wide.

Betty Jo butted in and told her husband, "Think Sierra meets Edie. But darker. Much darker."

Fin's jaw went sideways. Mine hung open until I realized what I was doing. How had she figured all that out in just a few minutes? And, how did she get Roishin to try on all the shit she got?

But I had to play it cool. Jackson's advice rang in my head. "You look amazing." It wouldn't hurt to praise Betty Jo either. Maybe she'd give me a discount? "Nice work."

Her eyes narrowed on me. "Don't bullshit me. And most of all, don't be such a tight ass. This woman deserves every cent in your wallet."

She was just goading me to barter.

Fin must have seen through it, because he snorted. "Bear already dumped a grand outside. What he ordered for her ain't cheap."

Roishin's eyes widened. "No." She took off the coat and handed it to Betty Jo.

What did she have on underneath? Practically nothing, that's what.

It could only be described as my fucking dream girl outfit. The leather hugged her curves and pushed her tits up into perfect half-moon mounds I wanted to taste. With her hair down, she looked feral and wild. No paint needed. I stared until she disappeared into the other room.

A slap upside the head knocked me out of my trance. "That was testing out something to sell at the rallies. She's not going home in what she had on, so stop gawking." Betty Jo hustled after her.

Meanwhile, Fin doodled on a piece of paper. Every once in a while, he'd stare off into space and then doodle some more. Finally, he asked me, "Where'd you find her?"

"Carl's."

Fin was far from retired, despite his lone-wolf status in Hagerstown. He and the club went back for decades now. And he knew all about our businesses and the players.

"No shit?" He squinted and listened to Betty Jo and Roishin argue about what she'd wear and what she wouldn't. "Fill me in."

I did as succinctly as possible. "He beat her. I have her now."

His low swear was quiet. "What's her take on that development?"

"She'll come around. She's a fighter."

He laughed. "Betty Jo was the same way." A rare smile spanned over his grisly face. I can't say it improved his looks much, but the lines around his eyes deepened while the ones on his forehead almost disappeared. He drew a few more lines.

Soon, Roishin came out in her jeans, leather riding chaps, and a decent coat. My thermals peeked out from the open collar. Her skin was flushed, and she'd tied her braids into a knot near the nape of her neck. They still hung to her waist, but they were out of the way enough to ride.

Betty Jo announced, "I had to fight her on the jacket and chaps, but she's good enough for the ride back." She dug into a crate. "Here's some gloves for her, too. Fin'll add them to the bill."

Fin leaned to push the paper toward Roishin. "Let me know if there's anything there you don't like. I'll change it."

She picked up the page and studied his drawing. Her hands shook.

I glanced over to see if Fin had noticed. His eyes met mine, and he raised an eyebrow. He'd noticed her nerves.

The last thing I wanted was to keep scaring her like this. Worse? If I didn't do something about it, there'd be questions. As carefully as I could, I rose and walked around to stand near Roishin. From my vantage point, I could see what Fin had planned. It was brilliant. Thorny ropes of rose briars twisted around the hilt creating a finger guard. The blade would be one of his multi-layered Damascus steel masterpieces which kept an edge for years with minimal maintenance. The scabbard had a triple moon signet embellishing the throat where the guard merged into the pattern; creating a locket to keep it from falling loose. The design was brilliant and far beyond what I'd imagined.

Roishin leaned into me. I steadied her with a hand on her hip. "What do you think?"

"It's perfect," she whispered. Then tacked on, "But too much. I can't…"

"Sold, Fin." I took the paper from her hands and passed it over. "When should we come back down?"

"How's the twenty-third work for you?"

I pulled Roishin closer and caught the faint smell of vanilla that clung to her hair. The sweetness pulled my face closer to hers. "Can you make do without it for that long?"

Her eyes met mine. "It's already been a month. I'll—"

Shit. "Can you work any faster, Fin?"

"You want fast? You don't get this." He pointed a finger at Roishin. "If *you* want cheap? You definitely won't get this." He held the paper in the air and shook it.

I gritted my teeth, waiting for Roishin's decision.

Roishin spoke. "I can wait. It's more than I could hope for. Most custom smiths take months." Under her breath she muttered to me, "Hopefully I'll be working soon to pay you back."

Fin's eyebrow rose. "And how would you know how long it takes?"

She swallowed. "I commissioned an athame once. It took four months."

And Carl took that from her. My fingers longed to wrap around his throat and squeeze the life out of him.

"Four months, that's amateur hour. In four months, I can get half a suit of armor done."

"Not without your arthritis acting up, you wouldn't," Betty Jo muttered. "Don't listen to him. He's just got a bad case of ego is all. We'll have it ready for you when it's ready." She picked up the saddle bags and passed them to me. "Your girl? Worth every damn penny. Don't forget it."

That was a warning, not commentary or a sales pitch.

Maybe Roishin had worked a miracle on Betty Jo? She didn't normally glom onto women that quickly. Unless… I glanced at Roishin's arm. Of course. Betty Jo was firmly in her corner because she had to have seen that bruise and asked questions about it.

Which meant, Betty Jo knew more about Roishin than I did. That was a scary thought. One that bothered me all the ride home.

I pulled up to the gates of the compound at a quarter to six.

"Where are we?" Roishin asked over the rumble of my bike.

"A junkyard."

"You're not buying anything *here*, are you?"

I leaned away so I could twist around to see her face. The scowl on it was funny. I laughed. "Only a whiskey. You want one?"

"They sell whiskey at a junkyard?"

The clatter of the gates drowned out any chance for a reply I had. But I hadn't intended on answering her, just showing her.

I pulled up to the club's building and shut down the bike. She wasn't as stiff or cold now and hopped off more gracefully than back at Fin's. I held her hand to steady her anyway.

And didn't let it go.

Why should I? This was the one place I needed to be the most convincing. Rumors would fly around about the new woman Bear was with. Hopefully, they'd get Carl angry. Even if they didn't, a plan formed in my head that I was going to win Roishin from him. No matter what hold he had over her, I was going to break it. And that plan started somewhere between seeing her pretty legs that first night and seeing her rounded tits a few hours ago.

And it was the perfect time for it. We had company tonight. A crew of wannabes from Allentown parked their bikes in the second row of machines surrounding the door. We'd met them several times before, and rode with them occasionally. Wolf and Jackson were eyeing them up because their presence filled the space on our club's border with the Demons. If they took the heat off us, we didn't have to work as hard to keep the peace.

But other clubs were wooing them, too.

And that made them dangerous, and valuable.

If we could insure they didn't swing to our biggest rival, the Wicked Legion, then our lives would be a lot simpler.

"Fair warning, you're not ready for this. But it's *showtime*. Follow my lead." I pushed open the door and a wall of noise blasted out. The night was kicking into high gear. A stripper stood on the bar,

half-naked already. The place was packed with hangers and brothers. I searched for any sign of old ladies, and saw none. Not even
Tits.

But Wolf was here. I beelined for him, weaving through the
crowd with an occasional shove to get some idiot drunk out of the
way so no one would molest Roishin. I stopped in front of him.
He'd propped up his leg on a barrel and leaned back in the fancy
barstool we'd gifted to him last year. His pose was relaxed, but his
gaze wasn't.

"Is this Rose?"

"Roishin," I corrected.

Wolf's eyes glittered as he studied her. "You've been to Betty
Jo's."

"Yes." Rose didn't need to answer, it hadn't been a question.
And now she had Wolf's attention. That was not a good thing.

"She needed riding gear. It didn't appear magically."

He laughed at my bluster. His eyes darted from me to Roishin
and back. "We need to talk before the meeting starts." Wolf snapped
his fingers and the prospect assigned to him hopped off his barstool
and joined us. "See to it that Ro—Roishin gets a drink and is unmo-
lested for the duration. She's Bear's."

That was exaggerating the situation slightly, but probably the
most succinct way to get the point across. Wolf hated to mess
around with unnecessary talk. I appreciated that about him. Jackson
used chit chat to find your weakness and didn't approach things
head on like his successor did. The honesty of Wolf's leadership
style was refreshing.

He led me into the meeting room. This meant our discussion
wouldn't be interrupted. I waited until he sat down at the head of
the table before joining him.

There was an uncomfortable pause before Wolf started his questions. "What did Fin and Betty Jo think of her?"

"They love her. Fin's making a custom dagger. Betty Jo tried to
sell her entire inventory to me."

He laughed. "You should be used to their tactics by now. How
much did they pinch off you?"

Over three grand if I paid for the shit I hadn't taken with me. "Eight hundred down, another twenty-two on delivery."

"Jesus." He leaned in and squinted at my forehead.

"What?"

"When did you tattoo 'sucker' up there?"

My hand covered my forehead, despite knowing he was teasing me. "I ain't a sucker. You've spent more on Tits."

His face turned dark. "That's because she's worth it."

"And Roishin ain't?"

My words stepped very close to insubordination. The tightness in Wolf's jaw warned me that I was treading on shaky ground. "You just met her…what was it, three days ago?"

I didn't back down. Instead, I explained, "There's a four-inch bruise on her right arm. Looks like a stick or a cane got blocked there. Carl did that. Of course, Betty Jo saw it and asked questions."

He leaned back, relaxing. Or at least, thinking. "Make sure my wife doesn't see it. I don't want her tangled up in Carl's shit."

"You might want to warn her before they meet. I'm going to take her on the ride tomorrow."

His eyebrow scrunched into a scowl. "Why?"

"Because Kate and Zoe met her, too."

That got his full attention. "Does Jackson know?"

"Of course. He'd have to be on Mars or something not to know every fucking detail of what went down." Kate knew far more dirty details of our operations than Tits did. Although, it wasn't because of any acrobatics on Wolf's part, Tits didn't *want* to know. That way, she wouldn't have to rat out her husband to her biker sisters who'd go vigilante on his ass.

Wolf speculated, "If Jackson knows, and Kate's in the mix, you shouldn't worry about my wife."

No shit. "I know that."

"What's your harem going to say?"

I didn't have a harem. Only a few women I hung around with for parties, and the working ladies who stayed around the club for a bite of my wallet. At least one of them was in the crowd just outside the door. But I played it cool. "Say about what?" I countered.

"About you getting an ol' lady."

"She ain't my ol' lady and you know what happens at the end of the month."

He glanced away. "Yeah, about that."

"Now what?"

"Carl's disappeared."

That was bad news, and good news. I focused on the bad part first. "He owes us eight grand. When did this happen?"

"Whoosh's guy, the one who saw him with the cop? Says he walked out of his house, hopped in his truck and never came back. That was the night you took his girl. There's been no movement inside for over twenty hours.

This was out of character for Carl. "I know he visited his sister's house the first night. And as far as I know, that was about ten, ten-thirty."

"Maybe he stayed there?"

I shook my head and relayed what I knew. The second conversation Roishin had with John seemed normal.

"I don't like this. First the cop, and now poof."

Wolf was right to be worried. "How's Sketch?" I asked.

"Pissed. Izzy insists she'll take the fall for anything that went down."

"We can't let her do that." Not only would that raise more questions, like why did the other gang members disappear, but the cops already knew she was with Sketch and admitting anything would implicate him.

"Sketch is on it."

"Do we bring her in, talk with her again?"

Wolf shot my suggestion down with a single shake of his head. "Let Sketch handle it, okay? Izzy will come around."

I frowned. Sketch had recently gotten custody of his kid. The situation had to be freaking him out. But there was another person we had to worry about. "Is Whoosh holding up?"

That earned a snort. "Fucker, he's acting like he's got his patch already. I'm thinking of putting a pause on it just to teach him a little humility. I might stall the vote tonight."

It would serve him right.

"But that's not what I needed to talk to you about. Sprout told me that you stepped up the other day."

Aw shit. This was a dressing down. I braced myself for the worst.

"And I appreciate that. The club agrees we need a VP who can handle decisions without calling a fucking meeting all the time. After all the bullshit we went through, we are all smart enough to know we can't have another Kush slacking off and leaving every decision up to the president.

"You did good making the moves you made, even if you kind of fucked up taking Rose—Roishin. I'm going to have a talk with Jackson about rotating you out of his protection detail, so we can install you as VP."

If I hadn't been sitting down, I'd have ass-planted on the chair. As it was, I had mixed emotions about all this. Foremost was the question I asked, "Who's going to be watching Kate and Zoe?"

"We'll keep doing what we're doing. Prospects, members, that sort of thing."

"And when a fucking prospect screws up?" I reminded him.

He grinned at me. "Guess who'd be in charge of picking 'em?"

Fuck. Me. Wolf sure knew his way around the role despite only being in it a few months. Or, maybe not… "I suppose that was Tits's idea?"

He grinned a little wider. "My wife might have had a say in it."

I scratched at my ear, pretending I hadn't heard that. Bad enough the club knew Wolf's soft spot for her, but if someone on the outside knew? We'd be laughed out of the organization.

"Fix this shit with Carl, and the job's yours."

Unspoken was, *fuck it up, and you'll never have a chance.*

No pressure.

13

ROISHIN

Follow my lead. How? Bear shoved his way to the bar, parked my ass on a stool, and left me stranded. I was an island of confusion inside a whirlwind of anarchy. The jukebox blasted out a familiar song and I couldn't help but tap my foot. And that led to swaying in my chair. And that attracted attention.

"What are you drinking?"

The prospect Wolf handed me off to waited for my reply. "Bear said there was whiskey for sale here?" I didn't particularly want whiskey, but he did say 'follow my lead' and that was all I had to go off of.

"Ha! It's already bought." The kid snapped his fingers and yelled over the bar. "Yo, Whoosh, get this sweet piece of ass a glass of Bear's private reserve. She's his ride for the night."

I caught about half of that, and didn't like the implications.

"Do I look like your bitch?" Whoosh stopped in front of me and looked me up and down. "You don't look like one of his regular girls." Something flickered in his eyes. "You sure that's what you want?"

He practically dared me with his tone. A challenge to my position. "I'll take Bear's private reserve." I tipped my head to the other guy, indicating that Whoosh should listen to him.

As I did, I remembered an overheard conversation. That last drug deal about a week ago. Whoosh didn't have the drugs Carl ordered. And I was deathly afraid Carl was going to kill him in front of where I was hiding.

The marks next to Carl's back door.

The glee Carl took over my part in them. The lust in his eyes as he anticipated more bloodshed.

That was an awful night. I didn't sleep at all for fear he'd visit me in my locked closet.

Whoosh, or Sketch, was a murderer.

Maybe that's why he didn't like me. These men knew about Carl, and probably all about me. I girded myself with bravado I hadn't used in years. "I'm sure."

Whoosh smirked at me. "Not that you deserve it, but Bear or Wolf will have my ass if I fuck up." He set a glass on the bar and then pulled a hand-labeled bottle down from the top shelf. There were many up there like that. Brands I'd never or rarely seen in any of the clubs I'd frequented. I braced myself for the worst.

And realized with one sniff, I'd misjudged alcohol my entire life. The aroma had nuance, measured complication, and most of all… promise. I took a tentative sip and marveled at the explosion of heat, flavor, and complexity.

Of course, drinking straight whiskey had side effects. Like the strong urge to cough out the flaming fumes that wafted up from the pit of my stomach and clung to the throat, or the sudden rush of heat to my skin.

I fought both reactions and managed to casually observe, "That's pretty good."

"Pretty good? Are you shitting me? That's handcrafted bourbon. It's seven years old."

I stared at him, mimicking Carl's best psychotically bland indifference. I may not be as violent as he could be, but I certainly observed the expression enough times to create a good facsimile.

Whoosh gave up, setting the bottle back in place with a

mumbled, "Whatever." Then in a lower voice, he said, "I hope Bear knows what he's doing," before walking to the other end of the bar to ogle the stripper and fill orders there.

After positioning himself two chairs away, the prospect assigned to me turned his back, also watching the stripper.

Which hurt. Sure, I deliberately donned that act, and wanted to avoid their interest. By doing so, I'd cut myself off from an opportunity to make a connection with these people.

And a month from now, would that matter?

No.

If everything went well, the only times I'd ever come back to this region would be holidays, and only then, to visit Beth and her family. Not hang out with bikers.

Fuck it. I sipped the whiskey in blissful solitude while the insanity of the Destroyers clubhouse spun around me like a wobbling top. Eventually, the party would end. Everything did. Friendships, dreams, lives…

"I heard you came in with Bear."

The woman who'd approached me had bleached blonde hair and obviously augmented lips and breasts. She sat down on the stool between the prospect and I, and set her drink on the bar.

I desperately wanted a lifeline. Could I trust her? Probably not. That didn't stop me from answering.

"I did."

She scanned my outfit. Thank goodness I wasn't still wearing the hobo look Betty Jo commented upon. "Are you from that bitch club that Tits runs with?"

Tits… I'd heard her mentioned as the president's wife. "No." I immediately regretted not saying yes, and adopting a temporary cloak of hierarchy, because her attitude shifted from nasty to worse.

"Funny, you look like one of them."

"Is that a good thing or a bad thing?"

Her eyes drifted up and fixed on my hair. "How long is your hair? And is it real?"

By rote I answered, "Real, and over four and a half feet."

"You're fucking shitting me."

If I only had a dollar for every time someone said that…
"Nope."

"Wow. I know a hairdresser who'd pay you for this." She petted a loose braid with an unhealthy compulsion, ignoring my personal space.

"Not for sale." I tugged it back and wound the mass into a tight bun that hid behind my neck. The helmet Bear gave me this morning wouldn't fit over my head if I fixed them higher.

As I did, she reached for my glass and sniffed. "What 'you drinking?"

I took the glass back as soon as her nose wrinkled.

"Whiskey."

"Are you sure you're not one of Tits's friends?"

This time, I ignored her. That did the trick because she said something rude and cruel and flounced off, taking time to flirt with the prospect, who finally paid attention.

But he was called off seconds later to run beers to a table.

These people invented their very own waitstaff of prospects to serve them. Two men crowded into the space left behind. One jostled me as he slid his wide body onto the barstool.

"I hear you're Bear's?"

I wasn't in truth. My eyes dipped to his leather vest. It was decorated similarly to Bear's but had different colored patches on it. Even without seeing the back, I guessed he wasn't from the club Bear rode with. "You must have excellent hearing," I deadpanned.

Out of habit, I held my hand over the glass of whiskey, turning it as I covered the rim.

The action caught his attention. He asked, "Whatcha drinking?"

What could I say to get him to leave me alone? "Bear's private reserve."

"Lemme smell." His hand shot out to grab, like the woman's had, and I was damn tired of this game.

"No." I slid the glass away and tucked it against the wall, now completely covered with my left hand.

"You're a bitch."

The other one leaned around his friend and scanned my outfit. "I don't see any property marks on her."

Like I needed them in order to not be harassed?

Of course, given the location, events surrounding me, and the general lack of order, I could be wearing a neon sign that read, "hazardous waste," and these assholes would probably still mess with me.

They didn't look like the picky type.

Speaking of marks. I traced a hex into the air in front of me and rattled off some Latin I'd memorized from a dystopian novel. Then added to the vibe with a real protection spell.

I even spit onto the floor at the closest one's feet to seal the deal. Then stared him down.

This would either end with me getting hit and dragged out of here, or they'd walk away. Odds were fifty-fifty. And since I was a long-ass way from the door, someone would have to step in, wouldn't they?

The bigger and hairier one of the two broke first. He had less to prove. But the smaller one goaded him. "Don't pussy out, Tilly. She's just a little thing."

"I think she cursed me."

"It's in your head. She's like that bitch in those videos. You know the one who says stupid shit to scare men." He kept his buddy's bulk as a wall between him and I, but sidled closer. "You're just a scared little girl…"

Of all the things he could say, that was the worst.

"I killed a man when I was fourteen. I'm almost thirty now and possess a much more effective imagination."

If only I had a knife, or something that would equalize this situation. I grinned, letting a little of my insanity shine through. Loathsome as it was, I empathized with Carl in this moment. He could do crazy like no one I'd ever seen. Of course with him, it was natural. Mine was earned.

The big guy hesitated. "She's Bear's." He hit his partner with the back of his hand to get his attention. Then he flagged down Whoosh. "Yo, prospect!"

Whoosh glared at him. "I ain't your prospect."

"My buddy here doesn't believe she's Bear's woman." His voice held a small tremor.

Whoosh's eyes narrowed on me. He could sink me with a single denial.

"She came in with him, and he's probably going to be leaving with her, so… yeah."

"Told ya!" The bigger one of the two shoved the smaller one away. But my antagonist bounced right back, sliding closer.

"I wanna touch."

A baseball bat hit the bar rail next to me with a loud clang that reverberated from our end of the bar to the other. Everyone turned to look.

There was a dent in the brass almost as wide as my palm.

"Touch her and die." Whoosh had stepped on something behind the bar because he stood taller than he had, and leaned forward, almost climbing over the bar as he did. One hand was on the bat, the other on his waist. There was a gun strapped there that I hadn't noticed before.

I leaned back in my barstool, still keeping one hand on the drink I'd barely touched, and the other rested in my lap, as if I hadn't a care in the world.

But my heart was racing and my ears rang from the shock of Whoosh's violent outburst.

Yet, I couldn't resist letting the corner of my mouth curve upward. Carl did that when he was particularly pleased at some tragedy. If this man was about to die, I'd wear that smile throughout the entire act.

Four Destroyers rushed from their closed meeting room and grabbed the men with the different colors on their vests and hauled them outside.

Boo. Now I wouldn't get to see the fun.

"You okay?" Whoosh didn't sound pleased.

I straightened my expression. "Thank you." He'd saved my hide. I let a little sincerity warm my tone.

"Don't thank me. Bear would have my ass if something

happened to you. That shit you did with the woo-woo and your face? You learned that from that fucktard, Carl, didn't you?"

The real story was much more complicated. "Yeah, I guess I did."

He nodded like he didn't quite believe me and was trying to convince himself. Then his face changed. "How long were you living with Carl?"

Too long? "A month."

I waited as the span of time sunk in.

His face paled. "You were there."

I nodded slowly.

"Fuck."

I rubbed the dent in the rail. "Consider us even. I didn't see or hear a thing."

He pointed the bat at me. "Make sure it stays that way."

"Get that thing out of her face." Bear shoved the bat away and pushed Whoosh from his perch on the bar. He landed with a stumble, but covered it with a tirade of expletives. They ended with, "What took you so long?"

Wolf stepped in. "Stand down… *prospect*."

Whoosh's face colored. "Sorry. To both of you. Bear, I'm sorry."

Wolf noted the dent in the brass rail. "You did this?"

His face reddened. "Yes."

Bear interrupted, "Next time, just make it their head and save yourself some scratch."

"I was trying not to add to my kill count," Whoosh protested.

Both Wolf and Bear snorted. Bear went as far as mocking the last two words.

"KC," Wolf muttered.

Bear stopped laughing. "It works."

"Well, KC, what you did was effective. And you managed okay. Where the fuck is that dickhead, Hammer?"

Whoosh, I guess now permanently dubbed "KC," pointed to the far end of the room.

"Hammer! Get your ass over here," Bear yelled.

The man practically ran across the room. He stopped short, glancing nervously between Wolf and Bear. "Sorry man, I was watching your girl, but we were short-handed." His pause fumbled his apology. "Whoosh was watching her."

"That's KC now. You'll call him that, and we're patching him in tomorrow after the run. You good with that, KC?"

The guy, formerly known as Whoosh grinned. "I'll try not to let it go to my head." His eyes shifted to me, then to Bear. "We need to talk."

"Everyone needs to talk to me. I'm fucking tired of talking, so it'll have to wait." He reached for my glass. I put a hand over the top and protested, but he tugged it away anyway.

"I haven't checked it since that girl took it. You shouldn't—"

He chugged down the entire glass like it was water. I stifled any protests and let him joke and talk over me with his "brothers."

The four who'd cleared out the guys harassing me returned and slapped Bear on the back. As if that were a cue, he turned and wrapped an arm over my shoulder, weighing me down. "This is my girl, Rose. *Mine.*"

Then he leaned in.

The smell of whiskey was strong on his breath. "Play along," he said right before kissing me.

There was no magic in it. And as we parted, his eyes met mine. They were slightly unfocused. "I didn't mean that," he said. Then he ran his nose along the side of my cheek, inhaling. The heat of his body pressed against me. I felt him wobble, planting a foot wider so he wouldn't topple. "I wish I could kiss you like I want to." His words slurred slightly.

"Are you okay?"

He blinked. "I don't know." Confusion scrunched his forehead into a peak of concern.

I dug under his beard to feel for his pulse. It beat sluggishly as it thumped in the hollow of his neck. "Do you feel dizzy?"

Another blink. "I'm drunk… on you." His smile was lopsided.

This was highly unusual. "You had one drink."

"Everything okay, Bear?" Wolf laid a hand on his shoulder.

"I think someone spiked the drink." I indicated the glass where he'd thumped it down after ignoring me.

Wolf raised the glass and scanned the liquid at the bottom. I went on tiptoe to peek at it.

While I didn't have the best view, what I could see looked cloudy. "Do you have a way to test it?"

Wolf's sharp glance accused me. "Why?"

"Because not only were those two assholes bothering me, but a woman approached me earlier and took my drink for a moment or two. I didn't have it in hand the entire time."

"Are you saying someone would dare to dose you in *our* bar?" Wolf's tone warned me to deny what I suspected.

But I couldn't lie. Not if Bear had been drugged. Anger I hadn't felt in years rose up inside and I braced for battle. "Listen, back in college, I was active with the campus security authority program. I lectured on the effects of date rape drugs. He's showing signs of a central nervous system depressant, my guess? Rohypnol. We need to get that glass tested, him to a safe place, and find a bitch with blonde hair and big Botox lips who I *think* dropped something in my drink. Move!"

I shoved Wolf with my free hand and coaxed Bear into following. "Come on, big guy we're going to find you a place to lie down."

Wolf's hand splayed across my chest. "You're not going anywhere."

"Hands off her boobs! That's my turf." Bear's words were barely distinguishable. But the way his hands fisted was clear enough.

Wolf held his hand up, then poked three fingers in the air. "How many fingers do I have up?"

"Three, ash-hooole." While he got the number right, his slur was getting worse.

"I give it fifteen minutes before he's immobile." I might have guessed a bit higher than usual. But Bear was larger than most college coeds. I turned to him, "Do you feel hot?" His brow was damp.

"Hot. Like you." His hands swept down my sides, lingering at my hips and pulling me in. "I wanna fuck you so bad."

Like that would happen in under fifteen minutes… "Follow me." I maintained eye contact with him as I shuffled backwards toward the door.

KC and Wolf directed me to a side door instead. A steep staircase loomed behind it. I shook my head. Getting him up it was going to be a nightmare if he went under too quickly. "We need to get him outside."

"No can do. We haven't cleared the place." Wolf slipped an arm under his friend. "One step at a time. Up!"

Bear wobbled, almost taking them both down.

I noticed Wolf's prosthetic and shoved him off, then wrapped both arms around Bear and took a step higher than him to use my thigh strength to drag him with me. All the while, I urged him on. "We're going upstairs, you and me, Bear."

"Hell, yeah. I can't wait until you ride me like a fucking sex jockey."

Unfortunately, that came out much clearer than his babbling earlier.

KC snickered. "I got his back. Let's do this." He wrapped around Bear's waist and I tugged from above as we led him up the steps. I almost fell on my ass when I cleared the top and stumbled into the open space. Bear slapped a hand on the wall to hold us both up. He pinned me against it and sagged a bit.

"We need a bed, Rose."

I nodded. "That's right, a bed. Come on."

It wasn't lost on me that there were at least three rooms with mattresses in them I could choose from. I picked the nearest one for expediency. Wolf swept around us and tugged the sheets off, tossing them into a pile in the corner.

"I'll grab clean ones from my room."

Bear fell to the mattress and landed diagonally across it. Face first was good, face-planted was not. I shoved his bulk to the side and curled in to use my body weight as leverage to position him better. His hand trapped my waist and tugged me close.

"This is what I'm talking about." The slur was back, worse than before.

I made certain he was on his side and comfortable before paying attention to anything else.

We'd gathered a crowd. Not only Wolf and KC, but almost a half-dozen more men stared at Bear and me.

This wasn't an audience participation moment. "Get out. Only one of you needs to stay to watch him, but not all of you."

"Woman, if you drugged him, we'll *all* stay to make sure he's safe from you." I couldn't identify who'd spoken, but the nods that got passed around meant they thought I'd done this. A few of them snickered and made crude comments about watching us follow through with Bear's sex jockey comment.

"Fine. This is my formal protest and a warning. You'll have to explain your voyeurism to him when he comes to. He doesn't deserve your ridicule. He needs help and a friendly face when he wakes up. Not your ugly mugs being dicks to him."

"That's so fierce. She's gonna give Tits a run for her money." KC nudged Wolf as he spoke.

Wolf's jaw worked to one side. "Everyone out. This is Bear's blue hair moment—Officers and KC *only* are allowed in. Rose stays. The rest of you assholes, find Skinner or Hickey and get them scrubbing through the interior feed. Find out who the blonde woman she mentioned was and detain her. Now!"

The room cleared almost instantaneously.

"Blue hair moment?" I asked.

KC pointed a thumb at Wolf. "Prez passed out at the wrong party and got a bad buzz cut and dye job he didn't want."

I flinched and gathered one of my loose braids.

Bear laughed and leaned heavier on me. "You smell so good. I wanna eat you." His breathing was too slow and heavy as he burrowed his face into my neck. I could barely move because his weight had trapped me. What hair hadn't fallen loose was stuck under my shoulder. I shifted, so it wasn't as uncomfortable.

KC held out a hand. "Need help?"

If it wasn't guaranteed that I'd rip my scalp off trying to break free, I'd have taken it. "I'm good."

"You sure? He's not small."

Bear certainly wasn't. "I'll survive. Do you know anyone who's got medical training? I don't like how slow his heart rate is." It was even more sluggish than before.

"Probably a good idea. KC, call Ma. Tell her what's going on." Wolf crouched near the mattress as soon as KC left the room. "She's a nurse. And you sound like her. Why?"

"In college, I was an RA with a biochemistry major and a past. Identifying date rape drugs and helping victims was an unlucky by-product of my history." I swallowed the memories. I'd given Wolf the sanitized version of my villain origin story. He didn't need to know the ugliest parts of it.

His scrutiny meant I hadn't sold it very well. Finally, he said, "You know Carl."

I sighed. "Duh. Why do you think I cultivated that unhealthy psychosis?" Sarcasm laced my words.

He thought about it for a moment before asking, "Did it work? Did you exorcize your demons?"

Unfortunately, I did not.

14

BEAR

My head felt like a bag of chisels. The chemical taste in my mouth was steeped in the toxicity of whatever was killing me. I barely moved and saw white stars behind my closed eyelids. I groaned because while I needed to move, it only meant more pain. But if I didn't move soon, I'd puke on myself.

Slowly, I rolled to one side and tried to breathe through the urge to hurl. The only thing that kept me from emptying my stomach was the acute understanding that if I did, it would hurt more.

I needed something cold to lean on.

Almost as if I'd conjured it, a wet cloth pressed against my head.

"Take it slow." Wolf's voice registered.

And there was something wrong about that. It should be someone else's voice. My memory was fuzzy, but there were at least two times in the haze that I remembered Rose's voice, and her gentle touch, not Wolf's sledgehammer mitts on my skin. "Take it off."

I rolled until I was on all fours. The floor was cooler than the mattress, and I hugged it, trying to find a position where, if I puked, the vomit would land somewhere I wasn't.

"Here."

A cold steel pan bumped my cheek.

Just what I needed.

What felt like an hour later, I finally rolled to my back and tried to open my eyes. The slicing pain returned and throbbed through every inch of me I could muster into motion. The rest of me was a grungy graveyard of confusion. "What the fuck happened?"

"You were roofied."

I squinted at Wolf's silhouette. The lights were off in the room, thank the Gods, but the hallway lights were too bright. "By who?"

"Remember that hooker who gave Baldy crabs last year?"

Could I possibly vomit more? *Naw.* But my head spun. Or the floor did. "Monica?"

"That's the one."

"Bitch." I felt my junk. Pants on, zipper up. Nothing funky going on down there. Good.

"You're cool. Rose played bodyguard for you most of the night. By the way, she's worse than Tits when it comes to people getting taken advantage of."

A memory drifted through my head along with a wave of heat. I'd kissed her. And it was awful. Not the whole kissing her part, but the rest of it. The reason why I'd done it. The force I'd used to make it look like we were an item. Her lack of response. The terror in her eyes when I pulled away... *Sweet Freya, I'd fucked up.*

"Where is she?"

"Tits?"

If I could have opened my eyes, I would've glared at him. "Rose. Roishin." I'd fucked that up, too. I'd begun to shorten her name like we were friends or something. "I need to apologize."

"She's crashed in my office. Under guard."

Oh, *hell.* She should be safe and free here, not a prisoner. "Why?"

Wolf made some noises as he shifted. "Because she pissed off just about everyone last night."

Great, another headache to deal with. "How?"

Wolf grunted. "Let's start with putting hands on me."

That I had to open an eye for, just to see if he was joking or serious. If he was joking, that was one hell of a bluff.

He wasn't joking, and told me as much. "She did."

I tried to stop the brain stew in my head from sloshing. "And?"

"*And*, she made Ma monitor your blood pressure until four A.M. Sprout was pissed."

That should have made sense, but it didn't. "What?"

"Your BP was way too low, man. She, Roishin, argued with Ma about your body mass, height, and the general average for a person your size and thought that one-ten over sixty was too low for you."

I'd never had a reading that low.

"About four or so, you stabilized at one-forty over ninety. That's when she let Ma go home."

Okay, while getting in Wolf's face, and Ma's was awful, it wasn't exactly *everybody*. "Who… or what else?"

Wolf started counting off on his fingers. "That club visiting last night? Yeah, two of their guys. Monica, because Roishin didn't drink the drink like she thought your girl should, and then she got blamed for your condition. Hammer, because he was supposed to be watching your girl, and paid too much attention to the stripper and hangers instead. Baldy, because he hates mouthy women, Skinner… but I have no fucking idea why he's pissed. And—"

I cut him off. "Who *didn't* she piss off?" That list might be shorter.

"Get this, KC."

"Who?"

"Kill Count."

It was as if I'd been dropped into an alternate universe. "Who the fuck is that?"

"Damn, that shit worked fast on you. Whoosh. You and I named him for fuck's sake."

"Why the heck did we do that?"

"Because, and I'm quoting what you said here, 'Next time, just make it their head and save yourself some scratch.' To which, Whoosh said, 'I'm trying not to add to my kill count.' Then I named him KC and you agreed."

Did I remember that?

Not really.

I scrunched my face to try to stave off the pressure between my temples, but it didn't work.

"And mostly, folks are pissed because I postponed the ride today."

"You didn't."

He got right in my face. "Yeah, I did. See, I wanted to announce your nomination after we got KC patched in, but I couldn't quite do that with you being the only asshole not along on the ride."

Wolf had a point. But a horrible one. "That announcement could have waited."

"Yeah, it could have, but more shit went down."

Did I want to hear this? "Can it wait?"

"No."

Wolf was firm in his answer. I sighed. "Lay it on me."

"I'd rather not while you're lying in your own puke."

"I'm not lying in puke." At least, I hoped not. I rolled over and did a push-up, and tried to see where the basin was, where I was, and what the fuck kind of shape I was in. That's when I noticed I didn't have my vest on. "Where's my vest?"

"Hanging up in my office. Your girl's been anointed its guardian until you're on your feet. I figured if she was good enough to sit with you all night and make sure no one fucked with you like they did me that one time, that she'd be a good choice to respect it. She knows not to let it touch the ground. Or to mess with it."

I curled onto my knees and tried to sit on my heels. It hurt, but I felt a little more human once I was upright. "And who knows you ordered this?" It was a bad look, giving a brand-new piece of ass a man's vest.

"You and I, and KC. He's on the door."

The alliance between those two was a mystery I couldn't unravel with my head hammering so hard. But Wolf said there was more shit going down, so I focused on that. "What else did you need to talk to me about?"

"Carl."

I didn't have to close my eyes, because they'd fallen shut on their own. "Has he surfaced?"

Wolf laughed, short and bitterly. "Yeah."

I didn't like the look on his face. "Well?"

He inhaled and let the air out slowly. "Monica fingered the visiting club. And while we don't normally just believe things on face value, Sprout, who— again, was pissed off because of Ma—went after the two who were bothering Roishin."

I gritted my teeth, waiting for bad news. Sprout did not do heavy lifting like that. Especially when it was two against one.

"Don't worry, Smoke backed him up."

Thank the Gods. "And?"

"And they claimed to have gotten it from a dealer in Harrisburg who approached them."

"Carl."

"Bingo."

"When did he do that?"

Wolf smiled. "The night he disappeared."

I pieced together the timing. "Before or after midnight?" I had to know whether he'd gone there directly after being at Beth and John's house or if there was a gap in there.

"Before."

So, he'd planned on going to the drop from his sister's. Or maybe he hadn't.

I replayed Rose and John's conversation in my memories. Rose was right to worry about the kids. If one pill could knock me out like it had, it would have killed a toddler.

But instead of doing that, Carl went to our feeder chapter, but only after confirming whether Roishin was with me or not, and testing John.

Even if he hadn't planned it all out like I suspected he had, Carl visited his sister's four kids while holding onto date rape drugs strong enough to knock me out. What a piece of work.

I laid out my concerns for Wolf. "Am I imagining things?" I asked.

"I don't think so. I'd bet he's not planning to let Roishin live once you return her. And, he's using the situation to set us up, or to weaken us."

"That's what Jackson thinks, too."

Wolf studied the wall for a moment. "We're one 'accident' away from getting framed. We've gotta move her."

"No."

"What do you mean, no? Dump her on Hagerstown. You said yourself that Betty Jo took a shine to her."

"Even if we did that, and nothing happened, which I highly doubt would be the case, Walt would bitch to his boss, our old boss, and you know what would happen then, right?"

Oh yeah, Wolf knew. "Jackson would get involved."

"Precisely."

There was a sports drink near the mattress. "Is that mine?"

"Yeah, no one's messed with it."

I cracked open the seal and hydrated slowly. Not only did I have to keep Roishin safe in order to keep our club out of hot water, but I had to watch everything I ate and drank because Carl had proven he could reach out and touch us where it hurt. "What's the verdict on our alliance with those bozos?"

"Broken. I sent a proverbial courier pigeon to the Demons. Just to let them know they have a rogue club in their territory."

"We're practically pushing them to our enemies."

"That's too fucking bad. I'd rather have them as enemies than friends. It's easier to deal with them that way."

"Does Tits agree with you?"

His nod wasn't convincing. "She's happy we're not courting them anymore."

"But?"

"She thinks it's a mistake to cut them off."

I held up the half-empty plastic bottle in my hand. "They tried to drug my girl, and by proxy got me. That's disrespectful." I sloshed the liquid around to keep his attention. "And if they think that little of us, they'll never be our allies."

His face was grim. "What do you suggest?"

"Nothing. I think you did the right thing, cutting them off and making them crawl to the Wicked Legion for help against the Demons. More than anything, it will humble them."

Wolf didn't find it as amusing as I did, so I poked him.

"We're ruthless. Just because we don't go around cutting down every single asshole who crosses us, doesn't mean we're weak. They'll suffer longer, and more this way. And our hands are clean."

That got a reluctant smile. "You're right."

I tapped my chest. "You gotta care to hold a grudge. Party line on this one? We don't give a shit. They're not worth it."

He slapped my shoulder. "Let's get moving. Maybe we can do a small ride, you game?"

That was questionable. "Where we going?"

"That place near Hershey with the burgers. I think we'd have ended up there anyway."

He was right about that. But did I have enough in me for all of that? "When are we leaving?" I needed to collect Roishin, shower the funk off, and get at least another bottle or two of electrolytes into me in order to feel human again.

"I figure, two?"

That didn't tell me much. "What time is it now?"

He laughed at me. "Noon. You got two hours to get your shit straight. I'm going to relieve KC. Don't make me wait in my office for too long."

Right.

I made quick work of showering in the public space across the hall from the room I'd spent most of the night in. KC flopped onto his back on the couch, ignoring me. When I got out, I dripped on him to get his attention.

"Fuck man, stop it. I'm tired."

"You're not patched in yet."

He groaned and rolled up to sitting position, but I slapped a hand on his chest to push him back down. "Just got a question, that's all."

"What?"

"What's going on with you and Rose?"

I was *not* jealous. At least it sounded that way in my head. But the growl in my tone spoke a different story.

He heard it, too. "She was there that night Sketch's girl got kidnapped."

This was confirmation of what Carl hinted at. Although I expected that hadn't been the first time she'd hidden behind his couch. "And?"

"And, she's cool. She's not going rat us out for it."

"How do you know that?"

He sat up again. "Because when I protected her last night, it clicked."

My fist stayed at my side. "What clicked?"

He grinned, his eyes dipping to the hand I'd clenched too tightly. Then he tapped his head. "It clicked in her head. That we're the *good* bad guys."

Considering my treatment of her, KC was delusional. Or maybe she'd only relegated that status for *him*.

Which was how it should be. This thing between us was temporary. I only needed to keep her safe and relatively happy for a month. Then she'd be free. "Speak for yourself." I slapped his head to knock some sense into it.

KC laughed. "Come on, man. Deep down, you'd like her to think that about you, too. Wouldn't you?"

"That's never gonna happen." Because I *was* the bad guy here. Like an idiot, I'd walked right into Carl's trap. And there was no way to extricate my foot from it. Roishin should hate me. It would be better for us all if she did.

Because, if she liked me, Carl would use that to hurt her.

15

ROISHIN

"When does the fun begin?"

I didn't recognize the man asking. And, he didn't have the telltale vest the Destroyers and their counterparts wore. But something about his voice was familiar. And because of that, he had my attention.

"Well?" His eyes dipped to my leather riding gear, which I hadn't had the luxury of changing from since yesterday. My braids were stiff from the cold ride of the day before, and the wet ride of today. Any makeup I'd tried to apply had smudged from smokey-eye to trash panda chic.

I said the two magic words that might get his eyes unglued from my tits. "I'm Bear's." It didn't work last night, and it certainly didn't work on this guy.

He hovered over the chair I'd claimed in the corner because Bear had abandoned me to stand outside, in front of the bar where everyone could see him as he drowned in the cold, misty air like an idiot. I was so *over* being cold. Finally, he said, "No, you ain't."

Did I need to say it louder? I opted to ignore him instead.

"You're Carl's." His eyes trailed down a braid that had escaped the hasty knot I'd made. "No one else has that long of hair. Nice trick with the make-up. I almost didn't recognize you."

His eyes locked on mine.

His were bloodshot and dilated. "You're one of Carl's dealers." An assumption that was statistically possible.

He squinted but didn't deny it. "My name's Fish. I'm going to be a Destroyer."

Nice to know.

"And when I am, you're going to suck my cock."

I'd rather not. "Did you know the Nile is over four thousand miles long? And that's about as far as you'll have to travel to hide from Bear when you attempt your little fantasy."

"Bullshit. I know you're only on *loan* to Bear. And you ain't his ol' lady. You're fair game in another month."

My heart rate picked up. Carl must have yapped to him. Or perhaps Bear or one of his brothers had. My jacket didn't have the magic 'stay away' lettering Kate or Danielle's had. It had no markings at all. And I'd quickly realized that this meant I was a target for just about any asshole who didn't pay attention—unless of course, you were Tits, and wore your own colors. I let the silence grow uncomfortable as I plotted avenues of escape.

KC slapped Fish on the back. "About time you showed up. I was about to send a posse out to find you." He gave him a side-armed hug and noticed me tucked against the wall. "Rose, this is my best friend. We go way back."

Shit. Now I had to play nice… or *not.* "Perfect. Since you're such good friends, tell him I'm *Bear's.*"

KC didn't strike me as a junkie, or someone who put up with the ultimate betrayals that would happen with someone like that, so those childhood bonds must have a deeply rose-tinted sheen painted on them. I hoped his bonds with the Destroyers ran deeper. Because one day, they'd be tested.

I stood up and sidestepped them both before heading straight for the tavern entrance. I needed to find that big hairy oaf and pretend I was who I said I was, not only to keep up the lie, but to strip Fish and any other horny asshole in the immediate vicinity of such delusions.

The surprisingly bright sun blinded me, and as it did, I hesitated. Why did I care whether KC got hurt or not? I was destined to go back to Carl. And hopefully by then, Beth would be cured, and I'd be the one four thousand miles away.

"Woman, get your ass over here."

That was Bear's growl. I blinked the spots out of my eyes and plastered on a smile I didn't feel.

He patted the seat of his bike. His long legs straddled the back hump and splayed wide, leaving space for me.

Instead of sitting, I stood by him.

"Where have you been?" he asked.

"Out of the rain."

His scrutiny lingered a bit too long. Sure, I hadn't answered directly. But that wasn't as criminal as he implied. "It's sunny now."

I set a hand on his shoulder and lifted my leg to straddle the seat in front of him. The maneuver placed my back to the handlebars and my ass landed halfway on his gas tank. I tried to make it as graceful as I could, but he quickly slipped his hands under my thighs and pulled them over his legs.

My crotch brushed his.

The stare grew more intense. He broke the tension by joking, "Now we're talking."

With an adjustment and a lot of manhandling, he tugged me so close I felt his dick getting hard between us. He leaned me backwards. The tank underneath me was hot from baking in the sun, and the gas cap bit into my spine. But I knew we'd attracted attention. I wrapped my arms over his shoulders to arch away from the hard metal digging into my back and hovered suspended by his grip.

His hands slipped up my rib bones, positioning to either side of the tank and cushioning the surface as he leaned further forward. My back rested against his arms, no longer in danger. I relaxed a little, trusting he'd figured out why I flinched.

"We should kiss," I whispered.

His eyes flicked to the men clustered around us. They were loud enough, my hushed worries were too low to be heard. "You good with that?"

I nodded.

Unlike the night before, Bear hesitated. His breath trailed along my skin and a tangle of his braid hid my face from the crowd.

My own fell loose. Likely touching the asphalt. But oddly, I didn't care. I licked my lips and arched to match his mouth to mine. I started softly. Just a brush of tender skin against his. I wetted my lips again and pressed harder, giving him a piece of my heart as I explored the forbidden. Doing this was safe. I could back off and claim it was good acting. That I intended it to look and feel real because we had to sell this stupid farce.

That didn't stop me from teasing his mouth open and slipping my tongue along the slightly parted fullness of his bottom lip, dipping inside to prime our kiss for more.

His arms tightened, and I was willingly surrounded by his power. It scared me and thrilled me like no other experience before. The fluttering pulse in my neck was too fast. My breathing hitched.

A long-buried grip of fear clutched at my throat. But my hips canted higher, riding the ridge of his erection with wanton abandon. I reveled in that power, the knowledge that this was too close and too fast. That made me wet. I wanted to throw away the terror and ride the wild passion. Prove that I was far beyond the things that had crushed my spirit and ripped away my trust.

A word crawled up my throat, begging to be heard. It tore from me, half plea, half question. "Bear?"

My fingernails curled into his neck. I needed him to stop. I needed him to rip my clothes off and fuck me right here in front of his friends. I needed safety and promises, and to forget who I'd been. I needed kindness in a world that was too harsh. I needed a man who could stand up to the storms and conquer the skies and coax the sun to come out. Like this man did.

His eyes cleared as our mouths broke apart. His chest heaved and our hips were still pulsing with unspent desire. The tension made his thighs quiver. Mine were far beyond that point and hovering on that cliff's-edge before leaping into a full body orgasm. My panted breaths were quick.

"Get a room," someone suggested.

Bear straightened, gently removing the cushion of his arms from behind my back. I held tense, arched away from the hard ridge of the cap. Waiting for him to help me up.

Instead, he ran his hands down my body. From breasts to belly-button, finally landing on my thighs. His thumbs curled in to brush my crotch, still too close to his. I arched further and bit down the moan that threatened to leak out.

Absently, he circled my clit through my jeans. His eyes scanned the parking lot to zero in on the source of the comment. "Fuck off, Skinner. I'll do what I want. Where I want." He looked down at me and winked. "How's that gas cap?"

I pulled myself off of his tank, using his shoulders for leverage. "It's too hard."

"That's what she said," Sprout snorted.

And suddenly, I wasn't so embarrassed. I laughed right along with Bear and his friends.

Bear pulled me close and whispered in my ear as the laughter died down. "You started it."

That I had. "Can we finish it?" *Later?*

His sudden movement had me clutching his neck and straddling his waist as he swung off his bike and locked it down.

"Don't mind us," he said to his brothers. He hefted me up, tossing me in his arms like I weighed nothing. My legs slipped free, and he used that to toss me higher until I was almost thrown over his shoulder.

"Duck." His hand covered the back of my head until I curled over his back. My braids swung free as I caught a good view of the floor and the bar door that slammed shut behind us.

The crowd parted for him, and the noise was significantly louder as he waded through the main room to the very opposite end of the building. He didn't stop until we dead-ended near the back door. Even there, people hung around. "Get gone," Bear growled.

But someone didn't listen. "Bear, there you are. I need to introduce you to—"

"KC? I'm busy." Bear turned, and I peeked over my shoulder. Fish hovered on his left.

"Put me down." I tapped Bear's head to get his attention.

"Nope. Not until these two leave. I don't want an audience."

I didn't like the undertone of anger in Bear's words. "We can do this later…" I lowered my voice and finished my thought as I whispered in his ear, "When it's just us." When I didn't have to pretend. It threaded through my worried plea.

He must have heard it because he set me on my feet. I didn't enjoy my freedom for too long because he pulled me behind him and kept a grip on my ass that was so tight, it pressed me against his back. "Lemme guess, this is your buddy from Harrisburg, right?"

Fish stuck out a hand and tried to introduce himself.

Bear ignored him and glared at KC. "Well?"

"Yeah. This is him. My friend." KC didn't sound as excited as he had earlier when introducing me to Fish.

Bear shifted, his body still blocking my view. "You're KC's buddy?" One fist curled at Bear's side.

"Yes. I…" His hesitation cost him. Bear cut him off.

"Cool. Leave. Take KC with you."

"But—" Fish tried to talk.

"Come on, man. He's busy." KC tugged his friend.

Fish, however, had other plans. "Carl told me to give you this."

Bear shoved me against the wall and drew his gun.

Fish had one hand in his jacket and both KC and Bear had their weapons out and aimed at his head.

"Move and you're dead." Bear's growl was lethal.

"Hold still, man. I'll take that." KC reached under Fish's coat and pulled out a plastic grocery bag. It crinkled as he tugged it free.

It was from the same store I shopped at only a few days ago. My shoulders stiffened as yet another reminder of Carl intruded on my life.

KC felt along the bag and handed it off to Bear, glancing down the hallway as he did. "I'm going to make sure no one sees this." He took a few steps and blocked the hallway, both arms crossed, feet planted wide.

Bear ripped the bag open.

Cash. Banded in the same fashion as the bundles I'd stolen from Carl. And just about as much. I sucked in a breath.

Bear's head tipped, acknowledging I was behind him, but not breaking his tense control over the situation.

"It's the payment. Carl said he wasn't going to be home, and he didn't want it late… or *stolen*."

His eyes slid to me. He stared at my face as he said the last two words. A subtle reminder that I'd done just that. And by this point, Carl had to know I'd taken his money.

Bear wrapped it back up and stuffed it in his vest. "Tell him, thanks."

Fish smiled, finally paying attention to Bear. "Will do." He held there, something else on the tip of his tongue.

"What?" Bear's gruffness should have been a warning to stay quiet, but Fish was clueless.

"One more thing." His attention shifted toward me.

Bear reached behind and found my hip. I slid closer to stand behind him and put my hands on his belt so he'd know where I was.

"Spit it out."

"Carl wants to know how you're enjoying his offering." His voice slid into the same sticky leer he'd vulgarly used on me.

"I'd be enjoying *it* more if you'd get the fuck out of here. That all you got?"

Fish's reply was short, followed by his retreat. KC was still at the end of the hall, arms crossed, feet planted wide.

Bear turned on me.

He was not happy. And he certainly was not the teasing man who'd carried me back here. His eyes caught a flare of the dim light and it glowed a reddish hue. "Rose?"

It. I was only an *it* to him. "A vow is a vow." I'd promised to pretend.

His nostrils flared and his fingers curled inward. His words gritted through his teeth. "No, it ain't. Not like this."

I took a step closer. My fingers touched his vest. I violated his rule to prove I could.

He blinked and stared at where I'd intruded. His much larger hand engulfed mine. Instead of removing it, he pressed it flat. "But since you insist, I vow—"

I shushed him. This was a public place, guarded hallway or not. Someone could overhear. The Gods could overhear. "Don't. Not here."

He twisted his head until his neck cracked. First one side, then the other. "No one tells me what to do except Wolf or Jackson."

I slipped my hand free. "Then I'm *suggesting* you don't do something you'll regret."

His knuckles went white as he clenched his fists harder this time. "I'm trying my damnedest to do just that. But you're tempting the fuck out of me. And I know KC has the hall guarded. Right KC?"

"That's right. No one gets past me until you say so." KC's voice was muffled slightly by the wall between us.

I frowned and directed my question to Bear. I desperately needed this answer. "What's stopping you?"

His jaw worked as he weighed his words. "Honor, Rose. I did vow that."

That I could admire and respect. Adore, even.

My breasts touched first as I moved to press against him. His hands slid over my ass and up to the small of my back. I splayed my palms on his waist. This was so different from the wild kiss on his bike. It was cautious. *Fragile.* One wrong move and the weight of outside expectations would crush us both. He bent to inhale the heat of my skin. I buried my face in his beard, pushing it aside to find his neck, or just drown in him so I could shut out the cacophony that clamored in my heart and mind. He deserved more than I could give. But he had my gratitude, nevertheless. "Thank you."

My words were soft. The drugging power of his scent much stronger than my voice. I clenched my fingers to hold him close. I inhaled again, making myself drunk on the sharp smell of leather, the heat of skin, the light fragrance of his beard oil, and the subtle musk that clung to his body like a long-forgotten memory of paradise.

KC whistled. Two staccato blasts that broke the spell. "Wolf's coming in hot. Look sharp."

Bear slipped his hands out of my clothes and straightened my shirt. Adjusting his raging erection wasn't as easy, and Wolf caught him mid-shift.

His president's face was grim. "The Demons are here."

16

BEAR

I slipped Carl's money into Rose's jacket and zipped her up tight. "Keep that safe." Tits was right behind Wolf and guided Rose through the bar to the waiting van where Kate and the other women huddled. Rescue mission complete, the group took off with little fanfare. Their escort included Tits on her rat bike and the few members we could afford to delegate.

I noted the patches present. The clubs were mostly the weekend types, with a few exceptions. Those I counted and weighed their loyalties toward our meager crew.

We were outnumbered.

As the Demons hung on the perimeter, a second group arrived. The colors on their back were from one of their feeder chapters. The bar's mood shifted quickly. The rattle of conversation died, and people cleared out, paying tabs, and making themselves scarce. Even the civilians knew we were outnumbered.

None of the newcomers left. That was good. Our women were safely gone.

I tipped my head to the road and back to Wolf. "Well? Shall we?"

He frowned, his eyes lingering a few moments too long on the highway Tits was on.

"She'll be fine."

"We're in our territory. They crossed without permission."

I shrugged. "Maybe they heard about that crew in Allentown?"

His face broadcasted his disgust. "Life would be a lot fucking easier if…"

He didn't finish his thought.

I could think of a dozen ways to do that for him. I wanted to be balls-deep in Rose right now; so I felt his frustration keenly. I matched his gait as we approached the mounted club.

Wolf held his hands loose by his hips, palms exposed as he addressed their leader. "Hey, Fry."

The man dipped his head. His eyes trailed to me. Unlike Wolf, I didn't pretend to be unarmed. I shifted until my vest hung open, exposing the gun I had strapped to my chest under it.

"I see there's been a regime change." Fry squinted at my patches, searching for a clue to give him the information he'd just hinted at.

Wolf stepped forward. "You didn't get the memo? Jackson's Regional President now."

Fry snorted. "Here I thought his fucking around finally killed him. Damn." His tone was sarcastic enough to be an insult. I held onto my temper by calculating how fast I could pop fifteen shots off to take him, his VP, his SoA, and any other motherfucker close enough to drill into with a bullet before the rest drowned me in a hailstorm of lead. We would not go down quietly.

"No such luck." Wolf laughed. "Got a present for you."

"I like presents." Fry licked his lips and searched the thin crowd behind us. It was only our brothers. I glanced to the left in time to see KC's buddy, Fish, work his way along our flank. He was positioning for a shot. I recognized the maneuver because it would be what I'd do if I wasn't standing in the middle of a parking lot with my ass waving in the breeze like a big red flag.

"We cut loose those bastards from Allentown. You're free to recruit 'em or shoot 'em. Don't give a fuck either way."

Fry smiled at Wolf. His eyes scanned our numbers. "Did you stop recruiting?" His tone hid a smirk as if he was a front row witness to our demise.

He had at least twenty men at his back. And the feeder chapter held another dozen or more. Numbers we would never be able to match. Not unless we wanted to give away the fortune Sprout stuck a ring on fair and square. This was what Jackson had worried most about. We might all be dangerous, but we also were far too few.

Wolf let him stew a moment before replying. "Tell me, if you were sitting on four hundred and fifty million, would you want to share it with a bunch of fucking idiots who can't even piss straight?"

Fry's quiet laugh didn't make a sound. His eyes drifted to Wolf's prosthetic leg. "I suppose if I was in your position, I'd be a little paranoid."

That *was* a threat. One I shouldn't let him get away with. If I were still the SoA for the chapter, I'd pull my gun, odds be damned.

Instead, I strolled forward, almost stopping within arm's reach of Fry's bike. I smiled and tipped my head to the guy on his left who had his hand jammed down his vest so hard it was going to get stuck that way. "Did you ever find out who shot your men up north?" As far as rumors went, Demons were supposedly very easy to kill. One half-out-of-it Destroyer and an old man wasted almost seven of Fry's crew. Hell, one woman killed four right under their own roof. Which would be a good thing to remind him about. "And Killer's getting better with a gun." I let my smile go wide and leaked a little crazy out. The kind that one day would get me killed.

But Fry loved crazy. He ate it up like candy.

"I like you, Bear. Wanna ride with the big boys?" He motioned to his crew.

His scrawny addict-infested bunch was no match for five well-armed Destroyers. "Wanna see how fast your house goes boom with some C4?" I winked.

His face dropped into a scowling pit of hatred. "Go fuck yourself."

He circled his hand once, and the bikes fired up. They roared around us three times before they took off in the opposite direction that Tits took.

Wolf let a silent sigh of relief leak out as soon as the thunder from their motors dimmed in the distance. "They still didn't ask for permission."

"I noticed that. They're going to be a problem in a couple of years." I muttered.

"They're a problem now." Wolf answered.

The Demons weren't technically our enemy. That was reserved for another group. The Wicked Legion had *always* been our enemy. And their biggest tactical mistake was making the Demons one, too. Which put us and the Demons on the same side.

That only worked if there was an even balance between our crews. But numbers didn't lie. Speaking of…

"Fish. Get your ass over here."

KC's tweaker friend crawled out of the shadows he'd taken residence in. I patted him down and pulled his nine-mil before introducing him to Wolf. "Meet KC's buddy, our eyes and ears on Carl. His name's Fish."

Wolf scanned him. Then motioned for me to hand over the gun I'd confiscated. He looked at it for barely a second. "Are you always armed?"

Fish *almost* lied. It was right there on his face. But he had at least one brain cell left. "No."

Wolf handed the gun back to him. "From now on, you will be. Understand?"

Despite whatever he was on, his nod was sober.

But Wolf wasn't done. "And whatever shit you're on? Get off it. I will not recruit anyone so fucked up they put my brothers' lives on the line like you just fucking did." He grabbed Fish's gun hand by the wrist and clamped down hard. "They saw you, you fucking idiot."

Sprout nonchalantly re-holstered his gun. He'd seen it, too, and kept his coverage hidden from even me.

Apparently, Wolf knew because he dipped his head at our very own class clown. "Sprout can hit dead center of a moving target at

80 meters. You may want to come to the lake house with KC and get some practice at being a little more…discreet." He let go abruptly. The marks from his grip turned white and then flushed into an angry red. Wolf was not a weak man. Too many people underestimated his abilities just because of a missing leg.

Hopefully, Fish would get the hint and begin taking advantage of our hospitality. It would be at least a year before anyone stepped forward to sponsor him, and double that long before we'd even think about patching him in.

Fry was right. We were down in numbers. Our feeder chapter down south had its own charter now, and we hadn't found anyone who could fill their shoes. West of us, Pittsburg was disintegrating. Maybe we could poach members from that implosion, but losing that chapter would leave a huge hole that someone needed to fill. And if we weren't careful, that someone would be the Demons or the Wicked Legion. Then we'd be screwed.

Jackson was right to swap me out for others. And we were damn stupid letting his wife and kid tag along on a border ride.

Even if it technically wasn't on our border. The Demons coming this far into our territory worried me. Truce or not, it had been a test. One we failed.

Wolf nudged my arm. "What's got you quiet?"

"You know what."

He snorted. "You need to get laid."

I let out a deep sigh. "I was this close, man." I held my fingers up, barely a millimeter of space between them.

He slapped my back. "You know what we need to do, right?"

I sent him a side-eye. "Lemme guess. Ride home and fix that?"

His grin spread wide. "Called it." He glanced at the sun. It hung over the trees. Not quite an urgent signal, but it would be close to dark before we all landed at the junkyard to patch KC in. I signaled for Sprout to gather the wagons. Wolf walked over and straddled his bike, walking it closer to mine. He reached over and put two fingers on my gas tank. "You know, Tits insisted I get a flush-mount. Best money I ever spent."

With that, he revved up his machine and took lead next to

Sprout. I hung back, letting Hickey and Smoke fill in the next set. I pulled alongside Sketch and sat firmly in the center of the pack. We tore out as one unit. Not nearly as impressive as the thunder of thirty-plus bikes, but it didn't suck.

The chaser van was parked inside the lot, close to the club's main building. Kate's car hadn't moved since early afternoon. Tits parked her bike where Wolf's should be. He idled in front of it, staring. "One of these days…" He shook his head and parked alongside it. Sprout was first off his bike, using his long legs to his advantage to beat us all inside.

By the time I caught up, he already had Danielle up against a wall and deep into a lip lock. Pregnant as she was, it was interesting he could even lift her into that position.

Speaking of… Rose sat at the bar. But so did Zoe. She'd kept to the perimeter of our crew during the ride, someone always outside with her and her mother, but damn it, they should be home. I included all three women in my announcement. "I'm escorting you ladies home soon. Kate, you good to drive?" She'd had a few beers during the milder moments of the trip. And Zoe was more than capable of getting her home, but for some reason, I wanted an excuse to sic a prospect on them.

Before she could answer, Wolf stuck his fingers in his mouth and whistled hard. "Yo, listen up. It is my profound pleasure to introduce the latest motherfucker who we call brother. KC? Get your ass over here."

I grinned because Wolf springing it on the crew wasn't necessarily a surprise, but he dragged out the timing to happen as soon as we were all mostly in one spot and safely tucked at home. Sprout scrambled to right his wife, then stood by Wolf's side. "Where's that fucking vest?" he yelled.

Someone dug it out from the meeting room where we'd hidden it. The name patch was a rush job we had Hagerstown ferry up while we were riding. Wolf slapped his hand on KC's name patch, hard.

"I know you got used to us calling you Whoosh, but Kill Count sounds *much* better for a Destroyer." He slammed his fist down hard in the same spot. KC staggered under the blow, but kept his feet.

"Have at him. Whoever takes him down first gets dibs on the best room upstairs." Five men rushed in.

I cupped my hands around my mouth so my voice would carry. "KC, you *can* fight back."

And with that, the melee began.

Poke went down. Smoke's heart wasn't in it. He wouldn't dream of taking his woman upstairs. Wolf had Tits, but already made his point, twice. Sprout laughed his ass off the whole time he swung wildly at KC.

Sketch was ruthless, but Isobel loudly reminded him she'd leave without him if he won a room. He caught a fist to the jaw when he tried to reason with her.

Cooper smacked KC in the vest. Almost exactly where Wolf had. That had to sting. Coop might be old, but that motherfucker was still fast with a right hook. He held out his hands and let KC know he'd taken his shot. Big Joe waded in and everyone paid attention. Money changed hands. KC slipped, but locked a leg. With KC's retaliatory kick, Joe went down to a knee and groaned. "Motherfucker. That's my bad leg." He limped away.

KC's hands flexed, adrenaline and pain mixing with his joy at finally getting a patch. His left hand rubbed the name plate leaving a smear of blood. Baldy took his time. Fists up and feet moving. I dissected his form. He was getting better.

Rocket used the distraction to hit KC on the blind-side and took him to the floor.

"Foul!" I yelled. "Doesn't count."

They rolled a moment, and KC let loose a flurry of punches that left the smaller man reeling. Baldy held a hand out to get KC on his feet again. Before he let go, he shot out a left hook that caught KC in the eyebrow. It rocked him, and it took two backwards staggered steps before KC shook it off.

"Damn. Thought I had him." Baldy held his hands out, having his shot and wisely not pushing it any further.

Hickey went down. Skinner, too. Cutty didn't stand a chance.

I pulled Rose close. "We *will* go home soon. Okay?"

She nodded and accepted the quick kiss I tapped on her cheekbone.

The club whistled as I walked up. Wisely, no one cast a bet.

KC's eye was starting to swell where Baldy caught him. "You need ice on that?"

I got a wary nod from KC.

He held ready for me. I shrugged. With a glance around at the men and a wink toward the ladies now clustered together at the bar, I squared off. "One shot." I held my arms wide.

KC balled up his fists.

He didn't pull his punch, but it barely glanced off my face. He stepped back, waiting to see what I'd do. I motioned for him to come closer.

A shake of the head. "Gotta catch me." His cocky grin was too cute.

I faked a right and while he twisted to block it, I came in with my left. His core was wide open, but I aimed higher. His arm managed to fling into place, giving just a modicum of resistance. I held my knuckles against his temple, proving that if I hadn't pulled the punch, he'd be dead.

"Consider yourself caught." I smiled and tapped his eyebrow. Then, with my other hand, I socked him right in the name patch where Wolf and Coop had nailed him.

He doubled over, wheezing. "Fuck, that hurts."

I helped him stand straight. "You good?"

He grinned as he panted. "When Griz and Hollywood get back, do they get shots at me?"

As much as being the bearer of bad news sucked, I let him down as gently as I could. "That's the rules."

He groaned, stretched, and looked around. His sights landed on one of the girls who wasn't claimed. "You."

She giggled and shot forward.

Wolf slapped him on the back as he slipped upstairs.

My private reserve came down from the top shelf.

I glanced at Rose, checking if she was going to throw a fit. Her mouth twisted into a half frown. She lifted her fingers and quietly asked for two glasses.

I tugged her close. The shot glasses were clean, the liquor straight out of the bottle and I poured both. As I lifted the glass, I spoke quietly so no one else except Rose heard me. "Remember last night?"

Her eyes widened. "I doubt you do."

"I owe you a debt." I tapped my glass against hers. "Anything you want tonight. *Anything.*"

Her gaze didn't stray from the laser lock she had on my eyes. I drank the shot down, and she followed suit, barely lifting her chin to let the whiskey slide down her throat.

I kissed her. If only to taste the liquor on her lips.

Her breath was heavy when I finally let her go.

"Anything?"

"That's a vow."

17

ROISHIN

Vow or promise, we were finally alone. The raw desire to touch my skin against his skin burned brighter now that we didn't have an audience. We left my coat, boots, and both of our shirts just inside the door. The jeans I'd been in for almost two days stayed on as I sashayed up the stairs with the hastily-wrapped bag of money in my hand.

I was tempted to break open the stacks and drop the Benjamins like bread crumbs. Instead, I laid the bag on Bear's dresser before tugging off the pants that clung to me like leeches.

My struggling caught his attention. His low laughter was at my expense.

"Getting rained on sucks." It didn't, really. I'd been almost too warm later in the day. And the leather chaps kept the wind at bay much better than my clothing ever would. But the moisture and ride made the exposed denim stick in place.

He picked me up and tossed me on the bed. "Lift." He pulled my leg toward him and tugged.

The material let loose, and he got one leg free. The other side released much easier, and I could finally breathe freely. I panted and let the cool air of his house dry my skin. "I need a shower." A *hot* one. And maybe a soak in the tub.

Instead of answering me, Bear tore off his pants and attacked my legs with open-mouthed kisses that began at my calves and moved rapidly to the inside of my thighs.

I tensed.

He paused, both hands curled over my thighs, fingers dangerously close to my underwear.

His weight made it impossible to move. He studied me and rested his chin on his hands. "Scared?"

A glitter of challenge winked in his eyes.

"No." That wasn't convincing because the word wavered in the air.

His eyebrow rose. He took a quick breath, then buried his nose against my underwear and inhaled deeply, twice. His groan of pleasure rumbled against my legs.

I flushed red. No one had ever savored me with such…abandon before.

"I need a shower."

"No, you don't. Not until I'm done with you. In the meantime, we're just going to get *dirtier*." He worked his fingers deeper between my clamped thighs, breaking my resolve to bar his access. Once successful, he pulled the gusset of my panties away from my skin and fingered under the edge of the elastic.

As he did, a knuckle or a fingertip brushed my clit. It repeated, circling my entrance, and the yearning for more than just that light touch took hold of my gut. My breath stuttered with longing. I arched to make the accidental contact hit the right spots, but he played with me instead. The brushes were more frequent, but still not hard or deep enough to be more than a whiff of sensation before they disappeared and left me keening with desire.

I pulled up my bra to roll my exposed nipples between my fingertips. The contrast of light touches with the hard squeezes I'd practiced on myself was unbearable. I begged.

"Bear, please."

His rumbled chuckle wasn't an answer.

I tried again. "I need more."

That got a response. He lifted his weight from my legs and pulled my panties off. Then he tugged me into sitting position and expertly unsnapped my bra. It landed on the floor somewhere over his shoulder.

Then he stopped.

Just stopped.

I covered my breasts with my hands because it was almost as if he'd never seen boobs before.

His eyes flicked to mine. A grin slid across his face and he settled onto his heels. Both hands slowly spread wide. "I'm waiting."

For what? "I said I need more."

"Yeah. You did." He glanced away, almost daring me to slap him for his distraction. The grin that had worked into place now quirked to one side.

He was toying with me.

I scooted forward to move closer. With one finger, I snapped the elastic band of his boxers. "Take these off, and find a condom."

For a moment I thought he'd disobey me. It was there, in the quick glance he gave me before standing up. He took his time, stretching tall, his lumberjack-thick form smoothing into sinewy muscles and an art-study of surfaces I desperately wanted to examine more closely.

Then his thumbs slipped under the waistband and tugged the cotton downward. It hung up on his impressive bulge for a moment. Another tug and his cock sprang loose, bounced slightly and swung free as he stepped out of one side of the boxers then the other.

Big. Maybe not gargantuan, but definitely on the "weighty" side of the well-endowed spectrum.

I needed my hands on it. One hand would definitely be inadequate. But he crossed to the nightstand and out of my reach.

The drawer squeaked with age. The rustle of plastic confirmed that he'd complied with the second part of my order.

"Good man. Set that down on the bed right here." I placed a fingertip on the fitted sheet just below the pillow closest to him.

"Then kneel on the bed, facing me." I moved to make room for him and patted the mattress so he'd know exactly where I wanted him. The position was eerily similar to where he'd frozen in place, realizing that he owed me "anything *I* wanted" rather than bossing me around like he'd been doing.

And while that was hot, it also was perilously close to one of my biggest triggers. I'd spent years overcoming fears and issues. However, some were hard lines that should never be desensitized. Like consent. We were consenting here. Or so I hoped.

I mirrored him. Kneeling in front of him, naked as he was. Not touching, not crossing the boundary he didn't know I'd established. I chose my words very carefully. "Tonight, I want to explore you. But…" I held a finger in the air, "…I do not want to break you. I want you willing and—" my voice faltered, the words log jamming on my tongue.

His head tilted to the side. "Rose?"

"A moment, please?" This was important. My hand quivered. I tucked it under my knee to hide the weakness. With a swallow and bravado I didn't feel, I plowed on. "I want you willing and fully participating. I want you. I want real, not ordered against your will, and not fake."

The rest of my churning thoughts fled. Cowards.

Bear leaned closer. With a careful touch, he moved one braid behind my shoulder. His fingers trailed along my arm softly. The skimming touch angled sharply inward and jumped from safe to sensual as the tips landed on my breast.

He circled my nipple twice before his hand stilled. The weight lightly bearing down as his hand flattened against my skin.

The quaking of my body turned into a quiver of anticipation. But he hesitated, trapping my gaze in his. In an echo of my own words, he said, "I want you willing. I want you begging. I *do* want to break you, but in the most…" his inhale shook, "*delightful* ways. I want you so perfectly undone that you come back reformed and stronger. Like steel. Are you with me, Rose?"

Tingles started at my shoulders and washed down my skin as goosebumps formed on my flesh. He'd seen through me. Into me. And spoke to my soul.

I nodded.

"Say it. Say you're with me."

"I am." Completely, utterly, unquestionably. The sirens' call to lean on his strength, kiss his warm skin, and soak up all the power he held trapped me in a magical state of wonder and shuddering bliss. With a man like this at my side, behind me, leading me, no matter where he was, I felt safe. And if I had to timidly admit, slightly frightened of the ease which he lifted me, arranged me for his needs, and how he held my fate in his hands as he let me ride him.

Undone wasn't a light word. The precipice of that mountain of trauma I carried was tall. Diving off it was a challenge of will and by doing so, I cracked open a door I'd kept locked for years. My heart's blood and hope spilled out, but in a congealed mass that clogged in place. Not only had I cut myself off from love, but from being able to love.

Sobered by that realization, I focused outward. Bear held me on his lap. I'd exhausted myself to the point my thighs shook and my knees ached. My breath was tight when I met his eyes.

"There you are." He lifted me once, lowering me slowly on his impressive dick.

I settled, this time not fighting gravity. He fixed in place deep inside me. *Goddess, why can't I let go?* Was I that broken that there was nothing left?

His heavy hand caressed my cheek and tangled in my hair. A ring caught, tugging one or two strands free. I slapped my hand over his. "Careful, you're caught."

With gentle care, he extracted his fingers.

The twin strands that had broken free clung to the jagged edge of his ring that had snared them. He pulled them free and handed them to me.

"Sorry about that." With me still deeply planted on his lap, he pulled off his rings and wrapped an arm around me to lean over and place each one on the nightstand. "Let's do that again. This time, I'll try not to pull your hair."

His fingers tangled and massaged my scalp. I leaned into the pressure and tried not to remember Carl pulling my hair free and casting his spell. The strands Bear had given me felt weightless, but as monolithic as a sacred artifact.

Quickly, I twisted the strands, wrapping them around my fingers and created a loop that doubled, then doubled again. In my thoughts, I composed a blessing of protection.

Bear kissed me, sealing the spell. As he broke away, his head tipped to the side. It was an attempt to see past my walls, into the shadows, and take a peek at my blackened soul. I set a hand on his chest to make space between us. I held up the small ring of hair I'd created. "Hold out your hand."

He did as asked. I slipped the featherlight loop on his smallest finger.

"A part of me, fleeting and insignificant, but freely given. May it protect you."

His eyes widened and his throat worked to swallow. He adjusted the loop, so it sat tight against his skin. "I have nothing for you."

"You've given me a chance to breathe again."

And just like that, I found strength. More than that, I found joy. Pleasure. Setting the pace and finding the right blend of arch and friction, I came. Just flutters like butterfly wings, but it was real, not pretended, not induced through mechanical means, and certainly not torn from my flesh through pain and blood.

I shoved those thoughts away and buried my nose against his skin. That subtle scent of his made my heart swell. I was free. Or at least willingly trapped here. Bear wasn't an ogre, and had proven himself over and over again.

"You don't need to buy me things."

He grunted and arched upward, still not sated. "Don't tell me what to do."

I grabbed his hair and tugged to get his attention. "Not even to suggest you flip me around to put me on my hands and knees so you can fuck me harder?"

His eyes flashed with desire. "Woman."

"Do it."

He lifted me completely off his dick and threw me on the bed. "Roll over. Now."

I hurried to comply, sticking my ass in the air so he could impale me again.

His thumb ran through my slick pussy. It stopped against my anus.

I shuddered. "No."

His hand lifted from me and the cool air of his house was not a substitute I wanted. "Fuck me, please?"

In response, he dragged his cock where his thumb had been, stopping short to notch at the opening to my vagina. "Here?"

"Bear," I warned. If he didn't start fucking me soon, I was going to rescind my invitation.

"Bossy, ain't ya?"

I lowered my ass and shot him a look over my shoulder.

But he had other plans.

Bear grabbed both of my ankles and tugged until I was splayed out on my stomach, my legs were forced wide by his thighs.

I quickly hooked my feet against his calves to balance in place. My sex open and ready for his cock.

This time, he thrust into me. The movement shoved me face first into the mattress as he pounded away. Each time his cock rammed home, I gasped. Not from pain or fear, but from the desire that sprung from a morbid hollow in my soul that reveled in dancing a knife's edge. I pressed my body against his, fighting for more power, more pressure, more danger. It longed for the moment when the snapping thread of sanity broke loose and ripped me apart so it could finally run wild and free.

Did it? Maybe. But it didn't take over. It fled to some unknown place in the spirit realm leaving me pulsing in ecstasy and drained.

Bear's grunt of pleasure punctuated the pulsing of his dick deep inside me. My matching flutters were double-timed to the heartbeats of his orgasm.

Until everything quieted. My breaths, his thrusts, my racing heart, his mindless curses, they all faded into peace.

He pulled out, holding the condom in place. "I didn't hurt you, did I?"

My groan was real. But I mourned the loss of him not the ache in my back. "I'm good," I slurred. I fell to my side, letting my body curl in on itself, so I could ride the wave of orgasmic bliss a bit longer.

His heavy hand stroked my ass and stopped on my thigh. "More than good." I soaked in the bliss of our connection as he paused in place.

Bear lifted his hand and slapped my ass. "Fucking great."

Dick.

He disappeared into his bathroom.

Just for that, I was going to roll to the other side and make him sleep in the wet spot. *Jerk.*

18

BEAR

A man's gotta do honest work once in a while. And Mondays meant a full day at the tattoo parlor. Inking others, not getting inked, although I had an idea to add something to my left calf. Maybe a little witch or thorns or something?

Rose was my fantasy formed as flesh. Not only was her body banging, but the things she did with her hips when she rode my dick were mind-blowing. And stamina? Damn. I didn't have the energy to jog this morning she rode me for so long.

But the best part was the look of wonder on her face when she finally let go.

At first, I thought I'd done something wrong. The change from vixen to joy was so complete. But her soft smile, the warmth in her eyes, and the languid way she collapsed on my chest, they all made me feel like I was the only man who'd ever made her feel that way. And that was just the first time. A man could lose his mind fucking her as much as I did in the last thirty-some hours.

I didn't dare think too long about that, knowing she'd been Carl's up until a few days ago. I doubted Carl ever coaxed those reactions from her.

I pulled the sterilized packs from the autoclave and sorted the bags into their respective bins. Doubt? No. Probability, and the amount of info I had on Carl made doubt seem generous. That man didn't know how to make a woman come. Not like I had.

So, I doubled down on what worked. I kept her within arm's reach yesterday, and kissed her fiercely this morning before I rode off.

But thinking about her wasn't getting shit done. I had books to manage, chair fees to total, and a couple of regulars on my schedule. That didn't stop me from adjusting the tiny hair ring she made for me. It was so delicate and fragile. One good tug would ruin it. Just like whatever Rose and I were doing with each other.

The bell above the front door jingled as my first client arrived. And with him, fantasizing about Rose got sidelined until I tugged off my gloves and immediately panicked. The ring had come off with it. Carefully, I pulled the glove from the trash and folded it between a bunch of paper towels. I needed to do a better job of protecting her, every piece of her.

Another customer came in, and I forgot about all of that until KC strolled in with Fish.

"Yo, Bear." KC flipped a finger salute in my direction.

"Hey Bro. How's it feel to be free?" I smiled because that first few days of being a patched Destroyer was a heady time. Pussy, booze, and the massive relief of not being anyone's bitch made for a wild ride. And several hangovers. KC had at least a three-day bender going by the glassiness of his eyes. I checked his buddy for wear and tear. Surprisingly, Fish looked sharp. So, I asked him, "Are you chauffeuring him around?"

Fish smiled quickly, but it fell with a wariness I didn't like at all. "Yeah."

"You got a minute?" KC glanced around at the nearly empty shop. I motioned to the other artist to take an early lunch and as soon as they exited, I flipped the sign to indicate someone would be back in a half hour. Then led them to the bullpen in the back. Out of habit, I flipped on the stereo and a jammer Skinner set up.

"What's up?" I asked as I settled onto a stool.

KC nudged Fish. "Go for it. Tell him what you told me."

Whatever it was, it wasn't good. His skin turned a little white. "Uh… Are you fucking that broad?"

I shot a look at KC, warning him that this was wasting my time.

"I—I mean, she was Carl's." Fish didn't know he was swimming in deep waters. But like any good predator, I let him get a little too comfortable, just to make the meat more tender.

"KC? Did you plan to waste my time?"

"Fish, spit it out."

His buddy must have picked up on the warning signs. "That bitch of his stole money from him."

"How much?"

Fish squirmed uncomfortably, then blurted out, "Twenty grand."

I barely let a beat go by before asking, "When?"

"When she lit out of there."

With me. I'd barely given her a minute and she'd executed a major heist in that time. If I wasn't pissed off, I might marvel at the impressiveness of it. "So?" I layered a bunch of sarcasm over the angry growl.

"Well, h-he thought you should know."

Ah. Fish was the messenger boy. Carrier pigeon. Stoolie? How much of this would go right back to Carl to give him ammunition against us?

Funny how my mind went there, rather than getting angry with Rose first. Maybe Jackson was wrong about me. Maybe I couldn't remain objective after getting my dick good and soaked.

"Does he think he's getting a discount for this?" I stood up and the stool knocked into a cabinet as it rolled away.

KC's eyes went a little wide.

Right. He didn't know the deal. Only the brothers who needed to know got that info.

Surprisingly, Fish wasn't alarmed. He was close enough to Carl to courier money and secrets. That meant I truly couldn't trust him. And KC shouldn't either. But that would have to wait.

I faked a smile and held out a hand to slap Fish's before gripping it and tugging him close. Once I had him trapped, with his gun hand gripped and the other pinned against his body, I whispered in his ear. "Carl's a nosy fuck who can't mind his own shit. So, word of advice, reconsider your loyalties." I let him go with a shove.

KC caught him, but his eyes were on me. I know I spoke quietly enough that he probably didn't hear me. "Go to the club. Send him home. Then call me."

There were reasons we made prospects wait as long as we did. Foremost was trust. We had to know whether or not they were all in or not. But another reason was conditioning. When orders were given, they had to be obeyed without question. Even with as long as I'd been in the club, I still did what I was told without bitching about it. There was always a good reason if a brother gave a direct order. And in the hierarchy of it all, KC had to answer to me whether I had an officer's patch or not.

KC let Fish lead. Right before KC dipped out, he said two words to me that made my blood run cold. "Sketch…Izzy?"

"You forgot to tack yourself onto that," I grumbled.

He tipped his head. "Well. At least you understand what's at stake here."

I lowered my voice. "Which is why *he* needs to keep a close eye on Carl, but not crawl into bed with him."

"It ain't like that." KC scowled at my accusation.

"For everyone's sake, I hope not."

"And what about you with Rose?" He insinuated the obvious hypocrisy.

Maybe not laying his ass out during his initiation was a mistake? "I got it under control."

"Yeah… right." His eyes dipped to the side, almost begging me to out myself by looking back to my chair where I'd wrapped that damn glove up.

In the wake of their departure, I relocked the door and sat in silence to sort my thoughts. Wolf and Jackson were right. Carl was playing us. Me.

But what was his game?

That was the biggest question. Were we the targets or someone else? Was Carl doing this to get revenge over something? Was he working for someone else?

There were no immediate answers.

Except one. Get my head back into the game and stop thinking with my dick. I swept up the bundle of waste and tossed it into the trash, ring and all.

Guilt or something like that itched under my skin. Like a fucking hair shirt.

It pestered me as I buried my nose in business.

By the time I finished the last session, I was ready to slice throats. I straddled my bike, weighing my choices. One was clear. Ride.

Ride until my head was straight. Ride until the road and wheels carried me somewhere I could find answers. Maybe even keep riding until all the choices were snatched away.

Of course, I ended up at the club, not my house. My ass hit the barstool and my bottle came off the shelf barely helped along by the pretty little hooker manning the boards that evening.

If she was there, and not on her back upstairs, nothing was happening. Even the jukebox was dark. Instead, someone had the stereo system behind the bar cranked into the speakers. And since there were no prospects in sight, the music was a far cry from usual. "Is this the same fucking club?" I mused aloud.

"It's a Monday. Everyone's sleeping it off, or at home recovering from the shock from the start of the work week." Shauna said as she poured me a glass.

I held my hand up to stop her from filling it to the top. She was right. I should be home. I wasn't a coward, was I? The old me would have stomped in that door and laid down the law. Feelings be damned.

"You lonely?" She played with the rim of her glass. I hadn't noticed her slip a dram of my private stock into the tumbler. Shauna's tone was flirty, but practiced. I'd have fallen for it a month ago. Willingly. But now? The combo pissed me off. Like she just assumed I'd bite, and worse? Share my shit with her.

No wonder I scraped clingers off within a couple of weeks.

"I ain't lonely."

Her finger circled the rim like it was her clit or something. She noticed my eyes tracking the motion. "You sure about that?" She paused to dip a finger into the liquid and bring the moistened tip to her mouth.

Her tongue swirled around it before she popped it in to suck the liquor off. That definitely would have broken my resolve.

Funny how my dick could get hard and I could still be angry. For a moment, I imagined Rose doing that. I'd pick her up, plaster her against the wall, raise the fabric of the loose, long dresses she preferred and—

Measuredly, I spoke two words, "I'm sure."

Shauna sighed. "I heard you're shacking up with some chick."

"That's right." I kept my answer short so she could hang herself on the conversation. It was always insightful to let people ramble their thoughts.

She shook her head. "How long did the last one hang around? Two weeks?"

This bitch could go fuck herself with that thinking. The trouble was, she was right. The longest relationship I had was with this club. It came before everything else. That's the way it was supposed to be. And it was the reason I came here to sort my head out. Rose had gotten under my skin. By doing that, she'd knocked me off balance and exposed a weakness I didn't know I had. I was immune to pretty. Case in point, Shauna here. She was a beauty. Soft auburn-brown hair, big doe-like eyes, a pouty mouth. Tits for days, and an ass that was perfect size and shape for any marathon banging you cared to sample. And she was professional enough to skirt that fine line of attachment but available.

If I wanted to, I could step up, seize the VP slot, give her a nod, let her jump on the back of my bike, have my position, a steady lay, and never have to worry about catty bitches sinking their hooks in, because Shauna was evil enough to claw their eyes out. And when I got tired of her, I could toss her back into the pool and she wouldn't get angry about it.

It was a shitty way to treat women. But useful.

And that aimed a realization that struck true, sunk deep into my chest, and skewered me with the sharp barbs of truth. I treated women like shit. I'd planned to treat Rose like shit for stealing from Carl. That's why I landed here.

Because I didn't want to treat her like that. I wanted someone in my bed who had my back. Someone would care enough to stay up all night fighting off my brothers and anyone else stupid enough to fuck with me. Someone who didn't raise an eyebrow when I stood in the rain sharing an ale with my Gods.

Most pointedly, a woman who could distract me from crafty hookers who knew all my weaknesses.

I poured the rest of my drink into Shauna's glass. "Here. I'm headed home."

"Good luck with that."

Whether she meant it or not, I'd need luck.

If only to control my temper… and maybe my stupid dick. It was going to fuck things up. I just knew it.

19

———

ROISHIN

The house was so quiet after Bear left. I took advantage of it by laying out all the things he'd purchased and tuning each item to my energy. As I worked, I called on the neutral nature of magic. Neither good nor evil, it existed as everything does, in its own state. My spirit extended outward, creating a vibration of awareness that sensed each element of magic within the house.

Bear's altar was bright, loud, boisterous. Laughing with gusto and tuned to the place he felt happiest. The bottle of ale in particular held that magical state of promise.

Surrounding and intertwining with that vibrance was something much darker. Powerful. Like the man himself.

I lit a candle and paced through the house. The bedroom sang with vigor. My skin heated. We'd consecrated that space well.

There were corners that sorely needed life. After opening a window, I blew blessings into their dusty spaces over the candle flame to dispel the negative void and bring life back into their stagnation. Even the basement needed a blessing or ten. And a good cleaning. I swept, blessed, and wiped through the entire house, working slowly, eventually rubbing the surfaces with mint-infused cleaning cloths until the place smelled fresh.

Then I laid out the remaining stones and what-not on the grass in the backyard to soak in the sunlight. In my eclectic practice, I did both shadow and light work. My blessings weren't as powerful as the shield spells or wardings which came to me as easily as breathing, but they were a part of my solitary craft, just the same. Moonlight alone wasn't enough to boost that magic.

Then I locked the house and took a long walk down the woodland path that eventually ended at the river. In daylight, it seemed so small and not nearly as ominous or wild as it had been that fateful night. I sat on the river bank between the last posts of the dock rooted in the mud. Meditation came easily for a change. My inner frantic pace calmed and thrummed with the languid pulse of the river and land.

Was this what happiness felt like?

I smiled to myself, knowing that it wasn't just happiness. My body ached in very good ways. Each little pang of exertion was a reminder of Bear.

He had amazing stamina.

"I've got it bad." It being the harmonious buzz of multiple orgasms.

I stretched and focused on the sunlight dappling the water in bright little shimmers of light. The hum of insects and the soft lapping of water sliding against the shoreline set the musical score I paced my chants to.

A cloud passed overhead, chilling my skin. I looked up, still dazed by the hypnotic state of inner peace I'd found. A noisy truck rumbled by on a distant highway. The susurrus of life stilled.

Someone was close. My senses, or the spirits, whispered a warning. I crouched low to hide my body amongst the weeds and grass that grew wild. The crunch of footsteps made me slip closer to the river bank where erosion had scooped the soil from the edge in a large curving bite that concealed my entire body.

Carefully, I climbed over tangled tree roots to creep further into the shadows there. I barely moved ten feet before the noises on the gravel ceased and the thump of tread on asphalt began. Whoever it was, they took the path toward the subdivision. And they weren't some random hiker walking casually. Nor were they a jogger, pacing their strides for maximum sustainable effort. This was a person with a purpose.

I avoided the path as much as I could, but the river bank quickly became too overgrown to follow, and I had to cut through the woods to work my way back to Bear's house. I was muddy and my dress was torn by the time I crested a hill and caught a glimpse of the neat little semi-circle of houses that made up that dead-end street I called home for now.

Something moved in Bear's backyard.

It definitely wasn't Bear. He told me his last appointment was at six. The sun wasn't far enough west in the sky for that. And the colorful flash meant it wasn't one of his brothers from the club. Not a one of them wore anything lighter than dark gray. And none of them wore anything bright.

Except when it came to bright neon pink running shoes. I smiled. Poor Bear.

The patch of blue appeared again on the path I'd taken earlier. It slipped south toward the crumbled dock and the river park.

I picked my way downhill. It took me a long time because of fence lines, steep drops, and overgrowth. Eventually, I emerged two houses down from Bear's, missing the path completely, with no clue how that happened. I'd have to go back and figure that out someday, but for now, I cut through a lawn to get to the opening that allowed me back into the yard.

I stopped dead in my tracks as I did.

My carefully blessed stones and tools had been rearranged.

Someone cut a pentagram into the lawn, dumping my items with no order whatsoever at each point.

But that wasn't what made me freeze in terror. In the center of the crudely inscribed star was a mutilated animal. Or maybe two?

I wouldn't know until I moved closer. Careful decision and inspection went into placing each step. Despite the randomness of the supposed casting circle, there was the genuine possibility someone had booby-trapped the lawn with non-magical weapons. Soon enough, I caught a glint in the grass. Gingerly, I picked up the caltrop. It was small, shaped like a vicious toy. There had to be more. This type of object was sold in bulk.

As I crept to the circle, I found two more. I collected them and the pieces of my altar. Finally, I stood over the poor creature who'd been savagely murdered to torment me. Or should I say, frame me? Because to an outsider, the grotesque display screamed "black magic."

But whoever did this had no clue what black magic looked like. If it wasn't so horrific, I'd laugh.

Feathers, brown—probably from a sparrow or some field bird—mingled with bits of rabbit flesh and fur.

The poor things.

I found the twisted, decapitated, and half-crushed head of the bird first. I knelt in the grass and cradled it in my palms. I chanted a quick prayer to commit its life to peace.

The rabbit hadn't been as lucky.

There was foam at its mouth. It died slowly.

I cried, feeling the gash of terror and loss surrounding me.

As the tears dried and my heart stopped hurting, truth whispered to my soul. *You know who did this.* The suggestion slithered around me, clutching at my neck and burrowing deep like a carnivorous worm.

Fucking Carl.

I repeated my hypothesis out loud. A breeze rustled through the treetops. The voices of nature and the spirits whispered in accord. The creak and clatter of branches bending and striking each other fit my mood perfectly. These creatures were murdered by one of the most twisted people I'd ever had the misfortune of meeting.

And deep down, I knew they'd been tormented because Carl was trying to control my life. I'd opened Pandora's box by coming back to help Beth beat cancer again. But this felt so much darker than before.

We were children then. Or at least inexperienced and child-like in the ways of evil. "When I was a child, I thought and spoke as a child." That damn bible verse bubbled up unbidden.

"Fuck him." I re-sketched the circle, finding three more of those damn caltrops as I did.

This time, I used his torture devices to reflect his poor attempt at spell work back upon him.

The nearly dried blood from the animals remained in the center of the circle, but their torn bodies, carefully collected and blessed, were far from this place. I wasn't about to bind their spirits to this work.

The sunlight angled sharply through the treetops, and I lit black candles to place at the sources for each of the four winds.

I cut and burned an offering of my own hair to seal the circle. Its acrid odor tainted the air.

Only then did I release my rage.

It fused into the magic I worked. A mirror reflected the dark purple sky and a flicker of candlelight.

"Benedicta est vis venti et terrae.
Benedicta est vita et potentia ignis et aquae.
Benedicta est lamina metallica non calcata.
Vos invoco, o dii cordis mei.
Vos invoco, dii benedicti huius terrae.
Quercum et spinam invoco,
serras urticae et aculeos hederae invoco.
Hoc malum aggredimini.
Utinam vindicta naturae in intrusum percutiat.
Surgant dii et inimici mei dispergantur ut fumus.
Utinam vis eorum deficiat.
Utinam astutia eorum vacillet.
Utinam consilia eorum dissolvantur.
Ita sit sicut supra et infra,
in vita et terra spirituum.
Fiat.
Instetur.
Fiat.
Malum abeat."

I moved the mirror thrice more, calling upon each wind to carry the curse back to Carl.

Finally, I knelt again, facing north. My blessings never came from any of the softer directions. Only the icy cold and harsh wind listened to my pleas. I called for resolve, justice, and let my will be the sacrifice for the spell. "Carl has no power here."

I spoke the affirmation seven times. Each time, I turned slightly and swept my hands in front of me to blanket the view with magic.

Then I meditated until the light was gone and the candles sputtered out. I must have been kneeling for hours because I could barely walk from the pain.

Only then did I break the circle and let the magic flow into the world. Carl would get what was coming to him. I had to trust the universe with that.

As I cleaned up, I found several more caltrops. The total hit seventeen. Either they were sold in batches of six and I'd missed one, or possibly tens, and I'd missed three. But it was too dark to find anything, and I needed to get dinner ready for Bear.

In fact, he should have arrived by now.

I cleaned my muddy hands, changed clothes and brushed the brambles out of my hair.

Still, no Bear.

Ah, well. I was hungry. I made short work of a quick chicken stir fry. And waited on the rice I'd tossed into the cooker. I should have timed it better. The vegetables softened as they simmered.

Then the distinct rumble of motorcycle and the clatter of the garage door announced Bear's arrival.

The door opened as the rice cooker beeped, letting me know the food was done.

"You're just in time."

Bear sniffed at the air. His eyes scanned the house like there were threats in every corner. "Dinner's ready?" His tone was cautious, as if he didn't trust the timing.

I ignored him and set two plates on the table. "You don't have chopsticks, do you?"

He grunted and bumped me as he shoved his way to the sink to wash his hands and face. "I don't fucking use chopsticks."

"I take that is a no. Rough day?"

He glared at me like his bad mood was my fault.

I sent him a placid, but neutrally firm stare back, daring him to start the fight. His body was tense. It caused his movements to slice through the space around me, leaving a wake of anger.

Something had set him off.

I quickly gathered utensils and pulled out two beers.

It had been that kind of day for both of us.

He sighed as he studied the table and the food I plated.

"How'd you know when I was coming home?"

"I didn't. Just coincidence."

He glanced at the clock. His forehead creased, grooving the narrow path between his eyebrows deeper.

"Do you think this is enough? Should I heat up—" My hands fluttered through the air as I spoke.

"Rose. Stop. I'm not fucking Carl."

I swallowed. He picked up on that? I hadn't even clued in on my nerves until he bludgeoned me with the truth. "Okay." I slid into my chair and tried to calm my mind to thank the Gods for the fortune I had.

Bear was a little more vocal. He cracked open the beer first, raising it high. "Hail, Thor Odinson. I raise my ale to you. Grant me strength through nourishment and grant me peace through alcohol." He slugged down a good portion of the can, then burped loudly. The can rattled, near empty, as he set it on the table with a heavy sigh.

I lifted a forkful of food. "I call to thee, Freya, the mistress of bounty and war. Thank you for your blessings of food and insight. May both bring this house peace."

Sure, that was a subtle hint. One that wasn't lost on Bear.

He shoveled food into his mouth, pausing as he chewed. The next bite was slower, more reverent. After the third, he set his fork down and looked skyward. "Thank you, Freya."

His eyes fell upon me, studying me as I ate.

"Is everything okay?"

The intense stare fell away as Bear looked inward. "Not really, but that's a me problem." He ate a little more. "The food's good. I appreciate it."

"I'd planned for more, but I got sidetracked today."

"By what?" His tone had gentled. I was loath to ruin the moment with my afternoon, but if I kept it secret, it would blow back on me.

I set the fork down carefully. "After I got breakfast cleaned up and did some cleansing spell work, I took a walk down to the river again." For an unknown reason, I smiled. "The dock's almost completely gone now."

"I'm surprised it didn't break while you were dancing on it."

"I wasn't dancing."

He chuckled quietly. "That would have been a nice bonus, just saying. Me fishing you out of the water all naked and shit." He peeked at me through his heavy eyebrows and licked his lips. The mischief in his expression displayed blatantly.

"I was going to pick berries but someone was on the path." I paused, parsing the subtle lie for truth. "Not exactly on the path, more like taking the path to get here. I hid."

His forkful of food fell back onto the plate when he froze. "Who?"

I weighed assumption versus fact. "I think it was Carl, but since I hid *really* well, I didn't get a good look."

"And?"

This was going south quickly. "I worked my way back here through the woods, so I wouldn't be seen, and got a little lost. When I finally made it to that hill behind the house, someone was in the yard. I waited until they left before coming back."

"Probably a good idea. Anything missing?"

No. Nothing was *materially* missing. "My blanket sense of security?"

There was silence between us.

I continued because he needed to know more before he walked out there and discovered it for himself. "You'll see it tomorrow, but

Carl, or whoever it was, dug a pentagram in the yard and scattered my shit all over to make it appear like I was using black magic. And, you will need to watch your step. He scattered some presents for us."

I left the table to collect a caltrop he'd dropped. "I found seventeen of these in the grass."

Bear took it from my hand and admired it for a moment. "Nasty fuckers. I used a bunch like this to hijack a semi-truck. Seventeen, you say?"

I nodded, ignoring his admission of a crime.

"They sell 'em online in twenty packs." He tossed it to the table.

That meant there were three more out there. "Be careful then."

He laughed as if the danger was nothing. But it was very real.

20

BEAR

My damn stomach was going to ruin me faster than my dick was. I'd walked in with every intention of laying down the law. And that witchy woman had food ready. Hot food. Fresh off the stove. It sapped the vinegar right out of me.

Worse? She'd been trapped outside with that asshole, or some other asshole I'd pissed off lately, who'd been sniffing in my lawn and laying down booby traps. Fucker.

I picked up the caltrop I'd tossed down.

"I think Sketch has a metal detector." He bought one for his son a while back. It had to be somewhere in his junk pile.

"That would be helpful." Rose picked at her food. I made sure she was eating it before I took another delicious bite.

Relying solely on her body language, something was still bothering her. Sure, having Carl creeping around was bad, but the tension in her shoulders and the way she wouldn't look me in the eye went beyond what she'd already relayed. "Anything else I should know?"

She set her fork down with a choked sigh. "He killed two animals."

I didn't realize I'd slammed my hands on the table as I jolted up from my chair. But I must have done it, or knocked the table, hard. Her beer tipped over and left a spilled trail of foam right to the edge where she caught it.

To remedy my outburst, I grabbed a towel from the rail by the sink and helped Rose clean up the mess. Her hands were shaking too much to do more than make the mess worse.

I caught one. "Hey. I'm sorry."

Hell, her whole body shook.

Now I've been known to make grown men piss their pants. It's just the way I'm built. And the image I've cultivated. With probably a good helping of very real actions propping up all the rumors of my violence. But I'm not the same guy around women.

Except, I'd pulled a gun on her. Pulled a knife on her, too. Hell. She had to be scared as fuck of me by now.

Was she scared of me last weekend? Was that why she slept with me? Fear?

My stomach went sour.

"Rose?"

It took her at least two tries to meet my eyes. As she did, her spine straightened. Her exhale was shaky. "We really need a damp washcloth so the table isn't sticky."

"Let's forget about the table for a minute and talk about this." I pulled her arm up. She fought me a little, making a fist as I brought her arm into view.

"You caught me by surprise. That's all."

"That's not all, and you know it."

Her nostrils flared.

"Do you know that when you lie, your chin goes down? It's almost as if your brain is saying, *dig in*. And that? Is one hell of a tell, woman. It means you've had to lie often."

The hard focus she stabbed me with told me a lot more than words. Roishin Black did not like anyone knowing her secrets. I recognized that trait because I guarded mine just as fiercely.

I tried again. "Why are you shaking?"

"I'm not shaking anymore."

And she wasn't. She'd controlled it or squashed it. The white knuckles of her tiny fist gave me a clue. "No, now you're pissed off."

She tugged harder to try to extract herself from my grip. Cute, but ineffective. I smiled. Maybe it was time to broach another mystery Roishin Black hid. "Carl says you stole money from him."

Her struggling ceased abruptly. "When did you talk to Carl?"

"I didn't. He sent Fish with the message." I noted that she didn't deny it.

Something shifted by her eyes. The anger or maybe the fear was gone. Whatever had changed morphed her face from unguarded to a careful mask. The same one she wore that first night at Carl's.

Odd.

I hated it because I knew my window of insight was gone.

To knock her off balance again, I pulled her fist to my lips and kissed it. "Keep your secrets, witch, but tell me everything that happened in my yard. And I'll know if you leave anything out because I've got cameras covering both mine and Jackson's house." I loosened my grip on her arm.

Her hand slipped free. "We need to clean this up first."

"No, eat and talk, then clean up. I'm not negotiating here."

"Are you going to blow up again?"

"I might. I might not. Was that the worst of it?"

She tilted her head from one side to the other, releasing tension. Then thought about my question. "Probably."

I motioned to the chairs. "Okay. Let's hash this out."

A few minutes later, I interrupted again. "What kind of spell did you cast?"

Roishin stared at her half-eaten plate. "A curse. I called on the Gods to avenge the deaths of its creatures and banish his evil intent from your land. I used a mirror so, it would, in theory, return the harm he intended for us back on him."

Sevenfold. Something whispered in my thoughts. Another whisper, this one I recognized as my own sarcastic and paranoid self reminded me that Carl getting in trouble could be awful for the club.

"You shouldn't do that shit."

"Are you telling me or ordering me?"

"Would you listen either way?"

"No."

I threw my hands up in the air. "I can't fucking win." This was exactly why I was single. No pussy is good enough to deal with the bullshit.

"At least this way you won't be targeted by a fucking lunatic."

"We."

"You," she fired back.

"No, woman. We. We're in this together. Whatever game Carl's playing, he's targeting both of us. You know that, right?"

Her mouth clamped shut.

"My yard, your woo-woo, and Carl's seeded a little crop of distrust. And I wonder why that is? Hum?"

Rose's face was blank.

"Don't you know why?"

She blinked. "No. If I knew… well, he wouldn't be doing it anymore."

I laughed, hard. "Woman—"

"Stop calling me that. My name is Roishin."

I licked my lips. "No, it ain't. It's Rose. Technically, Mary-Rose." Skinner did a lot of digging for me in the last couple of days. And I never even had to ask. He was so paranoid that Rose was selling us out, he practically moved into second-floor office space we all dubbed "the geek lodge."

Through gritted teeth she hissed, "*Never* call me that."

"Why?"

That face was back.

"Fine. But when your jealous ex-boyfriend escalates his bullshit, *we* are in this together."

"He's not my jealous ex-boyfriend."

Her chin didn't go down. Huh. But Skinner had photo proof. "Ex-lover?"

This time, she dug in, readying for the lie, but with bravado, her chin went back up as she looked me in the eye. "Love had nothing to do with it."

In a way, she was right. Teenagers get those feelings all twisted up and call it love. But it's just hormones and sex. At least she wasn't lying to herself about it now. Some women never get over their first crush.

"Whatever you call it, Carl's got a case of jealousy."

She stared at me like I was an alien. Then burst out laughing. She laughed so long, she had to wipe her eyes.

"It ain't funny, Rose."

"No, it totally is. Carl doesn't love me. He's not jealous."

"Bet you twenty K he is." I would be.

Her eyes went a little wider.

That's right, *I have details of your crime, woman.*

She waved a hand through the air. "The amount doesn't matter. You're wrong."

I snorted. "Gimme one good reason why."

"Carl only loves himself."

She hadn't even hesitated. Damn. And double-damn-it, that tracked with everything I knew about Carl. "Then it's jealousy because he's not number one."

She shook her head. But it soon stilled. "There may be a small amount of truth in that, but not nearly enough to drive him to mess with you like this. He's playing a game. One he wants you to get visibly upset with me about. Then, when I—"

She cut herself off abruptly.

"When you, what?"

The plate of food got shoved out of the way. "When I return at the end of the month, and am found dead, that public display of anger will bury you."

"That's twisted."

"That's Carl. He finds more pleasure in killing people by proxy than sex ever brought him. But god forbid he ever gets his own hands dirty."

"Then how is he going to kill you?"

"I'm sure I'm the exception."

I leaned in. Rose was candidly introspective. I softened my tone. "Why would that be?"

She looked me directly in the eye. "Because I've played this game with him before, and I lived long enough to walk away."

I stayed awake for hours after we cleaned up dinner and the mess on the table. It started innocently enough, scrubbing through the camera footage until I pinpointed the moment Carl walked into the yard.

Sure, by that point I'd gotten a little caught up watching Rose wipe my house down from ceiling to floor. Her ass looked good pointed at my cameras.

By the time I did watch Carl set the scene, then toss those damn spikes into my yard, I was fuming.

Rose entered, barely missing one of those damn things.

And her tears? Fuck me, those hurt.

I scrubbed through Jackson's footage to make sure Carl hadn't fucked with him, and came up empty. Which was a disappointment. If he had, I'd have full justification to take him out permanently.

Turning back to my feed, I noted when the sun set and the infrared system switched on. Rose knelt in the dark for so long I thought the feed froze. But the random flash from a bug flying past the lens proved it worked just fine.

She stumbled as she finally got up. I stopped the playback and noted the time. I'd just arrived at the club and sat down for a shot. It drove home the vulnerability of her situation. She'd been dealing with this all by herself.

While I debated on whether to take Shauna up on her offer.

What if I had?

What if Carl had come back?

Why hadn't he come back? Was Rose right? Did Carl want me to do his dirty work?

I dialed Skinner and had him download the feed from the time-stamps I gave him. "Do me a favor and translate that for me?" I'd picked out the part where Rose chanted something in Latin.

"You know, I have real work to do."

"Yeah, but this is the kind of stuff you enjoy."

He ran the recording back. "Carl's woman is a freak. What do you see in her?"

Did I dare answer that? Maybe I could give him a little hint. "She's like me. Twisted."

He swore and tapped away, trying to decode her spell. Finally, he sent me a file.

"I think that's what it says. I ran the audio through a translator, then back through a text translator. The sheer fact she knows Latin should be a huge red flag, brother."

A chuckle escaped me. "Hickey would love it."

"Well, I don't," he fired back. "She's a menace."

A compliment. I scanned the translation. Interesting and fairly spot-on her description. She didn't lie to me at least. "I wouldn't have her any other way."

"You're playing with fire."

Now that brought a full smile to my face. "Like I said, 'wouldn't have her any other way.'" Then I hung up on him and wiped the feed so he couldn't get nosy and discover Carl in my backyard.

He'd tell Wolf, who'd tell Jackson, who'd insist I take that motherfucker out. I had other plans for Carl Wingren.

If he wanted to play games with me, I'd play games with him. But first? I had a witch to bed.

21

ROISHIN

Don't bother cooking tonight. Mr. Bossy's text message caught me mid-rise of a tender batch of brioche. I was tempted to flatten it and toss it in the trash. Instead, I stuck to the recipe and the plan for it to be coming out of the oven when he pulled into the garage.

And that magic of chemistry and discipline worked out perfectly.

He froze mid-step, his keys still in hand and not tossed carelessly into a little ceramic bowl I'd found at the second-hand store. "Is that bread?"

I set the pans on their racks to cool. "Yes."

He visibly deflated. "I told you not to cook."

"I'd already proofed the dough." With a sweep of my arm, I included the rest of the kitchen. "And I didn't make anything else."

The conflict on his face was evident. He breathed in deeply through his nose, then confessed, "I'm an idiot."

Since he was a bossy jerk sometimes, I didn't argue with him.

He noticed. "Witch."

"Grumpy Bear."

We'd taken to calling each other those nicknames in private. Public displays were an entirely different story.

He chewed his lip. "Black dress with that lace up shit." He crossed his arms over his chest.

"The long one or the short one?"

His grin deepened. "Short."

I was going to freeze. "Are we going out or…?"

"We're going out. Oh, hang on… Betty Jo sent something up." He disappeared into the garage and returned with a garment bag.

This man and his presents. I'd never be able to pay him back for everything. Luckily, Skinner gave me my laptop back. I'd applied for four jobs in the last two days alone. And Regina hooked me up with an interview at a clinic. It was only part time, but work was work. I wouldn't turn any offer down at this point.

I took the bag from him and the unexpected weight almost tore my arm off. "What in the hell?" I unzipped it as Bear rocked in place with giddy impatience.

As soon as I saw the embossed knot-work and scrolling dragon heads, I gasped. "You really shouldn't have." This was the coat Betty Jo tried to thrust upon me that first week. I'd snuck a peek at the price tag as she dug out a corset. It started with a two and had three more numbers behind it. "I can't accept this."

"Too bad. I already did. Black dress, lace up thing that makes your tits rock harder than a heavy metal concert, and this. Five minutes."

"I can't get ready in five minutes."

"Woman."

I glared at him but ran up the stairs with a huff or twenty. "Bossy son of b—"

"I can hear you, witch!"

The laces were difficult to get even in such a short time. I struggled to tug each one into place. "A toad. I will turn him into a toad."

He snuck up behind me. "I'd be a well-hung toad. You know, the horny kind." He moved my hair and kissed my neck.

"Do you really want me ready in five minutes?" I glanced at him through the mirror we stood in front of.

He met my eyes. The hunger in them made me smile and quirk an eyebrow at him.

His fingers squeezed my waist. "I made reservations."

"Eight. And no more neck."

Bear growled as I slipped out of his grasp. After tying the dress on, I rushed through applying mascara, nearly blinding myself in the process, and barely swept on some lip gloss before he handed me a pair of sky-high heels that were better suited for starring in an adult film than a night out.

"I can't walk in those."

He grinned. "Try. Please?"

"I'll put them on downstairs. You don't want me breaking my ankle on the stairs, do you?"

He was too busy ogling my ass to understand the question I'd lobbed at him.

I rushed down the steps to avoid his grabby hands and quickly slipped the shoes on. Then grabbed the wall because, holy shit they were too fucking steep. "Who'd you get these from, a stripper?"

"Naw, Shauna loaned 'em to me."

"Who's Shauna?" I'd met a few of the old ladies by this point, and even fewer of the strippers his brothers collected like trophies. I had a sneaking suspicion she was one of the hookers who rotated through the three rooms upstairs.

"The dark-haired one with big eyes." He held his hand out to indicate her height.

Oh yeah. I knew which hooker she was.

"A friend of yours?"

He snorted. "She's everyone's friend."

"If you have a dick," I muttered.

"What's that?" He held the coat out so I could slip into it.

"Nothing."

"It sounded like jealousy."

I tipped my head at him. "Aren't we late?"

He shrugged, but opened the garage door so I could teeter down the measly two steps to the concrete. "I'm going to break my neck. That was her evil plan, wasn't it?"

Bear didn't answer, opting to open the passenger door to his SUV. We were taking the motorcade monster. That's what Kate and Zoe jokingly called it. "Need help?" He held out a hand.

Unfortunately, I did. "You're going to have to carry me."

Already my feet hurt. I kicked the shoes off and worked my toes to get the blood flowing to them again.

A few minutes later, he backed into the parking space behind his tattoo shop. The strung lights along the river walk glowed like tiny stars, and the street bustled with people of all types. His shop was still lit, a couple of artists working late, and assisting walk-in traffic should the light and the busy night entice someone in. Bear dragged me through there instead of walking around the buildings.

I barely caught names before he hustled me into the cold again.

"You should be nicer to your employees."

"We're late. Ain't got time to be nice."

I tripped on a crack. He caught me, then swung me up in his arms to go the meager fifty feet between his shop and the restaurant.

"Put me down!"

The brave few who sat at the tables outside the restaurant turned their heads to gape at my distress.

"Please?" I whispered. We were in public. I stroked his beard so he'd stop being such a caveman and work with me at my pace. Which was seriously hobbled by the damn shoes.

He kissed me before setting me on my feet.

Of course, I wobbled. He slipped an arm around my waist. "Lean on me if you have to."

Oh, I would.

Like any restaurant, they barely noticed we were five minutes late. Luckily, our table wasn't given away and we were seated before my toes could start screaming at me again. I slipped the shoes off and dug my toes into the carpet.

Bear smiled across the table as the waiter handed out menus and explained the special. His hand groped under the table until he found my knee.

Two could play that game. I slipped my free foot between his legs and rested my toes against his crotch.

He straightened and covered my foot with his warm palm. I almost groaned aloud as he gave it a squeeze. My eyes did blur a little as the bliss washed through my body. And I missed the waiter's question.

"Wine, red," Bear ordered. He motioned to me then back. "Leave the bottle."

Once the waiter left, I leaned in a little so we wouldn't be overheard. "This is a date?"

"Of course, woman."

I fought the urge to scowl. Instead, I pressed a little against his dick, warning him that he shouldn't call me that.

The bastard smiled.

Then we had to pretend again while the waiter fussed over our glasses and let Mr. Bossy pick my food.

No foot for you. I tucked both bare feet around the chair legs so he'd have to stretch all the way under the table to find my knees. He tried, but coming up short, he decided on a different strategy to drive me nuts.

"So, Fish says Carl's cutting back. No one's been able to score for a week."

The buzz of the restaurant around us drowned his casual discussion of drug dealing with its banality.

"Ask me if I care?" I smiled, pretending we were flirting instead of talking about the Devil Incarnate.

His finger tapped on the table, a sure sign he was agitated. "I have to wonder, where has he been?"

That was worrisome. I'd kept up with regular calls to John. Beth's blood counts still hadn't reacted to the donation. And he had his hands full with the kids and his parents. "Has he been to the church?" During my brief stint with him, he'd made noise about going back. The whole prodigal son thing had been a heady delusion he regularly fantasized about.

"Some. But not nearly enough to account for all his absences. Or the string of false alarms we've been having." He reached across and took my hand, fondling my fingers as he continued to talk about the one topic guaranteed to ruin my night. "I'm going to put up more trail cams and motion sensors. Skinner's coming by tomorrow to reset the alarm zones. You're going to have to stick around to get the new codes."

Great. I'd planned on going to a placement agency to apply.

He tugged my hand to his lips, forcing me to lean forward. "Where's the money, Rose? Maybe he'll back off if you hand it over."

That was my leverage. I couldn't just hand it over.

I pulled my hand away too quickly and his fist thunked on the table. The couple next to us noticed and their whispers increased.

Bear hadn't changed from his usual uniform of dark jeans and motorcycle vest and jacket. With his tattoos and piercings, I was shocked they even let us in the door. But apparently, flashing money around made those dirty looks quiet and the ripple of hastily whispered distrust less noticeable.

Except, like cancer, it spread.

Table after table began to shoot guarded glances our direction. I fiddled with my napkin to disguise the anger that made me drop his hand like a hot pan. Then I leaned in to caress his arm. *Convincingly willing*, in public. My vow was biting me in the ass. I couldn't even get angry with him. Maybe that's why he'd waited to spring the accusations and his follow up questions on me until now.

"When you're the underdog, how would you posture yourself to make people believe you're winning?"

He sipped wine and thought my question through. "Personally? I've never been the underdog."

"Not even when you prospected?" KC regaled me with stories of his torture during that phase. He was drunk, of course. And Bear wasn't too pleased with him but I found it enlightening.

Bear's beard shifted. "It's been a bit since I was that asshole."

His cursing attracted more attention. And he noticed this time.

"Fuck off and mind your own business."

One of the groups whispered louder, their heads clustered together as they plotted Bear's demise. He shifted in his seat to address them directly. "Listen up, Buttercup, I own half this town. Me and everyone who puts on this vest." He tugged at it, emphasizing the name tag that proudly announced him as "Bear." "Gape all you want, but I can buy you, your place of employment, and even the fucking church you attend every third Sunday. You might wanna think about that before you talk anymore shit about me and my woman here."

Great. He looped me into the circus. I rolled my head on my neck to work the tension free, then plastered on a sappy smile to grace him with. I even mouthed a perfidious, "I love you" at him.

He winked at me and mouthed back an exaggerated lie. Then he tacked on "witch" into his beard.

That was more like it. I didn't have to pretend the blush or the grin I tried to hide. He did like me, but not in the stupidly normal way that would drive me into insanity someday. Nope, this was unwholesome and wicked. Luckily, our food arrived and people stopped staring so blatantly.

And for all his bossiness, he got the order right. The food was amazing. The wine bottle ran dry about the same time I straightened my utensils in a cluster and placed my napkin to the side. The waiter fussed a bit then let us be in that short window between meal and check.

"I was upstairs figuring out how to untie that damn cilice. And you bellowed at me about tampons."

His eyebrow went up. He set his napkin down and mirrored my arrangement of utensils. The waiter came and fussed some more, suggesting dessert or coffees. Bear asked for the check. As soon as the server was out of earshot, he nodded to me to continue.

I double-checked to see if anyone was still eavesdropping. Most of the restaurant had cleared out of our section, not wanting to linger around the big bad Bear. "Carl has a stash point behind his toilet. I grabbed." I shrugged, trying to remember why it had been so important. Beth's hollow eyes flashed through my thoughts, nudging me to speak. "Beth, his sister, is going through her *second* battle with cancer. I started growing my hair when she got it the first time. By the time she beat it, it wasn't long enough."

I laughed, silently and bitterly. My nose stung with the memories. "She got better. We all thought that the chemo and stupid prayers fixed her."

I closed my eyes, remembering that horrible time. I'd been on the precipice of returning to the fold. For her. Luckily, science and healthcare intervened and I was free to continue exploring who I was and what I wanted out of life. "Three months ago, she found the first swollen lymph node. Within four weeks, it became more than one, and she started losing weight. Then she got sick. *Really* sick. I moved back to help her and John." My head shook back and forth without any will behind it. "Carl's a perfect match for donation. We all knew this the last time. But no one wanted anything to do with him because of—" The waiter arrived with Bear's card and discreetly set the leather folder beside his elbow before slipping away.

I swallowed the pain. "She'd gotten better. Then… *wham*, so much worse. Because he'd already been tested years ago, the medical team suggested she pursue the stem cell donation. But Carl wouldn't listen to anyone. Except me. I wouldn't have been at Carl's otherwise. Trust me when I say that. I wanted nothing to do with him. Nothing."

Bear shifted to sign the check and held the binder up for the waiter to grab. But he made no move to gather his coat or anything. Instead, he took another sip of wine and silently encouraged me to do the same.

I drained the glass. "I took the money so he'd have to come back, just in case the donation didn't work. I'm bound to this. So, I can't." *I can't give you the money.* "You are justified for getting angry with me about this. But I'm not going to back down." I stared at the table to hide my sad frown. I knew I was hurting him and the people he cared about. I knew stealing from Carl was a long shot, and likely would make me a bigger target for his evil. But if Beth got better, then it was all…

Well, evil would do some good for a change. Was it worth it? Maybe not. But hope and love were fickle things. Hard to shake, and even harder to hold onto.

22

BEAR

Wolf and Jackson both wouldn't fit through the front door of my shop at the same time, but that didn't stop them from trying. Wolf had led the charge from the curb. I'd just peeled off the second latex glove when the bell above the door sounded as Jackson elbowed past him.

Being who it was made when it was not matter. I motioned to my apprentice to clean up the client I'd been working on. "Reschedule him. Any time that works with his schedule."

Then turned my attention to the twin thunderheads in my front lobby.

"You're back." I held a hand out to Jackson.

"What's this shit with your ol' lady?"

Fuck. Jackson didn't mess around with preliminaries. At least he hadn't shot me yet. "She ain't my ol' lady."

Wolf snorted, but kept his speculation to himself otherwise.

Jackson had that face on. The one where he just had to prove his point. There was no arguing with him when he got like that. He flicked a finger up. "One, she's been living at your house since the first. Two, you ain't poked your face in the club for a whole fucking week."

No shit. Fridays were the only mandatory night. And seeing that it was Friday, I was due for another appearance. "I'll be there tonight."

"That doesn't fucking count. Three, you took her to that fancy as fuck restaurant." He pointed toward the place just down the block.

"That ain't a crime."

"It is when his wife hasn't gone there yet." Wolf kept his voice low. His usual tone when he insulted Jackson.

I laughed.

Wrong move.

"Lemme guess, you just made it home, Kate's pissed because it took longer than expected, and you plan to come to church tonight?"

"That ain't why, and you know it."

Beside him, Wolf brushed a finger on the tip of his nose to tell me I'd hit the truth right on the…well, nose.

Unfortunately for him, Jackson caught the movement out of the corner of his eye. "Knock it off. Kate's just fine with me going to church tonight."

Jackson was delusional. There's no way Kate was fine with the situation. She'd made a habit of showing up at the house every day for the last week because she missed her husband so much. Her and Zoe practically lived with me it was getting so bad. And Rose?

She was enabling their visits despite my warnings.

"Tell him the shit about Carl," Wolf prompted.

"What shit about Carl?" I checked behind me to make sure the client and my apprentice weren't listening in. "And let's take this somewhere a bit more discreet?"

"You know what I'm mad about."

Jackson could be mad at any number of things. A few of them related to Carl. More than a few were aggravated by the fact he hadn't spent time with his family. But was I going to open my mouth and stick my size elevens in it? Hell no.

I led them through the bullpen to the back alley. "Okay, bitch me out, but first, what thing about Carl?"

"The money," Wolf summarized.

Ah, that. I glanced at Jackson, who usually was more verbose. "Carl's money. The protection fee?"

"You're not stupid, Bear. The money Rose stole." Jackson leaned in closer. "How does it look when we charge for protection, and our client gets ripped off?"

Shit. I hadn't thought about that part of things. "She's got it. It ain't like she's going anywhere."

"Well, we need it."

My gaze jumped from Jackson to Wolf to hear it from him. Just because Jackson said jump didn't mean Wolf was going to make me go through with it. "We who?" I asked him.

"We, the club," Wolf confirmed.

I swallowed. After hearing Rose's side of the story, I had better insight into why she'd done what she did. Not that I fully accepted it, but it was a better reason than just wanting to take his money. Hell, I would have taken that as a reason and probably understood it. Carl hit her at least once. And with the way her voice trembled whenever she brought up her past with Carl, I'd guess that was not an isolated incident. It might even be a minor one, given her hatred of him. But I wasn't the kind of brother who'd pass along a sob story to try to change both Wolf's and Jackson's minds.

"How much time do I have to convince her to give it up willingly?"

Wolf's eyebrow went up.

Jackson, however scowled. "And you dare to say she's not your ol' lady?"

I squared off with him. Rank or not, he was pissing me off. "Let me remind you who asked me, no… ordered me to do this?"

"I didn't say stick your dick in it."

"You didn't exactly tell me not to, either."

Wolf's heavy sigh of disgust interrupted our argument.

"What?" Both Jackson and I said at the same time.

"Twenty grand." He held out his hand.

I stared at it. "The fuck?"

"Twenty grand from you. Buys out Carl. We meet him on his

turf and buy Rose for the money she stole. Walk away from all of it. You then go back to Rose and tell her she owes you. Make her work it off."

His plan was insane. "Who are you? And what if Tits hears you talking like that?"

Jackson laughed. "He's got you there."

"I'm serious. I won Tits fair and square. I know that's not how it's supposed to work but that's how it smooths out all the fucking feathers sticking out."

"You know, he's not completely wrong."

"Shut up, Jackson." I wasn't going to buy Rose from Carl. "There's a huge problem with that. Carl wants her back. In fact, he named at least thirty grand, if not closer to forty-eight K as his starting point."

The mere mention of how much I'd been quoted made the men with me scan the alley for eyes and ears.

"And I turned him down. I don't buy women. They come to me and for me all on their own." Sure, that sounded like bragging, but it was the truth.

Jackson held his hand over his mouth and muttered, "How much have you spent on the hookers upstairs?"

"That's different and you know it. Hell, you were once the best customer up there."

Jackson frowned. "That was then. Listen, I want to get home to my wife. Maybe I can squeeze at least one orgasm out of her before I have to come back and listen to you assholes ruin my club."

"Ain't your club anymore, old man," I joked.

"Who you calling old?"

"You." Wolf laughed with me.

"I ain't old."

Jackson's protests wouldn't fly.

"Your daughter drives," I pointed out.

"Hell, she dates."

Wolf's statement was met with a squinted glare. Slowly and grimly Jackson asked for the impossible. "Who? I need names, addresses, next of kin…"

"We're not helping you off a teenager."

"Which teenager?"

I traded a look with Wolf to see if he was going to back me up or not. There was no way would I rat Zoe out. The fact that she was doing normal teenage shit was a blessing. And Wolf knew where I stood on that hill.

Wolf slapped Jackson's arm. "We're just giving you shit."

"I need a name," He growled.

"You need to get laid. Go home. Otherwise, you're going to miss your window." We had about two hours before church. With the drive, Zoe, and just Jackson and Kate being who they were, he'd be late.

"Fuck all of you. Twenty grand, Bear. Or I will not endorse your promotion." He tapped a finger on my chest and slipped back inside. The spot where he'd touched hurt.

I turned to my president. "You told him?"

"I had to. That's his job."

"To meddle in our shit?"

Wolf shrugged. "What else is he going to do? It ain't like he's got a club to boss around anymore."

"He's got twenty clubs." And that wasn't enough for him.

"Go easy on him. We were his first."

Damn it. I caught Wolf's arm before he followed Jackson. "I'll fill you in on the whys of things after the meeting, okay?"

His eyes met mine. "There are whys?"

I nodded.

"Anything that's going to bite us in the ass?"

I filtered through everything I knew. "I doubt it. But it will bite at a conscience or two."

"You have a conscience?" He laughed, slapped my arm with a grip to the elbow before letting go, and followed his boss.

Big surprise, right?

An even bigger surprise for them would be to find out I've had one all along.

～

There was barely time during my pit stop at home for me to dump my plain jacket and shove on my colors. Rose had her hair up again. That left her pretty neck wide open to give her a peck and rub my beard against it as I inhaled the fragrance of the week. She changed up between flowers and the vanilla blends I preferred. Today's was a light lemon with an undertone of something richer. If I asked, she'd probably say something like dragon's blood or wormwood. I stopped asking and just buried my face in it. It was the best part of my day.

"Church tonight. I'll be late. Set the alarm for me, will ya?"

"Bear."

Her tone was serious. I quickly checked the clock. "I got five minutes before I'm late. Can it wait?"

That's when I noticed the red around her eyes. The puffy state of the skin. "What made you cry?"

"John called."

Called… my phone. I'd loaned Rose a burner. I tried to soften my tone as much as I could before asking, "And?"

"Beth's running a fever."

"She's still in the hospital, right?"

Rose nodded.

I shrugged. "She's in good hands then." I needed to go, but the pallor of Rose's face made me hesitate. "Rose?"

"She's supposed to be getting better, not worse. The stem cells aren't growing and reproducing."

My mouth shot its load before my brain could flag it. "Ha. Carl shot blanks."

Her face went even paler. Then it turned red as she got angry with me. "It's not a joking matter."

I was going to have to pay a fine for showing up late. "Babe, I can't do this right now. I'm sorry your girl is in a bad way but, I *can't*. I've got to leave."

"I need to find Carl."

"Oh, *fuck* no."

"You don't own me."

What a wrong thing to say. "No? Because of you, I owe twenty

K to pay off Carl because you stole his shit. I've paid for the clothes on your back, the food you've eaten, and put a fucking roof over your head." I grabbed hold of my temper and used it like a club. "Get your coat and boots on, you're coming with me. Because while I may not own you, you owe me two more weeks of your time." I pulled the shorter leather coat off the hook and tossed it at her. "Now!"

Her mutinous face told me what she wasn't saying. But I was too worked up to care. She was coming with me to the club.

Once we were there, I would be able to breathe easier and come up with a plan that wouldn't involve her getting within a thousand feet of Carl Wingren. Because going back to that asshole was not an option. Ever.

I intended to keep her.

23

———

ROISHIN

Like earlier, Bear gave me a warning before we walked in the doors of the club. "We're in public." A not-so-subtle reminder I'd made a vow.

He wrapped an arm over my shoulder and pulled me over the threshold. Once inside, he made a beeline for the bar area. On route, he spotted Kate and Zoe at one of the tables. He grabbed a chair and dumped it beside theirs. Then he snapped his fingers at Hammer, the same prospect who had been in charge of watching me previously.

"This time, don't fucking screw up."

As far as acting went, he sucked. His foul mood definitely didn't scream "happy." Nor did the way he stomped off to the meeting room. At the door, he stopped and dug out his wallet. A bill went into one hand and then he disappeared into the Destroyers bastardization of church.

"He's in a mood," Kate observed.

"He and Dad both," Zoe echoed.

I felt the urge to defend Bear, then the overwhelming urge to squash that sentiment into a bleeding pulp.

"Hammer? I need a whiskey. Please?" I spread my finger and thumb apart indicating a full tumbler.

"You sure about that? Last time…"

"Please? It's been a day."

"What about you two? Zoe, Cola. Kate, what do you want?"

"Why can't I drink?"

Kate ignored Zoe's question. "Beer, please."

Zoe grumbled about being the designated driver, *again.* "Bad enough I couldn't stay home by myself, but I can't even have fun."

Kate studied me. "How bad of a day?"

I wanted to pour out my pain at someone's feet, but also remembered everything I'd promised, including not dragging Kate and Zoe into fighting my battles. "My best friend isn't going to be able to come home from the hospital."

As far as conversation killers, I'd found a doozy.

Zoe finally worked up the nerve to ask, "Why is she in the hospital?"

"Cancer."

Hammer set the drinks down and straddled a chair so he could look out at the room while we sipped in silence.

"What kind of cancer, if I may ask?" Kate's question was quiet.

"Lymphoma."

"Any family?"

I nodded. "Four kids."

Even Zoe blanched. "That sucks."

It did. I drank more than a sip, hoping to numb the pain. I stared at the walls. Photos of bikers and half-naked women littered them. I recognized a few faces. Sprout, Wolf, Bear. There were more I didn't know. The age of them went back decades by the fashion choices and hairstyles. "How long has there been a chapter in Skilletsville?" I remember finding out about them when I was a teenager but knew very little about the story.

"It was going strong even before Jackson and I got together, so at least forty years? I don't know."

"Any of them die?" It was an odd question, but one I needed to know.

"A few. Sprout's dad was killed by the police. They ran him off the road. I'm a little fuzzy on the details of the others."

"Pinner is in prison."

I sent a silent question to Kate to explain Zoe's comment.

"Pinner is Lily's father. Lily and Zoe are closest in age of the children here."

It drove home that this was a family. Maybe it was a big, dysfunctional family. Yet it was light years stronger than mine. From the horrible example I had as birth parents, to the issues I brought to Carl and his family. Beth filled the void I had for an uncondi-tional bond.

And that bond was unraveling.

My phone buzzed at my hip. I took it, knowing it was John. It was too late for anything else.

"Hey, John."

"Where are you?" He wasn't his usual polite self.

I sat straighter. "I'm at the... the Destroyers club. Why?"

He swore.

That was completely unlike him. "What's wrong?"

Kate set her beer down to listen in.

"Beth stopped breathing."

I stood up. "She's not—" *Please don't tell me she's dead.*

"No, but they put her on a breathing machine. I've got to get to the hospital, but Mom and Dad aren't here—And I can't go with the kids."

"I'll be there in a half hour, max."

"Thank you, Rose. I owe you." The relief in his voice was clear.

Zoe, who'd also been listening in, pulled the keys off the little hook on her mom's purse. "Mom, you're on shotgun."

"We should tell someone. Where do you have to be?"

Kate and her daughter were angels. I rattled off John's address and explained the details as quickly as I could. Meanwhile, Kate motioned for Hammer to come with us. "No sense in getting him in trouble."

She also grabbed one of the prospects at the door and slipped him the address with directions to tell Jackson first, then Bear.

And within minutes, the four of us were AWOL.

Kate talked us through the gate. The whole time, Hammer cussed under his breath and texted a novel on his phone. Who he was ratting me out to didn't matter. I was doing this with the fully functional non-family I'd somehow conned into helping.

John met me at the door. He took one look at Hammer and the second thoughts on his face almost surfaced on his tongue. "Bear has him guarding me. He's harmless."

"Am not," Hammer argued.

Kate and Zoe joined us.

"We're here for your children," Zoe deadpanned.

John sent me a look of desperation, open mouthed and frantic. "We've got your back." I pointed at my group. "Hammer, Zoe, Kate." I made introductions as fast as I could. "Go. Drive safely."

On the heels of my order, June ran at my legs with a high-pitched, "Auntie RoRo!"

I swept her up and corralled the other children while John gave quick kisses before leaving in his truck.

That was my cue to create a calm circle for the children. I plopped down on the living room carpet and crossed my legs to make a nest for June. "Arthur, Guinevere, Harry, sit here, here, and here. Zoe, you can sit there. Hammer, don't scowl. Kate, you can have the couch."

I reached out and held Arthur and Harry's hands. Gwen, opposite of me, scooped up Zoe's, who really didn't know what to do, but Harry glommed onto her other hand so hard she winced. I should have warned her, but there wasn't time. "Okay." I squeezed Arthur's hand. "I'm so happy to be here."

Arthur picked up my thread. "I'm happy Daddy can go see Mommy."

June sobbed once and clung to my chest. I kissed her head but kept my grip on the two boys.

Gwen peeked at Zoe. "I'm happy Auntie Rose is safe... and has friends." She leaned over and relayed instructions to Zoe. "You're supposed to say one thing you're happy for."

"Oh. Whoa. I'm happy for...uh not wrecking Mom's car?"

"Ditto," Kate smiled from her perch on the couch. Then added, "I'm happy my husband is back from his trip. Too bad I can't be there, but…"

"It's my turn." Harry dropped Zoe's hand to shoot his complaint at Kate.

"Sorry."

Appeased, Harry thought hard. Finally, he said, "I'm happy Nana bought the new Lego Xbox for me."

Arthur shushed him. "We're supposed to be happy about people. Not toys."

"Well, I did include Nana."

I interceded quickly, "I'm very happy Nana spoils all of you. And I'm also happy you have the opportunity to share her presents."

To redirect things, I made sure all the children were properly introduced to Zoe and Kate, but Hammer got the greatest scrutiny. Mostly his tattoos. The boys wanted me to draw some on their arms. I handed a pen off to Hammer and told him to go for it.

He shot me a panicked look.

"What? It'll wash off. Like you never pretended to have tattoos when you were little?"

After a moment of introspection, he grinned. "Who's my first victim?"

Soon, he was the center of a mayhem sandwich, which freed me up to apologize to Kate and Zoe. "If you need to leave, I got this." I knew Hammer couldn't leave because of his direct order from Bear.

"No, I think we'll stick around. This should be enlightening."

Whatever had Kate grinning was not lost on Zoe. "Dad's going to freak."

"Bear's the one I need to watch."

And just like that, I had two willing accomplices.

An hour later, the roar of motorcycles sent Harry, Hammer, and Arthur to the windows.

To not leave the girls out, I pulled both of them to the door so we could watch the spectacle of Bear, Jackson, Sprout, and two others line their bikes up against John's suburban curb.

Kate laughed silently. Her crossed arms tapping against my back as she tried to keep a straight face. Zoe quietly laid odds. "Over and under on Bear freaking out first."

"No contest. He's going to go quiet. Sprout's going to say something stupid."

"That's not a bet, Mom, that's a given. Dad?"

"Five bucks he growls."

"Ten, he tosses you over his shoulder."

"Shit." Kate dug in her pocket readying for her inevitable loss.

Before any of the predictions came true, Sprout reached over and hit Bear with the back of his hand. "She looks hot with a kid on her hip, doesn't she?"

That made Bear hop off his bike abruptly. His face was angrier than it had been when I told him I wanted to find Carl. He stormed up to the house, towering over me and June. Gwen hugged my leg tighter.

"Hi, Bear. This is Guinevere, and this is June. Beth's daughters. And over there with Hammer are Arthur and Harry, her sons."

Bear's beard shifted. "Where's John?"

"With Beth, at the hospital." I tried to keep my tone as light as possible for the children's sake.

He scanned the chaos. Kate, Zoe, Hammer, Harry, Arthur, Gwen, and finally, June, who was trying very hard to hide.

"Kate, Zoe. Outside. Hammer, cover them."

He breathed hard through his nose between orders.

"I have to stay until John or his parents arrive."

Bear tipped his head to acknowledge that I'd spoken. "When's bedtime?"

"Probably an hour ago. John was a little stressed."

A nod. "I'll be back in a minute."

He walked back to the cluster of bikes. Zoe swung her leg over the back of Sprout's bike and Kate stood by Jackson's. After a quiet word or dozen, she climbed behind her husband while Hammer retrieved keys from Zoe. Their little cavalcade took off leaving Bear behind.

No yelling, no theatrics, just an organized exit despite the haste.

"You've got more tattoos than Hammer." Harry had no filter. And no fear. He put a sticky finger on Bear's hand, right on top of the warrior rune he had inked on his ring finger.

"Yeah. I suppose I do."

Gwen took his low rumble as an opportunity to release her death grip from my leg, but she fisted my dress in one hand. "Are you a friend of Auntie Rose?"

"Rose? Am I?"

"Yes, Gwen, he's my friend. So are all the others who were here."

I don't think she believed me because she didn't let go of my dress. But June did. She launched from my arms to reach for Bear. I almost toppled over trying to catch her and not get tripped up by Gwen.

"Whoa, hey. Which one are you again?"

June slapped a wet hand on his cheek. "Ju-ju."

"What's your name?" Gwen stared up at Bear.

"They call me Bear."

"You look like one."

"Bear!" June hugged him by wrapping her arms around his neck.

That made his eyes bug out a little. "Is she always like this?"

"Only for people she likes."

"She likes everybody," Gwen supplied.

"Can I draw tattoos on you?" Harry asked.

"No." Bear mouthed a silent "help" at me.

I smiled wickedly.

Arthur tugged his jacket, "Can you draw tattoos on me?" He twisted his arm to show off the blue ink that Hammer and Harry contributed to.

That was something Bear couldn't ignore. "Who drew that shit on you?"

Three little hands stuck out at the same time. June, who'd stuck one hand back in her mouth, pulled it out and patted Bear's mouth. "Bad bear."

"You owe a quarter for every swear word," I explained.

"To each of them?"

That only made their insistent hands waggle harder.

"Yep."

He dug out his chained wallet. "I only have—"

Gwen snatched a dollar from the stack and ran it to a bright blue mason jar aptly titled in bold black letters.

He held the wallet a little closer to his chest. June ran a finger across the skull design embossed on the outside.

"Not yours." He tucked it away while June rewrapped herself around his neck.

Finally, he sighed. "You had to, huh?"

I nodded. "I'll get them ready for bed if you can watch June for a bit?"

"Seeing as she's stuck to me like glue, I suppose."

"Thank you." I leaned in and gave him a kiss on the cheek. He could have gotten angry. Could have demanded and blustered, but instead, he adapted. For that, he deserved a bit of honesty. "We will talk about all of this and the stuff before. I promise."

He sighed. "Yeah. First things first."

At least an hour later I had all four children clean and if not sleeping, tucked in bed. Gwen was last to go down. She demanded I read her a bedtime story. Bear leaned against the door as I pulled out the worn copy of fairy tales I'd bought for them.

"Read the one about the bear." She snuck a sly look at the man in her doorframe.

I thumbed through until I landed on it.

When it ended, I kissed Gwen on the forehead and tucked the covers around her. "I'll be downstairs until your dad or grandparents get here, okay?"

"Rose?"

"Yeah?"

"He married the wrong one."

"Who?"

Gwen pointed at the book I'd placed on her nightstand. "The bear. He should have married Rose Red. Not her sister."

"Okay. Why?"

"Because Rose Red is you."

"And I suppose there's a prince over there?" I slid a mischievous look at Bear.

"He's in disguise," Gwen whispered loudly.

"Sorry, but that's his normal look," I told her.

She didn't believe me but let me finish tucking her in.

In the hallway, Bear put a hand against the other wall to block my path. "I'm not a prince."

"I know that."

His jaw tightened. "Probably more than most."

I stared up at him. "You're trying though. That's something."

His hand slipped and he walked away.

24

BEAR

John wasn't what I'd thought he be. I expected some beaten-down shell of a man, not someone I might have to tip my chin up at to stare in the eye.

And he was not happy with Rose at all. "They're bikers, Rose."

"And you're a construction worker. Labels, John."

He seethed quietly.

"How's Beth?" Rose asked quietly.

"Stable. But her ANC is way too low. They started looking wider for a different donor."

"What did her parents say about Carl's absence?"

John scratched his head obviously uncomfortable discussing this in front of me, but I wasn't moving. I needed this information almost as much as Rose did. Despite his demands, Carl was not following any of his usual patterns. The only person who'd seen hide or hair of him was Fish. And that was because of Carl's doing, not Fish's. "They haven't seen him either. He left their place a week ago."

That tracked.

I strode over and held a hand out. "Bear."

John stared at it for a second, then took it. His grip was strong, but the circles under his eyes told a different story. This was a man at the end of his rope. There was real desperation lurking behind his honest expression. "I'm John. You're Rose's…"

"Yeah. I'm hers. She's mine."

That admission did not make him happy. But Rose slid an arm around me, giving the lie a bit of weight.

I let go of his grip and wrapped my arm over her shoulders. "You ready to go?"

Rose nodded, "Give Beth my best."

"Will do." John stopped me. "Bear? I…" He was going to say something sappy, I just knew it.

"Keep your shit tight. That's all. Despite how it looked, I ain't no baby sitter. Understand?"

The look he shot Rose was a warning.

A well-deserved one. Like she'd told Gwen, I wasn't a prince. Far from it. I was a villain who shouldn't be around him or his kids.

"Let's go."

On the cold ride home, I fought visibility and the temptation to ride faster so Rose wouldn't shiver so much. I hadn't exactly given her time to dress for the ride, and John's house was tucked northeast of Harrisburg. That itself was a shit-show when Jackson found out his wife was that far away. His hand went to his gun before he even blinked. I stepped between him and the prospect who relayed the news. I showed him the scrolling feed Hammer had sent during the drive. "They're safe, man."

"I'll believe it when I see it." There'd been murder in his eyes.

And for his sake, I'd buttoned down my own anger and tucked it somewhere I couldn't even find now. I waited for a light and slipped my hand under Rose's skirt to rub her leg. "We'll be home soon."

"I know." She took the free moment to tuck her skirt tighter so her skin wouldn't be exposed. I tapped her knee to warn her the opposite light had turned yellow.

A car screamed through the intersection right after the light turned green on our side. I slammed the clutch down and braked hard. Rose's body bumped mine, and I steadied the bike so we wouldn't tip. With a little more caution I checked the intersection before ripping through it.

Rose squeezed my waist tighter. I took a moment to pat her hand and warn her to hang on. Fog or not, I never wanted her to let go. Random things like some moron blowing a light could tear us apart.

Or she could get cancer. I could die on a run. A million ways death could find us both knocked on my thoughts, begging to be let in so they could distract me. Or maybe eat me alive, like it had done to John. Even the oldest kids had that haunted *knowing* in their eyes. I hated it.

And the littlest? By the Allfather, she was a rare one. Fearless. And just a little too aware of how death can snatch someone you love away. It showed in the hugs. Those weren't innocent. They were driven by despair. She soaked in all of the good because it was going to go away, fast. And she knew she had to hang on as tight as she could because tomorrow?

Shit.

I pulled Rose's fingers to my lips. Then I put her hand over my heart and made sure it stayed there. I needed her. And I didn't want to fight anymore. She'd been right. Carl needed an incentive to show up for his sister. And if it took me pissing off both Jackson and Wolf, that's what it took.

The lights were on at Jackson's. Zoe's room was dark. The lounge upstairs lit by a blue glow. Someone was watching a movie.

The downstairs was lit up as well.

I rolled the bike into the garage and handed the keys off to Rose. "Go in, get warmed up. I need to talk to Jackson first, okay?" Before I let go of her hand, I pulled her close. "But I need you."

Her expression changed. "Why?"

Because you challenge me to be a better man? "I just do. We'll talk as soon as I get done over there." I ran a finger down her delicate skin. Why on earth did I think a ton of makeup was pretty? I preferred her light freckles, the slope of her nose…the way her eyes stared into my soul. She was far from perfect, but so damn strong. I was lost to her. "I'm yours."

It hurt.

I hurt.

She tangled her fingers in my beard. "And I'm yours. I don't know when that happened, but…"

Thank the Gods.

I kissed her nose. "Get inside."

"Bossy."

Not if Wolf or Jackson didn't want me to be.

For that, I needed to face up to the fuck up that tonight was. I knocked on Jackson's front door. While I waited, I sent him a text message to make sure he knew I was there.

He was not happy when he opened the door. "Get your ass in here."

Kate was on the couch. They'd started a fire that crackled perfectly. If you didn't look at Jackson's vest or his tattoos, you'd think you just stumbled into one of those cheesy movies where everything can be solved by a hug and maybe a cup of cocoa.

Jackson joined his wife and tucked her tightly at his side.

"Zoe?"

"Watching a movie," Kate said.

The sound of gunshots and an explosion clued me into any number of the choices she preferred. Luckily, the kid inherited her father's tastes.

I shuffled my feet, too aware of the cream carpeting. "I'm sorry about tonight."

"How's the kids and the dad?" Jackson's question caught me off guard.

"He's…rough." A thousand-yard stare was almost too mild to explain his status. "The kids are good. Rose got them all sorted."

"What do we know about them?"

Kate pretended not to listen. I'd seen that before. She stayed right where she was and soaked it all in, but kept her opinions and nose out of it. I'm sure that wasn't the case as soon as those two had a private word, but I wouldn't judge. She'd seen a hell of a lot worse than Jackson in her day.

"He works construction. I'd lay odds that the house must have been bought by their parents, or with their help. It's big and has his fingerprints on it. That means it's not a rental. I do know her parents are loaded. His, I don't know."

"And the cancer?"

At Jackson's question, Kate sucked in a gasp and looked down.

I watched her carefully. There was something they'd talked about already. Jackson played a mean game and was a difficult read, but Kate was an open book. "They're looking for another donor. Carl's in the wind."

"No, he ain't." Jackson's fingers tapped out his thoughts on Kate's shoulder.

"You heard from him?"

A grunt. "I'd barely gotten my ladies home and he called my fucking business phone."

That was downright suicidal. "Where is he? I'll take care of it."

He met my eyes. "No. He upped the amount. It's twenty-five now. I told him to speak that amount to my face so I could gut him."

Over an unsecured line. "And?"

His nostrils flared. "I want him dead. But I saw that oldest girl in the doorway and want her mom alive more." His fingers tightened on Kate's shoulder. "I'm sending the hospital's info to the national prayer chain. The club could use some good press. When she's better, we can kill that asshole for laughing at me."

Well, that was one way to fix things.

"Is Wolf on board?"

Jackson's frown deepened. "Nope. He's still concerned about keeping our asses out of trouble. And that's his job. So, I can't do jack shit about that." He slipped his arm free and leaned forward clasping his hands together between his knees. "Your woman played mine. She used bullets I couldn't dodge. Cancer and kids. Fucking low ass…" His fingers tightened so much the knuckles went white.

Kate put a hand on her husband's back. Her eyes met mine. "There's a lot more to her than meets the eye, isn't there?"

Unfortunately, yes. I nodded.

Her eyes bored into mine. "My husband does not want Zoe involved with anything dangerous. And I am one-hundred percent in agreement with him. However, I don't think Rose is as bad as he thinks. So, I need your insight. Is Zoe at risk?"

Jackson fixed on me to read my body language. My hesitation alone was enough of an answer. "Yeah. All of you are. Carl is…"

"He's a fucking nutcase." Jackson finished for me. "And your girl?"

"Rose is strong. She's dealt with his crazy before."

"That's not a good thing, Bear."

Jackson was right. I glanced up in time to see him slip a hand over to Kate's knee and squeeze it.

And maybe I wasn't seeing the whole picture? Kate knew crazy. Her ex was fifty times worse than Carl because he'd had power. Carl just had crazy going for him. Well, that and the people he sold to. Which in a small way was an army.

"She thinks she can talk Carl into donating bone marrow for his sister. He's already given blood."

Jackson sat back. A look of horror, if that's what it was, made him pale. The grooves of age, wind, and cares stood out bolder without his usual smirk. "You can't let her think like that."

Kate's mouth tightened. "She's going to, though. She's going to try to bargain with him."

Jackson faced his wife. Whatever he saw there made him spin to face me. "You have to lock her down. Whatever it takes."

"I know."

"She's going to hate you for that." Kate thought deeper. "She's going to hate all of us for that."

Unless we found a donor.

Then I could kill Carl and save everyone a lot of worry.

25

ROISHIN

The club had resources across the country. Members from every club volunteered to get tested. And thankfully, Beth responded to the antibiotics. They moved her back to a regular room, and she could have visitors again.

John called me first.

"Did you need me to watch the children?"

"No, Beth's been asking for you."

Thank the Goddess. "Let me check with Bear." He was hovering nearby, listening in as he always did, so I quickly told him the news.

"She wants to see me."

His brief deliberation was marked with a subtle grimace he tried to hide by licking his lips. "Okay."

I relayed it to John.

"Do you have to ask permission for everything?" The accusation in his tone was palpable.

"It's called respect."

The silence on his end told me what he thought about that. Finally, he said, "Only you, Rose. The doctors are clearing each person on a case-by-case basis."

As was protocol. You had to be healthy, go through thorough sanitary steps, and wear the protective gowns. We'd both been through this once before. "Fifteen minutes, right?"

"Ten. She's really weak."

My heart thumped harder. I pressed my lips together so I wouldn't cry. When I recovered, I told him, "I'll be there as soon as I can."

Bear was already pulling down my long coat from the hook. He handed it to me as I wiped the phone number from the call history.

"We're not taking your bike?" It was a nice day with no reason to ride enclosed.

He studied the keys hanging by the door. "You'll be more comfortable in the truck." With that, he grabbed his plain coat from the hook.

Before I climbed into the vehicle, I stopped in front of Bear and went up on tiptoe and framed his face with my hands. "Thank you. I know you would rather ride."

His dark eyes softened slightly. "Yeah, but I hate riding with a bitch crying on my back."

I rolled my eyes. This was the real him. Showing he cared by actions and burying it under layers of crassness. I squeezed his beard, tugging slightly. "I'm not a bitch."

His mouth tightened, fighting the smile that curled the corners. "Keep telling yourself that. Witch." There was a flare of heat that sparked between us. I inhaled, savoring the connection before letting go and climbing in the truck.

Even though we weren't on his bike, he reached over to keep a hand on my leg whenever he could. I covered it, caressing the rough skin and tracing the tattoos. Each finger had a runestone inked into the skin. I brushed the stroked lines and recited the meanings. Fehu, Uruz, Kano, Nauthiz. For the uninitiated, you'd see them and read, "fuck." But they really meant wealth, strength, creativity, and restraint. Bear knew the meanings. He had to.

"Did you do these?" They didn't match most of his artwork.

"I had to drill them left-handed. They're a little shaky, but… Yeah."

I lifted his hand and kissed each one.

A small smile twitched into place as I did.

I spoke to his fingers. "You're mine. And I'm yours."

He braked hard, pulling to the side of the road. I scanned for danger or the cause of his abrupt stop.

A hard kiss interrupted me. Bear's tongue pressed into my mouth. It caught me by surprise, but once I realized we weren't in danger, I leaned into the kiss.

He growled and kissed me harder.

A car whizzed past and rocked the SUV.

I was panting.

Bear wasn't much better. He stared at me hard. "You're mine, and I'm yours."

I nodded, unsure of what was happening, but it was significant.

He grinned.

With one more kiss, he let me collapse back into my seat while he buckled up and checked for traffic before slipping back onto the road.

"You pulled over for a kiss?"

"That wasn't just a kiss, woman."

My cheeks felt warm. It certainly wasn't. It might have been the single most romantic thing he'd done yet. All because I got a little lost in my thoughts and let my emotions slip out.

I let myself be vulnerable and it felt good.

This time, I reached across and put my hand on his knee.

He slipped his hand off the wheel and covered it.

We were still holding hands when we met John in the waiting room. He glanced down at the sight. Then took in Bear's leather, denim, tattoos, and piercings. And my floor-length black gown with skull eyelets and the black lace overlaying it all. A smile tilted at the corner of his mouth.

That's right. I finally found someone to be myself with.

John sized Bear up again. It was shocking to see they were almost the same size. I'd gotten so used to seeing both of them alone, or with people smaller than they were, that the shock of them together brought out comparisons. They both were giants compared to normal men. Bear had thicker legs and hands. John's fingers were slightly longer, and both had biceps for days. John was clean-cut, Bear wild. It was almost as if they came from the same mold, but were decorated to match Beth and my personalities. I pinned a mental note to tell Beth about that.

But first I had to make sure they didn't kill each other.

"Play nice. I'm going to check in and wash up. Bear? I'll be out in about a half hour. You good?" I moved close so I could brush my fingers against his scalp. He shaved the sides almost daily, but had missed a day or two. The stubble there was soft and velvety. I adored the feel of it under my fingertips.

"All good." He locked eyes with me. "You got this." He leaned in and kissed me, ending it before it could heat too far. His nose brushed mine. He was so close I couldn't focus, so I closed my eyes to soak in his strength. John didn't need to watch me break, he had enough on his plate. Somehow, Bear knew that and was giving me some of his abundant energy.

I dug my fingertips into the muscles of his neck to let him know I appreciated his offering. "Tonight." I kissed his cheek and let go before I lost control.

I'd give him everything. Lay myself out on a platter and let him take anything he wanted. I trusted him enough for that. It was a heady feeling. I barely felt the floor beneath my feet. The trance of his magic floated me through the ritual of hand-washing, wrapping my hair, putting the protective over layer on, and donning a surgical mask.

Then I was allowed in, and it all came crashing down.

I was fifteen again. And Beth was dying for the first time.

Sure, she was older, I was wiser, and we were both much more experienced at navigating death, but seeing her so frail knocked my walls down. Everything let loose at once. The pain, the tears, the rage… I couldn't feel so much at once.

I was barely able to walk the scant few feet to plant my butt in the chair next to her bed.

"Hi." Lame.

Beth smiled and started to say something just as lame, but opted to reach a hand out instead.

I took it immediately. She was mine. I poured power into our connection. The strength I'd gotten from Bear, the hope he'd given me when he announced the club was spreading the word nationally for donors, all of it. "You look like shit."

She laughed. "Feel like shit."

"I'm sorry."

She blinked. "No, you're not. You'd do it all over again five times ten."

"That's seven times seven."

"No, you know what I mean."

I did. We'd talked about so much when we were younger. Nothing was immune from dissection. "Did you hear about the donor search?"

She snorted lightly. "Bikers, huh?"

I shrugged. "They're not all bad."

Her eyes met mine. "I don't think they are. I think they're a lot like you. Good people doing everything they can to crawl out of the swamp. And learning to swim in the cesspool while doing so."

"That's not fair. You know my weaknesses."

"John says he's big."

I suppressed a laugh. That was an understatement. "Okay. I got a chance to study them both out in the waiting room. Picture John as a dark barbarian with thicker thighs, waist and neck. Longer hair, of course, and piercings."

Her mouth opened slightly. "I hear he's got a mohawk."

I frowned. "A Viking braid. And sure, probably not even close to authentic, but it's kind of sexy." I lifted an eyebrow remembering how good it felt to dig my fingers into it and moan his name.

"You're in love."

I dumped her hand and crossed my index fingers between us. "Stand back Satan."

She laughed.

That was balm to my soul. "I love you."

Her smile turned pensive. "I know, but you need someone to fly the night skies with."

Wow. I forgot I told her that. "That's only in dreams." It wasn't real. Even if I did feel it almost as acutely as if it were, my body stayed behind each time.

"Are you safe with him?"

No, but that was part of the appeal. "He's not a good man, if that's what you're asking. But he's one of those acts of service types. And he tried buying me. Twice."

"What?" Beth didn't believe me.

"Okay maybe the first time he turned Carl down, but—"

Her hand gripped mine, tightly. "What's that about Carl?"

Shit. I didn't want to tell her that. But I wouldn't lie to her either. "Your brother wouldn't let me leave that first night. And Bear showed up." I faltered for a moment but pushed on.

"Your brother offered to sell me to him." I laughed. But it cut short as my breath caught. "If it had been anybody else? I think I wouldn't be alive to tell you all this in person. Do you understand why I say that?"

She nodded. Her eyes held too many of our shared secrets.

"That's why… despite his grumpy exterior, I know I'm safe."

Beth smiled again. It was so pure and sweet, I wanted to touch it. But knew better, so I stroked her hand instead. "My life for yours. My heart beats at your side."

The smile fell. "Rose," she cautioned.

"I know. But I want to give you my strength. Lean on it for a bit, will ya?"

She squeezed my hand. "I might take you up on that."

"You better." A tear slipped out and dampened the edge of the mask. My trapped breath was hot and humid, making my cheeks sweat. I couldn't wipe away the moisture because then I'd have to go back out and wash my hands again. I sucked in snot and tried to focus outward.

Beth saved me from an embarrassing meltdown.

"I'm glad you found someone. So, buying you twice? What was the other time about?"

I told her all about the cold ride to Maryland, meeting Betty Jo and Fin, slipped a bit of my dress free from the covering to show her the lace, and finished with, "He ordered a custom athame for me. It's fucking expensive."

Her eyes got a little wide. "Do you think he gets his money… illegally?" Her volume dropped significantly on the last word.

"He's a biker. What do you think?"

"Oh, Jesus."

I snuck a glance at the door, waiting for a nurse or other person to interrupt us. "Carl buys from him."

"Holy shit, Rose!" This time, Beth's warning was clear.

"I know."

She frowned. "You can't stay with him."

I bit my lip and lowered my voice. "I've been paying attention. A couple of years ago or more, they somehow inherited half the town they are based in. It's legit. The club owns a lot of property, and I don't think they deal for money because they don't really need it." I lowered my voice to a whisper so soft, I had to lean in so Beth could hear me. "I think they're getting out. Bear demanded that Carl buy out their agreement with them, and I don't think it would make a difference in their income if Carl did."

Beth's eyes widened. "Then why do they keep doing it?"

"Appearances." I shrugged because that might not be accurate. "Maybe pride. I don't know." I sat back in my chair.

Beth wouldn't tell a soul this, but maybe I should ask for secrecy?

Nope. She carried enough of my crimes on her conscience, I didn't need to burden her with one more.

Too soon, the visit was over. I promised Beth I'd come more often. Her color was high, and her eyes less burdened with worry than when I'd arrived. She'd seen me. She knew first-hand I was safe, and now could focus on getting better. I reminded John I owed him and his parents a night off. "Maybe Friday. Bear won't be there then." I slid a joking glance at Bear. He shook his head, dismissing my barb. "You'll do it on a night I'm free, woman."

John squinted, not understanding.

I quickly translated. "He gets grumpy if I'm left all alone without protection."

There was a quick glance toward Bear before John faked a smile. "That's understandable. You're a menace left to your own devices."

"Always."

It felt so good to smile. Beth was going to get better. Soon. I sent the intent into the universe. Then set my will behind it, and vowed to take action when it was clear how to proceed.

Bear was much happier on the ride home. Maybe the promise of exploring this new balance between us, or just being free from the hospital made him smile more.

But that smile fell as soon as we opened the door. He raced upstairs, then to the basement, gun out and intent on killing something, but came up empty.

At first, I couldn't see anything wrong. But then I did.

My altar wasn't where it was supposed to be. All the objects were arranged on the dining room floor. The dark charcoal lines of a cross were thickly drawn. A page, ripped from a book lay in the center, under the toes of my goddess statue.

A passage was circled in red. I read it out loud. *"But as for the cowardly, the faithless, the detestable, as for murderers, the sexually immoral, sorcerers, idolaters, and all liars, their portion will be in the lake that burns with fire and sulfur, which is the second death."*

Bear crossed his arms.

The word, 'murderers' was underlined. Twice.

"Carl," I said through gritted teeth.

"Has he always been fucking suicidal?"

I glanced up at Bear. "What?" The last thing Carl wanted was to die. Nope, he wanted to live forever just to rub everyone's noses in shit.

"Breaking into my house? That ain't gonna fly."

Nothing but my altar was out of place. "He didn't touch anything of yours."

Bear pointed at his floor. "No?"

It would wash off. Hopefully.

"I'll clean it up."

"No." The ringing of his phone stopped him from saying anything else, and his upheld finger told me it was someone from his club. I sat on the floor silently waiting for the one-sided conversation to cease. But whoever was on the phone had a lot to say. Loudly.

Unfortunately, Bear had walked to the farthest side of the house to deal with the conversation. His low voice spoke in short bursts as the tirade went on.

He paced back to my side of the room. "Nothing else was touched." Bear's low grumble was audible. Then, "I know. I checked the house. Nothing."

He rolled his shoulders, as if adjusting a heavy weight. "Listen, this is about my shit. I'll take care of it."

The call ended abruptly after that. Bear's scowl spoke to how dire this situation was. I quickly moved everything I'd collected back to the table and grabbed the mop from the closet.

Within a minute or two all evidence of Carl's intrusion was gone. Except for the crumpled bible page in Bear's fist.

"I'll throw that out."

He snatched his hand away. "Nope. KC and I gotta take a ride."

"You're not going to go to Carl's."

My warning should have been clear, but obviously wasn't. Bear was on the phone, calling his 'brother' and setting the wheels in motion to retaliate.

As soon as he ended that call, I spoke up. "An eye for an eye makes the whole world blind."

Bear glared at me. "Ain't going to kill him." Under his breath, he muttered, "Yet."

I'd heard that before. "You are going to let this slide. It isn't your fight. He targeted *my* things."

"In *my* house. And let me just read this part again, *as for the murderers…*" He put emphasis on the final word. "That ain't about you."

"Yes. It is."

He froze. "I'm sorry, what?" He pretended to shake an ear out.

"You heard me. But I could argue that it would also extend to

Carl, but he'd never admit to what he did so that's what you call hypocrisy at its finest."

"Who'd you kill?"

He fired it off so quickly it took me by surprise. "It doesn't matter."

"Yes, it does. Who? You can't drop a bombshell like that and think I'd ignore it."

Bear was right. Somehow, I'd let my guard down around him and his friends. I'd foolishly thought I fit in. I didn't. I was ten times worse than any of them. I bit my lips to keep from blurting out my sins. But now that the deed was admitted, they'd dig. Eventually, they'd uncover my sealed juvenile records. And perhaps the court notes from my counselor. And when that happened, this lie I was living would come to an abrupt halt. "I was—" Instead of starting there I shifted the timeline. "An elder of the church, a deacon, caught Carl and I climbing on the girders of the new church. It was still under construction. The deacon tried to force me to climb down. As he reached to grab me, I jumped to a rope, and he fell."

"That's an accident, not murder."

Unless you'd lured the victim up there to make him fall. Not even my counselor got that part. Carl knew. He was the one who'd thought it up.

He also was the one who climbed down and made sure he was dead.

"Guilt is guilt. It doesn't listen to reason." That was something one of the psychologists said during the trial.

Bear's eyebrow lifted. "Listen, only the innocent feel guilt. The rest of us can't afford it."

The rest of us. He'd called KC. That's why he was angry with Carl. "Murderers. Plural."

"You don't know that."

"I was commenting on the underlined."

Whatever connection we'd created was gone.

26

———

BEAR

Carl's house turned up a big fat zilch. KC and I were thorough. We planted a couple of miniature cameras and motion detectors. I checked the hidden stash point behind his toilet that Rose mentioned. Empty. The computer he used to spy on the neighbors? Gone. No vehicles, nothing.

In an act of sheer spite, I ran my muddy boot across his rug. The mark I left was simple. It was a zig-zagged lightning bolt. In runic symbolism, it said, "see you on the dark side." That was an invitation to escalate. He'd know who made it. And since the mud came from his own backyard, no nosy cop could prove it was me.

KC stopped by the back door. He ran a finger down the scratched surface. "That's odd."

"What?"

He stopped with an index finger touching the bottom row of marks. There were twenty in total. "I could have sworn there were only three rows of five and that odd first row. Now there's four more. Carl's so weird." He shrugged and led the way out.

The neighbor hadn't replaced their dog yet. Which meant Carl had to have been spotted recently. I stomped over to their backyard and hammered on the door. A kid answered and promptly shut it.

Like that could keep me out if I wanted it. "Is a parent or adult home?"

"Not talking to you."

Fuck. Smart kid. "Listen, I just want to know if you've seen your neighbor recently?"

Silence.

"Dude, you scared the shit out of him."

"Did not." But I probably did. "You try."

KC knocked like a normal person. "You don't have to open the door, just say yes or no. Have you seen that weird guy next door in the last two days?"

"No!"

"In the last week?"

"Maybe?"

KC shot me a look. He was getting farther than I was, so I gave him the lead.

"Okay. What about in the last two weeks?"

"Yeah."

"Thanks kid. That's all I needed."

I bugged my eyes out at him. He was letting him off too easy. That little bastard knew things. I could feel it.

KC crowded me down the steps. I caught myself on the railing and stomped on the plywood someone laid at the bottom. "Don't fucking push me, I'll—"

The door cracked open slightly. Through the screen, the kid eyeballed me, then KC. "Did you find any bodies inside the house?" he asked with a tentative finger toward Carl's house.

That took KC by surprise. But I'd searched the basement for that very thing. It was too fucking clean if you ask me. "Nope. Bet he bleached the place before we got there."

The kid's eyes went wide. "I think he did. He kills people, you know?"

KC sent me a warning with a finger raised behind his back. "People?" he asked more nicely than I ever could.

"Yeah. He had a girl there. She's gone. And he killed our dog."

Figured as much. "The girl's fine. She's with me."

He breathed a visible sigh of relief. His little shoulders slumped with it. "Good. She was nice to me. I thought for sure he was going to slit her throat or something."

That wasn't Carl's style.

"Who else did he kill?"

KC shushed me, but the kid answered anyway. "The mail lady. She used to bring mom's checks to the door. But one day she talked to Carl and he got angry. Then the next day? Gone." He ran a finger across his throat.

"She could have retired or something," KC said.

"No man, you don't know. He makes people disappear." The kid looked around nervously, then slammed the door shut. The click of a deadbolt sounded first, then the snick of the handle lock.

"That was enlightening." *Not.*

KC wasn't as convinced. "Maybe we should go back in?" He did not want to. The hesitant way his eyes scanned the top windows of the house was a sure sign of fear.

A part of me had to admit there was a reason to be afraid. We'd scanned the neighborhood. Most of the houses had meager Halloween decorations planted randomly. Like a Jack-o-lantern on a front step, paper decorations taped inside of windows, some fake spiderwebs, but Carl's house was pristine. It stood apart. Almost as if just the house itself was spooky enough to creep anyone out so it didn't need decorating.

"I don't like this," he muttered.

Neither did I. He'd broken into *my* house, so I broke into his. Just for payback. An eye for an eye, break in for break in. Even though we'd met no resistance, my spine was crawling with warnings.

I put on a brave front and motioned at KC. "We did what we came to do. Let's go."

Once we got back to the clubhouse, Hammer caught me at the bar. "Fin's looking for you."

"He's here?"

The prospect nodded. "Out back. He's shooting the shit with Jackson."

The man hated being trapped indoors. Strange as hell, but since he'd done his years, we put up with the quirks. I slipped out the back door by the kitchen.

Jackson's wicked laughter flitted from the shadows. I followed it to find them sharing a joint. I wiggled my fingers for a hit. Once I had it between my fingertips, I inhaled deeply.

"Save some for the rest of us." I lifted my middle finger to tell them to wait their turn.

I sucked in a bite of air before handing it back. My lungs protested, but I stifled the coughing fit until I caught that first rush of tingling at the tip of my nose which meant the weed was working. I let go of the breath, blowing a light trail of smoke into the sky. "There you go, Odin." I coughed. "Is that dirt weed?" It was harsher than our shit.

Fin shrugged. "It came from Snake's old patch."

Jackson coughed his hit out. "I thought you burned that shit down."

"I did. It grew back. Kid saw it and started messing with the tops. That got his woman all pissy, and she took over. It ain't all bad now."

"I like her chili better than this." I passed the joint to Fin without hitting it. Despite the taste, the high slammed into me hard. It was one of those fuzzy kinds of buzzes that made you feel like you stood sideways. I almost wussed out and sat on the nearest junked car but stayed standing, barely. "What brought you north?"

Fin held up a finger to let me know he'd tell me as soon as he was done holding his breath. He let a little smoke leak out as he squeaked out, "Brought your woman's knife." He coughed and a cloud of smoke came with it.

He offered the nub to Jackson.

"Pass."

Fin snubbed it out between his fingers. Then got down to business. "I brought the truck. Betty Jo insisted I bring another box of clothes up with it. Damn woman."

Jackson tipped his head at the club. "You know, you're always welcome to—"

"Fuck off. My wife might be a bitch, but she's *my* bitch and I wouldn't have it any other way. You know that." He punched Jackson in the chest and said Kate's name as he did.

Luckily, he pulled it.

Jackson laughed. "Fuck. I know the feeling."

"Everything okay?" They'd just gotten married. I'd hate to think he was getting the itch already.

The smirk on Jackson's face wasn't comforting. "Ain't had time or opportunity to bust a decent nut is all. Maybe… Can Zoe sleep at your house for a night or two?"

"Jesus, man, I ain't a fucking hotel or a babysitter."

"I hear you were. Your woman had her hands full with four kids the other night, and you pitched right in. D'you and her have a secret you're not telling us?" Fin's bushy eyebrow went up with speculation.

"How in the fuck did you hear about that?"

Jackson chuckled.

Right. That asshole told him. Probably thought it was hilarious. "They ain't hers. They're her best friend's."

"Crotch goblins." Fin shuddered.

"Could you imagine kids with Betty Jo?" Jackson asked the air, but probably didn't mean to include Fin.

"They'd have murdered someone before they turned twelve," I said.

Fin laughed. "Damn straight they would have. And I'd've hid the bodies." A rare smile crossed his face. But it fell. "Speaking of bodies, Demons?"

Ah, yes. He kept abreast of the goings on, especially if it involved clubs inside our territory. "Thirty of 'em sniffing around. They also got that bitch-ass club of punks from West Chester riding with them."

"Fifty-eight then." He turned to Jackson, "How's 'Burgh. Still giving you shit?"

"Bandit rode with me on the trip last month. It's all good." Jackson sounded convincing.

However, Fin stared at him for too long. "You know it ain't."

"That's my problem, old man."

"Just saying." Fin brushed at his dirty jeans. He may look like he was giving up on the topic, but he had a serious hard-on about protecting territory, and we all knew it.

Jackson couldn't let it go. "No, ya weren't. You were meddling."

"I'm too old to meddle," Fin shot back.

"Bullshit." Jackson beat me to it, but mine echoed on its heels.

That's when Jackson finally let it go. "Let's see that knife. I'm curious what a one-thousand-dollar blade looks like."

"How in the hell do you know how much I—" Oh, right. Kate. Or Zoe. "Your women, I swear."

"Better watch yourself. Yours seems like a ringleader." He nudged Fin. "Sierra's got competition." Then he winked.

Fin laughed. "Ain't no competition. Betty Jo already declared a winner." He strode toward his truck as we joked around. But he couldn't just leave it hanging there, could he?

Jackson and I traded glances. Who was going to ask first? I doubted either of us wanted to know the truth.

Fin pulled out a plastic bin filled to the brim with black fabric and shiny shit. "I didn't buy that."

He glanced up. "Not yet."

Fuck my life.

Fin popped the lid. On top was a Ziplock bag filled with jewelry. Most of it was silver. There were stones of all colors and sizes embedded in rings, necklaces, and even a fragile-looking crown. He shifted that to the side and dug out a long package wrapped in a hide. "Here it is."

He unrolled the bundle, and the jeweled scabbard winked in the moonlight.

Jackson whistled. "Damn."

Fin tipped his head, accepting the appreciation. "Wait 'til you see the blade."

The important part, according to everything in Fin's world.

"Here, you do the honors." He held it out with both hands.

It was barely a foot long, but heavy. I took it by the hilt. The span was too small for my big hands, but probably perfect for Rose's. I fiddled with the catch that kept the knife locked in place. It was a crescent moon, hooked around a mounted black stone. In the dim light, I couldn't tell if the stone was clear or not, but it sparkled like a well deep in shadow.

"That's onyx. Edie says it wards of bad juju. Sierra won't touch it. Says it's cursed."

Perfect. I slipped the knife free and admired the veins in the steel. Damascus knives were always my favorite. The intricacies of each fold told a story. The honed edges glittered.

"Best be careful. It ain't been blooded yet. It'll be thirsty."

Fin and his superstitions. I slipped it back in the scabbard before handing it to Jackson. He admired it for a little too long. He went as far as to balance the unsheathed dagger on an outstretched finger. Not by the tip, but at a sweet spot above the bolster. "It's a little blade-heavy."

"That's better for cutting. She ain't got the upper arm strength for stabbing." Fin snatched the blade out of his hand and spun it before slipping it into its protective case. "I got a thigh belt for it, too. She can wear it under her skirts. Speaking of…" He set the knife on top of the jewelry bag and pulled out a long velvet dress.

Betty Jo had outdone herself. Unless…I eyed the fantasy-themed embroidery. "Did Edie make this?"

"Yup. And the jewelry. She heard about your woman from Betty Jo and got busy."

Busy wasn't the word for it. More like obsessive. I swallowed. Her work was *not* cheap. "How much?"

Fin made a noise that told me nothing. Then he clarified, "Indy doesn't know."

That meant Edie gave it away.

"And when he does?"

Fin shrugged. "I figure eight grand."

Holy Frigg. At least it wasn't five or six digits.

Jackson slapped my arm with the back of his hand. "Kate's wedding dress was nine large. Are you wussing out?"

"Fuck off." I pulled out my wallet and began counting out

Benjamins. "There's three grand. If Indy bitches, shut him up for me."

"That'd take another two hundred." Fin eyed my near-empty wallet.

I pulled out another pair of bills and shoved them in his hand. "Fucker."

"Nice doing business with you, Bear." He tipped an imaginary hat and handed off the box, jewelry and all.

It was almost morning before I slipped into bed with Rose. I dragged the rounded nub at the end of the scabbard along her bare skin. It skipped over her ribs as I slid it lower. The sheet pulled away, revealing a breast. And that I couldn't resist. I put the knife where she'd see it once she opened her eyes and bent over her body to suck on that pretty puckered nipple.

"Bear." She slipped her fingers into my hair. It was automatic. The one place she was guaranteed to know immediately who was assaulting her. She played with the beads near my ears. Her eyes opened. "Hi."

"Hey you. Got a present."

Her forehead creased. "Please don't tell me you killed Carl and cut off his finger or something." Her eyes darted around to make sure I wasn't bloody or worse.

"Not that good of a present. And I'd bring you his lungs. After he suffocates from a Blood Eagle. Here." I put the knife in her hand. Fin helped me attach the belt so she could wear it right away.

She squirmed out from underneath me and turned on the lamp to get a better look at it. Her breath caught. "It's beautiful." Her fingers stroked down the engraved surface, halting on each decorative inlay and mounted stone.

"Check out the blade."

She caressed the latch stone first.

"Onyx." At least I sounded like I knew what I'd bought.

She grinned. "That keeps evil spirits away."

According to Edie, yeah. I didn't know if I'd ever tell her Sierra's theory.

Rose slipped the latch open and tugged the knife out. Her eyes went a little wide as she took in the sharp edges and the intricate striations of tempered steel. "Wow. No one has a blade like this."

"Just you."

I didn't dare lean in for a kiss. Old wives' tales or not, Fin's blades were always sharp. And with it unsheathed in her hand, I let it own a healthy distance.

"Thank you. And thank Fin for me. Please?" She put it back together and spun the locking mechanism into place. Only then did I breathe easier. I stripped the sheet down and begged her to model it for me.

"I kind of have a kink for armed women." No sooner than I said that, I began to sweat. Why did I say something so …honest?

Rose crawled out of bed, stood naked beside it, and strapped the belt onto her thigh.

Then she posed.

I'd touched that goddess. And I'd get to touch her again soon.

"Wait." She slipped her hair free and unbraided it. The waves turned into curls as she shook out the mass.

Now she was beyond perfect.

I shut my mouth and swallowed a couple of times to talk. "I want you."

"Right now?" She twirled a lock of hair between her fingers. Her toes dug into the carpet.

"Fuck, yes." Now, always, forever. But I'd settle for right the fuck now.

27

ROISHIN

If I'd have known a man could get mesmerized by a woman wearing nothing but a dagger…well, Bear hadn't taken his eyes off me. Even as I circled the foot of the bed, he tracked me.

I halted on his side. The light from the bathroom silhouetted me from behind, casting him in shadow. I stepped closer so I could see him better. He was weary yet still so strong. He'd left so quickly and been gone so long I worried he'd been hurt, or worse. But here he was, whole, and looking like he'd stepped out of a very sexy nightmare. One where the monster wins.

And he gave me a knife so I could win, too.

I loved him. Every inch of him. From his thick eyebrows, to the tattoos snaking around his skull. The piercings, the warrior braids, his mighty neck and shoulders, all the way down to his black boots, which were damn hard to get off. But once they were, I pushed him backwards so he was half on the bed, under me, and submitting to my power.

The leather vest he wore had a special spot over the back of a chair next to the bed. I placed it there with reverence. While I'd been turned, Bear pulled off his shirt and tossed it to the floor. He'd reached for his pants. I stopped him to unbutton them myself.

Before I did, I traced the line of black hair that ran from his chest to his groin. My fingernails were long enough to scratch his skin and dig in slightly. He wanted an armed woman? I intended to prove I didn't need weapons. I had a sword for a tongue and claws for fingernails. And sharp teeth to bite with. I leaned in to lay my open mouth on his tender stomach.

He sucked in a breath. "Careful."

I bit down lightly just because I could.

He flinched, but then moaned my name. I licked the spot where I might have hurt him and watched his face. All I could see was beard and chest. But with patience, I got what I wanted. He curled to look at me. "Whatcha waiting for?"

I smiled. Then licked his stomach again. His mouth dropped open and his eyes fluttered shut.

That. That was what I wanted to see.

Him, losing control, forgetting how to feign indifference, a man falling under the spell of lust.

And to keep him mesmerized. I kept the tip of my tongue on his skin as I finished loosening his pants.

I had to sit up to help him tug them off, then straddled him again low on his thighs. I curled like a cat to nibble on a hip bone, lick that trail of happy black fur, and inhale deep as I soaked in his glory.

His dick was too heavy to stand straight up. But it was hard. The veins bulging in ropey purple ridges that twisted like the roots of a tree. Their paths snaking over one another, appearing and disappearing into his flesh. I traced those with my mouth.

Bear groaned. The tip of his cock leaked precum that I sucked off him, only to have to devour more as he shifted under me.

"Rose, you better get a condom out of that drawer, or suck me dry. I can't wait much longer."

That wasn't what I wanted. I wanted to edge him into insanity.

I stood up, stepping back from the bed, hand on the knife hilt. It fit perfectly. The natural fall of hand aligned with the handle. And with a twist of the wrist, I could grip the pommel, flip the catch and tug it free. The knowledge that I stood a meager second or two from murder thrilled me. And scared me.

If someone had given me this gift years ago, I would have followed them forever. I almost did. But back then the scales weren't balanced. I was a pawn.

Was I fooling myself to think Bear treated me like a queen? His queen. I lifted my hand, but didn't move.

Bear sat up. His dark eyes took in my hesitation. Then with a grim smile he raised his hand, curled his fingers against his thumb and with only his index finger free, silently ordered me to step closer.

I did.

One step, then another. And a third that brought my legs in contact with his. He swept his hands down my skin from ribcage to hips and finally landed on my ass with a finger-tightening squeeze. "You're mine."

"I'm yours."

With less grace, he trapped me one-handed and reached for the drawer, coming up with a condom held between two fingers. "Fuck or suck?"

"Fuck, please?" How could I resist?

He set it on the bed next to his leg. "What's going on in your head, Rose?"

"Power. Shame."

His eyes focused sharply on me. "There's no shame in wanting to be strong." With that spoken he swept his hands down my arms as if to punctuate exactly how brutally different we were. I had barely any definition tapering from thin biceps to even thinner fingers. Yet even his fingers were burly.

Those interlaced with mine.

"Strength is nothing without speed, agility, and most importantly, will." His eyes sought mine. "Your will is stronger than mine. I know that. It's stronger than anyone's I've ever met. And you wear it like armor." He blinked. "A knife just makes you more dangerous.

And frankly, I'm an idiot for giving one to you. You could kill me easily. I saw it in your eyes. You wanted to. You have the desire to do that. Not many do."

I swallowed.

"It should scare you, but it doesn't scare me." He slipped his hands around me to squeeze my ass again, then caress it. "Maybe I'm lying. Maybe I'm a fool. But you are perfect just the way you are. Don't be frightened of that."

Without thinking, I bent toward him. My hands tangled in his hair and my fingertips rubbed his scalp so I could pull his face close. "I'm yours."

"So am I, sweetheart. We'll own each other, okay?"

I nodded against his nose, relishing the feel of his skin against mine. Balancing against him, I slipped one knee, then the other onto the mattress until I straddled him.

He reached under me to retrieve the condom and get it placed before I lifted up so he could position at my entrance.

I sank down, feeling him stretch me wide. As turned on as I was, I was still lacking a little lubrication, and the movement sent a tiny twinge of pain, but I ignored it because even that felt exquisite.

Bear grunted as I tilted my hips to get him as deep as possible in this position.

"You're killing me, Rose." His breath came quickly, his eyes were shut tight.

I arched my back and used my thighs to work along his length. "I need you alive," I whispered against his ear.

His eyes shot open. "I'll show you alive."

With a heave and a mighty lift, he flipped our positions. I was the one on the bottom, my back resting on the mattress and my hips and legs cradled in his grip. The flex of his body hammered into me with intense passion. I met him with every thrust and tense arch. My fingers clawed at his arms because I couldn't break his grip. Nor did I want to. I wanted him to merge with me. To pound so hard that we fused as one.

My body was just a vessel for him to shatter against so our fires could merge as one flame.

"You. Are. Mine." He thrust with each word, the strain in his voice making his neck muscles bulge and his skin red.

Then he seated deep.

I cried out. "Mine!" The orgasm broke free and the walls between us shattered as he pulsed into me and I gripped around him. My heart beat wildly and I breathed shallowly to lengthen the moment into a trancelike state where my spirit form slipped into that other realm that shadowed the real world.

Once there, I touched him. He was a being of red power, not quite flame, but an essence of something caught between forge and hammer. Glowing like a molten god.

My essence was ghostlike, lit with white blue, ethereal and as solid as smoke. Were there cracks I could find to slip inside? Could I give him a piece of myself to carry under that iron hide? Would I burn?

I didn't care. I loved him. Trusted him. My lips met his in that world. He inhaled and I sent a tendril of life into his. He'd carry me with him until the end of time. Yet that piece clung to my conscious mind. Almost screaming that I'd abandoned it. I caressed his face. *Take care of that piece. Don't hurt m—*

His eyes snapped open, and I was in my body again.

The fear hung between us. "What did you…?"

I shook my head. I couldn't tell him. He'd never believe me.

He glanced at our bodies, still interlocked. He smiled and slid free. "I'm beat." He tapped my hip to get me to move to my side of the bed. Instead of joining me right away, he took care of the condom and brought a towel back from the bathroom. "Here. I'm going to crash for about a day or fucking three." He face-planted onto the mattress, but still had enough energy to wrap a hand around my leg. His fingers loosening as he lost the battle with Morpheus.

I cleaned up and sat beside him.

That glowing god was just a man.

I stroked down his broad back. One hell of a man.

He fought battles daily. Maybe not always physically, but always dominating others. He would never be fully happy unless he was at the top of the food chain.

There were few others who could beat him physically. And he'd proven he was able to see beyond appearances and view the intent under the surface. He could sense magic. That was dangerous. Without the power to thwart it, it left him open to be exploited.

I gently laid my palm on his back, right between the shoulder blades. With it in place, I called to the piece of me I'd left. Grow. Glow. Protect. Keep him safe from those foes. Make him stronger. Give him my will and my intent, and most of all build the walls he needed to keep the spirit realm out.

I kissed him there to seal any openings I'd made through the connection.

Then I went downstairs to put my own brand of security on the house. If Carl wanted to mess with us, he'd leave himself open to me.

I started with the besom over the door. The round broom was mostly symbolic. I studied it. It was dusty and brittle. A fakery sold for aesthetic value.

That had to change.

I searched the woods, gardens, and the banks of the river nearby for the right items. With luck I found two snail shells, some animal bones, dried hydrangea flowers, and a nasty wild rose briar with sharp thorns that demanded ten minims of my blood before yielding to my blade.

From the kitchen, I dug out rosemary and the bag of turnips I'd bought on the last grocery trip.

I worked at my altar, carving, pulling thorns, filling the snail shells and sealing them with wax, then binding the spell into the besom.

Bear came down some time in the midst of my work. He watched for a moment, but didn't interrupt. Instead opting to make a late breakfast before dressing in his usual uniform of black Destroyers shirt, jeans, vest, and leather coat.

He kissed me before leaving. "Heading to the shop. You good?"

I nodded, still focused on my work. But then realized that he was about to leave.

"Wait." I quickly tied a red string around his wrist. "There." I smiled at him.

He glanced down at the bright color twisted over his usual black leather wristbands. "Cute. What's it do?"

"Keeps you safe."

"So… don't take it off?"

I nodded again. "Not until it breaks. Then I'll give you a new one."

He slid a hand under my loose hair. "You're something else, Roishin Black." He pulled my face close for a dangerously hot kiss. I almost forgot everything as his tongue wound around mine. Except an underlying current of doubt that made me push against him.

"What do you mean, something else?"

He licked his lips. "I mean… I don't think I'll ever *not* be surprised by you. And that's a good thing. I'm working until eight. Call Hammer if you have trouble. He should be next door on kiddie watch."

I blinked; it wasn't like him to forget the schedule like that. "Zoe's at school. Jackson's home."

He scrunched his eyes, thinking. "Right. Make sure Hammer's with you. I'll confirm who's tailing Mini Me after I get to the shop. Jackson and Kate should be home all day, but don't bother them. They'll probably be doing what we did last night. Anywhere in that goddamn house, so don't peek through any windows, and ignore the screaming."

I laughed and shoved him to the door. "You're awful. Go."

He eyed my altar with a little trepidation. "Don't get in trouble."

I motioned to the pile there. "All this? It's meant to keep trouble away."

Bear wasn't convinced. "Well, Skinner or Hickey should stop by later to beef up security. Let them in and don't… hex 'em or anything."

"What if I put a seeing spell on them so they can find answers quicker?"

He winced. "Yeah…no. Skinner might shoot you. Play nice, please?"

I gave it a second or two of thought. "Maybe."

He kissed me again, harder but shorter. When he broke free, he said one word before slipping out the door. "Witch."

"Grumpy-ass Bear." I said to the wall after he drove away. Why was he so infuriating and so damn cute while doing it?

28

BEAR

Jackson was all smiles and looking for me on the one day he could guarantee I was captive to whatever insanity he'd cooked up.

"I hear church on Friday needs a visiting preacher or ten."

The shop was empty. I motioned at it. "You don't have to speak in code." Wolf had one delay after another to get everyone wrangled for the VP vote. But it was happening. The patch had been sitting in Wolf's desk for too long.

"Hagerstown, 'Burgh, and Scranton RSVP'd."

Cool. It would be a hell of a party. On fucking Halloween, too. I smiled. "Is Kate at the club?" They started decorating a week ago and still weren't done stretching fake spiderwebs all over the place. Rose was beside herself making witchy decorations and finally fitting in.

"Naw, she's back at the house. The fucking cable is out again."

"Hickey never tracked that down?"

Jackson groaned. "This is all new shit."

There went his smile. Damn it. "It'll all be fixed by the time you get back, then you've got…" I checked my clock and grinned, "all of a half hour to fuck her senseless again."

"Takes more than a half hour." Jackson stood a little wider and that smile peeked back out.

I pulled my phone out to text one of the prospects to meet Zoe at her school. Maybe even warn them not to take her directly home.

But it lit up in my hand before I could. I answered.

Skinner was talking too quickly.

"What do you mean, you can't get a hold of Wolf?" I glanced at Jackson, who was not making a secret of listening in. Skinner spat out some more info. It sounded like he said KC had been arrested.

"He's where?" *Fuck.*

I snapped my fingers and quickly relayed what I needed to Jackson while I listened to Skinner. "Write down that lawyer's number—the criminal one, not the fucking estate one."

I had it stored in my phone, but I needed to get Skinner on this right away. "Does KC have an alibi?"

Jackson's eyes widened. He jotted down a number from memory. It figured he'd have that one memorized. We all should. I stuck a pin in that thought and moved back to Skinner's conversation.

"Let me repeat what you said, Jackson's listening. Three minutes ago, you got the post-booking call from KC. He's facing a murder one charge." I glanced at Jackson to see how he'd handle that news.

His mouth tightened. I barely caught the silent, "fuck" he couldn't hold back.

And that was putting it mildly. We were all cooked. There were stipulations with the estate that applied specifically to this situation. The biggest were the morality clauses in the contracts that the club agreed to in order to get our hands on that money. No felonies. By any member.

We'd been relying on a silent addendum of '*They have to catch us and convict us first*' to every action since. Because not even the fear of losing millions was enough to stop us from being Destroyers. Or in this case, an idiot. I passed the number Jackson gave me to Skinner who had to be working on his laptop and his phone because he verified he had the firm on the line.

The next thing I said was worded very carefully because the line wasn't secure. Nor was my shop. "Have you run a roll call yet?" What I really wanted to know was if he'd located Sketch, his girlfriend, Izzy, and probably got them and his kid out of the fucking state. But I didn't dare say anything close to that over the phone.

Skinner said he'd send a thread out.

Sure as shit, my phone displayed the message. "Check me and Jackson off. Kate's at the house. Hickey should be there looking at her cable, but don't count them until you hear from them." I sent Jackson a tip of the head to make sure of that before anything else. "Pop it up and down the line. Use the *full* list. ASAP." That meant everyone, ol' ladies, hookers, prospects, everyone. Jackson got on his phone to check on his family rather than wait.

"What do you mean she doesn't have her cell on her?"

Shit. Jackson's skin had turned that ugly shade of red it got just before he beat the ever-loving shit out of someone. More than once, I'd had to tear him off so he wouldn't kill the unfortunate target of his anger.

I tapped his elbow carefully to ground him and silently ask, *who?*

"Zoe. Fucking school makes 'em lock up their damn phones." He turned back to the call with Kate. "Tell me you sent someone there in person to pick her up."

While I didn't hear her reply, I did see the dagger-stare Jackson sent in my direction. "And who's on her?"

No. Fuck *no.* Hammer was supposed to be with Rose. I quickly texted him, demanding his twenty.

Lake. Lockdown. Smoke n Sprout hdng here fr job site.

That meant at least two ol' ladies were under his care already. I sent a thumbs up to his message and waited while Jackson gave orders to Hickey to keep his wife safe.

That done, he kept the phone in hand. The black mirrored surface felt like a pit.

"Rose is on Zoe?" I asked carefully.

"If it's any consolation, they're both armed."

If Zoe couldn't keep her phone on her at school, there was no way she'd be able to bring her handgun in. "Where's Zoe's gun?"

He grimaced, realizing what I had. "Probably locked in her glove box."

I didn't have to roll my eyes to let Jackson know what kind of stupid place that was for it.

"She'll be fine."

Jackson didn't fire off platitudes recklessly. So, I dissected the disassociated way he spoke. He was telling himself that lie, not me.

"Ride with me. We're going to go make sure of that."

Our bikes waited outside. Jackson took lead, breaking laws to get to the school as fast as he could. I shadowed him, head on swivel so we wouldn't get busted.

About three blocks away, my efforts weren't enough. A cop pulled out from his blind all lit up. I gunned my bike to jump ahead of Jackson so I could tap my head, then downshifted fast so the cop would nab me, not him.

But that idiot circled around to join me.

Jackson smiled nicely and took the blame. Bear was just keeping up, officer. Give me the ticket, not him. I glared at my boss the whole time, not daring to say anything lest we get arrested on top of everything else.

Two tickets and twenty minutes later we pulled into the school lot. It was empty. My phone had been buzzing on my hip the entire time. I pulled it out and checked the messages from Rose.

"They're at the junkyard."

Jackson looked confused. "Why not home?"

I held up a finger and dialed Rose.

"Bear! Oh, thank the Goddess. Are you okay?" Her breathy, rapid-fire words barely registered.

"Is Zoe with you?"

"Yes, we're fine." I heard Zoe in the background say something.

"Tell her to call her dad, *now*."

Jackson's phone rang within seconds. "Baby girl, tell me something good," he answered.

I breathed out a quick thank you to the gods. To Rose I said,

"Stay there. I'll bring Jackson in. And if you could, please find out where Griz is? Let him know I'm on Jackson, and he should confirm Wolf's twenty."

"No shit?" Jackson's tone caught my attention. So did his laughter. "No, you can't have a shot until I get there, do you hear me?"

Zoe's "Da—ad" echoed through my speaker. "Why does Zoe want a drink?" I asked Rose.

"It's not that, and it's complicated, you might want to hear this in person."

With that cryptic warning, Jackson signaled I needed to end the call and get moving.

"What's going on?" I asked him before he could pull away.

"We get to kick some ass." His smile wasn't creepy at all. At least, that's what I told myself.

A tow truck—not one of ours—sat outside the club. Attached to it was Zoe's car. Next to them was my SUV.

Jackson took his time to walk around the vehicles to inspect for damage. His brows were down, casting his eyes into shadow. With the precision he carried himself, and the glowering seriousness of his expression, I knew he plotted murder.

Bad timing for it.

Then again, if the club was going down, maybe it was the perfect time to show everyone why we earned the moniker, "Destroyers."

I peeked into the cab of the tow truck out of curiosity more than anything else. No sooner than I did, I smacked Jackson's arm as he paced another slow circuit around the vehicles. "Check it out, blood."

His face flushed red and his eyes met mine. "That better be his because if it's not…"

"Boss?"

"What?!" He was at the end of his leash and ready to snap free at any second.

I kept my voice low. "If it isn't his, I think everyone would want a piece. I know I would appreciate at least one bite."

His body shook with rage. "We'll see.

He practically ripped the screen door off its hinges, then kicked more than opened the door as he powered into the club. The rumble of voices cut short.

Near the entrance, Baldy and Coop flanked a greasy pig of a human who wore filthy overalls, a squalid T-shirt yellowed by dirt and sweat, and mud-caked work boots. Blood dripped from the towel he had pressed to his neck, and more of it stained his clothing rust-red.

Zoe raced to her father with a high-pitched, "Daddy!" Her momentum practically took him down but he recovered quickly to put her at arms-length and check for damage. Seeing none, he smiled.

"May I please get my gun out of the car? Please, Daddy?"

He shot a glance at the bleeding man. "Give me a minute to catch up first."

"Who cut him?" I interjected, because that was important.

Rose stepped forward. Unlike Zoe, she did have blood on her hands and clothes. "I did."

My head went a little fuzzy.

Before I thought to blink, she was standing in front of me, holding out the athame I'd given her. "Long story, but he had Zoe's car attached to his truck when I got to the school to wait for her. I tried to make him unhook it but, well, eventually had to force him to see things my way."

I snatched the weapon from her hand and inspected the blade to make sure she'd cleaned it before sheathing it. There was a little residue near the pommel. I pulled out my bandana to clean it off.

Meanwhile, Jackson set Zoe to the side, drew his gun, and confronted the tow truck driver. "Before I kill you, do you have anything to say in your defense?" He was maybe a dozen words away from pulling the trigger.

I tipped my head to have Coop and Baldy stand clear of the splatter zone.

"I'd gotten a call." His defense was weak even to his ears.

"From who?" Jackson may have sounded calm, but he was far from it.

The driver licked his lips, preparing to fabricate a lie. His eyes shifted to my left where Rose stood.

She leaned in and whispered to me, "From Carl."

While that wasn't news to the driver, he had the good sense to look down and piss his pants.

"Gross," Zoe observed.

Jackson addressed his daughter, "Baby girl, if I had a dollar for every time some fucking moron pissed his pants in front of me? Well, your college tuition would be paid for already. Twice." He motioned for the knife in my hand. I passed it off, handle-first to Jackson.

Upon receiving it and inspecting the blade, Jackson shot Rose a look, then pointed it at the guy's throat. "You did that?"

"It was an accident. I was just holding it, and he hit a pot hole."

Like a snake, Jackson spun on the driver. "You had my daughter's car hooked up and you hit a fucking pot hole!"

As if that were the crime here. I snickered.

The man held both hands in the air. With the bloody towel pulled away, I caught sight of a two-inch wound that oozed blood. That sluggish flow meant nothing too major was nicked, but it had been deep enough to warrant at least a pint or maybe more. Fin was right, Rose's blade was bloodthirsty.

I almost had a mind to warn Jackson to be careful with it. Then again, a good blooding needed more than a pint to satiate a truly dangerous blade.

"Please don't kill me. I've got a family…a daughter, l-like yours."

Wrong thing to say. Ain't no one had a daughter like Jackson's.

My boss held the knife out, point-first, directly in front of that fucker's chest. "Where does this daughter live?"

His chin wobbled as he spoke. "I-in p-p-Pittsburgh w-with her mother."

Jackson nodded as if pleased by that answer.

"Skinner?" I sent a command with that one word toward the camera on the front door. Skinner had to be either in the war room, or remotely monitoring this shit. My phone buzzed a second or two later with an address. I showed it to Jackson who rattled it off to the driver.

He collapsed to the floor, begging us to not kill his daughter. He went as far as to touch Jackson's boots.

That wouldn't fly. I'd been on Jackson's protection detail long enough that I didn't think before I kicked him in the ribs and followed up with a stomp to the head. Blood flowed from the split in his scalp where I'd scraped my tread down hard. He curled up into a moaning ball of piss and blood. Between sobs, he pleaded for his life.

I almost took my gun out to end this bullshit. But that was too easy for him.

Instead, I checked Rose's hands once more. Then her arms.

There were fresh bruises on them. "Who did this?"

Her eyes dipped to the piece of shit on the floor.

"Did he touch Zoe?" I whispered that, because Jackson didn't need to hear this yet. It would drive this fiasco from fatherly anger right into first degree felony if she told me what I didn't want to hear.

"Just once. That's when I drew the blade."

Zoe had moved closer to Rose during this whole conversation.

"If I could've gotten my gun out of the car, I'd've shot him."

"In the school parking lot?" I had to drill home the risks and consequences of her hot-headedness. "And then what would your father say?"

"What would he say about what?" Jackson had given orders for the man to be tied up so the club could take pot shots at him until we decided what to do with him and the truck in our lot.

"All the cameras, witnesses, and evidence that connects that asshole to Zoe." I was thinking fast. Knowing Jackson had to figure this out for himself, but needed to use his devious, psycho-killer noggin on this one.

If we killed him, that would take us down faster than KC could.

Jackson's jaw was tight. He let out a careful sigh. "This happened right as school got out?" He asked Rose, not Zoe.

Rose nodded. "Dozens of witnesses."

"And they just walked by, ignoring the shit out of things, didn't they?"

Another nod, this time accompanied by a tight frown.

He stared at the knife he'd finally put back into the scabbard. Turned it twice. Then handed it back to her. "Keep this on you at all times. I want you at Fin's at least once a month for lessons on how to use it, how to kill a man with it, and most importantly, how to make sure this never leaves your hand. Got it?"

Rose swallowed and nodded. Her mouth opened but after shooting me a look, it closed.

"You got something to say?" I asked.

"I do."

She kept her eyes on me, rather than asking permission from Jackson. I'd drilled the rules into her head, and my smart little witch remembered them well. "Remember, respect first," I warned.

Rose nodded.

Her back straightened and her chin lifted straight forward. No digging in, no lies. "I arrived at the school just before the bell. As I pulled in, I saw the tow truck, Zoe's car, and I know that man. He's one of Carl's…minions for lack of a better word. He stole my car a month ago when I had a problem with vandalism. I haven't gotten it back because he claims there's been other problems with it." Her face showed her disgust and anger during that pause. But she continued.

"I confronted him. Not only about Zoe's car, but mine."

This time her head tilted a little and her eyes drifted from Jackson's. Then she dug in. I bit my lip to not give her away.

"We were still talking when the students started leaving. Zoe came up and was obviously angry. I tried to get her to ride with me in the SUV, but she didn't want to leave her car."

"My gun was in it." Zoe interrupted. Then tacked on, "Duh."

"We'll talk about *that* later," her father warned.

"Then he grabbed Rose, and I kicked his knee." Zoe obviously wasn't afraid of her father at all.

"And I pulled the knife to force him to drive the car here."

Zoe talked over Rose. "He wanted five hundred dollars to unhook it. That's robbery."

"I rode with him, and Zoe drove Bear's SUV."

"No dents," Zoe fired at me with a glance at my curled fists.

That wasn't what I was angry about. To Rose I muttered, "You got in the cab with him?"

She stared at me with intense focus. "Would you rather it was Zoe?"

Fuck no. But that wasn't the point. "You should have let him take the fucking car." My teeth wouldn't unclench.

"Like hell. Then Dad would've killed him."

Whether Zoe was right or not, it didn't excuse the danger Rose had been in. Knife at his throat or not. She was damn lucky the driver was a fucking idiot who didn't know how to handle danger.

Which reminded me keenly how Rose handled danger. She'd lived with Carl and survived. Whatever haunted her past hadn't killed her. She faced down a man twice, maybe even three times her size and didn't even think about backing down. "You and I need to talk."

My phone buzzed at my hip, giving her a reprieve. I answered it with a gruff, "It's your fucking quarter, talk."

Skinner's voice was loud and clear. "Just heard from KC's lawyer. The charges aren't going to stick. And... you really need to know who they thought he killed."

His voice was a little too gleeful for my patience.

"I ain't got time for games, asshole."

Skinner laughed. "I suppose you don't, but you might wanna let Jackson know KC's going to be released. Ain't no way he killed Fish."

Like a record scratch, my mind went blank. "Fish? He's dead?" Jackson caught the name. I reiterated the word "dead" on my lips so he wouldn't have to wait.

His glance immediately shot to the woman at my side.

29

ROISHIN

Bear dropped me off at the hospital with hurried instructions. "I'll be back by three. KC's arraignment and release shouldn't take that long. Don't leave without me. Don't stand by the doors, find somewhere public to stay, and for fuck's sake, don't get yourself tangled up with any of Carl's bullshit."

Obviously, his dark mood centered around me. Or at the very least, the hell I'd brought to the club. Every day it was something new. From break-ins at their businesses, to deals going wrong, Carl was doing his damnedest to make their life miserable.

Through it all, Bear siloed me from knowing why. Like I hadn't heard the twelve phone calls in the last three days? Or noticed how members greeted him with glee, but barely acknowledged my presence?

Thank goodness Kate hadn't snubbed me yet. In fact, she and her daughter went out of their way to include me in their little circle.

But I knew I didn't belong.

Worse? The clock was ticking down to the day I'd have to leave.

I knew that. Bear knew that.

Hell, all of the Destroyers knew I was gone as of November first.

But oddly, their women thought differently. Their friendship was the one bright point of this entire week. Yet, I still needed Beth. So, I begged Bear to take me to the hospital to see her.

It was bad timing for it. KC's arraignment was today. They'd delayed it twice, keeping him locked up for no reason. The Destroyers and their legal team were livid and threatening to sue.

KC couldn't properly mourn his friend's loss, and was getting blamed for it.

While Bear didn't outright say anything, I knew he stood like a wall between me and the club members blaming me for the situation. And the stress of it showed in his gruff demands.

"I'll be in that waiting room, or the cafeteria down the hall."

His beard shifted with the clench of his jaw. "You got your phone with you?"

I nodded.

But there was no one to call, save Bear. With all the problems and KC in jail, they were stretched thin. Jackson even postponed one of his trips to remain home with his family.

"I'll have mine off while in the courthouse, but…"

"I'll text you messages with updates. I'll be fine."

"I don't like this. Are you sure it can't wait?"

That I was completely certain of. The closest donor the club found didn't match. And searches elsewhere were taking too long. "Tomorrow is Fish's funeral and your Friday club meeting. And her visiting hours on weekends are limited because of how vulnerable she is. And by Monday, I'll be with Carl so—"

"No, you won't."

I didn't want to argue with him here. "He's going to keep causing problems for—"

"You ain't going back."

If only that were true. "You're going to be late for the court appointment. Go."

"Rose…"

"Bear, go. KC needs you. I'm fine here and I'm going to stay fine. Go."

He didn't move.

"Bear?"

"Vow to me that you'll be here when I get back."

I blinked. "What?"

"Vow. On your Goddess. You will be here when I get back. And, you're going to come home with me today."

He was serious. And also displaying a vulnerability I hadn't seen before. I moved close so our bodies touched from thigh to chest. "I vow, on the Goddesses of nature, home, fire, and moonlight that I will be here in this hospital waiting for you. And I vow I will return to your home tonight and any night I physically can until your bargain with Carl is done."

I touched his cheek, above his beard, and very quietly told him, "You're not losing me today."

His shoulders lost some of their tension as he bent. Our noses touched and he waited there for a moment, just connecting with me.

My lips hit his skin, and I trailed kisses up his cheekbone to his forehead. I ended between his brows where his third eye rested. To that spot I sent intent and will to back up my words. *"Because I fucking said so."*

If my words were out loud or not didn't matter. I stared him in the eye and showed him my desire to remain true to my word. "I will be here."

He kissed my lips and nodded.

The air was colder without his presence. Yet the warmth crept back in because I got a whole twenty minutes with Beth. They'd moved her to a room with a sunny southern exposure. Hand-colored pictures of different sizes, skillsets, and types of paper clung to every vertical surface. Even June contributed bright scribbles of pink, blue, green, and purple. They were god-awful, but proof that her children hadn't forgotten her.

"Hey." She slipped her hand into mine.

The shadows under her eyes were worse.

"Gwen is getting pretty good at cursive." I indicated a lovely hand-drawn card she'd made with "Get Well Soon, Mommy" written in carefully bold curves. It stood out against the backdrop of Harry and Arthur's block letters and June's shaky squiggles.

"She is." Beth was quiet, contemplating the wall of pictures. "I started working through my end of life plan."

The pain hit me like a hammer. I had to swallow at least twice to keep my tone positive. I knew this was coming. It shouldn't be such a shock. But it was. "How's John taking it?"

Her lips were tight. "He's in denial."

"Not bartering?" I was well-acquainted with the seven stages of grief. Although, acceptance was my enemy. I'd never accept losing her.

"No, you have that one covered."

Her dart struck home. "I intend to keep bartering until you're better."

Her sad eyes met mine. "Don't."

I didn't want to argue with her, either. "I love you. And you can't give up. I want you fighting every day for one more day."

She'd told me the same thing once.

A sad smile hit her lips. "We've been through some shit, haven't we?"

I nodded.

Beth changed the subject. "How'd you get here?"

"Bear dropped me off. But I'm getting my car back soon." One good thing about the confrontation in front of Zoe's school was that a good ass kicking miraculously saved my car from thousands of dollars of repairs. The tow truck driver agreed to drop it off next week, no charge.

It couldn't be this week while I was still with Bear, though. Funny how I could smell Carl's dirty fingers all over that agreement.

She squeezed my hand. "Take it and get far away. Find a lawyer and have him contact John or his father."

"I'm not leaving you."

"You have to."

My head shook all on its own. "I can't. And I won't. We're in this together. No take-backsies."

Her throat worked and triggered a coughing fit. I held her upright so she could sip some water. When she finally recovered enough to talk, she asked, "You're not going to listen to me, are you?"

"Not on this."

"But…"

"I'm not. You know you created a monster when you told me to get stubborn. I did. I listened then, and it saved my life. I can't give that up, and I won't ever. Now, I'm telling you to get stubborn."

Her lips turned up. "A monster. That's funny."

"Damn straight it is." The monster and the angel—that was us.

The smile didn't leave her face like it normally did. "That's why you like Bear."

She hit the truth there. It burst over me like a beam of sunlight in my soul, I brightened with joy. "He's the right kind of monster for me."

"Then grab onto him. With both hands and don't let go."

I wish I could. The silent thought flashed through my head before I could stop it. I smiled so it wouldn't show on my face. In case it did, I made sure to warn Beth not to get her hopes up for me. "He's not the kind who would be happy in a cage."

"Love isn't a cage."

No, it was torture. Loss. Pain. Anger. All masked under a polite facade. Unless you stripped away the falsity and embraced the ugliness of it.

Maybe that was my way to reach acceptance?

I'd stripped away at myself, at the raw nature of the beast inside me, and Beth still let me sit at her side. That was love.

And it was beautiful. "You're going to make me cry."

"We can't have that." Her laugh was weak.

"Nope." I took a breath. "When you get better this time, and the doctors release you from this place. Where are you going to go on vacation?"

This was something I'd done for her before. Plans, hopes, dreams…

"Disney World."

Ugh. *How about nope?* "With the kids?"

"Of course."

"Woman, you need better dreams."

"Oh, come on, they'd love it. And you'll come with us. They have a whole haunted mansion and the Tower of Terror and pirates… I bet Bear would fit right in."

"Pirates." I smiled. "Could you imagine a six-foot-something biker with piercings standing next to the park version of Jack Sparrow?" I could. Bear's beard and piercings would outstrip the fake ones any day.

"John said your man is quite scary."

"Only on days that end in 'y'."

She laughed. "Tell me about him."

I did. From the latest bobbin of bone wrapped in his beard to the size of his feet.

She stuck her tongue out at that. "We need to put his boots next to John's." A euphemism we'd discussed at length. Great length.

"Bear's bigger."

"You don't know that."

"Naw, but I bet I can talk him into stripping naked in front of you and John to prove I'm right."

Her shy smile meant she wasn't convinced. Then she pulled the trump card. "There's a reason I have four kids."

I held up my hands in defeat. "You win."

"You're just letting me win because I can't kick your ass right now."

Busted. "Well, you just have to get better. Then we'll see." With that challenge in place, I felt a lot more hopeful leaving her. We both knew Carl needed a nudge to do the right thing. But maybe there was still hope in finding a different donor, if she'd just dig in and stay alive long enough.

That plagued my thoughts as I sipped horrible coffee and waited for Bear to return.

"No bodyguards today?"

Carl slipped into the chair next to mine.

I set the cold cup down so I wouldn't spill it. "What are you doing here?"

He chuckled. "Following you."

That wasn't creepy at all…right? "Nice to see you care."

His grin deepened. "You know I don't."

I turned to face him. "Then why go through all this?"

There was a glitter of light that danced across the shadows of his eyes. "Because it brings me so much joy to see you sad."

"I think that's the first honest thing you've said to me."

"Don't get used to it." His eyes dipped to my clothing. "Harlot."

"Murderer."

Another grin. "It takes one to know one."

"How'd you kill Fish?" I could use that information to bring justice to the world. Maybe in prison he wouldn't have a choice whether to donate bone marrow or not.

His finger went up and wagged from side to side. "You don't get my secrets anymore, Mary-Rose."

I leaned back. "No? A shame. This conversation's going to be *so* short."

That made his eyes narrow as he tried to see through me. Then he leaned forward. "Did you know Beth has me banned from the visitor list? Her own donor can't see her to wish her well."

"You're not going to donate again."

"You and I know that. But the doctors don't. They're prepping me." He tipped his head as if to say, *See? I can play this game better.*

"When's your last shot?" They came in a series of daily doses. And if I could time a quick murder with his last dose, maybe…

"Monday. And I expect you to be with me for that one."

I saw the game clearly. "Not sooner?" Hopefully, he'd say no just to spite me.

His face twitched as he adjusted his plan. "*Yes.* Sooner.

Tomorrow in fact. Unless you want to come with me now and save *everyone* the grief."

"I can't go with you today. I promised I wouldn't."

There was a moment his face flushed red, but he remained infuriatingly calm in expression. "Tomorrow then."

"I can't tomorrow, that's a day early. You made a bargain. That's almost like making a vow."

He scanned the cafeteria for anyone paying attention. No one was. That emboldened him. "Did you know that two members of the Destroyers own houses on a public lake? It would be so easy for an early boater to pull out a sniper rifle and shoot that pregnant woman dead when she goes out to drink her morning tea.

Surely Sprout figured that out already. If not, I'd warn him as soon as I talked to Bear.

"Or the other one? The pretty dark-haired one? She's vulnerable every time she stops in front of the gate. It takes two seconds to register her car on the sensor. That's two seconds too many. And she's such a trusting soul. Or maybe I'll just go to Philadelphia and kill her sister. Lily is *all alone* there."

Carl didn't expect my reply. He motioned to the hospital around us. "And that old broad. The mom? She's a target every time she takes an emergency room shift. I don't even have to be there. I can pull in a favor. She'd be dead that very night. And you are already aware of how easy it is to get to Zoe. They can't watch everyone all at once."

He was right, there were too many variables to cover everyone. But he hadn't factored in the Destroyers' propensity for violence. I'd witnessed firsthand how quickly that escalated. Even Zoe was a party to it.

"How long do you think they'd let you live if you took one of their women out?"

"They let the tow truck driver live." He laughed. That drew attention because most of the people in here had seen so much sorrow, laughter was almost foreign. But with the clean-cut image he portrayed, and his easy smiles at the curious, they buried themselves back into their self-imposed misery to avoid thinking about joy.

"They are so worried about losing their millions, they're slipping. They've become the establishment and are *shackled* by it."

The sheer relish he put into that word sent skitters up my spine.

"Zoe was just a warning. Tomorrow, Rose. Come back to me before the sun sets, or someone else becomes a martyr on your altar of defiance." He stood up and leaned in for a parting shot, "I almost forgot, Happy Halloween."

30

———

BEAR

"I'm staying home. KC won't want me there."

Rose's words echoed in my head. She was wrong, dead wrong. When I showed up to the Friday mid-day funeral alone, KC noticed. His haunted eyes tracked the empty space to my right.

Finally, he worked up the nerve to ask me about her. "Was it your idea or hers?"

"Hers," I said bitterly. She cared more about other people's feelings than mine. Sprout's, Smoke's…even KC got more consideration than I did.

He chewed on his lip. "Sorry, man."

I snaked an arm around his shoulders and pulled him close. "Don't fucking be sorry. Fish was your bro. If anyone's got reason to be sorry, it's fucking Carl. He's going to regret this." And he'd get to that state. I vowed it.

KC leaned in and slapped my side to tap out of the PDA. "When you get that figured out, I want in."

"Absolutely."

He shuffled his feet and looked at the carpet. "That is, if you'll hang with me?"

His reluctance confused me. "What are you saying?"

KC glanced around. There were several people in dress clothes, the discount store version, but much more "formal" than we were in our Destroyers vests. They didn't understand that us wearing that symbol to Fish's funeral was an honor of the highest order.

"I might pull my membership."

I smacked the back of his head. The action causing several people to gape and whisper about us. I flipped the finger at the worst offenders, who quickly pretended they hadn't been nosy. "What the fuck are you talking about?" I tugged him close. "You need brothers now more than ever."

A hitch caught his breath, and he shook his head. "I don't think I can handle it. I just… This is fucked up."

No shit.

"The lawyer get back to you?"

He nodded. "They've cleared me completely."

I squeezed his shoulder. "Get drunk. Really fucking drunk. Don't worry about that shit, and just grieve. Okay?"

KC wasn't listening. He stared at the casket sitting all by itself on the other side of the room. It was as if no one had the balls to approach Fish's corpse. I tugged on his shirt and pulled him to the casket. I laid a hand on the wood and knocked three times. *For luck?*

The noise triggered a gasp from the bystanders. The room quieted and I swear some of them held their breath.

I waited long enough to let the silence get uncomfortable. "See? Dead. He ain't Jesus folks."

KC snorted. "You asshole." His laughter quickly turned into sobs. I held him up as he draped over Fish's coffin and poured out his pain. To everyone else, I shot the evil eye. If any one of those dicks got too close, I shifted a foot and clenched my fist. Even going as far as raising it once.

When KC finally got his shit together, he used his bandana to wipe his face and blow his nose hard. "I needed that."

He slapped my side, letting me know we were good.

After the funeral I rode with him to the club, poured him a glass of my private stock and left the bottle on the bar beside it.

Brothers approached him one at a time. Each one taking time to sit next to him. Offer an ear, slap his patch, or pour a fresh glass.

The mood was somber for a Friday. On everyone's mind was the upcoming meeting, but not a single person mentioned it. The clock was ticking, though.

I turned to Wolf. "I gotta go pick up Rose."

"You got two hours. Don't be late."

I laughed. "Don't start without me." The humor died too quickly. "You know? We don't have to do this tonight. I can wait."

"The club can't. It needs to get done."

I shook my head and looked at Fish. "Bad timing."

He scratched the scruff on his face and then gestured around the room. Plastic spiders hung from webbing the women had strung around each rafter. Orange and black streamers decorated the shelves of the bar. There were carved Jack-o-lanterns everywhere. Even decorated gourds and a random turnip troll or five. Rose's doing.

"It's Halloween night. The perfect time for *you* to take your rightful place."

My spine tingled. Tomorrow Carl would demand I give Rose back.

And for demanding that, I'd kill him.

"I think it should wait." I had a murder to plan. One that could take the club down if I was an officer. The cops sometimes looked no further than the source when it was just a member, but as a deci-sion-maker? That was a fast escalation to RICO charges.

Wolf shook his head. "Get your woman. This isn't waiting."

It took at least ten minutes to get out the door. Everyone wanted a piece of me today. My phone buzzed so often, I'd silenced it. I scrolled through the messages.

One number stood out. I'd memorized it almost a month ago, but I'd never dialed it.

"What's up?"

"Can we meet? I'm ready to talk."

I blurted out an address between the club and my house. It was for the park where I'd first seen Rose standing on that pier. But the last pylon was gone now. I pulled up next to John's truck. He'd parked in almost the same spot Rose had parked Carl's sports car.

I barely recognized John.

The last time I'd seen him, he was in a clean button-down dress shirt and khakis. Today, he wore dirty jeans caked in drywall dust and an insulated flannel overshirt that might have been brightly-colored at one point, but was almost as weathered as his jeans.

He approached my bike with a tired grin and a pending handshake.

"I got places to be, man," I ignored his outstretched hand.

"This is important. It's about Rose's past."

Fuck. I needed this information two weeks ago. My girl was cagey enough to keep her secrets quiet.

"What prompted the change of heart?" I shut my bike off and balanced it between my legs.

"Beth was moved to the ICU last night."

The shadows under his eyes told me he hadn't slept. "Your wife's in intensive care, and you went to work?"

He frowned. "Had to. I've used up my leave. And they're being assholes about it."

With four mouths to feed and a terminally ill wife, that wasn't the word I'd use. But I wasn't here for his sob story. "I have a half an hour, max. Get cracking."

John glanced around. "Some of this is pretty bad. Fair warning."

My fingertips drumming on my new flush mount gas cap filled the pause.

He glanced down and noted my visible impatience. "Right. Back before I met Beth, I think it was even before Rose and Beth knew each other, the church needed farmland to build their planned mega church on.

"They put the call out to the membership for donations. One family, Rose's, was pretty committed to making a name for them-selves, and put up the family farm."

That was news. I knew her parents were out of the picture, but I could finally see where the seeds for the split got planted.

"But it wasn't theirs."

"Lemme guess, it was Rose's?"

John grimaced. "Not exactly. The land was her grandmother's property. Her 'amma' wasn't keen on selling. So, she went to a lawyer to move the land into a trust for Rose if she died."

That was a smart move on her part.

"But it didn't work." He held up a hand to stop my interruption. "I don't know the particulars, but Rose's grandmother died about a week later, and no one mentioned that she'd filed the paperwork. So, the deed transfer went on. And the church jumped on groundbreaking almost immediately.

"Then it went to court." John's disgust was evident. "That's when it got complicated. Rose was way too young to make decisions, and she was influenced by her parents and the people of the church. I think that's how it all started. But it got worse."

Of course it did. "I don't have all day. What was this *it* that got started?"

"I'll explain, but you need to know this part because what happened *after* is related. The church board covered up their knowledge of the trust even though her lawyer went to the church's board. And since Rose's parents weren't fighting it, the lawyers for both parties swept it under the rug. And that became a habit." He made a face that was part disgust and part concern. "To influence Rose, her parents put her in special classes with one of the deacons who helped with the cover-up. He used their crime of stealing Rose's inheritance to keep them quiet about his...proclivities."

My stomach twisted. "Proclivities?"

John was solemn. "He singled out Rose. Groomed her."

The sourness churning in my gut intensified. I didn't want to know this part. I really didn't.

"Rose and Beth were friends by that point, and Beth suspected something was wrong. She went to her parents."

"And?"

John shrugged. "I don't know. Beth doesn't know why either, but she says the abuse didn't stop. I knew both of them by this point, and while Rose was odd, she was, for the most part, nice, kind. The type of girl who didn't make trouble. But Beth wouldn't let it go. She went to her brother."

Carl?

He must have seen the disbelief on my face.

"He helped, I guess. He…" John made a noise that wasn't natural. "Carl convinced Rose to videotape it."

Everything I knew about Carl tracked with that. "Lemme guess, he got to see it first."

John rolled his eyes. "I wouldn't bet against you on that."

He shook his head and continued.

"The evidence went to court. But since it wasn't clear that Rose didn't instigate it, the deacon got probation."

"You've got to be fucking kidding me. How old was she?"

There was fear in John's eyes. He studied my clenched fists. Eventually, he found his balls and stumbled on. "Twelve. Because of that, Carl and Rose got—I wouldn't say, 'close' because it was really twisted. But they were as thick as thieves for a while. And, uh… within a year they'd gathered enough additional evidence and ammunition to quite literally bury her abuser."

"Literally?" I scoffed at his word choice.

"The church building had to be put on hold because the issue with the trust was exposed. Her parents were exposed. The entire church board was exposed. That's when the former leaders stepped down and Carl's parents took over almost exclusively. They were fired up, using the leverage they had against the deacon and his faction of the board to approve the change in leadership. And it still didn't help Rose at all."

"Was that while Rose fostered with them?"

John searched his memories. "It was about that time. Her parents were brought up on charges for fraud. She was going to be a ward of the state, but… the judge thought she'd have a more consistent childhood with Beth's family. And she probably could have, if it weren't for Carl. He talked her into luring that asshole to the construction site. I think they killed him."

"I heard it was an accident."

John fired back the rebuttal evident in his scowl. "Carl was involved. I highly doubt it was an accident."

"How old was she then?"

"Almost fourteen."

Forget my gut. My heart hurt for her. "Is that when she went into the foster system?"

"Yeah. The investigation into the death prompted it. Apparently, Beth told her to tell the court adjudicator everything. I don't think she did, because Carl walked away Scott-free, and Beth's parents didn't get any blowback."

"And the church?"

John's shoulders lifted as if he was going to shrug but knew that wasn't the right response. "They had to find another building site. The congregation didn't want their building on a spot where two people died."

"Two?"

John held up a finger. "I forgot that part. Her grandmother was found dead there. Everyone thought it was natural causes at the time. They'd even planned a garden for her in memory."

"But with the deacon obviously murdered, that put a big question mark on things, didn't it." *Good riddance to bad news*, I thought.

"Well, I wouldn't say it was *obvious* murder, but there were enough questions to get the courts looking at Rose's life with a sharper lens."

"What happened to the land?"

"Rose sold it to the church when she turned eighteen and used the money for therapy and college."

"And Beth?"

"She stood by her the whole time, even through her first bout with cancer."

No wonder Rose put herself in this situation.

"Bear?" John broke my train of thoughts.

"What?"

"Beth asked me, no… told me that her dying wish is that you know everything about Rose so you can stop her from going back to Carl." Tears collected in his eyes. "Beth's dying. And—" his voice broke. He coughed to clear his throat before continuing. "And instead of letting Rose con her brother into saving her life, Beth asked me to beg you to save Rose's."

"But—"

"I know, my wife will die."

"And you're *okay* with that?" I wouldn't be if it were my wife. If it were Rose. I blinked, shocked as all hell that I'd gone there.

John studied his toes. "If Rose goes back to Carl, he'll kill her. I'm sure of that. And if Rose dies, Beth will, too. They're too close for one of them to survive if the other doesn't."

John made certain his next words were clear and looked me square in the eye as he spoke. "I'm telling you this to save my wife. The cancer could kill Beth tomorrow or in a month, but a broken heart? That will kill her faster."

His abrupt departure left me reeling.

I barely could breathe, let alone gather my emotions and thoughts into a coherent whole. John's life was falling apart, and he dumped this shit on my plate.

I drove home replaying the echoes of dead conversations in my mind.

"The cancer could kill Beth tomorrow."

"I'm not stupid. It's right after Halloween."

"It's the day to celebrate the martyrs!"

Above my head, the sky turned turbulent. As if the Gods' mood matched my own. I parked the bike inside the garage out of habit. The locked garage door snapped my attention to the present. I'd collect Rose, whether she wanted to come with me or not. We'd take the bike, hopefully dodging the impending rain, and get stuck at the clubhouse the entire night.

Tomorrow, I'd shut her inside Wolf's office and put two prospects on her as guard.

Then I'd kill Carl.

With that plan firmly in place, I unlocked the door.

My first instinct was to search for Rose. But she stood in the center of the room. As if she'd been waiting for me.

Her backpack was in her hand.

"Cool, you're ready. Let's go."

"I'm not going with you."

John's pleas echoed in my head on repeat. "Not an option."

Rose's face darkened. "Are you telling me what to do?"

"Damn straight I am. Come on. I'm going to be late for church."

Her jaw worked. "Church," she repeated.

"Yeah. Biker church. The best fucking kind of church and the only kind I'm ever going to force down your throat, got it?"

A flash of anger lit her eyes and tightened in her jawline. "No."

"Fine. We'll take the truck and I'll carry your damn ass to it."

She whipped out her dagger and held it like she knew what she was doing. I hesitated.

"Put that away."

"No."

"Beth's in the ICU," I blurted, trying to appeal to her softer side.

"Why do you think I'm doing this?" Her reply was short.

31

ROISHIN

"Don't do this, Rose. Beth doesn't want you to be a martyr."

There was no note of pleading in Bear's tone. Only a firm denial of what was inevitable. But that didn't hurt as badly as the smothering, strangling grasp that clutched at my heart. I didn't want to leave, didn't he see that? I *had* to.

Carl had backed me into too tight of a corner.

"Don't tell me what to do. And I don't plan on dying." I planned to kill him before that happened.

Bear roared in frustration and flailed his arms, but avoided me by rushing to the farthest side of the room. When his outburst ceased, he fired back at me, "You're *not* going to Carl."

On the contrary, I was. I'd only waited until he arrived to tell him myself. "I have to. The stem cell therapy didn't work. The match your club found fell through. I need to make sure Carl donates his bone marrow." *…And leaves your club and their women alone.*

Bear's nostrils flared. His face flushed red. "Do you know who I was talking to a few minutes ago?"

"Let me guess, John?" He'd called me right after I hung up on Carl.

"Yes, John."

I sucked in a breath. "No matter what he said, you don't have the full story."

"I know you and Carl murdered a man."

Maybe he did have the full story? Or at least as much as Beth suspected and told her husband. "Then you realize I have leverage on him."

"You don't have jack shit on Carl. What you do have is an almost two decades old cold case he could weasel out of and blame solely on *you*!"

He'd raised his voice.

"I didn't act alone."

Bear's breaths sucked in too quickly and his hands clenched tightly. I took a step back. Without thinking, I cast a sigil into the air for protection.

His focus homed in on my sudden movement. "I'm not fucking Carl."

Tell that to my shaking body.

Or, that part of me that was nine years old and locked in a room with a predator. "I am not that person anymore. I refuse to be influenced by past wrongs." I repeated the mantra under my breath.

"Rose? Are you even listening to me?"

His clenched fists were huge. Had I noticed that before? "I'm trying, but listening goes both ways, buddy."

His eyes flashed, but he changed tactics. "Don't 'buddy' me. We're meant to be together, I'm yours, Rose."

I waited for him to follow that up with, "You're mine." Even unsaid, it echoed in the air. I panted in the silence. It took a small eternity to meet his eyes. "I'm *not* yours."

His jaw tightened, shifting his beard with it. "I'm seeing that."

Animosity glittered in his eyes.

He chewed on his words, settling on, "I'm yours. I'm on *your* side, in *your* camp. Work with me here. Please?"

And deliver him to Carl? *Never.*

He must have seen my denial as I thought it. "I love you. Beth loves you. Don't *do* this."

"Carl…needs to die." After his last shot.

"We'll do that, together. Us. You don't have to do this alone."

Why did he have to say it that way? It was too close to the argument Carl used to manipulate me.

"*You* don't have to do this at all. Vow or otherwise, it's not your battle."

His lips turned white as he held in whatever he was thinking. His hoarse whisper hurt. "But I love you."

"Beth loved me first. She didn't have to. She could have given up on me like everyone else. It cost her a lot to stick by me when everyone thought I was evil and shipped me off to be a ward of the state. And I *owe* her for that." I motioned to the distance between Bear and me. "This thing with us, it was always supposed to be temporary. Don't you see? Carl *knew* your weaknesses. He *knows* mine. He understood all along that the best way to torture us both was to let us be together." It was so clear in hindsight. The worst way he could have hurt me was by giving me hope.

Not just hope, what I always wanted. Love, a home, friends, acceptance. I dug into my backpack and pulled out the stack of money I'd stolen. I'd planned to use it to placate Carl temporarily, but Bear needed it more.

"Here. There's twenty thousand, five hundred and eighty-five dollars in this bundle. I've counted it at least a dozen times. You can keep it or give it to Wolf. It's Carl's so, technically, you've been paid off."

He stared at my hand. "I don't want the money, I want you… I want you safe, Rose. Not stupidly walking right into a psychopath's trap. Please? If not for me, do it for Beth."

"I'm doing this for you *and* for Beth. And for everyone Carl could target around your club. Do you think Zoe and Fish were the end of it? He's just getting started. If I don't go back, someone else will die. But if I leave? That all stops. Don't you see that?

"No one is going to miss *me*. No one ever has. Not my parents, not the foster system, not even my jobs. I'm completely replaceable. But in this, I make up for a lifetime of anger." I set the cash down on his altar and continued to counter the arguments written on his face.

"You're *not* replaceable. Your friends, they need your leadership. You can always get another woman to warm your bed or play backpack. But you need to live. Beth needs to live. She's got kids. A husband, a life that needs her." I broke down, unable to continue. The things she had, I envied them. I wanted at least *one* person to need me.

But even if Bear *wanted* me, he truly didn't *need* me. In that, Carl actually had him beat. Carl needed an outlet for his madness. I served that end well. And maybe in doing so, I could do one small thing to help an innocent mother with everything to live for. Beth was a gentle soul who'd proven over and over again that she was the best of us. Her children shouldn't have to suffer or be alone. Not when there was an obvious solution.

Bear's shoulders drooped as he stared at the pile of cash next to his figurine of Thor. "You're not replaceable. You are a warrior-goddess, a spark—the fires of midsummer when the night is darkest. You're my North Star, Rose."

"Then trust me. If I'm all that, I'll survive this, maybe even triumph." Even if I didn't have hope, I could give it away.

Yet, given so falsely, it was worthless. And Bear saw through me.

"Even if you did survive, would you be the same? Do you think Carl would let you just come back? He wants you broken."

I didn't reply. I wouldn't lie to him.

He sighed. "You're right. I can't tell you what to do. It's fucking useless trying to change your mind. You're twisted, Rose. Carl did that to you, and you're blind that you can't see it." He swallowed and straightened to his full height. "I have pride. I'm a warrior. And you've disarmed me."

He laid a hand on Thor. "I vow—"

"Don't," I warned him not to make foolish vows.

He glared at me. "I vow, by my Gods, if you walk away from me to help Carl, you will be my enemy. Just like he is my enemy."

So mote it be. I didn't plan on helping him. I planned to kill him.

I tore the besom from its hook above the door. As it swung

down, I brushed the threshold with the tips, wiping away all traces of the protection spell I'd put on the house as my home.

Tingles started down my arm. In the backswing, I whispered a blessing. One on his house, his life, his friends, and anyone who crossed over the step of his home in peace.

The final stroke, a magical number in the third position, I cursed any being who would try to harm him, and *him alone*. The bristles of my broom stilled and I dropped it in place.

Even if the door hung open forever, nothing would cross that boundary without feeling my curse clinging to its essence.

Bear must have sensed the spell because he didn't cross the threshold. But he watched me walk away. His eyes followed my progress until I turned right at the end of his street and continued my journey.

An hour later, Carl stopped his truck in my path.

"Are you going to walk the entire way to Harrisburg?"

If I have to.

I remained mute.

He swore and shoved the vehicle into park. Then he jumped out of the truck and opened the passenger door. He stood by it, patiently waiting for me to acknowledge him.

I didn't even have to look to see him. His aura was a murky purplish black. And dark gray like soot. Marbled through the cracks in his essence were crimson streaks mimicking blood, but decaying rapidly into dusty tendrils of death. It was wrong, deeply wrong.

His aura had settled. The swirling madness of varying colors ceased, replaced by a fixed solidity. I peered at his face for clues.

"Do you have my money?" he asked.

"I gave it to Bear. That's what you wanted, isn't it?" In the subtext, I let him see how that act had broken me. Taken my hope and destroyed any future I'd imagined.

But he hadn't broken my will. If anything, it was as solid and fixed as his. We were two unbendable beings trapped in a mortal battle on a spiritual plane. One of us would die soon. The miasma of that fate clung to the air between us.

Strangely, it didn't frighten me. Nor did it thrill me. It was just…

inevitable. Like the tides, the seasons, the sun rising and setting. It was a thing carved into the bones of the earth. We'd formed that entity, and it doomed us both.

Carl's grin spread warily. "How did he react?"

My eyes struck his. "Badly," I said, my heart dead to the pain raging inside.

The grin disappeared, but the satisfaction in his eyes did not. "Get in. We're going to visit Beth."

"No hair shirt this time?"

The corner of his mouth flicked upward. "You're already wearing it."

His laugh was not comforting.

I buckled the seatbelt and ignored him.

Carl prattled as he drove. "I hope you don't mind if we stop at my house first? You're not dressed to visit."

"I'm dressed just fine. Beth has seen me like this." I was in black from head to toe. Betty Jo's tight bodice held me stiff when I wanted to collapse from the weight of it all.

"Mom hasn't."

I fired back, "Like I give a shit what she thinks."

Carl's fist hit the side of my head too quickly to counter. Blood trickled from my brow where the force of it broke my skin. I blotted at it with my sleeve. "What the fuck is wrong with you? Your dad's going to have a fit when he sees me like this."

He slowed the truck down and pulled to the side of the road. I grabbed for the door handle, readying to jump out, but the seatbelt slowed me down. Carl pounded on my head and hit my arms as I tried to defend myself.

Somewhere in that beating, I blacked out.

I came to, but my left eye was swollen shut and my right was blurry. I saw a lot of leaves, trees, and the darkness of wooded land, not the urban decay of Harrisburg.

My mouth fared much worse than my eyes. The swelling around my lips and the slow tickle of blood dripping down my chin was the first indication he'd beaten me even after I'd fallen unconscious. It hurt to move my jaw, so I stayed still and mute as I blinked at the grayish haze in my cyclopean vision.

The truck dipped as he drove off the paved road onto a gravel path. Branches brushed at the truck, scratching it like ragged hag's claws.

Carl hummed as he avoided the worst dips.

I recognized the hymn. The words all too familiar.

Trust and obey,
For there's no other way
To be happy in Jesus,
But to trust and obey.

Cautiously, I walked my fingers along my right thigh where Carl couldn't see the movement. The straps for my athame were in place, but the weight felt wrong.

"I took your knife. Too bad it's such a cursed thing. The craftsmanship is exceptional. Did Bear buy that for you?"

I nodded to avoid the pain in my throat.

A small chuckle emanated from Carl. "He was too easy to fool, wasn't he? You played your role masterfully."

"What role?" I rasped out.

"Why, Jezebel. Delilah. The original Eve, holding a poisoned apple and bringing God's Adam low."

If I could bring Carl low…

The hill we stopped on was barren. At first, it was unfamiliar. But in the distance, an oak tree twisted with familiar angles. Just a short walk down the hill from it, turn left at the creek, walk at least a hundred yards further, and when the meadow opened back up, I'd see the ruins of my grandmother's house.

"Why'd you bring me here?"

Carl's eyes lit up. "To finish what I started." He laughed again. "Did you really fall for my story about getting back what was mine? I never wanted that. I only needed access to this place."

My mouth was dry. Despite the efforts to bulldoze over the pit, fill in the scars on the earth, and remake a scene of death and destruction into paradise, the work was in vain. It was as if God himself had cursed the land.

And well he should.

The original foundation for the new church was rubble. The girders and support posts that had been lovingly blessed in a special sanctification ceremony, uprooted and removed. Only the cornerstone wall and its single smooth temporary flagpole remained. Embedded under it was a dedication plaque. It replaced the original one. The newer square of bronze had a name inscribed. Under it, the words, *Humble servant, faithful Deacon, loving father, child of God.*

The only truth in those lines was his position. The power he yielded that made others look away when his sins became too pronounced.

Like the sin of lust.

"Get out."

"No."

He studied me. "Defiant to the end, aren't you? Don't you realize you are doing the one thing that will keep you out of Heaven. You're denying God."

No, I was denying Carl. My Gods were *Goddesses*. They *empowered* women, they didn't rape them. They cherished the sacred connection to the elements and actions of life which we're all part of. They didn't force submission upon the earth and its creatures. "Are you speaking *for* God now?" That was a sin.

He hit me again and again.

32

———

BEAR

There were twenty-two marks carved into the wood by Carl's back door. Two more than when KC commented on them. With a hunch that bordered on clarity, I traced the top mark sitting all by itself.

"The deacon." That's the murder Carl and Rose committed together. It stood apart as if symbolic.

And it likely was. The first murder he'd orchestrated and gotten away with.

Then I traced the three rows of five marks each between that time and the fateful night KC and Sketch chased down the four gangbangers who took Sketch's girl.

Three rows of five. While KC used to drive us nuts by failing to see the obvious, sometimes he saw things we all missed. Like knowing new marks had been added. I didn't doubt him anymore. I traced the last full row of marks that was fresher than the previous three.

KC killed this one. I ran my thumb along the first mark in the row. Then moved to the next mark.

Sketch got that one. Self-defense, but still, we didn't need him getting fingered for the kill, justification or not.

My thumb lingered on the two marks that followed. Mine.

I'd gone to "talk" to the gangbanger KC and Sketch jumped in an alley and let walk away. He wasn't alone, though. His buddy, the fourth member of the squad was with him. I'd beaten confessions out of them both. Their bodies were at least sixty miles away. Maybe someday some curious sort might find their bones. If they dug deep enough.

Each mark told a story. I wondered at the ones between. Who were they? What had they done to warrant being enshrined on Carl's altar.

What bothered me most, Carl took credit for kills that weren't his.

Except for Fish taking up the diagonal. If only I could prove that one, we'd all sleep easier.

And perhaps the line in the last row. It sat all by itself, like the first one. *Rose.* Something whispered her name to me. The mark was faint, as if it wasn't a done deal yet.

I tore the hidden cameras and motion detectors KC and I planted down. Any evidence we'd ever been at Carl's got bagged. I called Skinner to let him know what I was doing.

"Wolf's pissed. Why aren't you here?"

"Carl's setting us up. It's going down tonight." Or tomorrow. Knowing Carl, it would be tomorrow. Which made it strange he wasn't here right now.

Skinner's silence wasn't comforting. "Are you sure?"

I stared at that mark. "Yeah. He's got Rose."

"The fuck, man? When? How'd he grab her? I'm getting my keys."

I stopped him from doing something stupid like leaving before a major meeting. "Sit your ass back down. She went to him all by herself."

The squeak of his rolling chair told me he'd followed orders. "You've got to be shitting me."

I wasn't. It had taken me too damn long to get pissed off enough to move. She'd *gutted* me. Watching her walk out that door almost took me out of the game. I tried to talk myself out of going after her. But then I remembered that KC and I planted shit at Carl's house. That gave me the incentive to come here, if only to protect the club. Because nothing else mattered.

They were all I had left. And even that connection felt empty, as if it had met some previously unknown expiration date and I was just acting out the motions without any meaning behind them. I cared enough to warn Skinner to stay put, but was I leading by example? No. I was doing unauthorized and likely unnecessary dirty work when I was supposed to be basking in a promotion.

The celebration, with all those clubs present, was important. Yet I was making no attempt to rush back.

A big part of my heart was asking, "So what if I was late for the vote?" I rationalized that ambivalence, telling myself that even if my actions here cost me the spot, I'd protect the club with my dying breath. Or, if killing Carl and Rose myself was what it took to keep my brothers out of the crosshairs, then, in the words of that damned woman, *so mote it be*.

Skinner sputtered out a single word. "Why?"

"What?" His question came at me sideways because my head was elsewhere.

"Why the fuck did she leave you? What the fuck did you do?"

"I didn't do anything."

"Oh, you fucking know you did something. You always do something. Did you boss her around or some shit? Did you threaten her again?"

Asshole. "Since when are you on her side?" I was hanging my ass out at Carl's house to protect the club, and he had the nerve to accuse me of causing this bullshit?

"Listen—"

"No."

"See? *That's* why she left your ass. You never fucking listen to anyone. FYI, I'm voting against you for that. We don't need another egomaniac like Jackson in this place."

"I'm not an egomaniac." I wasn't, was I? I listened to all their bullshit.

"When it comes to women, you sure the fuck are. You treat them like objects. I'm surprised it took her this long to wise up."

I stared at the screen of my phone trying to figure out where this was coming from. Skinner droned on about me ordering Rose around. Using Carl's bargain as a reason to force her to stay. Then went as far as saying I deserved to have my ass dumped.

"Go to hell," I told him during a strategic break in his rant.

"Seeing as you're there right now, I don't think there's room. Go find that woman and apologize."

I didn't have time for this. I hung up on his dumb ass and dialed Wolf because like it or not, I *was* running late.

"Where the fuck are you?"

Not him, too. "Covering the club's ass. We left shit at Carl's. And we sure as hell don't need it here anymore."

"And why's that?" His tone was measured, almost accusatory.

I wasn't going to tell him Rose left me. "A bunch of bullshit. I'll be there for the meeting as soon as I can. And tell Sprout that Danielle better keep her pregnant ass off the back deck until I find Carl." *And murder his sorry ass.*

"Where's Rose?"

Fucker. I was beginning to hate the fact Jackson picked Wolf as his successor. He knew me too damn well. But I knew my place, even if I never got rewarded for it. "With him," I begrudgingly admitted.

"Ah."

"*Ah*, nothing. I'll be there as soon as I get this shit secured. Then you all can do that damn vote."

"Don't bother." He hung up on me.

On *me*.

They fucking needed me. Wolf needed me.

No one needs me.

"Not now, Rose."

If I don't go back, someone else will die.

I placed a finger on the very last hash mark. "Yeah. You. And you left me anyway."

It hurt. Maybe Skinner was right. I was the bad guy here.

She's property. Carl's voice echoed in my head. With it, I remembered the evil glint in his eye when he spoke those words.

Property.

You treat women like objects.

Carl only loves himself.

I was a fucking idiot. That's what I missed in all this. Carl wasn't in love with Rose like I thought he was. He considered her property. Something he could loan out and take back at will. Someone who he needed to "break" in order to be perfect. As if Rose didn't have a will of her own, and was for sale. And he was such an…egomaniac —gods Skinner, get out of my head—he thought he could dictate the where and the when of all of it. I dialed John.

"What's the address of that land Rose sold?"

"What are you talking about?" His kids were loud in the background.

"The farm that the church wanted. You said they started to build a church on that land."

He rattled off an address, and I scribbled it onto the palm of my hand.

"Tell me that Rose is with you and safe."

John was as bad as Wolf. "I can't do that."

"You asshole."

More than one child piped up demanding a coin for the swear jar. "Blame that one on me. I'm going to try to find her, okay?"

"You are?"

Was I? *Yes.* Even if she hated me for being a demanding, ego-driven jerk, I'd save her from Carl. I finally answered his question. "Yeah."

He quickly relayed information where the church foundation had been laid, and described where her grandmother's old farm-house was just in case. "I'd guess Carl would choose the church, though."

It sounded like a place he'd choose. I thanked John and ended the call. Then entered the address into my GPS.

Right before I left Carl's, I touched the hammer hanging from the chain around my neck. As I did, I used my thumbnail to dig at that last hashmark as if I could cancel it out by will alone. "Odin, Thor, grant me strength, wisdom, and speed. I need that woman."

The night turned darker and more violent. Wind gusted across the road, pushing me around every time I broke into the open. I fought for each mile.

And the entrance to the property was blocked. It was one of those fancy electronic gates that only worked if you had a transmitter in your vehicle. I had to leave my bike there and slip under the gate to proceed on foot.

My boots slipped on the loose gravel as I ran along the road toward the hill that loomed in the distance. I missed my damn running shoes.

A flash of lightning bounced through the clouds. The distant rumble of thunder followed after a few moments. The wind picked up again, pushing against me.

My feet pounded on the soil. With each stride I drove myself to move faster than I ever had before. Visibility was for shit. Low clouds clung to the valleys as the storm overhead boiled in place. Another bolt flashed behind the clouds, with that meager light I picked out the shape of Carl's truck.

The cab was illuminated by the dome light. While I couldn't see what was going on, I sensed Carl was there. He was digging around for something, but I was too far away to rush up on him. And if I kept moving like I was, he'd be sure to notice me. I slowed down for stealth, crawling along the edges of the road and keeping hidden by the overgrowth of weeds that had taken over the slope.

The light cut off and I heard the soft thud of the door. Within minutes, I finally reached the top of the hill and slipped next to the truck.

I used it for cover to spy on Carl.

And froze.

Rose was strung up like a sacrifice. Naked and limp. Her skin was bruised and, in some places, cut. Blood trickled from a wound on her ribs. It snaked down her body and dripped from her toes.

My knees gave out.

I was too slow. My body had failed me.

33

ROISHIN

The cloudy day was now night, and the sky filled with roiling clouds, vengeful in their turbulence.

In the time I'd been knocked out Carl erected a stack of wooden pallets, sticks, logs, and other detritus. The odor of gasoline overpowered the ozone and ichor in the air. Red containers littered the grass around me like unlit candles in a gruesome hex circle.

He yanked on the rope he'd rigged to the flag pole and wrapped around my wrists. It lifted me a few more inches above the stack. I kicked and screamed trying to wiggle free, but like a fish on a reel, he methodically snared me in his trap.

Carl studied me. A scowl darkened his face. Suddenly, he brightened. "Oops! I forgot something." He said it almost as if it were an afterthought, but supremely important.

When he came back from digging in the truck, he held my athame in his hands.

I stopped all attempts to find footing and wrapped my ankles around the wooden post. It halted my flailing, which was probably a bad thing, but I'd be damned if I wasn't prepared for his attack.

Instead, he climbed up on the woodpile and sliced a slit in the hem of my dress. Then he tore it upward, baring my legs and only halting when the fabric met the stitched seam and the layers collected at my waist. Then he got closer. "Don't move, Mary-Rose. I might cut you."

His breath was fetid against my arm. He sliced again, this time with more force, powering through the layers of fabric and seams binding it together, rendering my clothing to rags.

He worked methodically, each time warning me of what would happen if the knife slipped. The cold, misty air hit my skin.

A breeze picked up from the west. It drove away the rancid fumes of gasoline, and brought with it the promise of rain. I inhaled deeply, getting cut as he sliced my bra band.

"I told you not to move." His low chuckle slid over me like worms.

The small line of red widened as blood trickled from the wound. He stopped, fascinated by it. As he traced the drip with the point of the blade, I barely sipped air through my nose to keep from moving.

Finally, the trail soaked into the band of my underwear. Only then did he pull the knife through the elastic and fabric twice to strip me of everything.

"Now you're ready." He eyed my figure, not even stepping off the platform of wood and tinder.

I chose that moment to strike. I kicked out, using the post as leverage. My foot connected with his shoulder, driving him off the platform and into the dirt below.

But it was futile. My hands were bound, so I couldn't run. He brushed himself off and laughed maniacally.

"You'll pay for that, Mary-Rose. God will make you pay."

My eyes watered from the pain and the fumes. He stalked the perimeter and piled up more logs and pallets as he moved from his truck to my funeral pyre. Every few moments, he'd stop, soak the wood with more gasoline, and winch me higher.

"Just light it already." I was sick of the torture.

He froze and stared at me. "Did you know they say witches orgasm when burned?"

My thoughts raced through all of his threats and the memories of his obsessiveness about religion in our childhood. He'd always been a bit…off, but this? This was sick. My mind couldn't rationalize it. But my heart, and more importantly, my *will* was thinking way ahead. I struggled to find a board or stick wedged hard enough to push against so I could get my foot on anything to take the weight off my arms. But I only knocked the pile away from my toes, leaving me with less than before.

So, I did what anyone would. I screamed for help. Screamed, "Fire!" Screamed for anyone to listen.

Deep down, I knew that help was at least a mile away. We were deep into the wooded area leased to the church. Not even the cemetery caretaker was close enough to hear me. The closest person was, or would have been, my grandmother. If she were alive. But she died on this very hill.

I cried to her ghost, hoping she'd hear me beyond the veil and call the Gods down on this asshole.

Carl stopped again to listen. "That's right, unburden yourself from your sin."

"Fuck you!"

His smile was eerie. "Another sin."

It was as if he was keeping a running tally of my… what? Who was he to judge? I spat an appropriate Bible verse at him. Then went further digging up every hypocrisy he committed.

Carl's unnatural calmness waited me out. Finally, he quoted Exodus 22, not stopping at verse eighteen, but moving directly into the nineteenth. "Whosoever lieth with a beast shall surely be put to death." He paused and took a step closer. "That's *you*, Rose. You didn't even fight your carnal urges. You willingly *fucked* that man. I cannot let you live, you know that, right?"

My jaw clenched hard. "Who sold me to him?"

He threw the gas can in his hands to the ground. "You weren't supposed to fall in love with him!"

Ah. That *was my sin.*

"I don't regret a thing."

Maybe one thing. When I was dead, there would be no one to

remind Carl he'd promised to help his sister. But maybe that was what he intended all along. String me, her, the family, the doctors, everyone through his little game and then pull the rug out from under everyone at that worst possible moment.

"You have regrets, I see it on your face. I know you, Mary-Rose. I've watched you your entire life."

"That's not creepy at all." My sarcasm was lost on him. I continued to poke around with my toe for something to brace against. The wind had picked up, and if I had to hang naked on some hill in the middle of nowhere freezing my ass off while Carl got his poop in a group, I'd die of hypothermia before burning.

"You're such a bitch." He kicked the gas can, spilling the contents in an arc over the grass. Then he dug in the cab of his truck and returned with a lighter. He tried lighting some grass first, but it fizzled out.

A light mist blew in from the west. The clouds grew thicker, and the sky hung low overhead.

He bent over the stack, attempting to light one of the smaller sticks. But the wind blew the flame sideways and he scorched his fingers.

I gave up trying to find something near my feet, opting instead to curl the soles of my feet against the wood post at my back. It gave a small amount of relief to my shoulders, but the angle made it difficult to hold.

He went back to the truck one more time and came out with a box of matches.

Meanwhile the mist turned into stinging rain that spat at my bare skin, chilling me.

Carl bent over, close now. I braced one foot on the post and swung the other leg at his head. I kicked as hard as I could, causing my body to swing loose. I screamed at the strain on my arms.

But I made contact, and my target fell on his ass, spilling the matches into the wet grass.

"You'll pay for that!" He picked up my athame.

"Thor, if you're listening? Fuck this asshole up."

The wind sucked inward and shifted, heralding a major front barreling down on us. Lightning cracked against the blackness.

Carl startled and dropped the knife.

Maybe he was scared of the Gods? The thunder rumbled. Three miles away. I'd counted the seconds from flash to sound.

Then there was calm.

In the stillness, Carl flicked the lighter with trembling hands, and caught one of the matches on fire. He tossed it onto the pile and it hit one of the larger logs soaked in so much gasoline it glistened. The match bounced once, then sputtered out as it landed in the puddle of fuel.

Carl skipped the science class about flammability.

I bit back my suggestion that he hold the next match in the fumes.

Another spear of lightning forked across the sky. The air erupted with a loud crack.

In the flash, I saw a creature rise up behind Carl's truck.

My heart beat faster. I knew that form. I knew that war braid. But Bear was in berserker mode and not the man I bedded. His eyes were streaked with black mud, and when he smiled, the flare of his capped canines flashed in the night.

He moved quickly, running with stealth and speed, knocking Carl from the pile and rolling with him. In the motion, Bear pulled a knife. But Carl managed to knock his aim off, and the blade hit a rock.

Carl grabbed another rock from the ground and slammed it against the side of Bear's head. Blood trickled down his face as they wrestled. They rolled out of view, and I tried to twist to see them but only managed to get a glimpse of Carl on top before my body swung back to stare at his truck.

The noise of battle was drowned out by the rising storm. Bolt after bolt of lightning flashed overhead making my hair rise. The wind picked up again and this time blew in straight across the hill and cold. Shivering, I tried to scale the post, aiming to free my bound hands from the pulley connected to it. My feet slipped against the slippery wood and I hung in place, staring at the metal cap at the top of the pole.

Almost directly overhead, the roiling clouds lit up and there was a flash that blinded my good eye. Pain seared around my wrists, then drove deeper as I fell from the post onto the piled wood. A spark dropped into the mess and caught. I scrambled forward, searching for the safety of the grass and ended up tumbling off the stack and rolling onto my back, stunned senseless.

I could barely see, the aftermath of the flare making the center of my vision a bright orange blob. But out of the corner of my bad eye, something glinted. I reached for the object and wrapped my fingers around my athame. With it in hand, I crawled away from the wood pile, but was tripped by my hair. I flung the mass over my back and managed another two feet before someone yanked on it hard.

Carl had a hank of it wrapped around his fist and used it to drag me back toward the wood pile that was now ablaze. I leaned away, trying to escape my fate, and realized that I had salvation literally in my hand.

Using my body weight to pull my hair taut, I cut across it with the knife. The blade was so sharp it swept through the strands cleanly.

I landed on my ass, and Carl fell forward into the fire.

Bear rose up from the shadows and pushed Carl back in when he tried to stumble out.

Against the backdrop of flames, Carl laughed and pushed to his feet. "You think you won?" He turned to me and taunted, "Say goodbye to Beth."

And with that, he tipped backwards, and was engulfed in the blaze.

"No!"

One of his feet was unlit, I grabbed it and tried to pull him out of the blaze, uncaring that sparks hit my arms.

Bear grabbed my waist and flung me away from the inferno. He rose up between me and Carl.

"Do you love him that much?"

"I don't love him. He can save Beth. Please?"

I love you. His words echoed in my memories.

"Please?"

Carl's laughter was little more than a wheeze.

34

BEAR

I tried to do everything right. I gave her time, space, autonomy, and respect. Everything Carl tried to take from her. Even her life. I don't know how she got free, but Rose was far from unharmed. Her wrists were bloody and raw. The jagged edge of her hair hung uneven from where she'd cut it to get free.

There were bruises, scrapes, scratches, and blood on her naked skin. Burns ran down her arms and along her spine from the pole as the entire pyre burst ablaze. She favored her left side as if it were broken or worse.

And she begged for that bastard's life.

I turned to the horror show behind me. The conflagration was high, but slowly being quelled by the downpour that dumped on us. The lightning that had struck the hill… no, the post she was tied to, moved on.

My head still hurt from the blows I took, and I tried to keep upright just in case Carl somehow walked out of those flames.

"Please, Bear. For Beth. Not for me."

My hammer necklace tapped against my chest with each labored puff of air I sucked in.

I heard her screams. And ran from the road at full speed. John told me where the place was, but didn't mention how fucking far everything was or how much that would slow me down. I'd poured so much into getting up that fucking hill I couldn't fight Carl. But I could watch him burn, right?

For Beth she pleaded. Rose loved her more than she ever could love me.

I was being selfish and jealous, and a weak-ass monster by doing nothing.

I caught one of that dickweed's feet and dragged him out of the flames. The rain continued to pour down, dowsing the blaze of his clothing almost instantly. He was charred from knee to shoulder. The side of his face was burnt. The other side, uncannily calm. That side's eye opened.

The fucker was still alive.

He stared at me with that single unburnt eye, accusing me. Judging me.

I hefted his sorry ass into the bed of his truck and tossed a tarp over him. "Get in the truck, Rose."

She limped blindly, falling to a crawl. I tossed her in the passenger seat with a little more care than I showed Carl. Her labored breathing didn't sound good. She shook from the cold or shock. I stripped off my outer layers and wrapped her in them to warm her, then tried to figure out how I'd get her out of here.

Luckily, barbecue boy had left the keys in the ignition. *Grand theft doesn't apply if you're carrying the owner in the bed, does it?* I shrugged off those intrusive thoughts and backed the truck around to pick my way out of this hellscape. A half hour later, we'd made it to the hospital, and I had to explain myself. Or *not*.

You show up with two burnt people in a stolen truck and there's not as many questions as you'd think. Until they notice one of them is wearing only a Destroyers leather coat and your bloody T-shirt as a skirt.

I sat my ass on the floor outside Rose's curtain-ringed cubicle in the emergency department. Carl was upstairs in the ICU or surgery somewhere. I hoped the motherfucker died.

As another doctor swept into Rose's space, a disgusted-looking nurse carried a bundle of bloody sheets out. I stopped her. "Do you have my coat?'

Her eyes held rage.

I could tell by the set of her jaw that she thought I'd done this.

"She was naked when I found her." The pause went on too long, so I filled in the gap. "I don't give a shit about my shirt, but my coat is… well, not as important as she is, but they're going to give me grief if I don't ask."

"Who's going to do that?"

Who indeed? I'd blown off church. "No one. Sorry." I doubted they would give two shits about me now. I sat back down, slouching against one of the columns that made up a corner of the room.

"Who did all that to her?"

"That asshole you guys are trying to save." I pointed at the ceiling.

"Why?"

That was a great question. Jealousy? Fanaticism? An egomaniacal possessive streak like a certain biker who was a fucking idiot? "He's a psycho, I guess." It took one to know one. That lesson hit hard.

The nurse shifted the bundle in her arms and pulled out my coat, blood and all. She pinched it between her fingers as if it were going to bite her for touching it.

I held out my hand, waiting for her to walk the distance between us.

"Are you *sure* you want to keep it?"

It had Rose's blood on it. The smell of ozone clung to it.

I nodded. "Yeah." If that's all I got to keep of her as a reminder of us, then I'd wear those damned stains with honor.

For as long as I could. Which would be tomorrow when Wolf came for my patch and everything tied to it.

A police officer stopped at the intersection of the hallways, first looking the wrong way, then he spotted me. His eyes took in my hair, the blood, my piercings, tattoos, the coat being offered, the blood on it, and you know what happened next, right?

"Hands in the air, you're under arrest."

Yeah. *That.*

I held my shaking hands above my head.

"What are you arresting *him* for?" The nurse stepped between us.

"Ma'am, step out of the way. This man is dangerous."

"For your information, *he* brought both of the victims in. That's called *heroic*. Get your words straight."

He peeked around her at me. "Heroic? *Him*?"

The things that were going through my head were probably written in my scowl. If he could hear them, I'd be locked up for life.

The nurse turned her back on the cop and addressed me, "You need to be treated for those head wounds you got defending the woman in there."

"How's she doing?" I tried to stand up, but it was tricky with my hands held safely where the cop could see them.

"Considering she was struck by lightning? As well as can be expected."

She was struck by lightning? My knees gave out, and I ended up on the floor again. This time, I stared at the ceiling. It was spinning.

"*Timber.* The big ones always go down the worst." The nurse directed orderlies to get me on a gurney and wheel me into another curtain-lined room.

The cop trailed behind to "get my statement" and was promptly barred from the cubicle. I was attached to monitors and several people scanned my pupils and asked me to do dumb things like press on their hands with first one arm then the other. Somewhere in there, they asked for an emergency number to call. I bit the bullet and gave them the club's private line.

It was an hour before Wolf showed up with his wife in tow. Tits flashed me a grin and disappeared.

"Where is she heading?"

"She hates hospitals. Did you know that?"

Wolf's tone was not jovial, certainly not forthcoming, and that set me off. "No one asked her to show up."

"She's meeting your lawyer outside, asshole."

Oh. *Good.* "Are you sure you want that?" I eyeballed him, not daring to back down because there's one thing Wolf respected more than respect, and that was strength. I'd shown enough weakness tonight.

"Yeah. Can't have my VP in jail, can I?"

I let out a cautious breath. "I missed the meeting."

"Yeah, well, KC stuck up for you. Once he voted your way, everyone else caved."

I cleared my throat. "He shouldn't have done that."

Wolf studied me for almost a minute before speaking. "He's staying."

Thank the Gods.

The silence stretched out longer than it should. "Is someone checking on Rose?"

Wolf sighed and crossed his arms. "I thought you two were done."

We might be. "She got hit by lightning."

He stared at me. His gaze dropped to my necklace. "I'm never giving you shit about your religion again."

"Fuck you." I couldn't help what happened next. A laugh leaked out. It was so damn tragic, and unbelievable that I couldn't stop. On the heels of its giggling death came a sob. I couldn't help that either. It caught in my throat and I coughed. Smoke and the smell of burnt hair clung to my lungs, and I wanted to get rid of all of it. I puked onto the floor and still couldn't get my breath.

"Nurse! Someone!"

They strapped me down and secured an oxygen mask to my face. My head swam. Wolf leaned over me, holding one hand tight. "Stay with me. This isn't going to kill you. You hear me?"

In reply, I lifted my middle finger. It stuck out of his grip. He felt the movement, turned my hand to witness it sticking out, and laughed. "You'll live." He sat back down, still holding onto my hand, but making room for the team of doctors to hook me up to more monitors and shit.

Hours later, they deemed me fit enough to discharge. The smoke inhalation symptoms had subsided, and my head scans were clear. I had a minor concussion, but responded well despite that. The cuts on my skull took fourteen stitches to close. I looked like a black and blue Frankenstein once they were done. I lingered in the lounge near Rose's room.

She was admitted for observation. Her heartbeat was irregular, her hearing impacted, and she was having trouble seeing out of her right eye. Her concussion was worse than mine, likely a result of the beating Carl gave her. She also had third-degree burns where the nylon cord melted into her skin at her wrists. Other, less dire burns were being treated as well. At least she hadn't been directly in the fire when it caught.

I pondered her close call and the events that still seemed too unreal to be believed. Who in their right mind burns someone alive? And why? Rose hadn't done anything to deserve that.

Tits sat with me, trading places with Wolf so he could talk to the lawyer about everything.

He came back with good news.

"They checked out the site. The fire's out, but there's enough evidence to back up your story. The receipts for all that gas were in the cab of Carl's truck. Cops matched them to Carl's credit card."

"Did that asshole survive?"

Wolf hesitated. "He's on life support. They're trying to figure out what to do."

"Pull the plug," I muttered. It was too good for him. Too clean. Maybe he should linger, racking up hospital bills until every cent he made of dirty money was gone.

Tits snickered. "That's the Bear we all know and piss ourselves around."

"It's not that simple. There's a standing order for his bone marrow to go to his sister. But his parents showed up ten minutes ago and asked to nullify the request."

"What?" I stood up and immediately regretted it. The room spun so badly I had to put a hand on the wall to keep my feet under me.

"They're claiming it will kill him."

"*Good.*" I hoped it killed him slowly.

"Beth is their daughter, right?" Tits asked to clarify.

"That's right," her husband answered.

"Don't they care about her?"

I shook my head. "They'd fuck her over for Carl. He's their golden boy." The room stopped spinning, but I was tired as fuck. I sat back down because this night was getting long. I still hadn't seen Rose, and that's what I really wanted.

No, *needed*. I had to apologize. Grovel. Beg her forgiveness. Even battered, bruised, drugged, scraped up, and struck by lightning, she had the compassion to think of her friend. "Did anyone call John or ask Beth?"

"The hospital did. John's on his way here to advocate for his wife."

That was good. Maybe he could talk some sense into her parents. And if he couldn't, well… maybe they should get a visit from Wolf and me? "You up to a haunting?"

"A what?" Wolf asked.

"You know, what bad little bikers do to good God-fearing folk on Halloween night."

Wolf grinned. "Who are you calling little? Cause that ain't me, and it certainly isn't you."

Tits flicked her blade out. "I think he means me."

"Oh yeah, like you'd scare anyone," I teased.

I came about one millimeter from having another cut requiring stitches. But Tits was a master of blade control. She pressed just hard enough to draw a single drop of blood.

I rubbed it away. "I've had paper cuts that bled more."

Tits examined her knife. "Didn't you lose enough blood tonight?"

"What's a few ounces more between friends?" I joked.

I'd bet Wolf regretted showing up. He leaned in and kissed his wife. "Stay here, guard Rose's room for Bear. We're going to go for a walk."

"Don't get arrested," she said right before giving him a quick smooch.

"That's it?" Wolf asked.

Tits shrugged. "I'm not bailing you out. You put me on baby-sitting detail…in a hospital."

"You know what I mean. Kiss me like you mean it." He locked lips with her for longer than was necessary.

I grunted to remind them this was a public hallway. Wolf flipped me off, and finished his mauling.

Finally, Tits broke the kiss.

Wolf frowned but gave her space. Then he motioned to me. "Come on, Bear."

We stopped outside the ER.

His mother looked like Carl used to. It was rather eerie.

John had arrived and held a pile of papers in the air.

"These have his signature on them, and the notary who witnessed it. You can't stop this."

"He's injured. He needs strength to recover."

"From trying to burn someone alive? Let him die!"

Whoa, John was doing a damn good job at playing badass. I cleared my throat. "Hey, John. How's Beth?"

His frown spoke volumes. "She'll be a hundred percent better if these two stop being hypocrites."

Wolf's raised eyebrows mirrored my own. We both slid our stares to the man and woman opposite us. In a subtle, for me, gesture of solidarity, I put my hand on John's shoulder, showing them he had our support.

"You're the ones to blame for this." Carl's father shook his finger at me.

I stepped forward and pulled open my coat. "See the stains there, that crusty stuff?" I waited until they saw it. "That's blood. I don't mind wearing it next to my skin because I know whose it is, and who made her bleed. Now, if you want to blame anyone? I'd look at your fucked up son who did this, and maybe take a good long look at your weird religion for putting psychopathic ideas into his head. That's the real reason we're all here tonight."

My hands shook. "He tried to burn my woman at the stake. That shit is illegal. Now I could tell you a dozen other things your so-called prodigal son did in the last month. Some of it would curl your hair. But honestly? You're not going to listen… not to me. But if you want to stick up for him, I suggest you talk to the Sheriff's department processing the scene. It's on *your* church's property. And that property has a security fence he had the transponder for. Why is that?"

Their faces paled.

I laughed at them. "You're going to have *so* much explaining to do. And let's just say you mention anything about your appreciation for your son trying to burn a witch at the stake? I'll personally make sure your church finds out about his *other* proclivities."

I was bluffing my ass off. Because Carl's proclivities would also implicate us. But since I was also the man who would deal out the swath of death that would ensue if anyone talked, maybe it wasn't a bluff at all. Maybe I was ready to do whatever it took to make sure Carl Windgren's good name was buried in ashes.

Carl's father looked to his wife for help. But her face was pale and scared. Whatever he deciphered from it wasn't good because he asked, "Where did this happen?"

John butted in, "The hill where Amma Dornberger and Deacon May died."

The collective sucked-in breath whispered secrets.

John's gaze narrowed. "I have a feeling the deacon's death wasn't an accident like Carl claimed it was, was it?"

Carl's father stiffened. "That was years ago."

"There's no statute of limitations on murder," Wolf rightly observed. "And party to murder? Bear, you wouldn't happen to know how long that span is?"

"I don't think there is one. Nor does it matter if it is before the fact, or after. Which means covering up a murder is still prosecutable. And Pennsylvania still has the death penalty." Jackson would know the particulars on all that. *Fucker.*

"The deacon's death *was* an accident," his mother spoke bluntly.

"If you don't want that theory tested, don't fight the transplant." John slapped the papers down onto the table. "These are copies. The hospital has another set. When Carl dies, you are more than welcome to collect his body. After my wife gets what is legally hers."

He stood up and left them to their sorrow.

Wolf and I followed to make sure he was protected. I wouldn't put it past those nut jobs to stick a knife in his back and blame it on the Holy Spirit or some shit. He stopped in the common area where it branched off to Rose's room and talked to the nurse behind the counter. He joined us, still flushed and clenching his hands like he wanted to tear someone's head off.

In a scary moment of realization, I realized John wasn't the goodie-two-shoes I'd pegged him as. "You ever think about riding motorcycles?"

He smiled, but it was grim. "Beth would kill me if I did."

That was a damn shame. "When she gets better, I'm going to have Rose talk her into a ride. She'll change her mind."

Wolf slapped my chest as he walked past to join Tits outside Rose's door. "You keep recruiting, I'm going to have to offer you the president's spot."

Maybe it was time I accepted the VP offer? As rotten as I'd be at the job, Wolf and the club wanted my help. And if I had to drown my sorrows over Rose, I'd need it to keep me busy.

Speaking of, I asked John, "Are they going to let you see Rose while you're here?"

He shrugged. "Depends."

"On what?"

"On how long your visit is going to take. She wants to see you."

35

ROISHIN

Despite the pain and the blurry vision through my swollen eye, the marks on my hands and arms were beautiful. I held my right arm up to see the spidery red lines better.

The door opened and closed, a large, dark figure slipped in, blocking the light from the hallway temporarily. By the size, it was John or Bear. I'd asked for Bear, but could have sworn I heard John's voice.

As he came into range, I realized it was Bear and held my hand out for him to admire. "Tattoo this." It came out as a raspy, slurred command. I didn't dare talk more than that because my throat and my jaw were in agony. I didn't know what caused it—Carl or the storm, or the horrible way my whole body clenched in seizure an hour ago. But I was alive.

And I'd stay alive as long as I could.

We'd made it to the hospital, and Carl wasn't dead yet. Which meant I couldn't die. Not now, not soon. And certainly not before I had a chance to run my dagger through his chest.

Bear took the hand I offered and carefully turned it, but avoided the padded bandages at my wrist. The other arm had a similar dressing where the nylon cord melted deep into my skin.

I couldn't feel that side, however.

"They look like tree roots."

"Lightning."

His jaw went tense. "Yeah." Without thought, his free hand covered the hammer hanging from his neck.

"Let me see." I couldn't sit up, so Bear leaned close so I could finger the tiny symbol of his faith. I'd prayed to him. "Thor."

Bear caught my hand and buried his head against the palm of it.

I whimpered a little because his grip slipped to my wrist.

He quickly corrected it and held my fingers where the lines stopped their snake-like trails with hundreds of little tendrils branching from the darker red lines that ran from my wrists.

"How far do these go?" He turned my arm carefully to check the path.

"I think everywhere." Because everything hurt. If they didn't travel the entire length of my body on the outside, they certainly did on the inside. Even my right foot stung like it was still on fire. Especially at the arch where I'd pressed it against the pole. That foot was wrapped. The other wasn't, but it was a curiosity to the doctors. They'd ran instruments along the bottom, testing my reflexes.

Their words frightened me. Paralysis. Nerve damage.

It might be temporary, and it might not be. No one knew.

"That would be one hell of a tattoo."

"Can you do it?"

His eyes met mine. His hand began to shake. Then, his head joined it. "I don't know." The anguish in his expression pleaded with me to not ask such a favor from him.

"I need photos so I can get it done later."

His nostrils flared. "Woman."

"Please?"

He blew out a breath, as if I'd asked him to give up something dear or perform a dire act.

"I'll get the doctors to—"

"No. I'll do it." His tongue darted out to lick his lips. "No one sees you but me."

Was that jealousy in his growl?

But he vowed to be my enemy. If… "I didn't help Carl."

So much swam on the surface of his expression. Horror, pain, relief, guilt… it was hard to keep up. "I can see that." His palm hovered over one of the bruises on my arm. I didn't need to be reminded of the blows that landed there and elsewhere. They throbbed in time with the bloody mess of my wrists, foot and back.

Electricity traveled from the clouds to the flagpole top. It exploded in a flash of white and seared down the wooden pole and the wet rope that looped around my wrist bindings before wrapping around the metal cleat buried under the stacked wood. In under a second, I'd been freed but at a terrible cost. I might not walk again. I might be blind in one eye. My skin had these pretty, but terrible burns called Lichtenberg figures etched into it. The lightning traveled through me, back to the pole, and into the ground. I was damn lucky to be alive.

In that brief flash, I'd seen what mortals shouldn't.

Pain was such a small price in hindsight. "You saved me," I told Bear.

He scoffed. "Hardly. I got my ass kicked. And I was too slow."

No, he'd saved me. His belief, his forgiveness… he found me. Which was a miracle of its own. "I asked Thor to fuck Carl up. Please tell me he's dead."

Bear frowned. "Hopefully soon. He's on life support."

I wanted to curse. But then remembered Beth. "The bone marrow?"

A slow nod answered. "John's here. He's quite bloodthirsty right now. And he's notified the staff that Carl is his wife's donor."

Good.

A wash of peace swept through me as I closed my eyes to send a silent thank you to the universe for watching out for Beth.

"Hey, don't pass out on me. I need you."

I opened my semi-good eye. "You need me?"

His face was pale. "More than you fucking know."

The knowledge that he'd openly admitted such a weakness

felt… amazing. Yet there was so much anguish in his voice. Was it because of my condition, or because of Carl? Or…

"Wait a minute, did you go to the meeting tonight?"

Bear shook his head. "I came after you."

He gave up his shot to be vice president. For *me*. "I'm so sorry."

He shrugged. "Nothing to be sorry for. They voted me in despite that. Something about keeping KC in line and looking out for the club's interests or some shit."

I tried and failed to snag a braid. He leaned closer so I could tangle my fingers in his beard. The pain lessened, and I couldn't remember what we were talking about for a moment.

"You with me?" Bear asked.

"I'm yours." It came out so easily. As naturally as breathing. Maybe even more so because breathing was a fragile thing right now.

He cupped his hands around the elbow I propped against the sidewall of the bed. "And I'm yours."

And the club's.

I smiled despite that reminder. "I love you. But…"

"No buts. I love you, too. When you're sprung from this place, we're going to figure out all the rest."

That was a tall order. There were complications, and more than just my tenuous grasp on health right now. "Beth?"

"She'll get better. Have some faith." His chin dipped, causing the chain and pendant to sway lightly.

Very slowly, I nodded. But tears gathered at my eyes. "I was awful to you."

"You were honest. That's not awful."

"I chose Beth over you."

He leaned over me so I could see his face plainly. "No. You didn't. You chose your friend, and my friends, and a bunch of stuff over yourself. You ain't going to do that anymore, got it?"

Oh, I got it. Bear was doing what he did best. "Bossy old bear."

"Witch."

That label felt so good.

"Don't leave me." I found a grip in his hair again.

He detangled my fingers gently. Then kissed each one, taking time to really look at the marks there. "You're right. These will make one hell of a tattoo. It's going to take forever, though."

"Don't leave me. Please?"

His stare was too intense. "I'm going to ask you the same thing. Don't you dare leave me. I wasn't kidding when I said I need you. It felt like someone took a big ass construction shovel to my chest when you left. I was hollow. I can't live like that."

I knew what he felt. "When it's all gone, there's nothing left, is there?"

His slow nod and tight lips spoke without words.

My grip tightened. "I *need* you."

"I know." He fiddled with the side of the bed so the rail was down and shifted around until he was half-lying next to me. His head pressed against my shoulder. His hand wrapped over my waist. The night nurse found us like that. She must have been used to such shenanigans because her directions were gentle.

"That chair folds into a bed. You'll be more comfortable." While she directed Bear, she checked the stitches on his head. I hadn't noticed before, but they were awful.

I felt more guilt.

Despite what I wanted, he needed more than I could give. I'd only hold him back.

When the next shift kicked him out and told him to return during visiting hours, I didn't fight it.

He didn't come back until late that afternoon.

In between, Tits sat with me, guarding my room like an angry tiger. I barely said two words to her, and likewise, she was scarily stoic.

But it was good to have someone around. I still couldn't move my left leg, and my arm on that side was clumsy at best. While my fingers tingled so badly they burned, I couldn't do more than make them twitch erratically.

And my toes had stopped curling in response to the external tests.

The burns that snaked over my body simmered with a raging

inferno of pain. Between tests I asked Tits to take pictures. The marks on my arms blistered already. They'd be ugly soon.

"Help me with this." I tried to reach the ties to my gown.

"You shouldn't be moving."

Right then, Bear strolled in. "What are you doing, woman?"

"Help me take this off." I got a hold of something back there, but it wasn't budging.

"She's trying to get a picture of the burns." Tits handed Bear the phone in her hand as if he were interested in the photos she'd taken. He barely gave it a glance.

"Go outside, no one in. Got it?"

Tits huffed out, "They're going to think you're killing her."

"Say it louder so the central desk can hear you."

"I might," she fired back.

"Just guard the door." Under his breath he added, "Damn woman."

"Was that directed at her, or me?" I asked.

"Your hearing's getting better," he muttered.

"At least something is." I tugged the string again. "Help."

He grunted and set Tits's phone down as he let me lean on his chest while he undid my hospital gown. But he kept it in place as he checked my face for clues. "Are you sure about this?"

I was. I wanted to capture the beauty of the marks before they became worse, or faded. "Yes. Can you handle that?"

His nostrils flared as if scenting the challenge I'd laid down. "I can." But his jaw was tight and his mood anything but happy.

"Do it."

He carefully moved my hair out of the way. The strands were haphazardly unequal. A fraction of the length escaped butchery, but the main body of it angled sharply where the blade had sliced through. "Did you find my athame?"

"I went up there with Sketch and his metal detector today. Found it."

I sighed with relief. "I hope the rain didn't ruin it."

He laughed tightly. "No, but I sent it to Fin."

That was curious. "Why?"

"Later. Are you sure you want to do this?"

I nodded.

He pulled my gown away and let it pile on my lap. His eyes traced the threads of red lines that shot wildly about in branches of scarring.

The cold air felt good. I breathed deeply, taking in the relief of having nothing touching my skin.

"That's damn beautiful."

But that wasn't what his face said. "What's wrong?"

"It's just… fuck…" His eyes met mine. "It's everywhere. You should be dead." There was fear in those dark depths.

"I know." That's what everyone told me today. How lucky I was. How amazing my recovery was. How miraculous it was that my heart hadn't stopped, or my body hadn't boiled from the inside out. I was a living breathing tribute to the one in a million people who get hit by lightning in a year. And of that, while 90 percent survived, rarely was a direct hit survivable. Most of the victims were near, but not at the point of contact.

My skin prickled from the chill, bringing pain with it. "Take those pictures."

Bear glanced at Tits's phone. "Like hell am I letting her see this." He dug out his own phone and began taking photos.

I rolled onto my stomach, getting my left arm slightly tangled as I did so, and an alarm blared. He snapped the photo right as a nurse barged in with Tits on her tail.

"You can't be in here." She fussed with the machine that was blaring. "And you, shouldn't be rolling around with your…whatever he is." Under her breath she was saying more, but I couldn't make it out. I looked to Bear for insight.

"She thinks we're being kinky."

"It's not kinky. I just wanted photos."

The nurse froze. She stared at the skin she hadn't covered with a blanket. "I shouldn't allow this, but… you're probably going to do it anyway, right?"

"Yes," I said.

"She's stubborn," Bear added.

Tits snorted but held up her hands when Bear and I both shot her a look. "I didn't say a word." With a twist of her right hand, she pointed at the hallway. "I'll be out there." As she left, she muttered, "God, I hate hospitals."

The nurse helped me turn so my back was exposed. There were pads taped to the skin she had to change because of the burns along my spine. She pointed out the worst to Bear as she worked. "That's where her spine made contact with the pole. The specialist believes over one million volts ran along her skin but her hair insulated most of her spine. It saved her."

I heard a thump.

"Aw, damn it. He went down again. Your boyfriend is a fainter."

I peered to the side where Bear was on the floor. "Are you going to do anything?"

She shrugged. "His head scans were good. And he's not bleeding anymore so…" She taped up my wounds. Then pulled the camera out of his hand and proceeded to help me finish taking photos.

Bear woke up when she'd just gotten me tucked into a fresh gown and upped the painkiller in my IV. "You'll be kind of sleepy for a while." Then she squatted by Bear. "Do you need some water?"

He blinked. "I passed out again, didn't I?"

The nurse nodded. "You may want to get your blood pressure checked. And stop pushing yourself so hard. Your girlfriend is going to live, and I think she wants you to live, too. So, go slow, okay?"

He sat up, slowly. "I hate that fucking word."

"Which one, stop or slow?"

"Slow."

The nurse made a frustrated noise. "Embrace it, big guy. We all have our weaknesses. Yours happens to be burn wounds. You didn't blink an eye at blood. But that"—she pointed at me—"had you down faster than a bullet."

She handed off his phone as she finished her tirade. Then she gave me one last set of instructions to rest, but only directed half of it at me. The remainder of instructions went to Bear.

He pulled up a chair and scrolled through the photos.

"Are you going to pass out again?"

He met my eyes. "Naw. Weird that I can look at you here and it doesn't do a thing. But…" Anguish covered his face when he met my eyes again. "I don't want you in pain."

"That makes two of us."

36

BEAR

Fin put the finishing touches on Rose's back and wiped the marks clean. I'd tried, really tried to do the bulk of the work. Her sleeve tattoos were easy. The tracing of lines practically child's play with my needles. But as soon as I had to work on her chest or back, I'd faint.

It was as if my body couldn't process the extent of her injury. Or maybe it was because those lines had faded leaving nothing but pure skin behind. I couldn't mark it up.

Anyone else who came in the shop got no mercy from me. But Rose? Damn it. She was my unicorn. The one person I just couldn't ink.

Fin gave me shit for all of three minutes. Then he saw the stencil.

That sobered him up.

Of course, the fucker named an outrageous price.

"I'll go somewhere else."

"Like hell you will. First hack who touches your woman, you'll go through the fucking ceiling. Then you'll kill 'em. At least you know it'll get done right by me."

And it was. I leaned in to admire the fine lines Fin had colored in. We decided it would be cool to do part of it in a deep rose flesh color to match the original scars, but then outline them with UV ink. I held up the black light to see the effect.

And practically fainted again.

Somehow, I managed to blink away the darkness hovering at the edges of my eyes and watch the light dance along her skin.

"That's one kick-ass tattoo." Fin wiped at her skin again to clean up a spot that wept a little. "Put that light up here." He held a mirror so Rose could look at the ceiling mirror and watch the little streaks of lightning shimmer and dance. It was a work of art.

And my worst nightmare sometimes. I loved every inch of her, and on those more tormented nights, I relived that moment when I glanced up and watched her fall. Then the fire flared up. And in its glow, Carl grabbed her by the hair. My stomach did a flip-flop even though I only thought about it.

"It's beautiful." Rose clutched the mirror and shifted to see the entire piece.

I traced one of the patterns that ran down the back of her leg like a striped stocking. The branches were so much smaller there. But that damn line went right down to her heel where the worst of the damage exited like a bullet wound. She could hardly put pressure on it for weeks.

Four skin grafts on her wrists, and two on her heel. She had macular holes in the vision of her right eye from the flash that might never fade completely.

But she was mobile now. There was only a slight hesitation with her left leg when she pushed too hard, or was tired. We jogged the trail together as therapy. And when she had rough days, we went to visit Beth.

Carl died on November first, the day of the martyrs, right about the moment I ass-planted on the floor again. Beth's transplant was only a few hours later. And almost immediately she improved. So did Rose.

It had been months since then, and the day after New Year's I'd made it official. Rose was mine. And I hers. A set of patches on her coat read "Property of Bear" and a crazy hodgepodge of witch symbols were sewn into mine, along with a custom, black hat patch that read, "Cross his witch and die."

I found room for that right under my heart.

And she wore a hammer necklace I'd given her at Yule. It was a miniature version of mine, more delicately made with little lightning bolts carved amongst the circlets of knot work. Tiny crescent moons flanked the handle. It was one of a kind, like my witch.

My finger stopped on her foot and I quickly ran it down the arch. She flinched and kicked her leg up. That cute divot behind her knee winked at me. I wanted this woman, badly.

"Hey Fin, do you mind?"

He read my face and the innuendo I'd broadcasted plainly. "Of course, I fucking mind. I need to wrap her up before you maul her."

"Bear."

I ignored Rose's warning. She was naked, barely a towel between her and Fin's elbows and hands as he worked. Meanwhile I had to watch him mark her up for the last two months. I'd shared her skin enough. "I got it. Leave, old man."

He sighed. "Hey Betty Jo, remember when you flashed your ass at me?"

"You keep telling all these idiots about that day, and you're never going to see my ass again."

Fin leaned in, conspiratorially. "I tattooed a shark on her ass."

I ran my hand up Rose's leg and under the towel. "Well, I guess I beat you for sheer coverage."

He snickered.

"Well, someone did." He stopped to give Rose some advice about care. "And if this asshole faints again, let me know. I'll—"

"You'll do nothing, Finnigan Curty. She's Bear's." Betty Jo led him out of the private room in my shop.

It took only a few moments to apply the Saniderm. I ran my hand under Rose's towel. "You heard what Betty Jo said?"

She rolled over, letting the towel fall away. "That you're mine?"

"Yeah, that's what you heard." I looked at the mirror on the ceiling because it reflected her tits nicely.

"Lock the door." Her hand ran through my hair, tugging on a braid as she finished ordering me around.

I did as asked and returned to her. "How do you feel?"

Her smile was blissful. "I love getting tattooed. It feels so good."

I glanced at her skin. There wasn't much of it left that was pristine. "I see that." With one fingertip, I lightly traced a line of burns that flowed up the slope of her breast and forked into fractals that framed the tawny peak of her tit. The other side matched, but like all things in nature, they weren't completely symmetrical. The pattern on each was different despite the illusion of balance. I knew each line, each fork, every sensitive root. My tongue traced each one as soon as it healed. Now, I traced the pattern again, not stopping where the tattoo ended, but sucking on her nipple with care and determination. She was mine, and I intended on celebrating that. Every chance I got.

Her fingers dug into my scalp. "Please?"

"Lift up." I stuck a pillow and a sterile sheet under her back, using care not to jostle the fresh bandage on her spine much. "Okay. Let's take this slow."

She laughed. "You, slow?"

"Woman," I warned.

Rose wrapped her legs around mine, drawing me closer. "I want you."

For as long as I lived, I'd never get tired of hearing that. I quickly shucked my jeans and slipped a condom on. Rose led me home and that first rush of heat surrounding my dick sent a shockwave of bliss straight up my back. It sunk into my skin and dropped right back down into my balls making me harder.

She moaned as I pushed deeper. I checked her face to make sure I wasn't hurting her.

Her eyes were open and staring at the ceiling. I glanced up to check the mirror. From my angle, I could see her body splayed on the table, but if I leaned back a little, I could view the place where we connected. I pulled out, almost to the tip and sunk back in while watching my dick slide into her.

Too soon, I forgot to look because it felt too damn good, and I quickened the pace.

Every few strokes I checked her face and where her eyes tracked in the reflection above us.

On a whim, I pulled out and powered up the blacklight so I could see the flash of ink that was invisible normally. Then I worked into her again and again, checking the mirror and reveling in the sheer perfection of each line on her skin.

Rose clutched at me, and her fingers dug deep into my shoulders. "Bear, I'm…"

Yeah, I was there, too. The experience was like fine whiskey and the smoothest open highway in the world. I couldn't stop touching her, watching the shift of lightning across her skin, and digging deep with each thrust. "Mine, Rose. You are mine."

"Yours!" She was desperate, arching into me hard, grinding her clit against me and letting the whole shop know we were more than halfway to heaven. And it was hell because I didn't want it to end. But the tingling at the base of my nuts wouldn't wait much longer. I pounded into her, trying to make the little forks of ink under her tits flash with each beat.

My hands looked dark orange against the backdrop of her ink. The electrified blues of the UV ink and shadowy rose-colored lines on her skin were obscured like a cloud covered the sky. My ink shrank into deep shadows of black, almost as dark as night. I gripped her waist and sank deep. A cry wrenched from her like a storm breaking wide open.

I waited for my own tsunami of lust to break free. But we were trapped in that liminal space between thinking and reality. Where nightmares slipped their bonds and spirits roamed like wild beasts.

And I was one of those creatures. Wild, dangerous, but one with the chaotic beating of my heart, and hers. She hadn't tamed me, but rather set me loose to run wild with the night horde. I had power at my fingertips and felt her magic under my hands, more wild, even more powerful, and deeply infinite like some ancient goddess made flesh. I loved this sorceress, and in return for that worship, was blessed with the noblest of mates a man could ever find.

My release pulsed out of me with a roar. I let the fury loose with a deep yearning to claim, conquer, and most of all, run wild. As long as this woman never let go.

Rose's grin lit like the flare of a bonfire but didn't fade. "Love you," she gasped.

"Oh, woman…" I couldn't speak. She'd driven thought away. I was possessed by her, owned.

"I like it when you say it that way."

I bet she did. "Witch."

A hum emanated from her that I felt in my balls.

"That, too," she purred.

If she could love me with all my gruffness, I could… conquer whole planets. Or maybe just one backwater town on the brink of gentrification. Someone needed to scare the townsfolk.

I leaned down to take a nip at her full bottom lip. "Get dressed, I wanna show you off."

"I could stay naked."

Oh, that was tempting. But I had a hard enough time trusting Fin with her skin, I doubted anyone else would survive. "Later." I pulled out and ran my hand down her leg one last time. "Perfect."

Her eyes flashed, as if arguing with my assessment. I flicked on the overhead lights, put the UV lamp away, and closed out the station while she slipped into stockings, then a set of black panties. I got a little distracted when she tugged on her bra and tore it back off.

"I can't wear it."

"Wear a tank top." There was one of the shop's black racer backs on the supply rack. I'd put it there earlier knowing she'd not want anything pressing hard against her skin.

She pouted. "It doesn't match."

She dangled the sequin top she'd worn to the shop from one finger.

"It matches just fine. No one's going to be looking at your clothes."

"Give me your shirt. I don't want to get cold."

She had a point there. I stripped off my thermal and handed it over. It was worse of a match than the shop shirt, but once she put it on and tugged the sleeves over her hands, it became something other than a fashion statement. It hung on her. And anyone with half a brain could see it was my shirt. If some idiot was stupid enough not to know, I'd educate them, fast.

Her perky tits poked at the fabric, proving there was no bra underneath. While I liked that view, I knew it would be a hard night of fighting my urge to pound someone's face in if they stared too long. "Wear the vest."

"No. I just know that will be too much under the coat."

I smiled. She still insisted on getting her own way. She'd taken to wearing the black duster any chance she got. She looked like a Goth gunslinger from Hell in it. And now that her hair was shorter, she wore a dark flat-brimmed hat on her head rather than braiding it all the time. The hat-band had skulls and feathers stitched to it. Not the cheap discount store varieties either. Real animal skulls and multiple, colorful and ebony tufts bound together with red thread. How she always managed to find those things on our runs was mind-boggling, but rarely did we go a week without a new addition to her growing altar. It merged with mine, taking up both tables and now a shelf in our living room. And I wasn't even mad about the takeover, or her defiance.

She'd never be a normal woman. I'd accepted that.

Because…

Fuck normal.

To quote from one of my favorite movies,
The end is only the beginning…

~

If you're like me, you want more…
[Looks around, puts a finger on her lips…]
Tell you what, go to this super-secret web page to read a
bonus scene. You may be asked to sign up for a newsletter
there. If you do subscribe, you will get two emails a month
with what's coming next, freebie links, and other great
content, but you can unsubscribe at ANY time.
shh…
caliawilde.com/roses/
The password is: witch

To find more Skilletsville stories, visit:
https://caliawilde.com/Skilletsville

ABOUT THE AUTHOR

Calia Wilde believes the hero isn't always the good guy. She believes some heroes and heroines cannot play by the rules to get their happily ever after.

She is a writer of misfits, anti-heroes, villains, underdogs, fringe elements, and other tropes that will likely get her barred from polite society.

As a feral Gen-Xer, she spent numerous hours roaming the woods in search of elves, fairies, dragons, or anything that would take her away from the dreaded curse of doing dishes. She once fell off a wardrobe, but instead of landing in Narnia, a very emphatic order of *"Don't tell Mom,"* was decreed. In case you are wondering, yes, she did land on her head.

Rainy days and dark nights landed the author in other worlds between written pages or immersing in her favorite space and time travel TV shows. Whether it was exploring the final frontier or simply disappearing down rabbit holes with shapeshifting aliens, the escape was the same, only the moonscape differed.

One time in Sturgis, she was offered twenty bucks to climb a ladder. She declined as there was some fine print regarding the quest that went beyond conquering a fear of heights and some activities which were definitely illegal for someone her age. But it was there... in that magical realm of bikers, booze, and foul language, that she came into the possession of her very first item of armor... aka, black clothing. The forbidden was in her grasp and became an life-long obsession to avoid anything pastel.

As she searched for a career that would indulge this penchant for wearing black, she stumbled upon the world of special effects and excitedly pursued the art of sleeping in strange hotels, working ungodly hours, and handling anything that could, and would, burn, blind, explode, freeze, or otherwise entertain wildlings like herself.

Her current fictional worlds are forged in a hippie world where music and nature peacefully co-exist away from modern conveniences, like bathtubs. Okay, there's a shower, but she has to share it with spiders. Yuck. Which is why she looks forward to going on the road once more where the hotel may have a real tub. Or a hot tub... maybe a heated pool... please?

So, she BEGS you to leave a review and do a good deed by encouraging others to read her books. With enough fans scattered across the globe, she'll have to travel, right? Then she'll have an excuse to leave the farm.

$\approx$

Want a FREE BOOK? Sign up for her newsletter.
CaliaWilde.com/newsletter-sign-up/
or
Become an ARC reader and get all the books FIRST.
CaliaWilde.com/become-an-arc-reader/

Walk on the Wilde side here:
CaliaWilde.com

ALSO BY CALIA WILDE

Destroyers Series

Motorcycle Club Romance, Contemporary Action/Adventure Romance
Novels and Short Stories

Devils Handmaidens Motorcycle Club

Motorcycle Club Romance, Contemporary Action/Adventure Romance
Novels — A shared MC universe with other MC authors

DeSantos Trilogy

Contemporary Romance/Romantic Suspense

Bones Series

Paranormal and Fantasy Romantic Short Stories, Mythology-inspired
Romantic Tales

TKI Logistics

Contemporary Romance, Military Romance Short Stories

Visit CaliaWilde.com/book-backlist for a full list of current publications.